Praise for Kath

"… the book is a nice balance of humour and compassion … "
– Lois Legge, *The Halifax Chronicle Herald*

"Kathy Chisholm's *Urban Tigers* is a must-read for all vets, vets-to-be and cat lovers … I guarantee you will love *Urban Tigers!*"
– Susan Little, DVM, Dip ABVP (feline practice)
Lecturer/researcher in feline medicine
Author of *The Cat: Clinical Medicine and Management*

"I laughed, I shed a few tears, and I couldn't stop reading … *Urban Tigers* is a novel, but it reads like a memoir. The stories are heart-warming and endearing, as well as humorous, and the book is hard to put down. This book will delight cat lovers and those who want to know more about what goes on behind the scenes of a feline veterinary clinic. I was delighted to hear that Kathy Chisholm is working on a sequel, because I didn't want this book to end."
– Ingrid King,
The Conscious Cat Blog (www.consciouscat.net)

"I laughed out loud a few times and the tears threatened to overflow on a few more occasions. The cast of characters, human and feline, carried this story and left me wishing for more! Chisholm tells her tale in a human, funny and realistic way and takes us behind the scenes with the people who care for our beloved four-legged family members … Whether you live with cats, love them from afar, or sit on the fence, this book will leave you delighted."
– Louise Denault-Jones
The Reader blog, Halifax Public Libraries

"I think *Urban Tigers* is quite delightful. I loved the adventures of Emily McB, and Dr. D … congratulations! – what a lovely addition to the veterinary canon."

– Alice Crook, BSc, DVM
Coordinator, Sir James Dunn Animal Welfare Centre
Atlantic Veterinary College

"*Urban Tigers* was our seventh bestseller for our entire fiscal year of February 2011 to February 2012. Thank you."

– Mike Hamm, Manager, Bookmark Halifax

Urban Tigers Two

More Tales of a Cat Vet

A novel by
Kathy Chisholm

Kathy Chisholm

Ailurophile Publishing

Library and Archives Canada Cataloguing in Publication

Chisholm, Kathy, 1955-, author
    Urban tigers two : more tales of a cat vet / by Kathy Chisholm.

Issued in print and electronic formats.
ISBN 978-0-9868301-2-9 (pbk.).– ISBN 978-0-9868301-3-6 (pdf)

    I. Title.

PS8605.H585U73 2013   C813'.6   C2013-903602-4
                                           C2013-903603-2

Copyright © 2013 Kathy Chisholm
All rights reserved.

Ailurophile Publishing
3650 Hammonds Plains Road
Unit 14, Suite 225
Upper Tantallon, Nova Scotia, Canada B3Z 4R3

Follow Kathy on Facebook: www.Facebook.com, Urban Tigers Tales of a Cat Vet
Twitter @UrbanTigersBook
Website: www.kathychisholm.ca

Editors: Robbie Beaver, Elizabeth Peirce
Cover photos: Hugh Chisholm, Ron Illingworth, Robert George Young, Getty Images
Author photo: Hugh Chisholm
Design and layout: Peggy & Co. Design
Printer: Etc Print, printed on recyled paper

Urban Tigers Two, More Tales of a Cat Vet is a work of fiction. Names and characters are products of the author's imagination or are used fictitiously. Any resemblance to persons living or dead is entirely coincidental.

Dedication

Many of you will recognize the cat who appears on the cover. His name is Tuxedo Stan and in the fall of 2012, he ran for mayor of Halifax Regional Municipality in Nova Scotia, Canada. He had but a single platform and that was to raise awareness about the tens of thousands of suffering stray cats in our municipality. After his story gained momentum with the local media, he was catapulted into the national spotlight and then made international headlines with endorsements from Ellen Degeneres and Anderson Cooper. Stan's message of hope and his belief that the world can be a better place inspired changes in countries as far away as Thailand and Kuwait.

In January 2013, Stan was diagnosed with renal lymphoma. In the same spirit of good humour and grace that marked his political campaign, he continues to fight this personal battle with the support of his veterinarians and thousands of friends he has made all over the world.

As *Urban Tigers Two* goes to print, change is in the wind. In a unanimous decision, the new city council voted to increase financial support to the SPCA for a low-cost spay and neuter clinic. This is an important first step and marks the first time in history that our municipal leaders have taken positive action to humanely address the issue of feline overpopulation. Stan will be celebrating his third birthday on May 28, 2013. With six weeks of chemotherapy remaining, he is happy, energetic, and robust. And we have learned that every day with this special little cat is a gift.

I dedicate this book to Stan, to my family and friends, and to people all over the world who believe that we need to be the caretakers, not the masters.

In the words of American cultural anthropologist Margaret Meade, "Never doubt that a small group of thoughtful, committed citizens can change the world. Indeed, it is the only thing that ever has."

Follow Tuxedo Stan on Facebook: www.Facebook.com, Tuxedo Party
Twitter: @TuxedoStan
Website: www.tuxedostan.com

Acknowledgements

I would like to thank graphic designer Peggy Issenman for her invaluable expertise and attention to detail; copy editor Robbie Beaver, for her patience and keen eye; Elizabeth Peirce for additional copy edits; ETC Press for their high standards and quality of work; professional photographer Robert George Young; veterinarian and amateur photographer Hugh Chisholm for the endearing photo of Tuxedo Stan; and last but not least Mike Hamm, the kind and thoughtful manager of the highly-respected independent bookstore Bookmark, in Halifax, Nova Scotia, Canada.

With much love and gratitude, I want to thank my husband, Hugh, and my sister, Judy; without both of you there would be no *Urban Tigers Two*.

I also want to extend my heartfelt thanks to everyone involved in Tuxedo Stan's health care, including the staff of Westwood Hills Animal Hospital who administer his chemotherapy and make sure he comes home to me; my readers throughout North America who loved the first *Urban Tigers – Tales of a Cat Vet* and made me feel like a real writer (many of you have become good friends and your support means more than I can say); the wonderful clients of Atlantic Cat Hospital for your loyalty, your friendship, and your stories; my long-suffering flute teacher, Jack Chen, who nurtures a place of stillness where music can grow and worries fade.

I would especially like to acknowledge the Tuxedo Party of Canada and its many supporters and followers world-wide. Cindy, Joe, and Linda, I am honoured to call you my friends.

And of course Cathy, my friend and "biggest first fan."

For Stanley

Urban Tigers Two

More Tales of a Cat Vet

Chapter 1

"Oh, Dr. McBride. Thank God! It's Verna Gillis," a breathless voice announced. "Sweet William's doing the revelations!"

"Revelations?" What I knew about revelations was limited to an admittedly unread chapter in the Bible and a tipsy roommate's confession that she'd slept with my boyfriend in vet school.

"It's like that nursery rhyme. You know … 'Round and round and round he goes,'" Verna chanted. "'And where he stops, nobody knows!'"

If it had been anyone but Verna, I would have suspected alcohol was involved, but Verna was a devout member of The Celestial Church of Truth. Parishioners believed that Christ was an alien from a superior race who had crash-landed on this planet and tried to make the best of things. Their rules were few, but liquor was strictly forbidden.

A few months ago, a moth-eaten stray had begun hanging out around the dumpster behind the church. One night he simply followed Verna home. New to the demands of cat ownership, Verna had lots of questions. Since she didn't remember most of the answers, she had to call Ocean View Cat Hospital regularly. Verna might be a few tomatoes short of a thick paste, but she had a big heart.

I looked at my watch and weighed my options. It was almost closing time. I could see Verna and Sweet William now, or possibly be on the receiving end of an emergency phone call at three o'clock in the morning. Who knew? … by then Sweet William might be spinning cartwheels and doing handstands while reciting poetry.

Verna didn't own a car and normally walked or took a bus to save money. She wasn't about to take any chances with her beloved Sweet William, however, and arrived at the hospital in a taxi. In spite of the cold, miserable night, the windows were rolled down part way. The taxi driver deposited his payload and sped off into the night.

"Oh!" Verna wailed as I opened the door for her. "Sweet William had to use the bathroom … Number Two," she wrinkled her nose. "Is it still okay to bring him in?"

I assured Verna that if I refused to see any patients who relieved themselves under stress, the hospital's appointment book would be only half full. In truth, I admired the dedication of cat lovers who made the trek to the vet's in spite of the accusations, the caterwauling, the vomit, and, more often than not, the gooey mound of poop in the carrier.

Grabbing my arm, she looked up mournfully from underneath a hand-crocheted hat that looked like an inverted flower pot. Her lower lip trembled. Too large for the mouth to which it had been assigned, it hung loosely in front of a row of neglected teeth.

"It's cancer, isn't it?"

Sweet William blinked at me in wide-eyed concern.

"Well, let's not jump to conclusions. Why don't you relax in that chair," I suggested, "and I'll have a look at him."

Verna nodded but remained standing.

Sweet William appeared perfectly normal. Although his heart was beating a little faster than usual, the rhythm was regular and strong. His lungs were clear. I did a few simple neurological tests, which he passed without any difficulty. Opening his mouth, I checked his gums and teeth then peered inside his ears with an otoscope.

"Mmm … "

Verna clapped a hand over her mouth. "Cancer?"

"No, no. He just has a little inflammation in his right ear and there's a waxy build-up. He might be a little disoriented and that's why he's doing … "

"The revelations?" Verna interrupted.

I nodded.

She thought for a moment. "How do you know it's not cancer?"

I resorted to a variation of one of my mother's standbys when we were growing up. "Because I just do."

The answer seemed to satisfy her.

"What about fleas?" Verna asked, switching gears. "I don't want fleas in the house. Mother would roll over in her grave. That'd be funny," she added with a grin.

"Well, he does have a few."

Verna shuddered. "I want to get rid of them instamatically!"

I began to discuss flea control, but Verna had her own agenda.

"He likes catnip, Dr. McBride. Is that OK? I don't want him addicted. My brother's addicted."

I hesitated. "To catnip?"

"No, gambling and … " Verna lowered her voice, "and whores," she whispered, shaking her head sadly. "I wish he'd come to church with me."

"Well," I quipped, "my grandmother always said the Lord helps those who help themselves."

"That's what I always say!" Verna clasped my hand as if we were soulmates, and gazed into my face. "What about his nails?"

"Your brother's?"

"No, Sweet William's."

"Oh, right." I was getting dizzy from all the conversational twists and turns. Digging through the drawer, I found a pair of nail trimmers. While Sweet William wiggled and squirmed his way through a manicure, Verna tossed questions into the air like confetti. I reached for a bottle of ear drops from the pharmacy shelf.

"This is Sweet William's ear medication," I told her. "It should get rid of the infection. Three drops twice daily for ten days."

Verna nodded as she studied the bottle. The manufacturer's warning, "Ear drops, veterinary use only" was splashed across the front along with my directions.

"Where do I put them?" she asked.

Many answers came to mind. I chose the one that would allow me to continue working at Ocean View Cat Hospital. I then showed Verna how to apply the drops and spent the next ten minutes typing detailed instructions beginning with "Hold the cat." I had her read the instructions back to me, and reminded her that I would like to see Sweet William in ten days for a recheck.

"I'd like to check his stool for parasites as well," I added. "Please bring a fresh fecal sample with you if you can." If Sweet William's past performance was any indicator of future performance, I doubted getting a fresh sample would be a problem.

"It'll be my New Year's Revolution!" Verna declared, although it was barely mid-October.

I called a taxi for Verna and waited with her in reception. I made several attempts at conversation but found it hard to follow Verna's train of thought. After awhile, I just smiled and nodded politely, sighing in quiet relief when the taxi finally arrived.

Verna rose to her feet. "I'm coming, I'm coming," she grumbled, as he tooted his horn impatiently. She put her hat on, tugging it fiercely down over her ears as if to keep the contents of her head secure. With my help, she fastened a handmade quilted cover over Sweet William's carrier and hoisted it into the air.

"Thank you, Dr. McBride. Goodnight," she called over her shoulder.

At the door, she paused. Silhouetted against the glare of the taxi's harsh light, she was an oddly-shaped figure in a coat three sizes too large that she had probably purchased at a thrift shop. The peculiar little hat had a mind of its own and was rising like a loaf of bread up over her ears. Sweet William shifted in his carrier, causing Verna to list dangerously to the left.

"Dr. McBride?" she asked hesitantly. "Are you sure it's not cancer?"

I squinted against the bright lights and nodded. "I'm sure."

The taxi driver tooted again. Verna hesitated, then scurried out the door with Sweet William in tow.

By the time I got home, it was almost ten. After a tongue-lashing from three hungry cats, I changed into a comfortable pair of old-lady, flannel pyjamas, the kind you don't wear in public unless you have a complete disregard for public opinion. Poking my head under the bed, I hauled out my favourite slippers, a pair of orange tabbies. Striped tails poked out of the heels and a softball-size head rested on each toe. They were my Christmas "Secret Santa" gift from Bernie, the hospital's head receptionist.

Still wide awake after my evening with Verna, I made myself a cup of warm milk and curled up with the cats and a book. Somewhere between Chapter 2 and Chapter 3, I nodded off, only to be awakened by a bone-jarring thud followed by an eerie silence. The cats scattered for safety, leaving me to deal with the end of the world alone. I crept down the hallway armed only with my book, and peered through the peephole in the door.

Lying on the hall floor was my upstairs neighbour, Ed. Standing over him was an attractive brunette in a short skirt.

"Eddy ... Eddy!" she hissed, shaking his shoulder. When he didn't respond, she looked at him thoughtfully. "Are you dead?

There was a brief lull, during which time I thought that Eddy might have indeed bought the farm. I needn't have worried. A former defensive tackle for the university football team, the man was built like a forklift. When I opened the door, he burped and smiled benignly at my feet. Two pairs of bulbous eyes stared back at him.

"Emily!" he gurgled happily in recognition.

"Did you break anything?" I asked. Eddy's date cackled appreciatively at my wit.

"Nah!" Ed scoffed at the idea and rose unsteadily to his feet. The brunette, who was only slightly less drunk than he was, held him on one side, and I held the other. Somehow we managed to get him up the stairs and onto the sofa, where he began to snore. The woman stared at the prone man while I cleaned and bandaged his head wound.

"Should we undress him?" she asked after a moment.

"You're on your own!" I shook my head and headed back downstairs in the hopes of getting a few more hours of sleep. I saw nothing of Ed or his girlfriend all day Sunday. In fact, there were no reported sightings of Ed all week long, although Mr. Chang, the property owner, confirmed that he had paid his November rent.

"Ha! Dr. Emily … you have thing for Mr. Ed?" He wiggled his eyebrows up and down.

"No! God, no!" I assured the skeptical Mr. Chang. Besides, wasn't Mr. Ed some sort of talking horse on a TV show from the sixties?

"Ha! He smooth operator," Mr. Chang commented. "Many beautiful women friends. Not for you, Dr. Emily. Ta-ta."

I stared at Mr. Chang's retreating back, wondering if he was merely concerned for my welfare or if he felt I didn't meet Ed's standards. I was still wondering when Verna showed up for her appointment a few days later.

"Here's your fetus sample, Dr. McBride!" she declared, shaking a yogurt container.

Cautiously, I lifted the lid and peered inside at a well-formed, foul-smelling fecal sample in its prime.

"That looks good," I said, snapping the lid shut.

Verna glowed with pride.

Microscopic examination revealed it was free of parasites. I passed on the good news to Verna, expecting she would be pleased. Instead, she threw her hands into the air. "Well, then, how come he still has the revelations?" she demanded.

I looked at Verna. "Are you getting the medication in okay?"

"Uh-huh." Verna bobbed her head up and down as she looked around the room in wide-eyed innocence.

"Verna!"

"Oh, it's so hard!" she wailed, collapsing under my stern voice. "He hates me."

I assured her that even I had trouble sometimes putting in ear drops, but that it was very, very important. Verna nodded solemnly. I showed her how to wrap Sweet William in a towel so he couldn't struggle. Then, holding him against my chest with one arm as he sat on the examining table, I applied the drops to his right ear.

"Remember to massage his ear afterwards so the medication goes in deep enough," I explained. Like most cats, Sweet William loved this part of the procedure and leaned his head into the massage.

"Now you try," I smiled.

Sweet William did not recognize Verna as an authority figure. It took her quite a while to get the hang of things and to convince Sweet William she wasn't trying to murder him. Ten minutes and half a bottle of ear drops later we emerged from the exam room, exhausted but victorious.

Verna plopped into a chair and fanned herself with her hat. "I'm just going to sit for a minute till I recover from that orgy." Al Whitehead, who was waiting with his cat Al Fresco, looked up with sudden interest.

Over the next ten days, I kept in daily touch with Verna so I was reasonably sure she was getting the medication in Sweet William's ears. She had increased her odds with a few flakes of tuna before, during, and after each treatment. According to Verna, Sweet William had never been happier.

His recheck was scheduled just a few days before Hallowe'en. Inside Ocean View's reception room, Verna gazed in delight at the black and orange streamers draped from each corner and meeting in an extravagant bow at the chandelier. Wisps of cotton batting had been stretched into filmy cobwebs on the retail shelves. Thanks to our receptionist's carving skills, a buck-toothed pumpkin surrounded by Hallowe'en cards flickered cheerfully on the reception counter.

"Oh, this is fun!" Verna clapped her hands together as she caught sight of a witch stocking the shelves and a pirate grooming a sedated cat.

"And what are you, Dr. McBride?" she asked.

"A veterinarian," I grinned.

"Ohhh." Verna knitted her brows together in a puzzled frown. Then, switching gears, she thrust an envelope into my hand. "Open it."

The envelope had been hermetically sealed with half a roll of Scotch tape. Impatient with my bumbling efforts to find a crack in the envelope's armour, Verna blurted out the contents with unrestrained joy. "Sweet William got you a card for Hallowe'en! It's real funny! There's a cat wearing white undershorts with red hearts on them. It says, 'My heart pants for you.' Get it?"

Giggling, Verna held a hand up to her mouth. The fact that it was a Valentine's Day card was lost on her. "I bet my card's the funniest of all them cards," Verna declared proudly as she studied the display of cards on our coffee table. And, in truth, it was.

I thanked Sweet William personally for his taste in cards and ushered the pair into the exam room to have a look at the cat's ear. There was a small amount of waxy brown discharge and his eardrum, instead of being smooth and uniformly opalescent, was a heterogeneous off-white.

"Mmm … "

"What?" asked Verna, instantly alert.

"Have you been massaging his ear after you apply the drops?" I asked.

Verna nodded vigorously.

"Well, I think he may have a polyp in his ear as well as an infection."

"Cancer?" Verna gasped.

"No, not cancer," I hastened to assure her. "It's probably a benign growth. They usually start in the Eustachian tube. That's the tube between the ear and the throat," I added, when Verna's forehead wrinkled in confusion. "Instead of growing down into the throat, it may have grown into the ear."

"More eardrops?" Verna sagged visibly in her chair.

"No, let's just leave it for a week or two and see how things go. If it gets worse, I may want to get a sample of the discharge from his ear." I hesitated. Sweet William's list of health concerns was growing like Jack's beanstalk, and no doubt Verna's savings account was shrinking proportionally.

"Have you noticed that Sweet William is losing fur on his face and ears?" I asked carefully. "His skin in those areas is a little blotchy too."

Verna opened her mouth to speak.

"It's not cancer," I added quickly. "I think he may have an allergy."

"An allergy? Like hay fever? Blessed Virgin!" Verna crossed herself. "Will he need drops?"

I explained that fur loss in these areas was typical of an allergy to the food, usually to a protein in the meat. All we had to do was switch his diet to a hypoallergenic formula and see if he improved.

"Oh no, Dr. McBride," Verna frowned, shaking her head, "he won't like that. He's very fussy. VERY FUSSY!" she added for emphasis, folding her arms across her chest.

I glanced at Sweet William as he sat Buddha-like on my examining table. Rolls of fat cascaded over his feet. Fussy was not a word I would have chosen to describe him. Forging ahead, I explained the importance of sticking with the special food for at least six weeks. "No treats, no table scraps, no cream – nothing extra. And I want to see him back in a couple of weeks. Sooner if his ear gets worse."

Verna grabbed onto her head with both hands, eyes wide. "My poor brain, Dr. McBride! It's swollen! It can only hold so much, you know."

I promised Verna I would write everything down for her. The staff knew by now to book me extra time whenever Verna and Sweet William came to town so I didn't fall behind with my other appointments.

When I pulled into the driveway that night, exhausted after another long day, I spied Ed at the mailbox. "Hey, Ed! How are you?"

"Eddy!" I shouted again when he didn't respond. "Are you deaf?"

"Oh. Emily. Hi," he replied, turning around as I came up the steps. "I didn't hear you. Ear infection," he grimaced. "I've had it pretty much since, well, you know. That night."

As he stood still under the bright porch light, I noticed the rash on his face and neck and took a few steps back. Ed was a decent-looking guy but the red skin and scaly patches were disturbing.

"Oh, yeah," he added. "I've got some kind of rash too. That just started. The doc doesn't think that it's contagious, though."

I murmured something sympathetic and decided to check my mail later. It struck me as an odd coincidence that both Sweet William and Ed exhibited remarkably similar symptoms, and I was the common denominator. I dismissed the thought as the overactive imagination of a veterinarian who had done one too many fecals.

But, over the next few months, Ed and Sweet William battled their remarkably similar ailments. Verna grew more stressed with each new bottle she took home. Ed cancelled a trip to Cuba. The doctor was worried that his ear didn't seem to be responding to treatment, and the rash had spread. The brunette had found herself a new boyfriend with smooth skin and an impressive net worth.

When there was no improvement in Sweet William's ear, Verna finally consented to an ear flush under anesthetic. I was able to examine his mouth and nasal cavity more closely and take X-rays of his skull. There appeared to be a small hole in his eardrum. I swabbed the debris in his ear canal but when we examined the slides under the microscope, we found nothing unusual. As luck would have it, the samples we sent to the lab for analysis and culture were lost en route so I had no way of knowing what antibiotic might be the most effective.

"His skin is improving, though," I told Verna with a bright smile.

Poor Verna. It was just one thing after another. To help with her ongoing medical expenses, I offered her a payment plan, which she promptly refused.

"I pay all my bills," she declared. "And I sell my hats at the flea market." When I dutifully admired Verna's hat, she pulled several variations on the flowerpot theme out of her bag.

"I sell them for $15 each. It only takes me an hour to make one while I watch them game shows. So it's good profit," Verna added proudly.

I bought a purple one.

Verna surfaced a few weeks later with a bag full of hats and Sweet William. She sat in the chair, nibbling her fingernails and casting furtive glances my way as I examined Sweet William's ear.

"Verna!" I exclaimed, clicking off the otoscope.

"What!" Startled, she bolted upright.

"Sweet William's ear is the best I've ever seen it!"

"Praise Jesus!" Verna looked up at the ceiling, then back down at me. "How is his crustacean tube?"

I assured Verna his Eustachian tube was fine. We chatted for a few moments longer. Sweet William looked good and smelled good and offered no resistance to my examination; I had become part of his normal routine. I had just plucked him off the table for a cuddle before returning him to his carrier when I noticed a small, ulcerated lump high inside his right foreleg.

Verna sat very still, her hands clasped in her lap. She fixed her sad-beagle eyes on me. "Cancer. I knew it."

"We don't know that, Verna," I replied. Despite my assurances to the contrary over the last few months, it was certainly possible that this lump was cancerous. It was just as possible that it wasn't. I explained that the only way to know for sure was to remove the whole thing and send it off to the pathologist for analysis.

Verna was silent.

"Everybody I know dies from cancer," she said at last. "Why, Dr. McBride? Why? And now my cat." She started to cry.

Verna loved Sweet William and she had continued to trust my judgment when others would have given up and gone elsewhere. I reached over and hugged her like I held my nephew when the older boys wouldn't let him play road hockey. Sometimes words alone are cold comfort when what we really need is to feel that we are not alone. I imagined that Verna felt very much alone sometimes, a child trapped inside an adult's body.

Wiping away her tears, she scheduled Sweet William's lump removal for the following Tuesday when she would be back on day shifts. "Can we fix him then?"

"You mean his castration?" I asked.

Verna nodded.

"I think it would be best to wait until we get the results from the pathologist," I answered. "I don't want to stress him too much right now."

Verna turned to Bernie at the reception counter. "He has The Cancer," Verna explained, lowering her voice so Sweet William wouldn't hear.

While Bernie murmured sympathetically, I hastened to remind Verna that we didn't know that for sure. "Cancer's only one possibility among many."

Verna looked at me and managed a feeble smile but her eyes glistened with barely restrained tears. I bought two more hats and Bernie picked out a lime green one for herself. Hughie found a pink one in the pile that his great-aunt Louise simply had to have.

On Friday night, I ran into Ed at the checkout counter of the liquor store. He was barely visible behind a tower of beer.

"Party tonight, Eddy?" I asked with a grin. His skin looked much better.

"Yup. Could be my last one," he confided. "Doc found a lump under my armpit."

"Oh, Eddy!" I gasped. "I'm sorry. It's probably nothing, you know," I added hastily. "I get them all the time from shaving. Sometimes a lymph node gets a little infected."

Eddy looked at me oddly. "Em, I don't shave my armpits. In fact, most guys don't. You need to get out more," he chuckled.

I laughed along with Eddy as I studied the pattern on the tile floor. The truth was I wished I did get out more.

He slapped me on the back. "I'm just teasin' ya, Em. I'm not worried. I feel great!" He smiled encouragingly at a giggling cluster of co-eds around a wine display.

I assured Ed that everything would be fine, then avoided him for the next several weeks. It was the stuff out of a Stephen King novel. For every symptom in every location that Sweet William exhibited, Eddy had one to match. Maybe somehow I had cursed the two of them. I popped a get-well card in his mail box and hoped for the best.

When I look back now, I can see I needn't have worried. Ed's lump was nothing more than a fatty cyst and Sweet William had a benign mast cell tumour with complete excision. He went home the day after his surgery.

Verna was ecstatic. "When can I schedule his catastrophe?"

Mercifully, Ed was on a cruise ship in the Caribbean when I castrated Sweet William.

Chapter 2

"She's not getting any better, Dr. McBride."

Jocelyn Pitman stared accusingly at me. So did Bathsheba, her Egyptian Mau. Jocelyn kept a stranglehold on her cash, refusing any diagnostic tests that would identify the cause of the problem. So, for the last several months, I had been treating her cat's recurring cystitis with antibiotics and a special diet. I hoped one or the other would solve Bathsheba's annoying habit of peeing wherever the urge overtook her.

"We really should do those X-rays," I repeated. "Bathsheba could have stones in her bladder that might need to be surgically removed."

"Well, if it's absolutely necessary." In a dramatic gesture, Jocelyn shook her mane of auburn hair and sighed. She was an attractive woman in her mid-thirties, but her boyfriend's state-of-the-art stereo speakers had just been sprayed with cat urine and Jocelyn realized that even her beauty paled in comparison with a 265-watt home theatre system.

"How long will it take?" she asked.

The morning had been a bubbling cauldron of chaos that threatened to boil over at any minute. Jocelyn's late arrival hadn't helped.

"Well," I began, "I'm a little behind schedule but we can admit her until I have a chance to … "

Jocelyn's cell phone shrieked inside her purse. Rather than ignore it, she withdrew a tiny silver phone that fit into the palm of her hand. I admired its slim lines. Hughie had purchased a cell phone for on-call emergency use several years earlier, a sensible model favoured by construction workers and telephone linesmen. It came with its own suitcase and could survive a nuclear holocaust.

"Yes?" Jocelyn's voice was crisp with authority. "I'm still at the vet's. Where are you?" She paused. "I know. I know!" she repeated, rolling her eyes. "Fine. I'll meet you there."

Jocelyn snapped her phone shut and grabbed her coat. "I have to go," she announced without apology. "Just call me when you're done."

Shaking my head, I carried Bathsheba to the recovery ward, where several patients lolled about in a drug-induced euphoria. The Egyptian Mau was particularly offended by a drooling grey tomcat with an overbite, who was sprawled upside down in his kennel, staring at her. Squirming against my grasp, she jumped into the open kennel and curled her bright pink tongue around a most unladylike hiss. Templeton's Milady Bathsheba of Aurora Kennels was clearly annoyed to be housed with a bunch of alley cats who couldn't trace their ancestry past one generation, if that. I gave her a litter pan and a bowl of water, then bolted to my next appointment.

Dan Baker had been waiting almost three-quarters of an hour with his six-year-old son and four-year-old daughter. He had read stories, played games, and accompanied each child on several bathroom excursions. Finally, he had bought three doughnuts next door. One was now floating in the fish tank and its owner was sobbing uncontrollably.

"I'm so sorry to keep you waiting," I apologized above the howls.

"That's okay," Dan managed with a weak smile.

I ushered everyone into the exam room. Andrew was reluctant to leave his doughnut behind. His little sister Beth dutifully cried in sympathy. Only Matilda, their neutered male cat, seemed to be enjoying the visit; the big orange tabby was accustomed to chaos and being dragged around the house in doll clothes. He was scheduled for a routine checkup and vaccination, so I hoped to make up some time.

Andrew's sniffles slowed when he saw my stethoscope.

"Do you want to listen?" I offered.

He nodded shyly. I put the stethoscope to his ears and held the diaphragm on Matilda's chest. When he heard the sound of a beating heart for the first time, his eyes opened wide in delight. Then he listened to his own chest.

"Isn't that something, Andy?" Dan asked.

"Me! Me!" Beth cried. She tried to grab the stethoscope from her brother but was scooped into the air by her dad before a tug-of-war could erupt. Though I admired his cat-like reflexes, no doubt honed by parenthood, Beth howled at the injustice. She continued to pout even as I shared the stethoscope with her. Unimpressed, she squirmed off her father's lap and plopped onto the floor while I continued examining Matilda.

"Daddy! Beth's eating boogers again!" Andy cried.

Dan sighed and made a face. "Bethie, honey, don't eat boogers." Turning to me, he added, "Their mother's better at this sort of thing."

Beth tugged on my lab coat. "Do you know Captain Underpants?"

"Not personally." I shrugged my shoulders and looked at Dan.

"Saturday morning TV," he explained. "Captain Underpants and the Perilous Plot of Professor Poopypants."

I shook my head. Whatever happened to Bugs Bunny and the Roadrunner? Foghorn Leghorn? Elmer Fudd?

"Captain Underpants is COOL!" Andrew declared as his sister nodded solemnly. "He can turn his enemies into mounds of poo!"

"Poo!" Beth echoed, clapping her hands.

"Ooey, gooey pooey!" Andrew sang.

"POOPY BUM!" Beth screeched. The two of them rolled on the floor in fits of laughter.

Poopy bum pretty much described the rest of my day. By the time the Bakers left, I was an hour behind schedule and sinking further into the abyss. With help from Susan, our head technician, I collected a blood sample from one of my in-patients in isolation. The complete blood count (CBC) was inconclusive, so I prepared a blood smear for a closer look under the microscope, which was tucked under one of the cupboards. (During one of his efficiency excursions throughout the hospital, Hughie had decided the microscope would take up less space there.)

"Dr. McBride?"

I jumped, banging my head in the process. Bernie had traded in her clogs for a sensible pair of Hush Puppies and could materialize anywhere without warning.

"Mr. Martinello says Daisy is depressed again."

"Not today, Bernie," I sighed, massaging my head. "He just wants to talk."

Once a month, Delbert and Daisy made the trek to Ocean View Cat Hospital. Daisy's monthly bout with depression coincided with the arrival of the old age pension cheque and was cured by a vitamin shot and some conversation. Daisy was healthier than the proverbial horse and would likely outlast her owner.

Bernie waited.

"He's a sweet old man but I've got that abscess to drain, two sick cats in isolation, Bathsheba's X-rays, plus I'm an hour behind." I sighed and turned back to the microscope. "Daisy's fine. Just book them sometime later this week."

Somehow I managed to get through the rest of the busy day without committing any felonies. As it turned out, Bathsheba had six stones in her bladder which had likely been there for months. Jocelyn raved at the cost but eventually consented to surgery, which I scheduled for the following morning.

I arrived at work early, hoping to get a good start on a day that didn't look any better than its predecessor and would likely be fueled by chocolate bars and coffee. An unscheduled appointment waited anxiously in my exam room. Overnight, Wiggles MacFarlane had somehow managed to nearly sever her tail in what was probably a cat-car dispute.

A three-inch piece of tendon was all that connected the two sections. While the entire family wept, I assured them that Wiggles would be fine following a partial amputation, and admitted her for surgery.

In the meantime, my mother called to remind me that the Diabetes Association would be by at noon tomorrow. I had promised to help her round up two decades' worth of obsolete clothes and household items, from which the association would somehow manage to squeeze a profit.

"In case you've forgotten, Emily," she added.

"I didn't," I lied, quickly scribbling a reminder on a piece of paper. Sighing, I hung up the phone and scanned my next patient's chart.

"Dr. McBride?" Hilary, one of our veterinary technicians, poked her head in the door. "Jason's pulled out his catheter."

"Oh, for God's sake!" I pushed back my chair and followed Hilary into the recovery ward. Jason was an ill-tempered grey and white cat who had helped himself to the supply of twist ties in the kitchen cupboard. I had surgically removed them from his stomach yesterday and installed an IV line to provide supportive fluids while he recovered from the ordeal. As he defiantly resisted our efforts to reinstall the line and clean him up, Bernie loomed large in front of the isolation window.

"Mr. Martinello says Daisy is VERY depressed!" she hollered above Jason's blood-curdling threats.

"So am I!" I hollered back.

Bernie didn't flinch.

"Squeeze him in somewhere tonight then," I added, hoping to get rid of Bernie, who had planted her feet in a defiant, red-headed gesture, not unlike Jason. It occurred to me, as Jason tried to shred my forearm, that a statistically significant number of boys in junior high school who didn't do their homework, fought with their classmates, sassed the teacher, and smoked in the bathroom were named Jason. Owners should never name their cats Jason. Or Lucky; the latter are usually anything but.

It was noon before I finally went into surgery with Bathsheba. We had withheld food since nine o'clock the previous evening in preparation for surgery. Jocelyn had been predictably annoyed with the delay but was more concerned that we were starving her cat to death.

Unconcerned, Bathsheba lay sprawled on her back, far away in the mysterious realm of the anesthetized cat. A tube inserted into her airway delivered a mix of oxygen and isoflurane anesthetic. I cut a round hole in the blue surgical drape, exposing her shaved belly.

"Are you going to take some X-rays?" Hilary asked as I picked up the scalpel blade.

"No, I took a pair yesterday," I answered, tracing an almost bloodless line down Bathsheba's abdomen. "Those stones have been there at least three months. They're not going anywhere."

Hilary nodded.

"Besides, Jocelyn will think I'm just trying to squeeze more money out of her."

Bathsheba was in good shape, without the pendulous belly common among her middle-aged peers. Reaching the bladder easily, I attached two long pieces of suture material at each end. Hilary held the leathery walls of the bladder open with these two "stay" sutures while I made a small incision. We were anxious to avoid contamination of the abdomen with urine. I withdrew about 30 cc's of bloody fluid and squirted it into a small blue dish. Then I inserted a finger into the bladder, hoping to palpate the stones. Hilary leaned over. Our heads were inches apart.

"Feel anything?" she asked through her face mask.

"No. Must still be in there."

Humming, I probed the small organ thoroughly but felt nothing unusual. The forceps that would be used to remove any stones lay idle on the sterile instrument tray.

"They must be stuck to the bladder wall," Hilary said at last.

I had stopped humming. Moisture was forming on the ridge of my nose underneath the face mask. "Can you shine the flashlight into her bladder?"

As Hilary's light exposed the angry, red walls of an irritated bladder, I searched in vain for six wayward stones. Nothing. No matter which excruciating angle I craned my neck for a better view, the stones eluded me.

"Shit!"

Hilary looked up.

"Let's take another pair of X-rays."

The Nova Scotia Veterinary Medical Association prohibited X-ray machines in surgery. To avoid contamination, we had to suture the bladder and three layers of the abdominal wall closed before wheeling Bathsheba into radiology. I was reasonably certain the stones were gone but I had to make sure.

For five long minutes I waited with Bathsheba while Hilary developed the X-rays. The heart monitor beeped with a comforting regularity. As I watched the clock, I wondered about the six missing stones and that elusive wisdom known as hindsight. Bathsheba, secure in her mother's love and still anesthetized, did not share my anxiety.

Hilary emerged from the darkroom, the dripping films in her hand. She turned on the light and slipped the two views onto the viewer.

"I can't believe it!" I groaned, staring at the black and white images. "She must have passed them overnight." Where yesterday six stones had glowed like stars in a nighttime sky, not a single one now showed its face.

I looked at Hilary and shook my head. "She was full of them for three months. I finally convince Jocelyn to have surgery to remove them and guess what? No stones!"

Above her face mask, Hilary's eyes crinkled in sympathy as we shared the same thought. Anybody but Jocelyn Pitman. I turned off the anesthetic and we waited for Bathsheba to wake up.

Her recovery was uneventful. She was in some discomfort but painkillers and anti-inflammatory drugs reduced it to a dull ache. By evening, she seemed happier and had devoured a plate of food. She would need to stay at the hospital for a few days while we monitored her progress.

"Oh my poor baby! My poor baby!" Jocelyn cried, as she buried her face in Bathsheba's thick, spotted coat. I apologized and added that we were not going to charge Jocelyn for the surgery.

"It isn't the money, Dr. McBride." As Jocelyn turned to face me, I felt the temperature in the room drop. Her words stabbed the frosty air like icicles. "You subjected my cat to needless trauma and risk. I'll be reporting you to the veterinary association."

Before I could respond, she stormed out of the hospital, nearly bowling over Hilary.

Frustrated and shaken by Jocelyn's outburst, I lingered in the isolation ward straightening Bathsheba's blanket and adjusting the flow rate on her IV. As if echoing her owner's sentiments, Bathsheba looked at me and hissed.

"Dr. McBride?" Hilary timidly poked her head inside. "Mr. Martinello is here." She handed me the chart and retreated.

I picked up a bottle of injectable vitamins from a cupboard in the treatment room and headed down the hall. I didn't see Carter, one of the resident cats, chasing his tail while his buddy Ernie cheered him on. I didn't hear Bernie and Susan laughing as they folded laundry together. I just wanted the day to end.

Mr. Martinello was my last patient of the evening. At the door to the exam room, I paused. Gathering a deep breath, I turned the knob and stepped inside. A wave of Old Spice rolled over me.

"You know, 8:30 is awfully late for me," Mr. Martinello began, "but your girl said that's all you had available."

"We actually closed at eight," I replied, more curtly than I had intended.

Seeing my face, Mr. Martinello hastened to add an apology. "Oh, don't mind me. I'm just a whiny old fart!"

"No, no. It's okay. How have you been?" I asked, trying on a smile.

Delbert's hair had been neatly combed and his face freshly shaven. Coming to the vet's was an exciting event in his life, worthy of a suit and tie. A starched, monogrammed handkerchief peeked out of his breast pocket. Instead of dress shoes however, he wore a comfortable pair of sneakers.

"Well, pretty good for an old fella," Delbert answered, his standard reply. "But Daisy's depressed."

I patted my lab coat pocket. "I have some vitamins in here. Let's see if that picks her up a bit. Then I want to know how your swimming lessons are going."

I opened the kennel door. "C'mon out, Daisy." Usually, Daisy didn't need any coaxing to come out of her carrier. She enjoyed her monthly visits as much as Delbert did.

"I think she has a cold," Delbert added. "She's very depressed."

I got down on my knees and shook the jar of treats encouragingly. Daisy stared at me in wide-eyed concern. She lay on her side with her mouth open as she struggled for each breath. Horrified, I lifted her out of the carrier and laid her on the examining table.

"How long has she been like this?" I asked Delbert.

Startled, Mr. Martinello could only shake his head helplessly.

"How long, Mr. Martinello?" I repeated, grabbing my stethoscope.

"I … well … she was quiet yesterday. I thought she was just tired." His hand shook as he reached up to pat Daisy's head. "She didn't come home the night before and she always comes home. But then she got this cold."

"This isn't a cold," I said, as I listened to her chest. "She's in serious trouble."

"Can't you just give her some vitamins?" he asked, looking up at me. "They always seem to pick her up."

I shook my head. "No. I'm afraid vitamins won't help her right now. I'm going to get her on some oxygen," I explained, scooping Daisy into my arms, "then I can examine her better."

"Can I come with you?" Delbert whispered.

I hesitated. "I think it would be better if you stayed here until I find out what's wrong."

Delbert nodded. Leaning against the table for support, he watched in silence as I left with his cat.

Their work done, most of the staff had already left for the evening. In the treatment area, Susan was staining a slide for cytology to be sent by overnight courier to a lab in Ontario. She jumped up as I came running into the room, and followed me into surgery.

I laid Daisy on a warm afghan while Susan held the Plexiglas face mask over her nose and mouth. With each gasp, pure oxygen flowed into her lungs. We rolled the X-ray machine into position and snapped a set of chest and abdominal X-rays. While Susan developed them, I inserted a small-gauge needle into Daisy's chest cavity, expecting to withdraw the fluid associated with heart failure. Instead, I withdrew only air.

Since the lungs are constantly in motion within the chest cavity, care must be taken to avoid puncturing them with a needle. Using a flexible device known as a butterfly catheter, I positioned the needle against the chest wall then safely removed 40 cc's of air. Daisy's breathing immediately improved. Her frantic gasps slowed until she was breathing almost normally.

"Pneumothorax," I murmured.

"Air in the chest?" Susan asked as she rinsed the X-rays and hung them over the sink to drip. "How would that happen?"

"Trauma, usually," I replied. "Once air seeps into the chest cavity, the lungs can't expand properly."

I snatched the dripping X-ray off its clip and held it up to the brightly lit viewer. "Hmm."

In the black-and-white group photo of Daisy's internal organs, everyone appeared to be behaving themselves. The stomach wasn't jostling the lungs, the spleen was snuggled beside the liver, and the intestines were coiled up in their own little world.

"Well, everything's in the right place so her diaphragm's probably intact," I murmured. "Looks like we're dealing with a tear in one of the small airways in the lung."

"How do you fix that?" Susan asked, reaching for a bag of IV fluids. She held Daisy while I inserted a catheter into a vein on her right front leg. I taped it into position then attached the IV line.

"Well, hopefully it will repair itself. Otherwise, she'll have to go to the vet college in P.E.I. for surgery. I don't know if Mr. Martinello can afford that or even how he would get there."

We carried Daisy to a kennel in the recovery ward. Once she was settled and reasonably comfortable, I brought Mr. Martinello back to visit. Years ago, he had taught piano at the conservatory. Hundreds of children, some willingly, had spent their after-school hours practicing scales, commanding their fingers to produce magic under Delbert's patient guidance. Now his gnarled, arthritic fingers struggled to open the latch on Daisy's kennel door.

"She looks so much better," he smiled hopefully. "Did you give her a vitamin shot?"

I explained that we were treating Daisy for shock and that I hoped, in time, the torn airway would repair itself. "The main thing now," I added, "is to keep her comfortable and quiet."

"When can I take her home?" Delbert asked.

"Probably in a few days, but … "

"Thank you, Dr. McBride," he interrupted in a husky voice. "Thank you. Daisy means the world to me." He studied his little cat, smiling as her chest rose and fell in a relaxed cadence, then reluctantly turned to leave.

"I'm sorry to keep you so late," he apologized.

"No need to apologize," I assured him. "I'm glad we could help."

Delbert gathered his coat and gloves then lumbered into reception. I could hear Susan wishing him a good night as she unlocked the hospital doors, ushering him into the night.

After Mr. Martinello left, I drove Susan home.

"You're quiet," she said as we pulled up to the house. Her little ones had been in bed for a couple of hours. The faint glow of a nightlight that warmed their room and kept it safe from monsters was just noticeable from the street. Her husband had supper waiting.

"Is everything okay?"

I hesitated.

"I guess I'm just worried about Daisy," I answered at last. "Another couple of hours and we would have lost her."

"But we didn't," she said with a bright smile. "I'll see you in the morning. Get a good night's sleep."

In spite of my exhaustion, I slept fitfully. My brain tried, with little success, to file away the events of the previous day in preparation for a new day. Jocelyn Pitman's angry, disembodied face floated in and out of my dreams. To be reported to the veterinary association was a very big deal and, depending upon the outcome, could affect my future at Ocean View. I also felt guilty about Mr. Martinello. I should have made time for him earlier. And I didn't get up to the house to help Mom with the stuff for the Diabetes Association. She was being uncharacteristically stoic about it. For a while the cats endured my erratic twists and turns, but one by one they eventually left my bed for the calm of the sofa.

All too soon, dark traded places with light. I showered, grabbed a muffin, and went to work. Daisy was stable. I noticed she hadn't eaten anything but I wasn't too surprised, given her recent ordeal. Hughie was studying an ECG tracing in the cramped office that we shared. I took off my coat and plopped down into a chair.

"Jocelyn Pitman is going to report me to the NSVMA."

Hughie looked up. "I heard."

"I'm sorry. I suppose I should have taken a second set of X-rays but she's always complaining about cost and ... "

Hughie shook his head. "Look, Em, if that cat had half a dozen stones for three months, I wouldn't have taken another set of X-rays either. I don't know of any vet who would have."

I took a deep breath and sighed. "I hope you're right."

"I usually am," he grinned.

I tried to push Jocelyn to the back of my mind. In truth, I did feel better after talking with Hughie. Confession was good for the soul. I was always a bit envious of my Catholic friends who were absolved of a week's worth of sin at confessional. The United Church had no such Get Out of Jail Free card.

By suppertime, that absolved feeling had given way to growing dread. Bathsheba was doing well, but Daisy had not eaten all day. Huddled in the back of her kennel, she seemed to be working harder and harder for each breath she took. With Hilary's help, I repeated the X-rays. As soon as I held them up to the light, I saw what had happened. Telling Hilary to prep Daisy for surgery, I called Delbert.

The second set of X-rays, taken almost 24 hours later, showed a dramatic change. Part of Daisy's liver and stomach had oozed into her chest cavity through a tear in the diaphragm that I hadn't been able to detect earlier. Her lungs couldn't expand properly. With Delbert's permission, we repaired the tear surgically; with no further complications, Daisy could go home in four to five days.

"I wasn't worried, Dr. McBride," Mr. Martinello said simply when the surgery was over. "I knew you would fix her."

I rode my bike to work on Thursday. Thank God I had a three-day weekend coming up. As my legs churned furiously, the wind whipped my hair and reddened my cheeks. My bike cut a path through the mosaic of leaves littering the sidewalk. Somehow it felt better to be struggling against the wind than sitting in comfort behind the steering wheel of my car.

Mr. Martinello was already at the hospital when I arrived. Susan had wheeled in a chair and he was settled happily beside Daisy's open kennel, stroking her head. He turned toward me, his old eyes bright within the weathered canvas of his face.

"Did you see the sunrise this morning, Dr. McBride? Beautiful." He began humming Edvard Grieg's "Morning Mood."

"Not really." I shook my head. The truth was I had seen the sunrise and pulled a pillow over my head. Delbert had seen the same sunrise and heard a symphony.

"I get up early," he explained as Daisy nibbled his fingers and rubbed her cheek against his hand. "I like to see the new day start."

Daisy thrust her face against Delbert's. Her purr, soft at first, gained momentum, spilling out from the kennel and filling the recovery ward as her happiness grew into a feline rendition of "Morning Mood." Except for her shaved chest and abdomen, no one would know she'd ever had surgery. She rolled onto her back and blinked at Delbert.

"Just look at my Daisy," he beamed.

As it turned out, Hughie was right. Jocelyn didn't file a complaint and in fact continued to bring Bathsheba to Ocean View. She always complained about cost and Bathsheba always hissed at me. Wiggles MacFarlane did just fine as a bobtail. Two weeks after he was home, Jason swallowed the red rubber band holding a broccoli bunch together and had surgery to remove that. He was as ungrateful as ever. The Baker children registered Matilda in the housecat category of the local cat club show, where he won first prize.

And once a month, a lonely old man dressed in a suit and tie brought his cat to the hospital for her vitamin shot. I made sure the staff always booked a half-hour appointment so there was time for tea.

Chapter 3

HUGHIE LOOKED POSITIVELY SMUG as he handed me a steaming triple-triple from Tim Hortons, my first of the morning. I mumbled a thank-you and continued studying an ECG tracing. The narrow strip of hills and valleys that assessed my patient's heart health was two metres long. As it dangled enticingly over the edge of the desk, Carter opened one eye, weighed his options, and went back to sleep.

Not so Hughie.

"What a glorious day!" he declared as he hung his jacket on the hook behind the door. Humming cheerfully, he sharpened all his pencils then began sorting through the mail, a task he normally put off until it arrived stamped with bold red overdue notices.

I grunted a reply. Admittedly, I was in a foul mood. Last night, I found out that Mom had called Benny Mombourquette to help her gather items for the Diabetes Association. No wonder she hadn't complained when I couldn't make it. There were half a dozen neighbours who gladly would have helped her, but Mom was determined that the boy who used to pee on visitors from the top of the pine tree in his front yard was somehow the perfect match for me.

I had known Benny since kindergarten but in Grade 9 he had moved away and we lost touch. This past year when I returned home from a mixed-animal practice in British Columbia to work at Ocean View, we had reconnected through a series of mishaps. Prodded no doubt by my mother, Benny had called last night wondering if I wanted to go for coffee sometime. I made up an excuse about long, unpredictable hours and the onset of a cold.

When Hughie throttled up and began singing Marvin Gaye's "I

Heard It Through the Grapevine," complete with choreography, I could stand it no longer.

"All right." I laid my pen down on the desk. "What?"

Hughie looked at me with a benevolent smile then sat down. He leaned slowly back into the chair and with a sigh of contentment, rested his arms behind his head.

"You'll never guess who I saw when I was driving past X-tra X-citing X-perience this morning," he grinned. "Dropping off a video rental."

I bit. "Who?"

"Dr. Dick!" he hissed.

"Oh my God!" I clapped a hand over my mouth and burst out laughing.

Dr. Richard Johnson, or Dr. Dick-Dick as he was known at Ocean View, had begun practicing while dinosaurs still roamed the earth. He was fond of criticizing other veterinarians in general and Hughie in particular. Rather than reprimand him, the veterinary association hoped he would either die or retire, whichever came first.

Over the years, Dr. Dick (his shortened moniker) had made shrewd business decisions and had allegedly amassed a small fortune. He had eight children and a very religious wife who was well known in the city for her charitable endeavours. Nevertheless, I couldn't get past the fact that his parents had combined Richard and Johnson without considering the result.

"Did he see you?" I asked.

"Oh yeah!" Hughie grinned. "I tooted the horn and waved."

Picking up the chart for his next patient, he winked. "Have a good day, Em."

The day got even more interesting later on when Dr. Johnson called the hospital to ask a favour. I knew who it was as soon as I heard the preamble of snorts and grunts on the other end of the line. I cringed as I held the phone to my ear, even though I knew I couldn't catch anything.

"It's Johnson," he began. It was a statement, not an introduction.

"Dick Johnson?" I couldn't help myself.

"Yeah. Look. Joyce, my tech, is off sick. Some female thing. I'm sending a patient down to you."

"A cat?" I asked.

"Well, of course a cat!" Dr. Dick snapped. In a softer tone he added, "You have a wonderful practice down there; I've always said that. And I'm too busy to see this patient. I know there's other practices closer, but I want them to see the best."

I hesitated. Dr. Dick never referred clients; he hoarded them. I'm sure the first penny he ever earned was making money in a high-yield investment somewhere.

"Well?" he grunted.

Caught off guard, all I could manage was a feeble, "Okay."

"Good! I'll send them right down. And Emily?"

"Ye-e-es?" I replied warily.

"Keep up the good work. Dr. Doucette is an admirable mentor and you'll learn a lot from him." The last remark sent Dr. Johnson into respiratory distress and he had to hang up the phone.

An elegant-looking couple arrived about half an hour later with a silent carrier. They thanked me for seeing them on such short notice. While her husband coaxed the stoic cat out of the carrier, Mrs. Agnappi explained that Malcolm had been missing for over two weeks and had just returned home. Even so, I was shocked by his appearance. A big-boned tabby, he was gaunt to the point of emaciation and severely dehydrated as well. Uncharacteristic for a cat, his mouth was wide open.

I slipped on a pair of gloves and pried apart the matted fur on each side of his face revealing the pus-filled, necrotic tissue underneath. Somehow, Malcolm's collar had been pulled halfway off and had become lodged between his jaws. He may have done this himself or it may have become snagged on something. It was also possible he had been the victim of abuse. The roof of his mouth was black and grotesquely swollen. Judging by his condition, I suspected he had been this way for at least a week, probably longer.

Mrs. Agnappi gasped and covered her mouth. Mr. Agnappi flinched but did not look away. He was tall with an almost regal bearing. Grey at the temples, he was a handsome man, and when he spoke he commanded attention, not because he was loud but because he was not. Each word was clearly articulated and bore faint traces of his African heritage.

"Can you help him, Dr. McBride?" he asked.

I looked up. Mr. Agnappi was studying me. His eyes were dark brown, his pupils invisible.

"Bernard found Malcolm when he was just a kitten wandering in the street," Mrs. Agnappi explained, holding onto her husband's arm.

I nodded and turned my attention back to Malcolm. Most cats considered a trip to the vet as a threat to their personal well-being. But Malcolm seemed to understand we were here to help, that we knew, as he did, something was terribly wrong. In that instant of clarity, a bond of trust forms between patient and veterinarian. I ran a reassuring hand along his back. Hilary was standing beside me, ready to help.

"Hilary," I said in a soft voice, as I continued to stroke Malcolm, "hand me those scissors, will you?"

I began cutting the collar away in several places. Parts of the fabric were embedded in the decaying flesh. With sterile gauze and saline, we pried them from the surrounding tissue and carefully shaved the fur around the wounds. Even with the collar gone, however, Malcolm was unable to close his mouth.

As I flushed his wounds and applied antibiotic ointment, Mr. Agnappi spoke softly to Malcolm in a language I didn't recognize, but whose intention I clearly understood. Like a lullaby, they ebbed and flowed in a gentle rhythm while I continued to work. Because the cat was so dehydrated, we inserted a catheter in his front leg and attached the line from a bag of fluids. To prevent the line from kinking, we kept the leg straight by taping it to a splint. The big, gentle tabby studied the cumbersome appendage but made no attempt to interfere. I administered some painkiller through the port in the IV line.

I then carried him into the recovery ward while Hilary wheeled the IV pump and fluid pole behind me. The Agnappis watched through the window. I laid him gently on a warm afghan with a heated thermal pack against his back. Closing the kennel door, I turned off the bright fluorescent light overhead, leaving only the small table lamp lit. As the room dissolved into warm hues and indistinct lines, Malcolm lay his head down on the blanket. The pump hummed softly as it worked.

Slipping out of the recovery ward, I closed the door behind me with a gentle twist on the knob. The Agnappis turned away from the window then and gazed expectantly at me. Mrs. Agnappi's hand rested on her husband's arm. He patted it reassuringly. Malcolm lay in his kennel, eyes closed. We had given him a helping hand but if he survived this ordeal, it would be a testament to his own strength and will to survive. Some would say it was God's will.

"We'll see how he is in the morning," I told them.

Mr. Agnappi bowed his head slightly in acknowledgement and murmured a reply in the same language he had used with Malcolm. Placing a hand under his wife's elbow, he guided her down the hall and into reception.

"Don't you worry, luv," I heard Bernie say kindly. "We'll take good care of your wee puss."

Malcolm was my last appointment of the evening. As I headed toward the office to update my charts and check for messages, I could hear Hughie on the phone with one of his regular clients, Mrs. Archie

MacDonald. The devoted owner of five cats, she had recently acquired a goofy, lovable lab who enjoyed supplementing his expensive dog food with treats from the litter box.

"Yes, that's a normal canine behaviour. They love poop in general but cat poop … well, that's the best. It's like dessert!" Hughie added, in a flash of inspiration. "Just make sure he can't get at those litter boxes anymore!"

"One man's trash is another man's treasure," he grinned at me as he hung up the phone.

In spite of my worry over Malcolm, I laughed. This was the nature of a veterinary practice. One harrowing moment, we could be treating a cat hit by a car and fighting for his life; the next we'd be vaccinating a kitten whose off-the-wall exuberance was a welcome reminder that life will find a way. And with the cats came the owners who loved them.

"Hey, how's that cat Dr. Dick sent over?" Hughie asked.

I shook my head. "We cleaned him up and got him on antibiotics, pain-killer, and fluids, but it may be too late. I don't know."

Hughie nodded. "Hilary said it was one of the worst cases of soft-tissue trauma she'd ever seen."

"It's really bad," I agreed. "He's a great cat and they're such nice people."

"Not the kind ol' Dick would send our way, no matter how busy he was." Hughie nibbled thoughtfully on a fingernail.

I checked on Malcolm one more time before I left for the evening. Hilary had arranged a buffet of temptations but the dishes remained untouched. Malcolm still lay in his kennel, eyes closed as if shutting out his misery. I adjusted his IV line and gently rubbed his forehead. Although he didn't open his eyes, I could hear an unmistakable croak as he tried to purr. Encouraged, I dipped my finger in some cat food and held it to his nose but the great head turned away. I watched him for a few moments longer until Susan came in with a load of clean laundry to be folded and put away.

I arrived at work early the next morning only to find that Dr. Dick had commandeered the storage room and was single-handedly unloading our weekly order of cat food from his van.

"What's going on?" I whispered to Susan.

"Our food order was delivered to his place by mistake. He called this morning to say he was bringing it over personally," Susan shrugged.

"You're kidding me."

"Uh-uh. God's truth. Cross my heart." She folded her arms across her chest and continued to stare in disbelief at the scene unfolding in our storage room. "Someone should get a camera."

As the piles of food grew, so did Dr. Dick's discomfort. He was not a young man and after a particularly alarming bout of wheezing and grunting, I suggested someone should help him.

"We already offered," Hilary replied. "He said he wants the exercise."

Since I was the only one with a current first aid certificate, I hoped he didn't drop dead of a heart attack and need mouth-to-mouth resuscitation. If that happened, Mrs. Johnson was going to be a widow. I left to check on Malcolm.

Malcolm was lying down, his splinted leg with the IV line stretched out to one side. The line was running smoothly and Hilary had administered his morning medications through the IV's port with no difficulty. She had replaced the untouched food from last night with another tantalizing buffet, but Malcolm showed no interest. I applied more antibiotic ointment on each side of his face, telling Malcolm what a wonderful and handsome boy he was.

Bernie tapped on the window, waving Gus MacKinnon's chart. I had seen Gus earlier in the week. Reportedly, he had swallowed a condom but had seemed fine. I was reluctant to proceed with a potentially unnecessary surgery so I advised his owners to keep a close watch on him and check his stool regularly for any evidence of the wayward condom. The fact that he was back, and so early in the morning, wasn't a good sign.

I rubbed Malcolm's chin, kissed his forehead, and told him he was going to get better. Then I hurried down the hall to the exam room where Gus and his owner, Mia, were waiting. This time Mia had brought along her boyfriend, who sat in the corner avoiding eye contact.

"He's not eating," Mia declared, "and he's vomiting gross piles of frothy yellow stuff."

According to Mia, he had produced only a single bowel movement in three days, which she had meticulously examined and declared condom-free.

"You're sure he swallowed a condom?" I asked.

"Uh huh. Oh yeah." Mia's earrings bounced up and down as she chomped on her gum and glared at her boyfriend. "Do you want the brand name?"

"No, that's not … "

"Golden Glove," Mia declared.

I thanked her and laid the consent form on the table. "Well, I'll just get you to read this over and sign it for me."

Mia thrust the paper at her boyfriend, who glanced sideways then slowly picked up the form and began to read.

"Three hundred dollars!" he gasped, blanching. Dressed in a well-worn trench coat and a pair of army boots, he looked like he could barely afford three dollars.

The orange hair on Mia's head bristled. "Is there a problem, Roger?" she asked, her voice glacial.

Roger picked up the pen and hastily scribbled his signature. Gus was the apple of Mia's heavily made up eye. I suspected that once the bill was paid, Roger would find himself on the doorstep with his luggage and any leftover condoms.

Bernie rescheduled my morning appointments so that we could

begin Gus's surgery right away. X-rays showed nothing unusual other than a build-up of gas in the large intestine. With Gus anesthetized and lying on his back, I made an incision the length of his shaved belly. Then I manually began examining every inch of his glistening intestines with my gloved fingers. I struck gold, Golden Glove gold, in the small intestine.

Somehow, it had slipped through the narrow opening leading from the stomach but had become lodged in the small intestine. There it formed a plug through which nothing could pass. I made a small incision just behind the inflamed area and, with a pair of forceps, gently removed the obstruction. Susan held out a pill vial and I deposited the remains inside. I was fairly certain Mia was the kind of owner who would want a keepsake.

We stitched Gus back up. I removed his endotracheal tube then transferred him to the recovery ward where Malcolm, the only other occupant, lay quiet and withdrawn. Some cats continue to doze peacefully as the effect of the anesthetic wears off, but Gus was not one of them. His unearthly moans and thrashing convinced Malcolm it might be a good idea to open his eyes and see what was going on.

I don't know if he was concerned that the wild thing two doors down might steal his food, or if hunger overcame pain. I held my breath as he shifted position, his head coming into contact with the nearest plate of food. He licked at the plate and seemed confused when it slid out of reach. With the splint on his leg he didn't have much room to manoeuver, so I opened the kennel door and held the plate in place.

It took Malcolm nearly twenty minutes to eat a tablespoon of food. Unwilling to break the spell, I stood perfectly still, hands locked on that plate. When he was finished, he looked up at me and meowed for more. These are the moments that vets remember when they are old and grey: not the grueling schedule, the ringing phones, or the difficult clients, but the small triumphs.

I called Mrs. Agnappi with the good news.

"Oh," she cried, "this is so wonderful, Dr. McBride! Bernard will be so happy! He did not sleep well last night. And if the husband does not sleep well, the wife does not sleep well," she giggled.

"Mrs. Agnappi?" I hesitated for a moment. "Your husband said something to me last night just as you were leaving. Do you know what it was?"

"Ah, yes." I could hear the smile in her voice. "He said your hands are strong but gentle, like the butterflies around you."

We chatted for a few moments longer and made plans to discharge Malcolm that evening. After Mrs. Agnappi hung up, I held my hands out in front of me and studied them. They were big, dry, and wrinkled. In truth, I had always been a bit embarrassed by them. No amount of hand lotion, manicures, or nail polish had ever made them look more respectable. One of my aunts had suggested it was a pity gloves had gone out of fashion.

But the butterflies …

"Dr. McBride!" Bernie loomed large in the doorway, interrupting my thoughts. "What are you doing?"

"Nothing." I thrust my hands into my lab coat pockets.

She held out the chart for my next patient and shooed me out of the office. "Get to work, luv," she grinned.

The Agnappis arrived just before closing to take Malcolm home. He had polished off two more plates of food. The swelling in his mouth was noticeably lessened, and I felt they would have no trouble continuing with his medications. Mia was visiting Gus in the recovery ward and clapped a hand over her mouth when she caught sight of Malcolm.

"Oh my gawd! What's wrong with your cat? That is SO gross! Ooooh!" She wrinkled her face in horror.

Mr. Agnappi explained what had happened in his precise, measured English.

"You're shittin' me!" Mia exclaimed.

"No, I most certainly am not," Mr. Agnappi smiled. "Dr. McBride, however, has worked her magic with young Malcolm and now he is going home."

"What is wrong with your cat, dear?" Mrs. Agnappi asked.

"He swallowed a rub ... prophylactic," Mia corrected herself.

Mrs. Agnappi nodded wisely.

Before Mia could unleash the details of Gus's misadventure, I whisked Malcolm into his carrier. He was much happier now that both the cumbersome splint and IV line had been removed. I went over his discharge instructions and reminded the Agnappis I wanted to see Malcolm in a few days for a recheck.

"I wish you well with your Gus," Mr. Agnappi said to Mia as they were leaving.

"Thanks," Mia replied. "Say, where are you guys from? I love your wife's dress."

"Uganda," Mr. Agnappi said. "But we live here now."

I was just a teenager worrying about pimples and school dances when news of General Idi Amin's atrocities in Uganda began making headlines. Mia would have been a toddler. I waited for her to forge ahead but instead, with a wisdom beyond her years, she just nodded.

"Well," she said, "good luck with Malcolm."

Mr. Agnappi thanked her, then picked up Malcolm's carrier. With the kennel in one hand and a case of food in the other, he strode through reception, head held high. At the counter, he and his wife stopped to thank everyone for their kindness to Malcolm and made an appointment for the next week. At the door, he once more acknowledged me with a slight bow of his head and a fleeting smile.

The Agnappis became loyal clients and I saw them many times over the years. I always wanted to ask Mr. Agnappi about the butterflies he had seen hovering around me but I never did. When I am sad or frightened or feeling alone, I hear the voice of a very dear client who once told me that butterflies are the souls of those we love, reborn. It is a fanciful idea, but it gives me comfort because, sometimes, not knowing is more powerful, more beautiful, than knowing.

Dr. Richard Johnson, on the other hand, was a man who dealt in practicalities. When he called Hughie to get his colleague's "valuable opinion" on a case any first-year veterinary student could figure out, my boss could stand it no longer. During the course of conversation, Hughie voiced his opinion that what a man does in his spare time is that man's business and no one else's. The entire staff was relieved when a client reported a few weeks later that she had stopped in at "that queer little man's place" to buy food. Dr. Johnson told her that our prices were outrageous and that we had a flea infestation and should be shut down.

"Dickie's back!" Hughie grinned.

Chapter 4

Tapered white candles!

I stopped typing discharge notes for a patient long enough to scribble a note on my to-do list. With only two weeks to go before Christmas, the list was growing faster than the checkout line at Walmart. These were the things that had to be purchased, delivered, mailed, baked, decorated, wrapped, and cleaned to make Christmas a success.

It had begun as an insignificant piece of scrap paper and had swollen to a full-size sheet of lined paper with writing on both sides. I was considering the addition of a second page when I heard my boss exclaim, "My name's Hughie, too!"

In the mid-nineties, with the world population approaching six billion, meeting another Hughie should have come as no surprise. Curious, I looked up. Across the hall, my boss was face to face with an odd-looking creature perched at the edge of the examining table. Apparently just as surprised by the coincidence, the cat tilted his head at a peculiar angle as he studied his vet.

Hughie the cat was a Devon Rex. Friendly and inquisitive, the Rex is best described as a dehydrated domestic shorthair. A genetic mutation resulted in the now standardized breed's short wavy coat and shrivelled whiskers. A generous pair of ears and bulbous eyes adds to its gnome-like appearance.

"He's started spraying around the house." There was a note of anxiety in Mrs. Becker's voice. "It's not like he walks up to something and just sprays," she continued. "That's bad enough. But Hughie's blind. And he sort of walks in circles. So it goes EVERYWHERE!"

"Like machine-gun fire," Mr. Becker added.

"We would have had him neutered before but … "

"He's got more problems than Heinz has pickles," Mr. Becker interjected. "His other vet didn't think it'd be safe. We'd like to get a second opinion before Frances here loses her mind."

Mrs. Becker nodded vigorously, as if confirming the possibility.

"What kind of problems?" Hughie asked.

"Get out your list, Frances," Mr. Becker sighed, as Hughie slowly closed the door.

I added sweet potatoes to my own list then entered the second exam room where Jasmine Houlihan was waiting for me. Jasmine was a short, squat, epithet-hurling tabby that should have been named after a Russian weightlifter on steroids, maybe Helga or Olga, rather than a delicately scented flower. My mission, as always, was to vaccinate Jasmine as quickly as possible before she had a chance to dwell on the negative. With my mission accomplished, I popped her back into the kennel. For good measure, I tossed in a few treats so I could talk to her owner in peace.

By the time I finished, the door to Hughie's exam room was still shut. In reception I smiled at my next appointment, a new client with a tiny black kitten in his lap.

As Bernie ushered them into the exam room, Hilary grabbed my arm and pulled me aside. "Make sure you check the kitten's collar," she whispered.

"Why? Is it too tight?"

"Just check the collar," she smirked.

I shrugged and shook my head. The staff had their own unique brand of humour, and I often found myself on the receiving end of their jokes. For my birthday last summer, they had somehow managed to find an entrepreneur who specialized in something other than the standard pink flamingos. I arrived at work to find an 11" × 14" glossy of me surrounded by 33 double-D pink lace bras swaying in the breeze, along with the earthshaking headline: "Thirty-Three Today!" It was a memorable day for the Tim Hortons crowd next door.

I closed the door to the exam room. Bernie and Hilary continued to stare in through the window, grinning like idiots. Unceremoniously, I closed the blinds then turned back toward my client and introduced myself.

"Hi. I'm Dr. McBride."

"Pete MacDonnell." He smiled and shook my hand. So far, so good. I noticed a bulging knapsack filled with books on the floor.

"You must be a student," I smiled.

"Third-year science," he replied.

Turning to the kitten, I continued, "And you are … ?" I checked the name on the chart. "Amanda."

My young patient was busy studying a furry orange leg that alternately appeared and disappeared underneath the door. Carter, one of our five resident cats, was its exuberant owner.

"She's a Christmas present for my girlfriend," Pete explained as Amanda pounced on Carter's invitation to play. He chirped in delight from the other side of the door. Kittens were easy. Adults, on the other hand, were a tougher crowd. They were already in a bad mood after being stuffed in a carrier and transported through space and time to cat hell where the devil's minions wore white lab coats. The sight of an unknown cat leg flailing the air often sent them over the edge.

"Well, let's see how much she weighs," I suggested. A machine-gun purr erupted from the tiny body as Pete picked up Amanda. Cradling her in his arms he kissed her on the forehead then placed her on the pediatric scale.

"600 grams," I noted.

"Is that OK?" Pete asked. "She seems so tiny."

"That's perfect for her age and bone structure." I smiled as Amanda tried to grab my pen.

"Good." Pete was relieved. "I just want to make sure she's healthy. You know, get her vaccinated, started on the right food. All that stuff. I guess it's like having a kid."

I nodded and began my examination. Amanda settled into the palm of my hand. Her lungs were clear and her little heart raced with the excitement of being alive. She purred at my touch, even the business-like, probing touch of a veterinarian. When I leaned over to examine her mouth, I slipped a finger under the pink collar but the tension was fine. What had Hilary been so secretive about?

Then I noticed a faint flicker against her throat, a solitary star in a black, furry sky.

"What a pretty little crystal," I told Pete. "It really catches the light." I parted the fur around Amanda's neck for a closer look. Cat "bling" was becoming popular among owners and ranged from simple rhinestone-studded jewellery to elaborate gold charms.

"Oh, it's a ring. That's cute," I looked over at Pete. A wide smile cracked his face in half.

"Wait a minute." I took a closer look. "Is that an engagement ring?" I asked, my voice rising in excitement.

Pete nodded. "I'm giving Amanda to my girlfriend tonight. An early Christmas gift. She loves cats … and engagement rings, I hope," he added with a grin.

"Oh, that's so romantic!" I smiled goofily. "She'll be thrilled."

Now that I had decoded Hilary's cryptic message, I could enjoy the rest of the appointment. By the end of it, I was grinning like an idiot too. What a wonderful Christmas it was going to be for all of them. Word had spread quickly among the female staff and they treated Pete MacDonnell like royalty. Free samples flowed into his hands along with a catnip mouse for Amanda and a tour of the hospital. For days afterwards, they sighed whenever his name was mentioned.

As Christmas approached, the river of cats we saw on a daily basis slowed to a trickle. Most people were consumed by the commercial frenzy of the holiday season. Shopping centres became asylums for the temporarily insane, a condition aggravated by a greater number of cars than available parking spaces. The last thing on anyone's mind was a trip to the vet's.

Not so the Beckers. Hughie's neuter had been scheduled for December 21. The sun made a brief appearance that morning but quickly disappeared behind an advancing wall of grey. By the time Mrs. Becker arrived with Hughie in tow, an icy rain was pelting the pavement. Both were smartly dressed in matching red coats with black trim. At the reception counter, Mrs. Becker signed the consent form then looked at Bernie expectantly. So did Hughie.

"Now, you'll call as soon as he's done?" Mrs. Becker asked, her forehead rippled with worry.

"Oh yes, luv, of course," Bernie replied. "Don't you worry now."

With no other appointments that morning, Hughie was able to examine and pre-medicate his namesake right away. As the drugs took effect, the Rex lazed in his kennel, blissfully unaware he was about to lose his close companions of several years. Because of a heart murmur, anesthetic was a risk, so Hughie had decided on gas induction with isoflurane. This was less likely to cause a dangerously irregular heart rhythm, and also the patient would wake up sooner.

Susan placed him on a blanket inside the clear Plexiglas box and attached the lid. With each breath, his body relaxed more as the oxygen-isoflurane mix flowed into his lungs. When he was sound asleep, Hughie removed him from the box and laid him on the surgery table. I attached a plastic, cup-shaped gas mask over his mouth and nose. While Hughie concentrated on the surgery, I would monitor the anesthetic and ECG tracing. Hughie listened to his heart one more time then picked up the scalpel.

"Here we go." He took a deep breath.

A week earlier, we had sent a sample of Hughie's blood to a lab in the United States for typing. Most cats are Type A but many Rexes are Type B. They also have clotting problems. Results could be disastrous if the wrong blood type was transfused in an emergency. Fortunately, Hughie Becker had escaped his breed's Achilles heel, though he more than made up for it with his other quirks. That list of problems was on my mind, and no doubt my boss's too, as we began surgery.

Fortunately, the castration was routine with no complications. In less than fifteen minutes, Hughie was back in his kennel. With two carefully placed incisions, he had been taken out of the gene pool and would probably never again feel the urge to spray. Not that he had much opportunity to impress the girls in the neighbourhood anyway. His outdoor activity was restricted to walking in circles on a leash.

As Hughie the cat rested comfortably, the mood in the recovery ward became giddy. Given the Rex's history, we had been prepared for any number of medical emergencies. In the afterglow of a successful surgery, Hughie the vet did his impression of Louis Armstrong singing "Hello Dolly." I countered with a variety of barnyard noises. I had risen to fame in Grade 2 as the voice behind our class play Farmer Andy's Animals, then spent years refining my skills. At vet school, where parties depended on beer, contraband, and cheap entertainment, I was always in demand.

When Hughie called Mrs. Becker with the good news, she admitted she had just downed a rum and eggnog. In keeping with the euphoria we all felt, she cried happily, "Well, I think I'll just go and pour myself another!"

As the day progressed, the cold rain that had gotten the morning off to a bad start turned into freezing rain, followed by fifteen centimetres of snow. City streets were transformed into icy conveyor belts that only the foolhardy or those with hospitalized cats dared attempt. The Beckers fit both those categories and arrived at the hospital early that evening, white-faced but anxious to take Hughie home.

He was still groggy from the pain medication and his red-rimmed eyeballs bore glossy traces of the lubricant applied earlier to keep his corneas moist. A pink tongue protruded listlessly between enormous white fangs. Hughie was a lovable but homely cat before surgery. Tonight he was downright ugly, and the Beckers loved him all the more for it.

After wrapping Hughie in swaddling clothes, Mrs. Becker followed her husband as he blazed a trail through the maze of chairs in reception. Rushing ahead, he thrust the first set of doors wide open for his wife and cat. Outside, the wind licked the second set of doors, seeking entry.

"Thanks so much, Doc! Merry Christmas!" Mr. Becker waved.

"Drive carefully!" Hughie shouted above the rush of wind as Mr. Becker opened the outside door.

Wrapping an arm around his wife, Mr. Becker guided her to the car. Then pulling his hat down against the wind, he hurried to the driver's side and struggled inside. The brave little Mazda roared to life, headlights glowing and windshield wipers slashing ferociously against the elements. As the Beckers inched their way home, the car lights receded then disappeared altogether, leaving the parking lot deserted.

Hughie locked the doors. "Might as well close early. No one's gonna be out on a night like this."

As they completed their evening chores, the staff left one by one until only Bernie and I remained. Bernie had turned the lights off in reception and was counting the cash when we heard a frantic pounding outside. Two people huddled by the door, trying to shield a cat carrier from the wind.

"Oh dear! The poor, wee things!" Grabbing her keys, Bernie rushed to open the door. "Come in! Come in!"

Grateful for sanctuary, the young couple slipped inside the vestibule.

As they tried to shake the miserable night off their clothes, a kitten's high-pitched voice rose in concern from inside the carrier. A young woman, probably in her early twenties, slipped her fingers through the plastic mesh of the door and the kitten nuzzled against them.

"Thank God you're still here." I recognized Pete MacDonnell as he pulled back the hood of his winter jacket. "It's Amanda. We think she's broken her leg."

"Bring her right into the exam room," I said, and motioned for them to follow me. Pete laid Amanda's carrier on top of the examining table and opened the door. Amanda hobbled out on three legs then flopped on the table.

"Did you see what happened?" I asked.

"No," Pete shook his head, "we were watching TV. She was running around playing, and then we heard this crash from the bedroom."

"I think she jumped up on the dresser and slipped on the lace runner," the woman added. "When we got to the bedroom, everything was on the floor and she was under the bed."

"This is Carole, my fiancée," Pete explained, introducing us.

Carole smiled shyly. I noticed a familiar sparkle on her left hand as she tried to comfort the kitten. Things must have gone well in the romance department. Bending over Amanda, I gently began my examination. Every time I touched her leg she tried to bite me, although she was not a mean-spirited little creature by nature.

"Is it broken?" Pete asked, seeing me frown.

"It's certainly painful," I said. "She doesn't want me to go near that leg. I'd like to do some X-rays."

Pete and Carole readily agreed. In place of a stretcher, we removed the top half of Amanda's carrier and gently placed her inside. When Pete opened the exam room door, I nearly banged into Bernie who had obviously been eavesdropping. Her face turned the same shade of red as her hair.

"What are you going to do?" she asked, padding behind me down the hallway.

"We're going to take some X-rays."

"Who is?"

"We are. You and me."

She grabbed my arm. "But I'm a receptionist! I don't know anything about X-rays!"

"Well, it's your lucky day." I hauled the lead apron off the wooden rack. "Put on this dosimetry badge and hold your arms out."

"What about my ovaries?"

"Bernie, you're fifty-six. Besides, the lead apron protects you."

Still complaining, Bernie reluctantly held her arms out as I helped her struggle into the heavy lead apron and lead gauntlets. Then I slipped a pair of protective goggles over her wide eyes. Lastly, I fastened the lead thyroid protector in place, rendering her mute. I placed Amanda in position on the X-ray plate, explaining to Bernie how to hold her in position while I focused the beam over her right hind leg. We took a pair of X-rays then I grabbed the plates and headed to the darkroom. Bernie's muffled cries overtook me and I looped back to help her out her suit of armour.

"Praise the Almighty!" Bernie gasped as she wrestled free of the heavy garment. Her face was red and her freckles looked ready to explode. Strands of frizzy red hair corkscrewed out from her head. She raced to the back door and, yanking it open, stuck her head outside. A frigid blast of Arctic air swept through the storage room.

"Damn hot flashes," she grimaced.

I stifled a laugh as I headed into the darkroom to develop the X-rays. No doubt my turn would come soon enough. By the time I returned to the exam room, Amanda was asleep in her carrier. Carole and Pete each held a steaming cup of tea, grinning as Bernie described in vivid detail the horrors of combining radiology with menopause. They looked up expectantly when I entered.

"Well, you're right," I began. "Her leg is definitely broken. It's an unusual fracture though."

"Can you fix it?" Pete asked.

"Why don't you come have a look at the X-rays? Bernie can stay here with Amanda."

Bernie looked relieved. Carole and Pete followed me to radiology where I had left the X-rays on the viewer. I turned off the overhead lights and pointed to the break, visible as a thin shadow across the right femur. Carole and Pete leaned in closer for a better look.

"Most breaks are jagged. Uneven," I explained. "When we put them together they tend to be stable. But this break is clean and very smooth. That means it's slippery and doesn't hold position well. So we have to plate the bones together instead of pinning them."

Carole nodded.

"The problem is that it's a much more expensive procedure. It's not something we would do here," I continued. "I would refer you to another practice that specializes in orthopedics."

"Dr. McBride?" Pete hesitated. "I hate to ask you this, but how much would the operation cost?"

"Well, I would guess around a thousand dollars."

In the silence that followed, Carole looked up at Pete. "We could ask my dad for help," she suggested.

Taking her hand in his, Pete said nothing.

"Look," I jumped in, "it's a miserable night. Amanda needs to stay anyway. I'll give her something for the pain and in the morning I'll make some phone calls."

Amanda was still asleep and Bernie not too far behind when we returned. Pete helped Carole on with her coat, then they tiptoed out of the exam room. I locked the hospital doors behind them and waved goodbye. Holding onto each other for support, they soon disappeared, consumed by the swirling snow and starless night like the Beckers before them.

※ ※ ※

By mid-morning, two things had happened. The sun made a glorious return and the orthopedic specialist in nearby Bedford returned my call. His estimate was $1,200, with 60% down and the balance payable in bi-weekly instalments. The Atlantic Veterinary College in Charlottetown would do the surgery for less but required full payment. By the time travel costs and accommodations were added on, Pete would be no further ahead financially.

I was dreading my next phone call.

"Any luck?" Hughie asked, sticking his head in the door.

"Not really." I shook my head sadly. "I was just about to call Pete."

"You know, Em, I've been thinking." Hughie grabbed a piece of paper off the desk and without bothering to sit down, began to scribble furiously. I craned my neck trying to follow the maze of squiggles and arrows.

"See? Here. And here!" He thrust the piece of paper in front of me. "You won't find this in the books anymore, but I think it'll work."

As I studied the paper, he added, "Tell them I'll do the surgery at no charge but they'll have to cover all the other medical costs. It'll probably be around three, four hundred."

I looked at him in surprise. "Are you sure?"

Hughie waved his hand absently, claiming it was a good opportunity for him to practice his rusty orthopedic skills. When Mr. Becker called later that day to speak with Dr. Doucette, Bernie rather grandly explained he was preparing for a ground-breaking surgery the following day. Mr. Becker then demanded to speak to "that other doctor." Fearing the worst, I picked up the phone in the office.

"Hi, Mr. Becker. It's Dr. McBride. Is everything OK?"

Mr. Becker assured me that everything was just fine. His speech was a bit slurred as he freely admitted to his third rum and coke of the evening. But, as he pointed out, how often do all your kids make it home for Christmas and your cat, once blind, can now see?

"Pardon me?"

"Hu-Hughie!" Mr. Becker hiccupped. "He can see!"

"Mr. Becker, what do you mean, 'He can see?'" I asked, raising my voice against the party that was in full swing at the Becker household.

Mr. Becker sighed, frustrated at my inability to grasp the obvious.

"Bert, give that phone to me!" There were muffled complaints as control of the phone shifted hands and Mrs. Becker came on the line.

"Oh, Dr. McBride! Thank you for calling." I didn't bother to point out that her inebriated husband had called me. "Hughie is just marvellous!"

"He can see!" Bert gurgled cheerfully from somewhere nearby.

"That's just it, Dr. McBride!" Mrs. Becker's voice rose in excitement. "We think Hughie can see. Is that possible?"

I hesitated. It was late and the Beckers had admittedly been celebrating.

"Probably not," I said at last. "Maybe he just seems more active now that he's recovered from surgery."

"I suppose you're right," Mrs. Becker agreed. "It does seem crazy."

I wished her a merry Christmas and was hanging up the phone when she cried out in desperation, "You're sure Dr. Doucette didn't do anything special?"

If Hughie Becker had miraculously regained his eyesight, it wasn't because my boss had removed two marble-sized testicles from the other end.

"No, it was a routine surgery," I replied.

"All right, then," Mrs. Becker sighed. "Thank you, doctor."

I spent the remainder of the evening at the nearby shopping centre. For the good of humanity, malls were open until midnight. By 2:00 a.m., a stack of wrapped presents were safely stored in the spare closet, away from the reach of prying paws, and a container of homemade Nanaimo bars sat on the kitchen counter. I wiggled into bed, trying not to disturb the cats, who had been sensibly napping for hours.

As I waited for sleep that would not come, I lay awake wondering when Christmas had been reduced to crossing things off a list. When I was a child, December 25th was the most important day of my life. The day after, I began counting down the remaining 364 until Christmas returned with its magical boxes of shining ornaments, the plastic reindeer family, and the miniature village under the Christmas tree, which I always helped Dad pick out. Over the years, there were casualties; the numbers were particularly high the year our cat Bootsie climbed the tree and knocked it over. But a three-legged reindeer could always be propped up against a miniature house or a fence. And the tree could be moved to a corner where no one would notice that it was only decorated on one side.

I struggled to continue believing in Santa Claus for a long time, not to preserve the bounty of presents that came my way but to preserve the magic. When my mother tried to talk me out of Santa Claus, I stubbornly stood up for him, defying all logical arguments to the contrary. In the end, I was right – when I no longer believed, it was different. For all of us.

But in the brightness of morning, there was no time to be philosophical. As we scrubbed for Amanda's operation, Hughie hummed a non-stop version of "Deck the Halls." Lather flew outward in every direction, littering the floor with soapy polka dots.

In surgery, Hilary prepped Amanda's shaved right hind leg. Using sterile technique, she worked from the inside to the outside, never contaminating an area that had already been cleaned and disinfected.

Gowned and gloved, with our hands held above our waists, we waited for Hilary to finish. When she looked up, Hughie nodded.

"Here we go, Em."

I felt a tingle of electricity buzz through me. It was always exciting to watch a new technique or, in this case, a very old one that I had never seen done before. With Hilary and me on one side of the table, Hughie positioned himself on the other.

"Pulse ox is 100%," Hilary reported. "Respiration's good. Heart rate's 170."

Amanda lay on a warming pad, her tiny body just a blip on the vast surgery table. Only her head peeked out from underneath the blue surgical drape. From a bag suspended above the table, fluids dripped silently into a vein. She slept as a mixture of isoflurane and oxygen flowed into her lungs through an endotracheal tube.

Taking a small pair of scissors from the sterile surgical kit, Hughie cut a hole in the drape to access the broken leg. So the drape wouldn't shift during surgery, he clamped it in place. He then picked up the scalpel and made a small incision through the skin and layers of tissue to the bone. The two ends of the fractured femur glistened like pearls in the exposed bed of red muscle.

"Hil, can you grab those X-rays and hold them up to the light?"

Hughie studied the films then selected an orthopedic pin from the tray. Starting at the break, he began threading the pin through the bone marrow toward the hip. He continued until one end was flush with the break and the other extended through the trochanter, the thick heavy bone at the end of the femur. He repeated the procedure with a second pin.

"Em, hold those two pieces of bone together," Hughie ordered.

While I held the bones in position, he began threading the exposed end of the first pin back through the lower half of the break. Once it was securely anchored in both parts of the bone, he cut the pin but left a small piece extruding at the trochanter. When the break had healed in six to eight weeks, the pin would be removed through here in a relatively simple procedure.

The break was now held together, but the bones would rotate out of position without any secondary support. Hughie began easing the second pin into position. He worked with the confidence and gentle authority born of experience. The second pin, now attached at both ends of the femur, would provide stability.

The procedure was beautiful in its simplicity. They didn't teach this stuff at vet school – we learned only the newest techniques and medical advances. But the average small animal practice didn't have the resources of a government-funded veterinary college.

Leaning back, Hughie shrugged the stiffness out of his shoulders and neck, then studied a second set of X-rays. Later this afternoon, he and his beloved Jack Russell terrier, Sullivan, were heading home to Cape Breton for a few days. Half the island's population would be descending upon the Doucette household on Christmas Eve to eat, drink, and attend midnight mass. Santa Claus, who had a day job as a cat vet in Halifax, would hand out presents the following morning to a swarm of nieces and nephews.

"Whaddya think?" he asked, as I peered over his shoulder.

"Perfect alignment," I breathed. "Wow! That was really cool. Good job."

Hughie brushed aside the compliment. "OK. Let's start closing."

Just as Hughie picked up the suture needle, there was a tap on the surgery window. We looked up to see Mr. Becker clutching his cat. Bernie hovered in the background, her arms raised heavenward in resignation.

Mr. Becker's lips moved and he pointed at his cat in excitement. Puzzled, Hughie looked over at me.

"It's an interesting story," I smiled behind my mask. "You should hear it first-hand."

Hughie hesitated.

"Go on. I'll finish."

Intrigued, he peeled off his gloves and stepped out of surgery.

While Hilary monitored Amanda's vital signs, I began closing. When I finished the last layer of sutures, I turned off the anesthetic and waited for Amanda to wake up. By the time she was stable and settled in the recovery ward, a crowd had gathered in reception. The two Hughies were the center of attention.

"I'm not a religious man," Mr. Becker admitted to the mailman, who himself was a cat lover. The mail delivery invariably stalled at Ocean View while he chatted with the staff and played with the feline residents. "But this ... " Mr. Becker shook his head, unable to continue.

The shift boss from Tim Hortons, a large black woman named Fern, rifled through her purse and handed him a tissue. Mr. Becker smiled gratefully. After blowing his nose, he continued in a choked voice, "This is a miracle!"

"Praise Jesus!" Fern added.

The crowd murmured in agreement. And indeed, Hughie did seem able to see. While he still had a head tilt, he was able to walk in a straight line and avoided banging into chairs.

Still clad in his surgical scrubs, my boss sat cross-legged in the middle of it all, smiling benignly. He had given up denying any involvement, his mild protests drowned out by a cat-loving, miracle-needy group. Hughie left for Cape Breton a short while later with a Christmas miracle under his belt and a forty-ouncer of rum from the Beckers in his briefcase.

I, on the other hand, was on call for the next three days. To be fair, I had agreed to cover Christmas and Hughie would cover New Year's, but already I was regretting that decision. I had so much left to do before Christmas and no plans for New Year's Eve unless you counted

Rummoli with Mom's cronies and Fuzzy Navels, her newest discovery, made from peach juice and vodka. It was a neighbourhood hit.

I packed the emergency cell phone, itself the size of a shoe, into its personal suitcase then raced home that evening to scrub my flat. Mom and my oldest brother's family from Athens, Ohio, were coming for supper on Christmas Eve. Beverly, his wife, an experienced mother of four, had suggested we just order pizza or at the very least, have something that didn't require cutlery. She remembered me only as a tomboy with scraped knees and a worm collection. I wanted to impress everyone with my grown-up, domestic side.

Although I had only two scheduled appointments on the morning of December 24th, the hospital was very busy with food sales and last-minute toy purchases. Many of our clients hung up stockings for their cats, and most made sure there was a present under the tree.

"If Claude didn't get his catnip mouse … " Anne Cummings left the sentence unfinished. Anne was a loyal client but her cat Claude had little use for me, the vet profession in general, and, apparently, life without catnip.

By noon, the river of retail purchases and gifts from clients had slowed to a trickle. I studied the mound of home-baked treats, alcohol, and chocolates with enthusiasm. Except for the alcohol, most had already been sampled by an appreciative staff. Someone, probably Hughie, had sliced open the cellophane on a box of candy addressed to me, eaten a chocolate, and replaced the cellophane.

Pete and Carole arrived to take Amanda home just before we closed at three o'clock. She was bright, happy, and anxious to leave. It would be hard to keep her quiet for the next eight weeks but I was confident she would make a full recovery, thanks to Hughie.

"Thank you both so much." Carole's eyes were bright as she shook my hand. "This is the best Christmas of my life."

After they left, Bernie turned off the overhead lights. Instantly, the Christmas tree bathed the darkened room in a rainbow of colour. Miraculously, it was still standing, although it listed to the right after Carter's ambitious, but ill-advised, climb to the top. The scent of cinnamon candles hung in the air. Bernie looked round the room and sighed as she pulled the plug on the tree lights.

"When we come back, Christmas will be all over. I just hate taking down all the beautiful cards and decorations, don't you?"

"No, not really. Christmas is a lot of work. I like getting back to normal." I threw on my coat and grabbed my grocery list. "By the way, did you get Pete to sign the payment schedule?"

"No dear, I didn't have to." Balancing a cheesecake and several parcels, Bernie slipped through the door I held open for her. "They paid in full."

"Oh." I turned my key in the lock. "I guess Carole must have got some money from her father."

"No, luv," Bernie said softly, as we stepped outside into a whitewash of fat, wet snowflakes. "They took the engagement ring back. You didn't know?" she asked, seeing the look on my face.

I shook my head.

Bernie studied me for a moment, then wrapped me in a bear hug that the cheesecake somehow survived.

"Merry Christmas!" she whispered.

After a moment, she released her grip and smiled at me. Then she turned and headed down the street to her car. I watched her erratic path as she flitted among the snowflakes, trying to catch them on her tongue. Her green and purple scarf trailed behind, a colourful beacon in the sea of white.

Slowly I crumpled my list and tossed it into the garbage can.

Chapter 5

On a gorgeous Halifax morning in February, an event more rare than the winged migration of elephants in pink tutus, I decided to walk to work. My bicycle was still hibernating and my aging, second-hand Volvo could use the rest.

I preferred walking along the quiet city side streets rather than the fume-choked main artery to the hospital, although the route was longer. Where the sun poked through the naked limbs of the trees, I noticed the occasional yellow coltsfoot poking its head through the ground in wide-eyed wonder. My neighbour Harold, an avid gardener, was on his hands and knees scouring his front yard for over-wintering poop. He waved cheerfully as I went past.

I arrived at Ocean View invigorated by the fresh air and the promise of spring, although we were likely in for a few good storms and some general weather-lashing before that happened.

"Morning!" I shouted to Lewis, the parking lot attendant. He could only grunt a brief reply as he set off in pursuit of a pair of seniors who had parked illegally and were shuffling down the street to the yoga studio. They just might make it: Lewis had a bad back, trick knees, and weight issues.

I opened the hospital doors and stepped inside. Instead of the usual mix of wailing cats and harried owners, the place seemed deserted. There had been a series of robberies on our street lately so I picked up a broom, always the weapon of choice in an armed conflict, and tiptoed toward the treatment area. On the other side of the door, I could hear soft moaning and muffled voices. Gripping the broom handle, I cautiously turned the doorknob and poked my head inside. A group of people were clustered around a cardboard box.

"Doc! Over here!" a familiar voice cried.

Cecil's bald head popped up from the crowd. Waving his arm, he beckoned me closer. As if taking a breath, the cluster of onlookers expanded to let me in, then quickly closed the circle behind me.

"Oh, they're so sweet," Susan cooed.

Inside the carrier, three little kittens cuddled together on a warm, woolen sweater.

"Their mom just up and died," Cecil explained sadly. "No one knows what happened. The owners brought the kittens to me this mornin'. Guess people know I'm a bit of a cat expert," he added, visibly swelling with pride.

Cecil had ridden to fame in Halifax's north end as the cherubic owner of a neighbourhood pub and, more recently, a cryptorchid cat named P.C. Instead of descending as he matured, P.C's testicles remained hidden away inside his abdomen. For some reason, the bar's largely male, blue-collar clientele found this entertaining. Word spread, and Cecil had more business than he could handle.

Cecil hovered anxiously as I lifted each kitten out of the box to be examined. They squawked in healthy protest at being plucked from their warm nest. I noticed an old-fashioned hot water bottle underneath.

"'Tis the wife's," Cecil explained. "Uses it to keep her feet warm at night. Gawd, them things is cold," he shuddered. "But oh," he winked, "dat heart's some warm!"

Then his face became grave. Cecil may have been shaped by the navy after twenty-odd years at sea, but underneath a sometimes crusty exterior lurked a heart with the consistency of a marshmallow (unless the subject was his wife's nephew, Henry).

"Joking aside, Doc, I'm worried about 'em. The wife warmed up a saucer of milk but they wouldn't touch it."

"That's because they're too young to lap up milk," I explained.

"Their eyes probably just opened. I'd say they're less than two weeks old. You'll have to bottle feed them for a couple of weeks, every two to three hours," I added.

"Every two to three hours?" Cecil repeated dully as he sat down in a chair.

I took some kitten milk replacer off the shelf and poured it into a pet nurser bottle. "You get to be mama cat," I grinned at Cecil, holding out the nurser.

He looked at the bottle dubiously. I handed him the largest kitten. Gently cradling the kitten in one hand, he held the nurser enticingly close to the small wizened face with the other. "C'mon, little fella," he pleaded. "You want to grow up big and strong like P.C., don't you? With testicles though," he added as an afterthought.

The kitten showed no interest in the nurser and cried piteously. Cecil was distraught. "What am I doing wrong, Doc?"

"Just give him a minute," I reassured Cecil. "He has to get used to the idea."

"'Tis a whole lot easier with natural packaging, if you know what I mean. No offense, ladies," he added.

I dipped the end of the nipple into some leftover milk replacer, hoping the kitten could smell it, and then Cecil tried again. As the kitten's little head bobbed with interest, Cecil wiggled the small nipple against his mouth.

"C'mon, c'mon, " he urged, "you can do it." With that, the little mouth closed around the nipple and the kitten began to nurse.

"Look at the little bugger go," Cecil whispered proudly. The kitten's tiny, perfectly formed feet began kneading against Cecil's calloused hand as his empty belly began to fill. Cecil looked up at me and smiled. When the kitten was full, I wiped his mouth with a damp piece of gauze.

"What do we do now, Doc? Should we burp him?"

"No, it's the other end we have to look after."

"The other end?"

"We have to stimulate his bowels and bladder." Seeing Cecil's puzzled face, I explained, "He's too young to pee and poop on his own. His mom does that by washing down there with her tongue."

Cecil paled. "Doc, I … "

"We'll use another damp piece of gauze."

A relieved Cecil nodded and watched as I massaged the little belly. In just a few seconds I was rewarded with a small pee. I moistened another piece of gauze and held it out to Cecil.

"Your turn."

Sighing, Cecil dutifully held the gauze between his thumb and forefinger. It took a bit longer but we finally had a healthy string of caramel-coloured poo.

"Good boy!" Cecil gushed. "What a smart boy! Now what, Doc? We feed the other two?"

I nodded. "Hilary can give you a hand if you need any help. I have an appointment waiting. You did very well," I smiled. As I turned to leave, I bumped into Bernie.

"Oh dear," she began. "Your wife just called, Mr. Cecil. She said to tell you to get your …" Bernie hesitated. "It's very busy. They need you back at work. There's something wrong with the freezer, too."

"But what about the kittens?" Cecil looked up at me in mute appeal. Mrs. Cecil was not a woman to be toyed with.

"We'll look after the kittens until you can get back," I told him.

"Thanks, Doc!" Cecil grabbed his coat and hurried through the door as fast as his chubby bowed legs could carry him. "I'll be back as soon as I can."

"I'm a new dad," he told my waiting client, who offered her congratulations. "Kids don't look anythin' like me, though," he added cheerfully.

Henry, Mrs. Cecil's nephew, arrived later that morning to pick up the kittens. At her urging, he was employed at the pub as a short-order cook with general gofer duties.

"Nepotism! That's what it is!" Cecil complained. He was fond of discussing Henry's shortcomings, from his pierced eyebrow to the way he cooked fish. If a bus overturned in India killing everyone aboard, Henry was somehow to blame.

I had barely spoken two words to Henry in the year of Fridays that Hughie and I popped in for lunch. He was always plugged into his music or chopping something in the kitchen. On his breaks, he sat in the pool room with a cigarette in one hand, a book in the other, and P.C. curled up in his lap. It annoyed Cecil that P.C. preferred Henry's lap to his own, but to be fair, Cecil didn't have a lap.

Henry had spent some time in a correctional facility as a teenager. According to Cecil, he had fallen in with the wrong crowd. After a series of misdemeanors, he was found guilty of breaking and entering, although he had supposedly only driven the getaway car. The latter had run out of gas on the mile-long bridge that spanned Halifax Harbour.

I would guess that Henry was close to thirty. Although he shaved his head regularly, his face always bore the manly look of needing a quick buzz. He stood at the reception counter quietly waiting for Bernie to finish her phone order.

"Sorry to keep you waiting, luv," she smiled, hanging up the phone. "How may I hold you?"

In the silence which followed, the corners of Henry's mouth curved upwards ever so slightly.

"Oh dear … oh my," Bernie stammered, turning crimson. "I meant help. How may I help you. Oh dear." She fanned her flushed face.

"I'm here to pick up Uncle Cecil's kittens," Henry told her.

"Yes, of course," Bernie managed. "Just follow me."

Henry dutifully fell in behind the mortified Bernie, who rolled her eyes and shook her head as she passed me.

"Must be a busy day at the pub," I smiled at Henry.

"Yup," he acknowledged on the way past.

Henry was a man of few words. Maybe he had learned along the way that life was less complicated if you were seen and not heard.

Cecil, on the other hand, called me every day with an update. The kittens were doing great. One of the regulars had donated a playpen to contain them, but it wouldn't be too long before the youngsters would be able to crawl up and over the mesh netting. Mrs. Cecil had drawn up a feeding schedule and posted it on the fridge in the storage room where the little trio was currently being housed. Unexpectedly, Henry's initials appeared the most often.

Several Fridays passed before Hughie and I managed to slip away for our customary end-of-the-week lunch at Cecil's. The place was packed. The noon-hour patrons were a loyal bunch lured by the mostly good food, the cheerful company, and the cheap draft, although Hughie and I never drank anything stronger than coffee (which was pretty hair-raising by itself). Into the melee walked Phil Henderson. Silence followed. Poor Phil took it as a sign of respect.

"Hello, everyone," he boomed. Light bounced off his shiny three-piece suit. "Don't mind me," he added graciously. "You good folks go right on eating your lunch."

He approached the nearest table and stuck out a meaty hand. "Phil Henderson. I'm running for city council."

"Phil Henderson," he continued moving on to the next table. "I hope I can count on your support."

In an effort to dislodge the incumbent, Phil was shaking every voting hand in Ward 11. He had already visited Ocean View with a briefcase full of glossy brochures that highlighted his career to date. This included three rosy-faced children and a chain of car washes. Bernie had planted her feet and advised him that soliciting was not permitted. He had countered by asking if she was the enchanting seductress who owned such a magnificent facility.

"No, that would be me," Hughie had said, poking his ahead around the corner.

At Cecil's pub, Phil met with even stiffer resistance. Standing beside Billy MacNeil's table, he asked, "What can I do for you?"

Immersed in his mashed potatoes, Billy barely looked up.

"More strip bars," Al jumped in. "With free admission for seniors." This was met with a round of applause. Al beamed and tipped his ball cap to the appreciative crowd.

Cecil grabbed a large mayonnaise jar filled with money and waddled over to the table. I noticed that Henry had poked his head through the door and was watching the proceedings with interest.

Phil turned to Cecil and flashed a well-practiced smile. "Phil Henderson. And you are?"

"Cecil. This is my pub."

"Well, Mr. Cecil, delighted to meet you!" Phil gushed.

Cecil thrust the jar in front of Phil. "Would you like to make a donation to a worthy cause?"

"Well, I, let's see. I suppose I could." Phil rummaged in his pocket. "What's the cause?"

"Homeless kittens. That's their vit'nery right over there," Cecil added, pointing to me.

Smiling, Phil poked his head over Cecil's shoulder as he dropped a few coins into the jar. "Veterinarian," he nodded wisely. "That's a noble profession."

When he turned back, Cecil was still holding out the jar. The two looked at each other for a moment. Cecil shook the jar encouragingly.

"Oh. Well, I don't have my wallet with me right now," Phil explained.

Billy's buddies looked at each other knowingly.

"Aren't there, you know, charities for this sort of thing?" Phil asked helplessly. "All I have is a twenty for emergencies."

"This is an emergency," Cecil declared.

Slowly, oh so slowly, Phil raised his arm toward the jar, then stopped. "It's pretty full," he remarked.

Cecil turned to Billy. "Give Mr. Henderson here a hand, will ya, Billy?"

Billy took the bill, folded it into a neat sliver and stuffed it through the narrow opening. "There ya go," he declared, turning back to his mashed potatoes.

"Good luck with yer campaign there, buddy," Al added, raising his beer in salute. "If cats had the vote, you'd win by a landslide!"

Phil nodded weakly.

It was at that moment the three kittens, led by P.C., tumbled into the pub. The latter had long ago learned that the pub was off-limits and spent his time lounging on the pool tables batting at the balls, or frolicking in the apartment upstairs. Cecil had even built a lovely fenced-in patio on the roof for him.

But the forbidden was always the most tempting. Just ask Adam and Eve. Like any older brother, P.C. might have figured that repercussions were less likely with the three adorable musketeers in tow.

Someone must have left the storage room door open. Judging by the look on his face, I suspected it might have been Henry. I scooped up one kitten as he scampered past the table, Henry grabbed the second, and the third tried to climb up Phil Henderson's leg. Phil's face turned an unbecoming shade of red as the kitten dug his needle-sharp claws into his calf. Cecil quickly extricated the kitten and apologized to Phil. The latter had recovered his saccharine smile and assured Cecil he adored kittens.

Cecil was furious with Henry and threatened to fire him. No one took it seriously; Cecil threatened to fire Henry at least once a week. All that changed, though, when an official letter arrived several weeks later advising the proprietor that his premises were going to be inspected.

Cecil was convinced that Phil had filed a complaint, even after his wife pointed out that it was the provincial department of agriculture and not any municipal office that carried out restaurant inspections.

"Phil Henderson is running for city council," she declared.

"Don't matter," Cecil said glumly. "Them fellas is all in bed together."

On the day of the inspection, the mood in the pub was dark in spite of the hours spent scrubbing the place to bright, shimmering cleanliness. Cecil had asked Hughie and me to be present as "professionals" who could attest to the health of the kittens and swear that this had been their first venture into the pub. The kittens and P.C. were secreted away in the apartment upstairs. Henry had orders to wear a hairnet, wash the pots, sweep the floors, and keep his head down.

"He's here," Cecil hissed from his strategic position behind the window curtain.

A tall man dressed in a trench coat and gripping a clipboard entered the pub. His hair was buzzed short, more for efficiency than style. Removing his sunglasses, he glanced around the room with the air of a man who had an eye for detail. He looked more like a covert mission specialist than a restaurant inspector.

"Come in, come in," Cecil gushed. "You must be the inspector."

"And you are …" the man glanced at his clipboard, "Cecil Cavanaugh?"

"That's me. In the flesh," Cecil beamed.

"And you are the proprietor?"

Cecil bobbed his head up and down. "Yes, indeedy."

The inspector made a few notes on his chart. Cecil leaned forward for a better look but quickly jumped back when the inspector raised his head.

"I thought we could start with the washrooms," Cecil said brightly.

Thanks to a cousin who was a plumber with a weakness for beer and fried food, Cecil had redone the washrooms at very little expense.

The stained urinals and toilet bowls had been replaced with porcelain pieces of art. It almost seemed a shame to use them for the purposes for which they were designed. Cecil himself had laid a new ceramic tile floor. Today, a rose bowl filled with petals appeared in each washroom. If the pub was an oyster, the washrooms were the pearl.

"No, I'll go through on my own," the inspector announced as he gazed past Cecil. "I prefer to do it that way."

Cecil could only nod agreeably. "Of course. Let me know if you have any questions."

"Rest assured, Mr. Cavanaugh," the inspector replied.

With that, he and his clipboard began their search of the premises. Cecil slunk behind him, lurking in the shadows and nibbling on his fingernails until a stern look from Mrs. Cecil sent him scurrying back to the bar.

The inspector re-emerged less than twenty minutes later.

"There you go," Hughie smiled encouragingly at Cecil. "He's all done."

Cecil remained unconvinced. "On the TV it's never good when the jury comes back fast."

"Mr. Cavanaugh?" The inspector caught Cecil's eye. "A moment please?"

"Of course." Cecil cast a worried glance at us, then ushered the inspector to a small table in the corner. "You just make yourself comfy. Would you like anything to eat? A cup of coffee?"

"No, thank you. Now, Mr. Cavanaugh, I have discovered a number of serious infractions."

As I strained to hear the conversation, I noticed Henry's face in the porthole of the door leading to the kitchen. Cecil sat upright, his hands folded on the table like a child being reprimanded. As the conversation continued, he began to look more and more haggard.

"Oh, and one more thing," I heard the inspector say. "Most

establishments in this city seem to have rodent problems." The inspector looked up from his notes and peered at Cecil, his eyes narrowing. "Except you, Mr. Cavanaugh. Who is your exterminator?"

"My exterminator?" Cecil repeated.

"Yes." The inspector waited.

"Um … " Cecil hesitated. He couldn't very well give the name of his exterminator since acknowledging his presence of one was an infraction in itself.

"We don't have one," he replied at last.

"Oh? And why is that?"

"Just lucky, I guess." Cecil managed a weak smile.

The inspector stared at Cecil and clicked his pen vigorously. Halifax is an old port city. Rats came over on sailing ships from Europe centuries ago and decided they liked the place. Restaurants, sewers, and grain elevators were delightful locations to raise a family; even some of the city's most expensive private homes harboured rats.

Just as the inspector began writing with a flourish, Henry pushed the kitchen door open and strolled toward the table. Cecil stared at the top of his hairnet-free head in horror.

Cecil glared at Henry. "Well, what is it? We're very busy," he added, flashing a smile at the inspector.

Ignoring Cecil, Henry looked at the man seated across from him. "I know you."

"Shouldn't you be washing pots?" Cecil asked.

The inspector looked puzzled. "I don't believe we've met."

"Yeah, we have. You're Sabrina's dad. We met at Shelburne."

"The correctional facility?"

Cecil, who had been following the conversation with growing dread, groaned and held his head in both hands.

"I'm Henry."

"Henry? Henry Whittaker?" the inspector asked in disbelief.

Henry nodded.

The inspector stood up and gripped Henry's hand in both of his. "It's a pleasure to see you again, son. I never would have recognized you. You had a lot more hair back then," he smiled.

Raising his head, Cecil stole a peek from behind his chubby fingers.

"How's Sabrina doing?" Henry asked.

"She's doing absolutely great. She's married now. I have two grandchildren." The inspector reached into his wallet and pulled out a couple of pictures.

Cecil leaned over. "Beautiful! Simply beautiful children."

"So, Henry," the inspector asked, "what are you doing now?"

"I play in a band. Heavy metal mostly," he added. "And I work here. Cecil's my uncle. He and my aunt have been really good to me. Gave me a place to stay. And a job."

The inspector flashed a glance at Cecil who smiled beatifically. Turning back to Henry, he held out a business card.

"Henry, if I can ever help you in any way, please let me know. I can't thank you enough for all the help you gave Sabrina. You were her friend when everyone else turned their back."

With a slight nod, Henry thanked the inspector and slipped back into the kitchen. Cecil stared at his departure with an open mouth.

"What a wonderful young man," the inspector said quietly.

"That he is!" Cecil readily agreed. "I'm always tellin' his aunt that."

The inspector picked up his clipboard. "Well, Mr. Cavanaugh, I'll be leaving now."

Cecil looked hopeful. "You're done then, are ya?"

"Yes, I'm sure the few things I mentioned can be cleared up without any further disruptions to your business."

"I'll see to 'em right away," a dazed Cecil agreed.

In addition to following the inspector's recommendations, Cecil gave Henry the new title of head chef, though his job description didn't change. He still washed the pots, peeled the potatoes, and did the short-order cooking. But along with the elevated status came a raise in pay. With some savings and the security of a pay raise plus a regular gig with his band, he was able to afford the down payment on a small townhouse outside the city. He also adopted one of the kittens, an affectionate little tabby with big, round eyes and a vivid imagination.

One Friday afternoon, while I sat across from Hughie half-listening to him rant about last night's basketball game, I took a sip of my Coke and glanced over his shoulder. The enigmatic Henry was leaning against the counter as he took a break. I smiled at him. He smiled back.

"Henry! Git off yer arse!" Cecil hollered from across the room. "There's two orders up."

Grinning, Henry slipped the hairnet back over his head and disappeared into the kitchen.

Chapter 6

Linda Robichaud-Comeau stared at me, her eyebrows knit in an angry French knot. Her cat, Noireaud, glared at me with equal distaste. Had I known Linda was loose in reception, I would have waited until hell froze over before venturing out to return Bernie's favourite pair of scissors. Linda disliked me, the staff, commercial fiction, and particle board. She pointed to the lit candle on the reception counter and muttered something behind the filtering mask that covered her mouth and nose.

I looked at her blankly. "Pardon me?"

Linda yanked her mask down. "I said," she began in a measured voice, "if you don't do something about the smells in here, I won't be back. "

As I was considering that option, Bernie extinguished the candle. "Sorry, luv."

Linda was about to say something more when Hughie unwittingly burst through the exam room door. "Linda!" his voice boomed. "What a pleasure to see you."

"Oh, Dr. Doucette … "

The woman turned to putty before my eyes. While Hughie nodded sympathetically, Linda discussed her health, including a stubborn urinary tract infection and recently diagnosed environmental sensitivities, in painstaking detail.

"And on top of all that I'm PMS-ing … "

Linda's voice faded into the distance as I scurried back into the treatment area where Mrs. Redmond and Tallulah Belle waited. Both were delightful seniors. The former was a bit forgetful and a little unsteady on her feet sometimes, but a demon behind the wheel, refusing to relinquish command of her late husband's cavernous Buick. It was currently parked broadside against the curb in front of the hospital, straddling three parking spaces. Fortunately, Lewis the parking lot attendant was off having his prostate examined that morning. I was privy to this kind of information because Lewis had cornered me in the parking lot, wondering if cats suffered from the same affliction.

Both Mrs. Redmond and Tallulah Belle took propranolol for their heart conditions. On more than one occasion, Mrs. Redmond had downed the cat's medication and chased it with a swig of sherry. She had also unwittingly washed her hair with flea shampoo and once served "ocean fish formula" on crackers to her bridge group. They asked for the recipe.

The pair was close in age and enjoyed each other's company. But lately, Tallulah Belle had been hiding in closets and refusing to eat. When Mrs. Redmond brought her in for a checkup last week, I had noticed an abscessed canine tooth. I would have preferred to avoid anesthetic on such a risky patient but the tooth had to be removed. I had started her on a course of antibiotics to temporarily improve the situation before we went ahead with the extraction.

Mrs. Redmond's son arrived just as I was going over the admitting form with his mother. He had the same flowing white hair and blue eyes as his mother. I wondered if he had only just now found his way out of the gas-guzzling Buick that could comfortably sleep a baseball team, their coach, and the general manager.

"Mother? I thought I was supposed to drive. You left without me."

Mrs. Redmond raised a delicate, veined hand to her mouth. "Oops! I forgot, dear." Then, turning toward me, she explained, "This is my son, Samuel. He's a doctor. A Ph.D. doctor," she added with a touch of pride. "He works with mushrooms. He even has a mushroom named after him!"

"That's all right, Mom," her son sighed. "I got a taxi. Please, go ahead," he said, looking at me. Both mother and son listened attentively as I explained the procedure and the steps we would take to minimize the health risks for a cardiac patient with aging kidneys.

"Now you take good care of my Tallulah Belle," Mrs. Redmond smiled as she signed the authorization form.

Samuel picked up his briefcase and headed toward the door. "Let's go, Mother. I'll drive," he added.

Mrs. Redmond took my hand and clasping it in both of hers, whispered, "I didn't really forget him this morning." She winked at me.

I winked back. "I didn't really think you did."

I had several appointments scheduled that morning, after which I planned to extract Tallulah Belle's tooth. Of course, none of those appointments turned out to be the routine checkups and vaccinations that the appointment book promised.

Hughie's morning was equally hectic as he split his time among surgeries, outpatients, and the quarrelsome Noireaud, who was boarding for the day. On the advice of her health-care provider, Linda was having all the carpet in her home torn up. She didn't want a "careless workman with s*** for brains" accidentally leaving the door open and letting Noireaud escape.

"Ah, the romance of the French language," I grinned. "Noireaud is so much more dignified than Blackie."

Hughie looked at me and grunted.

We stopped outside the isolation window. Since Linda didn't believe in vaccinations, Noireaud couldn't stay with the other boarders in the luxurious Cat Nap Inn. Spying us through the window, he screamed and lunged at the bars of his kennel. Hughie pulled a bottle of little orange tablets from the health food store out of his lab coat pocket.

"What are those for?" I asked.

"Anxiety." Hughie looked doubtful. "I'm supposed to give him one every hour."

"Oh," I nodded.

We stood side by side, staring through the window. Noireaud defiantly glared back at us.

"So," Hughie said after a moment. "Do you think he's anxious?"

"Oh, yeah," I replied, my arms folded across my chest.

"How anxious?"

"Very."

"Mmm," Hughie thought for a moment. "On a scale of one to ten?"

"Ten."

"Ten? Really? I think he'll settle down after he's been here for awhile."

I shrugged. "Suit yourself."

Hughie was still staring at Noireaud when I passed by a few moments later. His face bore the look of a condemned man.

"I'm going in," he announced, clutching the bottle of pills. "If I don't come out, I want you to have my NBA Superstar collection, Em."

Hughie was the proud owner of fifteen plastic bobblehead basketball players, including such notables as Michael Jordan, John Stockton, and Reggie Miller. These gentlemen lined one of the shelves in the office. On a quiet day, I used to see if I could get all fifteen heads bobbling at once.

With each passing hour, Hughie's mood worsened. At noon, I found him hunched over the counter in the lab looking like he'd just gone through the rinse cycle. His tie lay in tattered shreds on the counter.

"What're you doing?" I asked, noticing his bandaged right hand.

"Counting pills," he muttered. "Linda'll be back around suppertime. So that's about six hours, right?" He gathered six tablets in his hand and tossed them into the garbage can.

"And there, Dr. McBride," he declared with a satisfied sigh, "you have the art and science of veterinary medicine. When the cure is worse than the disease, common sense must prevail!" Humming cheerfully, he picked up the chart for his next patient and sauntered down the hall.

When Hilary returned from lunch, we took a small blood sample from Tallulah Belle for pre-surgical testing. The results were all within normal range, so I drew up her pre-med, a mix of narcotic and tranquilizer. The little cat was thrilled to be the centre of attention and didn't even notice the injection into her thigh. When she was completely relaxed, we placed her on a soft blanket in the gas induction box. Oxygen and isoflurane anesthetic flowed into the box through one hose, and a second hose safely removed the waste gas through what is called an active scavenging system. Once Tallulah Belle had reached a deep enough plane of anesthesia, I lifted her out of the box and sprayed her vocal cords with xylocaine. This would relax her vocal cords enough so that I could pass an endotracheal tube down her throat.

While Hilary began an IV line, I attached an ECG cable at each knee and elbow. We then shaved a small spot on her wrist and secured the Doppler blood pressure sensor. Lastly, we attached the pulse oximeter cable to her ear. The pulse oximeter measures the amount of oxygen in the blood; in humans, it is clipped to a finger. By the time we were done, poor Tallulah Belle looked like she was hooked up for deep space exploration.

I listened to her heart one more time and checked her gums. So far, so good. Everything was going well. While Hilary monitored her vital signs, I began the extraction. The decayed tooth broke with only the slightest pressure, but the infected root had to be removed as well. Canine teeth in cats have long, tenacious roots and this one was no exception. Using a variety of instruments I poked, prodded, elevated, and drilled. Twenty minutes and one sweat-soaked surgical cap later, the remains of that stubborn root lay on my instrument tray.

"Whew!" I removed my protective goggles and shrugged the muscle cramps out of my shoulders.

Hilary turned off the anesthetic so that only pure oxygen flowed into Tallulah Belle's lungs. We chatted amiably for a few moments as we waited for the little cat to wake up. Her ECG, though atypical, was normal for her, and all the other vital signs were good. Taking a small piece of gauze off the instrument tray, I began wiping away a bit of drool around her mouth.

"Uh-oh. Dr. McBride?"

"What is it?" I asked, looking up.

"Her pulse ox is down to 54%!"

"That's impossible. Check the cable." Before removing the endotracheal tube in Tallulah Belle's throat only a moment earlier, I had checked the reading and it showed 100% saturation. That meant her blood was well-oxygenated.

"Cable's fine," Hilary announced.

"Let's get her back on full oxygen, quick!" I ordered.

The little cat was too awake to insert the tube again so while I held her still, Hilary placed the Plexiglas face mask over her nose and mouth. Once she started breathing the pure oxygen again, her pulse ox shot back up to 99%. We secured the mask in place behind her ears and I listened to her chest. I could hear the crackle associated with a buildup of fluid in the lungs. With heart patients, fluid can leak from the capillaries into the spaces between the lung tissues, producing what is termed interstitial edema. This makes oxygen exchange from the lungs into the blood very difficult. Tallulah Belle had been able to compensate on pure oxygen but at normal room levels of 22% oxygen, she just couldn't cope. I gave her an injection of furosemide, a diuretic that would help her body get rid of the excess fluid.

We tried to wean her onto room air once again, but the levels of oxygen in her blood plummeted. As the diuretic began to take effect, however, we were gradually able to reduce the amount of time she spent on pure oxygen. Eventually, she seemed to be doing fine on room air and we transferred her to the recovery ward, but it had been a harrowing couple of hours.

I just had time to call Mrs. Redmond with an update before the evening outpatient clinic began. She took the news of her cat's condition in stride, although she admitted it would be hard to sleep without Tallulah Belle curled up beside her on the pillow.

"I read to her every night," Mrs. Redmond confessed. "We just finished Stuart Little. Tallulah Belle really enjoyed that one," she giggled.

Apparently, Tallulah Belle and I had the same taste in literature. The adventures of the plucky little mouse had always been one of my favourites too, along with The Wind in the Willows and The Rats of NIMH. I seemed drawn to stories about talking rodents. And yet, here I was at Ocean View Cat Hospital, doing my best to help their arch-enemies live long, productive lives.

Hanging up the phone, I bought a chocolate bar from a six-year-old entrepreneur who had the good sense to show up at suppertime with two full boxes. Dressed in a hockey jersey down to his knees, he was polite and irresistible. He was followed in short order by Linda Robichaud-Comeau, who was neither. She rushed through the doors, skidding to a stop at the reception counter.

"Well?" Her eyebrows arched like question marks over her face. "Is he ready to go?"

With no one prying open his jaws every hour and shoving down a pill, Noireaud's attitude had improved considerably. Still, Hilary wasn't taking any chances with this feline Jekyll and Hyde. Scooping him up with a pair of Kevlar gloves, she transferred him to his carrier and carried it out to reception where Linda waited anxiously. I had always heard that French was one of the romance languages but had never before seen it in action. As Linda gushed in what I assume was French baby talk, Noireaud responded with seductive chirps and meows. He rubbed his body against the bars of the kennel and blinked eye kisses like Morse code.

Linda placed his carrier on the counter and the two chatted back and forth as she paid her bill. When they were ready to go, Linda turned back to Bernie. "Where are his anxiety pills?" she demanded.

"Oh … right here, luv." Bernie rooted underneath the counter.

Linda shook the contents and, holding the vial up to her face, studied it suspiciously. "Did Dr. Doucette have any trouble?" she asked.

"Not that he mentioned to me," Bernie answered truthfully.

"Look how happy he is," she said to Bernie. "I don't know why you people can't sell these here. Then I wouldn't have to go all the way downtown to buy them. It's very inconvenient." With a deep sigh, she dropped the pills into her purse and left with Noireaud.

I winked at Hilary, then picked up the chart for my next patient, a big male tabby named Verne. He had been found playing with a mauled package of birth control pills, several of which were missing, and his owner was distraught. Verne, on the other hand, was sprawled on the examining table washing himself. In the second exam room, a thin woman with a high-pitched laugh that she unleashed at random was waiting to see Hughie. I hoped she was just reading a funny book, but you never knew. Meanwhile the black-and-white mascot of Phi Kappa Delta fraternity was strolling calmly throughout the hospital. The boys of Phi Kappa had christened her "Nipples" and loved calling her by name. The phones were ringing incessantly and the lineup of clients at the counter was growing like a weed.

Into this bubbling cauldron of chaos strode four men in bullet-proof vests. Silence followed them.

"Are you in charge here, Ma'am?" one of them asked Bernie.

Mute, Bernie shook her head and pointed to me. Four closely cropped heads turned in my direction. Their leader stepped forward and flashed a badge.

"Captain John Morgan, HPD."

"Emily McBride, DVM."

Not a titter ran through the crowded reception room, which had taken on the pallor and hushed tones of a funeral parlour. These were not middle-aged men with bulging bellies who talked to pre-schoolers about stranger-danger. This group wore jackets with SWAT plastered across the back in big, bold letters. They were streamlined and built for maximum fuel efficiency.

"Ma'am," Captain Morgan began, "we have a situation."

All heads turned as a familiar silver-grey Buick roared up to the hospital, one wheel coming to rest on top of the curb. The waiting room held its breath then parted like the Red Sea as Mrs. Redmond, followed by her ashen-faced son, entered the building.

"Hello, everyone," Mrs. Redmond said cheerfully. "I've come to visit Tallulah Belle."

Captain Morgan turned to face her. "Ma'am, I'm going to have to ask you … "

"Call me Sylvia," Mrs. Redmond smiled, extending a gloved hand.

"Ah, Sylvia?"

Mrs. Redmond smiled encouragingly.

"I'm going to have to ask you to leave," Captain Morgan said.

"Leave?" Mrs. Redmond was incredulous. "But I just got here."

"Yes, ma'am, I know, but this is police business."

"Well, I have cat business," Mrs. Redmond replied indignantly.

"I understand that, ma'am. Sylvia." Captain Morgan corrected himself as Mrs. Redmond's eyes narrowed. "But we have a situation down the street."

"Then be a good boy and run along."

Captain Morgan opened his mouth to speak but no words came out. One of his men coughed discreetly.

"She's got five minutes to visit that cat," Captain Morgan declared as soon as he had recovered his voice. "We have an armed stand-off down the street and we are evacuating nearby businesses and residences."

That was all anyone needed to hear. The hospital quickly emptied as clients rushed home to watch the ensuing drama from the safety of their living rooms. Down the street, several news teams were gathering where a barricade had been set up. Blue and white lights atop the police cars flashed eerily against the trees and houses on the street.

"Mom, we really should go," Samuel said, grabbing the car keys off the counter. He had joined his mother in the recovery ward where she sat beside Tallulah Belle, lovingly running a little pink brush through her fur. Sighing, she kissed Tallulah Belle on the head then reluctantly closed the kennel door.

"Nice to see you again," I told Samuel as he ushered his mother toward the door.

"Oh, no, you haven't met," Mrs. Redmond shook her head "This is my son Lawrence. He's a … " Mrs. Redmond hesitated. "What's the word? Litigator. That's it. Why do I always want to say alligator?" she asked of no one in particular.

Lawrence shook my hand. Except for a pair of black-rimmed glasses, he looked exactly like his brother.

They had no sooner left than Linda burst back in through the doors she had recently exited. She was breathless and even more agitated than usual.

"Thank God you're still here!" she exclaimed, plunking Noireaud back up on the reception counter. "Everyone's being evacuated!"

Linda was desperate to find accommodation for Noireaud after finding herself in the unenviable position of being right next door to the action. The police had commandeered her home and Linda had been relocated to a no-pets hotel, courtesy of the taxpayers of Nova Scotia. According to Linda, the dispute had begun when a child protection worker had been met at the door with a rifle. She returned with a police escort. Local residents comforted themselves with the knowledge that the man and his common-law-wife were from "away".

We settled a disgusted Noireaud back in the isolation ward. When I arrived home that evening, the answering machine was blinking out of control. I called Mom first since she had left the greatest number of messages, each one more urgent than the one before. After we had established that I was indeed still alive, she poured herself a glass of sherry and we discussed her dentures. These had been burned beyond recognition in an outdoor fire pit, apparently when she and George had been roasting hot dogs. A new set would take at least a week, so until then Mom had cancelled anything that would require her to be out in public, toothless. As a result she had a list of chores for me.

The other message was from Benny. He had heard about the stand-off on the news and knew that the location was very close to the cat hospital. He was worried and asked me to call when I got a chance. I played the message a couple of times. I made supper. I put a load of laundry in the washing machine. I played the message again.

Then I picked up the phone.

By morning, the stalemate was over. The house was still separated from the rest of the law-abiding residences by yellow warning tape, but the media and police cruisers were gone. The couple had surrendered to the police and the child was found in good health. Linda and Noireaud were back in their own home. We all breathed a little bit easier.

"Have a cookie, dear," Mrs. Redmond offered, opening up a very large can of homemade peanut butter cookies. She had arrived with Samuel, or maybe Lawrence, to take Tallulah Belle home. The little cat was doing well and showed no ill effects from her recent ordeal. Now that the nagging tooth had been removed, she was back to her old cheerful self.

"You know," Mrs. Redmond smiled, "I think a good-old fashioned peanut butter cookie just makes the world a better place, don't you?"

My mouth was full so I could only nod in vigorous agreement.

"Come along, William," she said to what was apparently a third son.

"Little Miss Tallulah Belle is ready to go home and be spoiled rotten."

With an indulgent smile, William obediently picked up the carrier and held the door open for his mother. He looked a bit more rakish than his brothers, dressed in a pair of cords and hiking boots. Part of his flowing white hair was held back in a short ponytail.

"I know you're not supposed to have favourites," Mrs. Redmond whispered, "but William lets me drive."

I looked out into the parking lot. Mrs. Redmond's car was not in its usual spot. Instead, I spied an impatient line of cars weaving around a familiar shape which appeared to be stationary in the middle of the lot. Lewis was frantically directing traffic around it. Mrs. Redmond's Buick.

Mrs. Redmond shrugged helplessly. "Your parking spots are too small."

Chapter 7

"This weather sucks," Tanya whined. "I'm tired of shovelling."

Tanya had joined the staff at Ocean View as a veterinary assistant just over a year ago. She was wallowing in debt and, as a result, still lived at home. Her parents had a long driveway and no qualms about child labour since the child in question was still living at home, rent-free. Unfortunately for Tanya, it was the whitest winter on record in at least a decade.

The back door opened. A frigid gust of wind rattled the storage shelves and deposited a film of snow inside the door. Sullivan, the impetuous Jack Russell terrier, burst through the opening followed by Hughie. Both stopped to shake the snow off their respective coats. Hughie tried to towel-dry an impatient Sully, who was more interested in what the resident cats had for breakfast and, more importantly, if there were any leftovers.

Hughie hung up his own coat to dry and draped a colourful scarf across a chair. It had been a Christmas gift from his elderly grandmother who had grown up during the Depression and refused to throw anything out, including balls of leftover yarn. Not only was Mrs. Doucette Senior frugal, she was also colour-blind. This combination of factors resulted in one-of-a-kind gifts for the brood of Doucettes that she and her late husband begat. Even on mild days, Hughie wore the gaudy scarf around his neck like a badge of honour.

"So, what's on the books today?" he asked, rubbing his hands together. Like his little terrier, Hughie was endlessly enthusiastic.

"A spay and two neuters," Hilary replied. "Their blood work was all normal."

"Right! Let's get to it."

While Hilary and Hughie prepped for surgery, I awaited the arrival of Rachel MacDonald, a regular client who was, predictably, late. Frances and Bertram, her Maine Coon cats, were not fond of visits to the vet and hid whenever the carriers came out of storage. When the doors chimed, I assumed the trio had arrived and stepped out into reception. Instead, I found an irate, middle-aged woman standing at the reception counter with a box of kittens.

"Well, why can't you take them?" she asked, glaring at Bernie.

"I wish we could, luv, but we already have two moggies we're trying to find homes for. And we have four others that live here full-time," Bernie explained. "Plus we need space for our patients."

"What am I supposed to do then?" the woman demanded.

Bernie smiled at the fuzzy orange head that appeared over the edge of the box. The little fellow had leapt into the air and managed to grip the edge of the box while his hind legs scrabbled for purchase inside. His round blue eyes had just a few seconds to glimpse an exciting new world before he slipped back inside the box, where his siblings pounced on him in delight.

"Have you tried the shelters?" Bernie asked.

"They're full."

"Keep trying," Bernie suggested. "You can place ads for free on the radio and in some of the papers too. And we keep an adoption book. I can take your name and number so that … "

"I don't have time for all that!" the woman interrupted. "This is her fourth litter. I'm going to have to get rid of her."

Grabbing the box of kittens, she stormed out the door.

Bernie was visibly upset. A gentle soul, Bernie loved animals and enjoyed helping people. Her hands shook and she tried to control the tremor in her voice when someone called to ask about flea control.

It is a sad fact that shelters across North America are filled to overflowing and hundreds of thousands of animals are killed annually due to lack of space. Like many vet hospitals, Ocean View offered spays and neuters at substantially reduced costs from our normal surgical fee to encourage responsible pet ownership, but that was a drop in the proverbial bucket. There were tens of thousands of homeless cats in the city and a mere handful of private citizens trying to help them.

Less than twenty-four hours later, as Bernie was returning from the storage room with an armload of food, she heard the door chimes. She hurried into reception, but no one was there. Instead, a familiar cardboard box sat in the vestibule between the two sets of doors. I was in the middle of an examination when I heard Bernie's strangled cry.

"No!" she moaned. "Oh, nooo!"

Grabbing the box she hurried to the treatment area. Hughie got there ahead of me and took the box from Bernie's outstretched arms. Two of the kittens were trying to climb out of the box. The third, the little orange tabby, lay gasping for air on the bottom.

Hughie looked round the room and grabbed his scarf. Bunching it into a blanket, he gingerly placed the kitten on top, sheltering his small body from the cold stainless steel table.

"Oh, God." Susan struggled to hold back tears but Bernie's seeped from her eyes and fell silently onto the scarf. Hilary was silent.

The tiny kitten had been mangled, probably by a dog, and was beyond our help. Even as Hughie drew up the Euthanol to end his suffering, he took his last breath. In reception, the telephone rang, but no one moved and the caller finally gave up.

We gathered around the small body that lay silent and still. His round baby eyes, forever blue, stared blankly at a lost world. They had only opened a few short weeks ago. I found myself wondering what they had seen in their short time on this earth. Tanya reached out to touch the soft, fuzzy baby fur and, leaning over, kissed the small head.

"I'm so sorry, little one," she whispered. "I'm so sorry."

Hughie wrapped his scarf around the kitten and reverently placed the small body in a box. A shipment of glass microtainers, used to collect, store and transport blood specimens, had arrived in it only last week. On the outside of the box was stamped a single word: "Fragile." Wordlessly, Susan carried the cardboard box to a small room in the back of the hospital.

"If only I'd taken them in yesterday," Bernie sobbed, "this wouldn't have happened."

I put my hand on hers. "It's not your fault."

Bernie removed her glasses. Without the funky green and white frames, she looked different somehow. Her face was bare, exposed. Picking up a tissue, she wiped her eyes then looked at me. "No? Then whose fault is it?" she asked in a choked voice.

The phone rang again. Steadying her hands, Bernie replaced the glasses. Behind them, her lids were still red and smudged with traces of mascara. With a sigh, she slowly walked down the hall toward reception, closing the door behind her.

In the days that followed, the two remaining kittens blossomed with the kind and loving attention of the staff. They were dubbed Bonnie and Clyde for the happy trail of destruction they left in their wake. Cardboard beds were systematically shredded, water bowls overturned, and litter scattered to the far corners of the kennel and beyond. Where water and litter mixed, concrete pancakes formed that had to be scraped off the walls and floor. We adored the irrepressible pair. Their enthusiasm for life helped ease the pain we felt over the tragic loss of their brother.

When they were old enough, they were adopted by clients who had recently lost their cat of sixteen years to heart disease. Their little boy Craig had been devastated to lose his best friend. The kittens spent their first night, and every night thereafter, on the foot of Craig's bed. And when that little boy was a strapping six-foot-tall point guard recruited by Carleton University in Ontario, he wept to be leaving his cats behind.

To find such a wonderful home for Bonnie and Clyde helped ease Bernie's guilt. Nevertheless, when Miranda Gebhardt asked if we could take in a pregnant feral cat, Bernie said yes immediately. Hughie didn't flinch when he heard the news, although it would stretch our resources even further.

Miranda had been feeding the cat for two years but had never been able to approach her. Now she was pregnant again. Last year, the city pound employees had trapped and euthanized several of her spring kittens. Worried for the family's safety, Miranda bought a live trap. After catching Tiny, the neighbour's charming but obese grey tabby on two separate occasions, she was finally able to snare the stray. With the delivery of kittens imminent, perhaps the cat had been desperate for easy food and less cautious than usual.

Now she cowered in the corner of the wire mesh cage, her belly swollen and distended. Like any wild animal, she was terrified by the confinement. Ears flattened, she snarled in fear at the humans who towered above, her eyes infinite black holes.

"I hate to do this," Miranda sighed as Hughie picked up the cage.

"What will happen to her?" Miranda's friend asked. She was a pretty woman, plump but not fat. Her naturally blonde hair lay in tousled disarray from the March winds that also whipped her cheeks a smooth, frosty pink.

"Well, we'll spay her once the babies are weaned," Hughie replied. "But she may not be adoptable."

Miranda nodded. "I know. She's still terrified of me and I've been feeding her for two years."

"You won't put her down, will you?" Miranda's friend persisted.

"No, no," Hughie hastened to reassure her. "What we'll probably have to do is spay her and release her back into the same area, so long as Miranda is able to feed her."

"But I thought the city wants to round up all the stray cats and euthanize them." Miranda looked alarmed.

She was right. Every spring, there were a few complaints about roaming cats, unwanted kittens, and garden soiling. This year, a small but vocal anti-cat lobby had forced a showdown with city council. Apparently, the most serious crimes in our community were committed by cats, so for five months, issues like poverty, youth violence, potholes, sewers, and urban sprawl were put on hold. At public meetings, the overwhelming majority of speakers were against the proposed changes that would allow citizens to trap nuisance cats and take them to the "shelter" where, if unclaimed after three days, the cats would be euthanized.

The estimated cost to build such a shelter varied from six hundred thousand to twelve million dollars. Humane and highly effective solutions such as TNR (Trap-Neuter-Return), financial support for spay, neuter, and microchipping programs for low-income groups, and intensive public education, were ignored. City council had flip-flopped on its decision several times. It was, after all, an election year. A final decision was to be made in early April.

Hughie shrugged his shoulders. "I guess we'll have to see what happens at the next council meeting and take it from there."

Tanya and Susan prepared a suite at the back of the Cat Nap Inn, away from the hustle and bustle of the hospital. For two days, the terrified cat didn't move, refusing to eat or drink. On the morning of the third day, Jim discovered five mewling kittens lined up against their mama's body when he arrived for work.

A few months earlier, Hughie had received an earnest letter from Jim, a Grade 12 student, offering his services as a volunteer. We received many such requests but most people only lasted a short time when they found out they would not be assisting in surgery or cuddling cats all day. Jim, on the other hand, had proven himself to be a reliable, hard-working young man whose dream was to become a veterinarian. He quickly earned a spot as a paid part-time employee. The staff loved him and he joined their circle as a lovable, sometimes goofy, younger brother. Today, he had trudged for half an hour in the middle of a snowstorm to feed the in-patients and boarders. The city's transit system wasn't running nor were the streets plowed.

It was March 17th, St. Patrick's Day.

"Dr. McBride! Five babies!" Jim shouted into the phone.

Shivering in my bare feet, I glanced at the kitchen clock. It was seven in the morning; I was supposed to be in bed, warm and comatose, for at least another hour.

"There's two white ones, an orange one, a black one, and a calico," Jim continued. "What should I do?"

"Are they all nursing?" I asked groggily.

"Just a second, I'll go check!" Jim dropped the phone in his excitement and raced back to the Inn.

For the first time, I noticed the buildup of snow against the window. None of my cats had stirred from underneath the duvet even though I was in the kitchen, their favourite room. I reached for a sweater hanging over a chair and pulled it close. The first day of spring was four days away. Or so the calendar said.

I heard Jim's footsteps echoing down the hall. "I think so. It's hard to tell," was his breathless reply as he picked up the receiver. "A couple of them are asleep. Should I clean the kennel? It looks like a tornado went through."

"No, just leave it for now," I replied, stifling a yawn. "I don't want to disturb the mom."

Jim's sigh of relief was audible. Molly's low throaty growl and flattened ears reminded anyone who strayed too close to her kennel that they could lose, if not life and limb, at least a finger.

"I'll stay till more people get here," he offered. "School's closed so

I'm free as a bird."

I chuckled in spite of the cold and the hour. Jim's enthusiasm was contagious. He was the only teenager I knew who didn't seem burdened with his peer group's need to be like everyone else. He preferred to take his dog for a walk or play chess than play games on the computer. His hair was short when everyone else's was long. He played bass guitar in a rock band called Chemistry; sadly, they had none. This didn't deter a gaggle of lovestruck Grade 5 girls from hanging around when they practiced in Jim's garage.

By the time I arrived, all the babies had been christened with Irish names in honour of the day: Sean, Erin, Meghan, Patrick, and Siobhan. Jim had installed a privacy screen and managed to slip a bowl of fresh water and food into the suite. We stole peeks throughout the day at the little miracle hidden away in the farthest corner of the Cat Nap Inn.

Molly was an experienced mom. She stretched out on the soft blanket inside the nesting box, making sure all the kittens had easy access to her milk. Her eyes were closed and her chest rose and fell rapidly in a soft, purring lullaby. If she sensed our presence, however, she would look up. Instantly, her eyes became narrow slits of suspicion and hatred. But the babies demanded her attention and for now she had no choice. She would never leave them while they were helpless.

With Molly occupied, we were able to clean her kennel and litter box, although she threatened us throughout the procedure. Only when the door was safely closed and the privacy screen back in place did Molly close her eyes again. The babies were lined up in the warm crescent of her body, alternately nursing and sleeping. It would be just over a week before their eyes would open and they would meet their mother face to face. In the meantime, she would provide for their every need. She was their world and they, hers.

By mid-afternoon of the second day, we noticed that Molly had removed the black kitten from the box where his siblings lay in a satisfied, sleepy mound, their tummies full. She lay down with her single kitten and encouraged him to nurse. Throughout the day and into the night, she maintained her vigil. Every few hours, she would get up to feed her other youngsters, always returning to her smallest baby.

In the morning, little Sean was dead. Molly allowed us to remove him from the kennel as she nursed her surviving kittens. Her eyes never left us, but it was our faces she watched, not our hands. If eyes truly are the window to the soul, maybe Molly was trying in her own way to understand us just as we were trying to understand her.

Death, when it comes, can be malevolent and without meaning or it can be silent and merciful. Upon examination, we discovered the kitten had been born with a cleft palate. When he tried to nurse, he aspirated milk into his lungs. There was nothing we could have done to save him. It was his mother who lay with him, who tried to comfort him and who, with age-old wisdom, separated him from the rest of her healthy brood. She stayed with him until she knew with certainty there was nothing more she could do.

As the days passed, the surviving kittens flourished. At first, their rubbery legs were nothing more than useless flippers. As they grew stronger and their eyes opened, they took their first tottering steps. With the indulgent grace that only a parent possesses, Molly allowed her ears to be bitten, her tail attacked, and her body used as a springboard. "These are my kids," her half-closed eyes said. Yet with us, she remained wild and unrelenting.

Jim visited every day between classes. He had been there with Molly in the early morning hours following birth. And he had sat spellbound as she shared with him a moment of complete vulnerability. He began bringing his camera on these visits, an old 35mm Rolleiflex that had belonged to his uncle. Using only natural light so as not to disturb the family, he began collecting images: Molly as a gentle, patient mother, her kittens' first tottering steps beyond the nesting box and their joyous recognition of each other as playmates, little Patrick as he rode around in Hilary's lab coat pocket.

The only surviving male, Patrick was adored by his sisters and could usually be found at the bottom of the heap of kittens with only a tail or part of a leg protruding. The little fellow was always being washed by one or more females in his family. He had been born with partial nerve paralysis on the left side of his face, resulting in a lopsided quirky grin. His left ear pointed out instead of up and he was unable to blink his left eye. Worried that he might need ongoing medical care and surgery to have the eye removed, we made the decision to adopt him as a hospital mascot.

During the process of feline development, there is a critical time period between birth and twelve weeks when socialization with humans must occur. We handled the kittens every day, preparing them for the time they would leave their mother to live with people. Molly, on the other hand, had been born into the wild and would always be feral. The kindest thing we could do was to spay her and release her back into the territory she knew: a feral colony maintained by Miranda and a loyal group of supporters.

While one little family was growing up protected within the walls of our hospital, the city's cat controversy raged. Hughie was scheduled to speak at the last public hearing before council made its final decision. It had been a couple of hectic weeks at the hospital and he was exhausted.

"I don't know what I can say that will make any difference," he sighed, gathering his notes for the meeting and stuffing them into his briefcase.

"But you're a vet," I insisted. "A professional. That should carry some weight with city council."

Hughie shook his head. "It hasn't so far." He had been working with one of the Trap-Neuter-Return groups as well as one of the local shelters in a public education campaign.

"We live in a disposable society, Em. The answer's not bigger and bigger shelters." He sighed and ran a calloused hand through his hair. "We just have to care more," he said simply.

Grabbing his jacket from the hanger on the back door, he rummaged through the pockets for his car keys. Sullivan looked up hopefully, wagging his tail.

"Not yet, little buddy. Sorry." Hughie reached down to pat him, then, straightening his lanky frame, said goodbye and headed out into the starless and frigid night that belonged more to January than the first week of April.

But the difference between January and April is hope. No matter how bleak, we know that the burden of winter is about to be lifted from our shoulders when the first weed pokes its head out of the snow, the first robin is sighted and, in Halifax, the first university student, clutching a cup of coffee, strolls down the street in a pair of shorts and sandals while the rest of the populace is wrapped in parkas.

With that same hope, I decided to pack up early and head down to City Hall to support Hughie. City council met every second Tuesday in one of the oldest public buildings in Nova Scotia, a national historic site. Made from red sandstone and granite, it featured fine Victorian architecture and a seven-story clock tower. The northern face of the clock was fixed at 9:04 to commemorate the time of the 1917 Halifax Explosion. This gracious old building sat adjacent to the modern 9,000-seat Metro Centre.

Parking is always at a premium at the downtown core but tonight it looked like a rock star was in town, or perhaps the Halifax Mooseheads hockey team was playing their long-time rivals, the Cape Breton Screaming Eagles. In frustration, I wiggled into a questionable parking space too close to both a fire hydrant and a driveway and hoped for the best.

I was frozen by the time I hiked the three blocks to City Hall. In the foyer, I stomped the snow off my feet and blew on my hands while furiously rubbing them together. The bored security guard, who had been watching my performance with interest, pointed upstairs when I was done.

I ascended a wide, red-carpeted stairway, feeling like Scarlett O'Hara in Gone with the Wind. Two and a half centuries of municipal leaders immortalized on oil and canvas lined the walls, staring at me with unseeing eyes. At the top of the stairs, the hallway leading to council chambers was jammed with concerned citizens. I squeezed and oozed and pardoned my way through until I reached the entrance. There I struggled for a view of the podium.

The current speaker finished amid scattered applause and was followed by two more. Spying Hughie, I eased my way through the crowd.

"Em, what are you doing here? You should be back at the hospital making money," he grinned.

"No money to be made tonight," I replied with a grimace. "It's too damn cold. When are you on?"

"I'm not," Hughie replied, "but you're in time to hear Jim."

"Jim. Our Jim? What's he doing here?"

Hughie nodded. "He didn't know you had to request a time slot. I gave him mine."

Reading from a list, the Mayor announced that the next speaker would be Jim McCafferty. I watched as a lean young man with neatly trimmed blond hair rose from his seat and carefully picked his way to the front of the room. At the podium, he adjusted his wire-rimmed glasses and waited for the crowd to settle.

It was hot in the room. People had removed their winter coats and were fanning themselves with copies of the agenda. Some of the councillors were doodling on sheets of paper, others were whispering amongst themselves. Jim waited. One by one, they looked up. Only when he had everyone's attention did he begin.

"Hello," he said, leaning into the microphone. "I'm a Grade 12 student and I work part time at Ocean View Cat Hospital. One day I hope to become a veterinarian. I don't know anything about your budget," he continued, addressing the councillors. "I don't know the best way to help the cats in this city. But I'm going to tell you what I do know."

The audience was silent, quietly expectant, as Jim dimmed the houselights. The image of a short-haired calico with five nursing kittens filled the screen at the front of the room.

"This is Molly," he began.

Chapter 8

I STUDIED THE NEON MENU BOARD that stretched to infinity and beyond. There were too many choices, none of them good. I was trying to eat more sensibly after a harrowing experience with a bathing suit in the Sears dressing room. Who was the genius behind the three angled mirrors? There were parts I would just rather not see. Most of my shopping was done in outdoor recreation stores; one mirror, one view. Everyone goes home happy.

"Wait till you have kids," one of my friends said cheerfully. "It only gets worse."

The growing line behind me shuffled impatiently. In a fast-food restaurant, indecision is frowned upon.

"What's in the chicken burger?" I asked.

The clerk, a pimply-faced teenager wearing a hairnet and a badge that said "Smiles are free," stared at me without smiling. "Chicken."

I nodded as if this was exactly the information I was looking for and promptly ordered one. "Without the bun," I added.

The clerk shrugged. "It'll cost you the same."

"That's fine."

"CHICKENBURGER," he hollered from his cash register to the kitchen. "NO BUN!"

"NO BUN?" the incredulous short-order cook hollered back.

"No bun, right?" the clerk asked.

I nodded.

"NO BUN!" he bellowed and motioned for me to go wait in a corner where the bunless people were apparently kept separate from the normal fast-food crowd. Hughie was almost done by the time I joined him at the table, my mood foul. Beside us, a trio of seniors was thoroughly enjoying their cheeseburgers, fries, and Cokes. They all liked pink, patronized the same hairdresser, and agreed that Ronnie in 4B should be invited to the bridge party. When they finished eating, the youngest stopped to measure her height on the growth chart by the children's playroom.

"Still five feet," she giggled.

Her companions cracked up, leaving a trail of laughter as they exited the restaurant and piled into a pick-up truck.

"That's what I want to be like when I'm older," Hughie grinned.

"What? Old and wrinkled?" I grumbled.

"No! Full of life, Em. Carpe diem!" Hughie waved his arms expansively. "We live our lives in boxes, afraid to let loose. To show our true feelings! To be all we can be!"

"Are you on medication?" I took a mouthful of chicken.

Hughie shook his head. "Eat up, Em. We have patients to see. Wisdom to impart."

Back at the hospital, Bernie met us with a fistful of messages for Hughie. He thanked her and continued on to the office, whistling cheerfully. While I examined Nathan Murphy, one of my in-patients, I could hear Hughie's voice rising and falling as he called each client. He discussed lab results, sympathized with owners of problem cats, and laughed at cat stories he'd heard a million times, answering the most mundane questions with charm and grace.

And then … silence.

I gave Nathan his medications then put him back in the kennel. Nathan adored humans but was terrified of his own species, so Hilary had cut a cat-size hole in a cardboard box and put it in his kennel. A grateful Nathan scurried back inside. As I made some notes on his chart, I heard footsteps down the hall. Hughie soon appeared, clutching a piece of paper. He looked around and, satisfied that no one was within earshot, waved the paper in my face.

"It's Michele," he hissed, his face ashen. "She got a cat. She wants to make an appointment."

Michele was Hughie's ex-wife and an accountant. In an unusual arrangement, she still managed the hospital's finances, albeit with ill-humour and an iron fist.

"I thought she didn't like cats," I ventured.

Hughie sighed. "It was more that she didn't like me."

"Oh." I picked up my pen.

"Em! What am I going to do?"

I thought for a moment. "Well, the usual things, I guess. Physical exam, vaccination, maybe … "

"No, no," he moaned, "I can't do that. But you could," he added, his face brightening. "We could say I got stuck in surgery and that you were just helping out. Or, better yet, I got delayed on a house call."

"Hughie, don't be ridiculous. She wants you to see the cat because she knows you're a good vet. It's a compliment."

My boss looked doubtful. "Yes, but … "

"No buts! Climb out of that box. Carpe diem!" I grinned. "You have wisdom to impart!"

With slumped shoulders, Hughie headed back down the hall. It was hard to argue against your own convictions delivered so convincingly less than an hour earlier. An appointment was made and then cancelled at the last minute when Michele got called out of town on business. Hughie's rejoicing, however, was short-lived; she returned the following day with a cat in tow.

"She's here," Hilary announced, racing out back. The staff was not particularly fond of Michele. Tyrannosaurus Rex was a mere lizard compared to Hughie's ex.

Hughie sat rigid at his desk while Bernie chatted fearlessly in reception. Her warm voice with its soothing Irish lilt melted some of the chill in the air.

"Hello, luv," I heard her say. "What have we got here?"

From the treatment area, I struggled to hear Michele's side of the conversation. Susan and Hilary debated whether or not they should turn on the intercom.

"I can't hear a thing," Susan complained.

Both looked up with a guilty start as I walked past. "Don't do it," I warned them. "She'll know." Opening the door to reception, I was immediately rushed by an exuberant but very thin mackerel tabby.

"Hello, Emily!"

Michele's smile nearly bowled me over. If I was to believe my boss, Michele was the spawn of the devil who just happened to be good with numbers. She and I had never been friends, but I admired her efficiency and dedication to her work. And I had produced a detailed inventory count at Ocean View's fiscal year-end, which left her smiling.

I patted the little cat at my feet. "This guy's a charmer. How long have you had him?"

"About a month," Michele sighed. "He just showed up at the door, starving. I put ads everywhere but no one's claimed him. I really don't need a cat right now."

"Does he have a name?

"Well, you know what happens once you name them," Michele smiled in resignation. "Hank."

As she cuddled Hank, I heard a familiar cackle followed by static. Bernie eyed the intercom with suspicion then turned it off. She picked up Michele's large black coffee and headed for the exam room. Michele caught the scent and, following on Bernie's heels, settled down in one of the chairs in the exam room.

"Here you go, luv." Bernie handed her the coffee.

"Thanks," Michele said as Bernie smiled and quickly shut the door behind her.

"Good work, Bernie," I whispered. "You've caged the wild animal."

Hughie's scheduled thirty-minute appointment with Michele stretched into an hour, during which time I castrated the aptly named Mr. Big and vaccinated Pickles Downey. Hughie emerged only once, to enlist Hilary's help with blood collection. All cats dislike having needles poked in their veins. Older cats in particular are frail, reluctant to be restrained, and, like my aging mother, feel it is their God-given right after all these years to dispense with tact. They caterwaul relentlessly and bite without warning.

Not so Hank. Hilary was in and out in less than a minute and had little to report. Michele, fortified by a second cup of black coffee thanks to Bernie, was in a good mood and Hank was a sweetheart.

His CBC, which measures the type and quantity of blood cells, was normal. The serum chemistry panel that we ran in our hospital lab showed normal kidney and liver function. However, the T4 test revealed Hank was hyperthyroid. His thyroid gland was enlarged and producing too much thyroxin. This hormone interacts with almost every cell in the body to speed up metabolism. In a healthy cat, it is part of an intricate, beautifully designed system of checks and balances. In Hank's case, it was forcing his body dangerously into overdrive.

Hughie prescribed a drug called Tapazole and cautioned Michele that he wanted to recheck Hank's thyroid function in a couple of weeks. Most cats tolerate Tapazole very well, but it can sometimes cause nausea, vomiting, and lethargy. In extreme cases, cats may stop eating and become so ill from the medication that we need to take them off it altogether.

After Michele left, Hughie plopped down in the chair and let out a deep breath. I looked up from my notes.

"So you survived."

"Yup. But she's coming back in two weeks."

I shrugged. "It could be worse. You could still be married to her."

"Yeah." He hesitated. "She's getting married again, actually. To a neurosurgeon. Can you believe it?"

"How did they meet?" I asked. "At a conference?" Michele was a tax specialist with a nationally known accounting firm and was often asked to speak at conferences for professionals.

"Why do women always want to know that stuff?"

"Because it's interesting … and we're nosy," I grinned.

Hughie rolled his eyes. "They met at a bowling alley, if you must know. A bowling alley!" he repeated, shaking his head.

I turned away, not trusting myself to keep a straight face in what was clearly an emotionally charged situation for my boss. Last year, Jack Cruickshank, a retired naval petty officer with a soft spot for cats, had revealed that Hughie's ex was the top bowler on his team. Michele, who wore only designer labels and vacationed in Paris, denied enjoying the game and claimed she only bowled for charity. We might have believed her until Jack mentioned that she had her own ball: pink and engraved with a big M.

"Humph!" Hughie snorted. "Probably a gift from lover-boy." He looked at me. "How many neurosurgeons do you know that like to bowl in their spare time?"

I didn't know any neurosurgeons and said so, adding that I supposed anything was possible.

Hughie shook his head.

"Are you jealous?" I asked in disbelief.

Hughie was silent, staring at the computer screen. "No," he said after a moment.

I waited.

"She's moving to Philadelphia."

"Oh. Well, that's a good thing, right?" I joked. "Year-end will be a lot less stressful."

Hughie looked up with a polite smile. "I suppose so."

"Dr. McBride?" Hilary poked her head through the door. "Mrs. Murphy's here to pick up Nathan. She has a few questions."

"Tell her I'll be right there." I looked at Hughie but he had turned back to the computer screen and was busy entering notes. By the time I had finished talking to Nathan's mom, he was immersed in his next appointment.

Word spread faster than the bubonic plague that Michele was getting married and moving to the States. The staff was delighted. Jack was disappointed to be losing his best bowler just before the Halifax Superbowl, but felt that Mitchy and Steve were well-suited to each other.

"They've got so much in common," he had declared, producing a team photo. Hughie leaned over for a better look.

"That's Steve," Jack said, pointing to a tall athletic-looking man.

"Looks a bit like a pug," Hughie commented later when Jack was out of earshot. "Did you see the overbite?"

Nevertheless, Hughie was back to his old, charming self when Michele returned a few weeks later with a cup of black coffee and the lovable Hank. While Hughie ran another T4, blood chemistry, and CBC, we chatted for a moment. According to Michele, Hank seemed happy, but he was sleeping more and eating less.

I nodded. "It may be that we just need to adjust his dosage. Most cats do fine on Tapazole."

"He's a good cat," Michele said. "We never had any pets growing up. And then I met Douce," she smiled.

Curiosity got the better of me. Hughie rarely talked about his personal life. "So how did you guys meet?"

"At university. I saw this good-looking guy hunched over something on the road. Turns out it was a dead squirrel. I'm not into rodents," Michele shuddered, "but he felt bad for the squirrel and I thought, well, here's a sensitive guy, you know. We started dating … " Michele's voice trailed off.

I clucked encouragingly, but Michele just continued to pat Hank. In the uncomfortable silence, I offered to check on his blood results. I figured Hughie had stalled somewhere and was merely delaying the inevitable. I found him hunched over not a dead squirrel but the microscope. A copy of Feline Medicine lay open on the counter.

"Looks like AIHA," Hughie muttered without looking up.

"You're kidding!"

Hughie handed me a copy of the blood results. "I wish I was."

AIHA, otherwise known as Auto Immune Hemolytic Anemia, is a rare reaction to Tapazole. The very medication that Hughie had prescribed to treat Hank's hyperthyroidism caused antibodies to identify normal red blood cells as foreign invaders. These knights in shining armour rushed to protect Hank by destroying his red blood cells. New ones weren't being produced fast enough to keep up with the demand and, as a result, Hank was anemic.

"What are you going to do?" I asked. "It's not usually curable, is it?"

"No," Hughie sighed, "but they can do really well on prednisone."

I nodded. The steroid would help suppress the immune system and slow down the destruction of the red blood cells.

"Murphy's law." Hughie shook his head in disbelief. He turned off the light on the microscope and headed up the hall to break the news to Michele. She left a short while later with pursed lips and a bottle of prednisone.

Fortunately, however, Hank seemed to do well on the prednisone. Because of the side effects associated with prolonged steroid use in cats, including kidney disease, diabetes, and heart problems, Hughie wanted Hank on the lowest dose possible that managed his anemia. All went well until Michele began lowering the dosage as Hughie instructed. Even after returning to the original levels, Hank only improved marginally. He started sleeping in closets, refusing to eat, and ignoring Michele. Hughie recommended sending a sample of Hank's blood to the vet college on Prince Edward Island for further analysis.

Michele was worried. The bowling neurosurgeon with the overbite called Hughie to discuss the case and offer his professional recommendations. Hughie's grip on the phone tightened with each suggestion. In a rather terse voice, he explained that feline medicine was considerably different than human medicine.

And then I heard him ask, "Steve, do you play basketball?"

I looked up. Hughie's Saturday morning "gentleman's" league was a cutthroat, brawling cesspool of testosterone.

"Oh, that's too bad. Another time." Hughie hung up the phone.

"Gutless shit," he muttered.

Despite Dr. Steve's offer to run another CBC in his state-of-the-art lab, Michele agreed with Hughie that an animal lab would be more likely to detect abnormalities peculiar to animals. Nevertheless, when she arrived for her appointment, her heels clicked in a way that discouraged small talk. I kept my distance while Hughie and Susan collected another blood sample that would be delivered by courier to the vet college in Charlottetown.

When they were done, Hughie scooped the little cat into his arms and carried him back down the hallway to the exam room where Michele waited. At first, there was only the odd murmur of voices. And then I heard Michele crying softly. The exam room door opened. Without a word, Hughie grabbed a box of tissues off the desk and returned to the exam room, closing the door behind him. A short while later, he and Michele left. They were gone a long time.

The lab faxed Hank's results the following day. When the technician had examined his red blood cells, she discovered the presence of hemobartonella, a parasite which attaches itself to the red blood cells. An infected cat would exhibit the same symptoms as AIHA. As in AIHA, the body recognizes these blood cells as foreign and rushes to destroy them. Hank had likely been a carrier for a long time without showing any symptoms until his immune system was stressed. Today, hemobartonella has been reclassified as a bacteria, but the same six-week course of tetracycline still cures the infection.

Hughie called Michele with the good news, but her betrothed answered the phone instead. Apparently, Michele was shoe-shopping for the upcoming nuptials. "She's already got a closet full," Steve laughed.

Dr. Steve had the kind of voice that could leap tall buildings with a single bound. Hughie grimaced as he held the phone a safe distance from his ear.

"Why don't you come to the wedding?" Steve added. "I know she'd like you to be there."

I nearly choked on my sandwich.

"Yes, she already asked me," Hughie said quietly.

The talk that followed was merely the polite conversation of two men who had little in common except for Michele. After a few moments, Hughie explained that his next appointment was waiting and after wishing the couple well, said goodbye. He hung up the phone and rubbed Sullivan's tummy.

"Are you going to the wedding?" I asked, incredulous.

It was to be a simple ceremony at the Royal Nova Scotia Yacht Squadron overlooking the Northwest Arm, a picturesque ocean inlet which reached into the heart of the city. On a warm spring day, kayaks skirted among the throngs of sailboats that skimmed the shimmering surface. When I was very little, I asked my dad where the stars went in the daytime. He told me that this sparkling sea held all the stars for safekeeping until nighttime and then let them go so they could shine. Even now, when I drive past on a sunny day, I see the stars trembling in excitement just underneath the water, waiting to be freed.

Hughie reached for Sullivan's leash. The little dog was instantly on his feet, his stumpy tail a blur of excitement.

"Probably not," Hughie replied, shaking his head. He snapped the leash in place and strode down the hall to the back door.

Steve and Michele were married on a spectacular day in May. The buds on the maple trees were almost ready to burst open and the fragrant scent of lilacs floated like a whisper on the air. Hughie didn't go to the wedding, but he purchased a hand-carved wooden box and placed a pair of season tickets to the Philadelphia Orchestra inside.

"Wow! That's a nice gift," I commented.

Hughie fumbled with glossy silver wedding paper, folding and refolding the sides until he was satisfied, then taped them in place. He wrapped a pale blue ribbon around the box and, with a pair of scissors, curled the ends.

"There," he said, stepping back.

"Looks nice," I nodded.

We stared at the box.

"She always wanted me to go the symphony with her," Hughie said, breaking the silence. "I never did."

❈ ❈ ❈

In the weeks and months post-Michele, Ocean View Cat Hospital began receiving envelopes proclaiming "Past Due!" in angry red letters. Crumpled petty cash receipts stuffed into a Tim Hortons coffee can spilled out over the shelf and onto the floor. With four resident cats, those that fell were quickly dispatched. On paydays, Hughie told the staff to guesstimate their earnings and scribbled his signature at the bottom of each cheque. Not until the phone company threatened to cut off service did he shake off his shroud of fiscal apathy.

Prior to her departure, Michele had provided Hughie with a list of bookkeepers and accountants that she recommended. Hughie had thanked her then promptly misplaced the list. He rifled through the desk drawers with increasing frustration before finally striking gold on a remote shelf in the coat closet. Clasping an envelope to his chest, he sighed deeply then ripped it open and phoned the first name on the list. On Monday morning, Mrs. Isabelle Tuttle, of Tuttle & Tuttle Inc., was temporarily installed at Hughie's desk. He sat at attention in a chair beside her, hands folded meekly in his lap. It was as if a famous scene from veterinarian James Herriott's book If Only They Could Talk was playing out before my eyes. Instead of Siegfried Farnon and Miss Harbottle, it was Hughie Doucette and Mrs. Isabelle Tuttle.

"Dr. Doucette," Mrs. Tuttle said in a stern voice. "What is this?" She pointed to an entry in the petty cash journal.

Hughie leaned over. "Oh. That's a purchase at the drugstore for an antibiotic," he said proudly.

"Yes. I can see that." Mrs. Tuttle peered at him over the rims of her bifocals. She tapped the entry with her forefinger. "What is the date, please?"

Hughie squinted. "Ah, I can't quite make that out," he said, smiling at Mrs. Tuttle. "Let me just put on my reading glasses. Old age, you know."

Mrs. Tuttle did not smile.

Hughie fumbled in his pocket. "There, that's better," he said, slipping on a pair of thumbprint-glazed glasses. "Now, what was it you wanted to know, Mrs. Tuttle?"

"The date, Dr. Doucette. The date."

Hughie leaned over. "Mmm," he said with a puzzled frown. Taking a tissue from the box, he removed his glasses, blew on them, and cleaned the glass with slow, circular strokes. He held them up to his face. Still not satisfied, he pulled a small bottle of eyeglass cleaner from the desk drawer and squirted a few drops onto the front and back of each lens. When the glasses were cleaner than I had ever known them to be, he leaned over the desk once more.

"Now, let's see. The date ... " Hughie inspected the book.

"April 20th!" Mrs. Tuttle blurted out.

"Yes, I believe you're correct," Hughie agreed.

"And what is today's date, Dr. Doucette?"

Hughie looked at me.

"July 5th," I said helpfully.

"July 5th," Hughie repeated.

"Exactly." Mrs. Tuttle removed her glasses. "Dr. Doucette, why are there no entries since April 20th?"

"Well, you see, Mrs. Tuttle, my accountant left town."

"In a hurry?" Mrs. Tuttle's eyes narrowed.

"No, no, nothing like that. She got married."

"I see."

Hughie's eyes drifted to the coffee can on the shelf. Mrs. Tuttle followed his gaze with mounting horror.

"Mrs. Tuttle? Would you like a cup of coffee?" Hughie asked brightly.

Mrs. Tuttle nodded. "Herbal tea, if you don't mind, Dr. Doucette. I might become violent if I have caffeine."

Hughie rose to leave.

"Dr. Doucette?"

"Yes, Mrs. Tuttle?"

"No dawdling."

Chapter 9

Susan poked her head in the door. Overnight it had gone from a rich chestnut brown with red undertones to a greenish blonde. The female staff were always experimenting with their hair, changing the colour, style, and length with every paycheque, but this time something had gone wrong. Hughie opened his mouth to ask, then thought better of it. Wordlessly, Susan handed me the chart for my next patient, one Virgil Vaughan. It sounded like a stage name; his real name was probably Fluffy or Lucky. I thanked Susan, who grunted something unintelligible and trudged back down the hall.

"Good morning," I said brightly as I opened the exam room door.

"It's supposed to rain."

I looked up. The voice had trickled down from somewhere near the ceiling. A lanky man in ill-fitting clothes stood in the corner, breathing the rarefied air. He looked at me with one eye while the other seemed to drift in an altogether different direction. I didn't know which one to focus on and I felt my gaze drifting too.

"Starting in the west and moving east," he continued. "Should be here by noon. At least 15 millimetres. Possibility of high winds in the afternoon."

"I heard it was going to clear at noon."

I looked down. Mrs. Vaughan was comfortably seated in a chair. Even if stretched end to end, she would probably be prohibited from most of the rides at Disneyland. Unlike her husband, whose arms and legs extended beyond the capacity of his clothes to contain them, Mrs. Vaughan was impeccably dressed and accessorized. A skittish black and white cat flitted through the exam room.

"This must be Virgil," I smiled.

Hearing his name, the little cat screeched to a halt and looked around inquiringly, then resumed his madcap inspection of my exam room.

"I wanted to call him Blackie," Mr. Vaughan announced. "Whoever heard of a cat named Virgil?"

Mrs. Vaughan shook her head. "That's so common. I named him Virgil after reading The Aeneid. I belong to a book club. I'm an avid reader."

Not to be outdone, Mr. Vaughan added, "I golf."

I glanced at Virgil's chart, searching for common ground. Bernie's notes were a bit sketchy but she had recorded a birth date in August of last year.

"So Virgil is almost a year old?" I asked.

Mrs. Vaughan nodded in agreement. "Yes, that's right."

"Well, we don't know for sure," Mr. Vaughan corrected his wife. "He was a stray."

"It's an approximation, Horace," Mrs. Vaughan sighed, shifting in her chair. "I think I know cats."

I scooped Virgil from the floor and peeked inside his mouth. He had all his adult teeth. Judging by his weight and size, I agreed with Mrs. Vaughan, who beamed in smug satisfaction. As I began to examine Virgil, a monster-truck purr arose from the depths of his little feline soul. He was a one-cat band: his heart the drum, his purr the rhythm guitar, and his meows the woodwinds. His white feet kneaded the air as I palpated his internal organs.

When I was done, Virgil jumped down on the floor and scratched himself.

"See that?" Mr. Vaughan said. "He has fleas."

"He does not have fleas. There are no fleas in my house," Mrs. Vaughan retorted.

Mr. Vaughan raised his arms heavenward and rolled his eyes in mute appeal. His fingers almost grazed the ceiling.

"Dr. McBride?" Mrs. Vaughan turned to me.

The Vaughans needed a marriage counsellor more than a vet. "Well," I began carefully, "there was no evidence of fleas on his physical exam and his skin is in excellent condition. Sometimes they just get itchy," I added with a smile.

Mrs. Vaughan folded her arms across her chest and leaned back in her chair.

"I still think … "

"Horace!" Mrs. Vaughan hissed. There was an edge to her voice, a line etched between the decibels that Mr. Vaughan dared not cross.

It was at this moment that a chorus of female giggles erupted from the second exam room.

"Oooh," a male voice crooned. "A little bit lower." There were more giggles followed by the hum of a battery-powered instrument.

"Oh … YES! Girls, that's lovely!"

I thought Mr. Vaughan's good eye was going to pop out of his head.

"So," I continued in a louder voice, "Virgil's a healthy little guy."

The Vaughans were staring at the wall. My framed credentials and a glossy anatomical poster of a cat's insides were all that separated them from God knows what debauchery was going on next door. Meanwhile, Virgil discovered the cupboard door. Its repeated thuds of protest seemed to refocus his owners.

"I'm sorry, Dr. McBride," Mrs. Vaughan said after a moment. "What did you say?"

"Just that you're doing a great job," I replied. "Virgil is one healthy, happy little guy."

The Vaughans looked at each other.

"How can that be?" Mrs. Vaughan asked at last.

I shook my head, puzzled. "What do you mean?"

"He's peeing around the house," Mr. Vaughan announced.

"It's not the whole house, Horace. Just the bathroom."

Mr. Vaughan shrugged his shoulders.

"It's not the whole house," his wife repeated to me.

I glanced at Virgil who was trying to catch the butterflies Bernie had recently stencilled on the wall. "Well, he's certainly bright and active. Sometimes, unneutered male cats like to mark their territory. It's a normal behaviour, but obviously one we don't appreciate in our homes," I added.

"So what do we do?" Mrs. Vaughan wanted to know. "I've just had the entire bathroom remodelled ... a pedestal sink, new bathtub, a wonderful hung toilet that I just adore, and new flooring. It's really lovely."

"Well, in the short term, remember to keep the door closed so he doesn't freshen up his territory and ... "

"We have teenagers, Dr. McBride," Mrs. Vaughan shook her head. "Half the time they don't remember their own names."

"Do your best," I told her. "We can schedule a neuter for next week and get a urine sample at the same time just to make sure there isn't a medical reason for what he's doing, like an infection or something irritating his bladder."

"Oh, dear," Mrs. Vaughan sighed as she rose from her chair. "I'm so worried about him," she added, glancing expectantly at her husband.

"I have an ear infection," Mr. Vaughan explained.

"No, Horace!" Mrs. Vaughan shook her head and pointed to her coat draped against the back of the chair.

While Mr. Vaughan helped his wife on with her coat, I coaxed Virgil back into his carrier with some catnip and fastened the door.

"It might rain tomorrow," Mr. Vaughan informed me as he bent down to pick up the carrier. It rocked like a thing possessed as Virgil twisted and turned for the best views from his new vantage point. "Don't plan on any outdoor events like a barbecue or tennis match."

I promised that I wouldn't, and followed the pair into reception. While Mrs. Vaughan paid the bill, her husband loitered outside the door to the second exam room, irresistibly drawn to the low murmur of voices.

When she was done, Mrs. Vaughan looked around impatiently. "Horace!" she cried, clicking her heels. "Come along."

Shortly after the Vaughans left, the second exam room door opened. Teddy Angelopoulos and Sherman, who looked much like the tank for which he was named, emerged surrounded by a gaggle of staff. The latter affectionately referred to Mr. Angelopoulos as Teddy Bear. In his early sixties, large in size, gentle in spirit, and always generous with homemade Greek delicacies, Mr. Angelopoulos was one of our favourite clients. He owned a flower shop known simply as Teddy's. He had an uncanny knack for matching flowers with people and took a genuine interest in their lives. As a result, he was very successful. The flower shop had put five Angelopoulos children through university. Numbers six and seven were still in high school and wanted to be an accountant and a doctor respectively. Number eight, unexpected but very much loved, was in Grade 3. Her current career goal was to be a cashier at the movie theatre and make popcorn.

Sherman was the family pet. He had been a skinny little stray with frostbitten ears and toes when Teddy discovered him behind his shop one winter morning. He was seriously ill for several months, but with medical intervention and a loving home, he blossomed. And blossomed. He developed a persnickety colon as a result of his large appetite and had to endure multiple enemas. Now he was on a special food. Teddy lived nearby and stopped in almost every day to buy a few cans of the food and chat with the staff. Sherman had lost some weight but I suspected we weren't the only ones who enjoyed Mrs. Angelopoulos's cooking.

Sherman spent his days in the sunny window of Teddy's shop,

sprawled amidst an ever-changing display of seasonal flower arrangements. For exercise he sniffed the flowers. Because he was too large to groom himself properly, he visited us regularly for "butt shaves" and, every six months, a lion cut. As the name suggests, most of the fur is shaved close to the skin but a beautiful mane is left around the face and tufts of fur on the feet and tail. Everyone goes home happy – in this case, everyone except for the Vaughans. At this moment, they were probably sitting at home, coffees in hand, wondering if Ocean View had found a way to supplement its income during the economic downturn.

"Dr. McBride!" Teddy rushed forward and grabbed me in a crushing embrace, kissing the air on each side of my cheeks. Then he held me at arms' length and studied my face.

"My wonderful doctor!" he gushed. "You look magnificent as always. But something is different, no?" He pursed his lips and studied my face. "Aha!" he said at last. "You are wearing earrings."

I blushed. He was right. I rarely wore earrings to work but Benny had just given me a pair he had bought at an open-air market on the weekend: silver cats with sparkling blue eyes. I just couldn't leave them home alone in their box.

"Aha!" Teddy declared again. "They are from a boyfriend, yes?"

"Yes they are!" Susan bobbed her head up and down enthusiastically. "He's good-looking too." I noticed her mood had changed considerably with Teddy's visit. "He teaches Grade 5 and he really likes cats," she continued.

"Wonderful, wonderful!" Teddy clasped his hands together as I turned crimson and radiated solar flares.

"And ... you are serious with this young man?"

"He broke up with his other girlfriend because he wanted to date Dr. McBride," Hilary chimed in.

Teddy became very solemn and leaned closer. "Ah! He is an honourable man. You come see me when the gentleman proposes and I will make a special bouquet for my special doctor."

"Oh, Teddy, we're just good friends," I replied, glaring at Susan and Hilary.

Teddy took my hand and patted it in a fatherly way. "This is how it was with myself and Mother Angelopoulos," he beamed. "And then before you know it, there will be little Emilys running around and then little … " Teddy paused and looked at Susan.

"Benjamin," she said helpfully.

"Little Benjamins." Teddy clasped his hands together over his heart. "So beautiful."

Ocean View was the National Enquirer of veterinary hospitals. It never ceased to amaze me how the staff seemed to know things about my private life. Although she denied it, my mother was, in all likelihood, their oft-quoted, unnamed source of information. I had taken to calling her Deep Throat. She reminded me on a regular basis that my biological clock was ticking. And I reminded her that I had no interest in reproducing, joining the PTA, and wiping dirty bums.

"How is that any different from cleaning four litter boxes every day?" she countered.

Despite Teddy's confidence and Mom's best-laid plans, I had no intention of getting married. Just look at the Vaughans. Single-handedly, they could fund a marriage counsellor's early retirement. Virgil's neuter had gone well and there was no evidence of any abnormalities on his urinalysis. However, three weeks later, he was still peeing in the bathroom and this was a source of tension between them, as were most things.

"Why is he still peeing in the bathroom?" Mrs. Vaughan asked.

"It's not just the bathroom," Mr. Vaughan piped up.

"Well, that's the only place I've ever found it," Mrs. Vaughan retorted.

So. We were back in familiar territory.

"Dr. McBride?" Mrs. Vaughan continued, "You mentioned we could do X-rays and possibly an ultrasound? I'm very worried about him."

"Well, we could," I began, "but that would be down the road. Right now, he's healthy, he's young, and you have him on a high-quality canned food. There's no reason to suspect anything out of the ordinary like a bladder stone or some kind of growth. I still think it's a behavioural issue."

"Maybe you're right," Mrs. Vaughan sighed. "You know, one thing I've noticed is that it only seems to happen when Horace is home. He has to travel a lot for work."

Cat behaviour is a fascinating subject. We sometimes forget that these little creatures, while domesticated, still share the same urges as their wild counterparts. I wondered aloud if Virgil was marking his territory because he was felt like he was in competition with Mr. Vaughan.

"Me? Competing with a cat?" Mr. Vaughan laughed. "That's ridiculous!"

Mrs. Vaughan's pursed lips suggested otherwise. If push came to shove for her affections, I'd bet on Virgil.

"We can put him on a mild sedative to try and modify his behaviour," I continued, "but I don't want to do that just yet. Put a litter box in the bathroom. Temporarily," I added, seeing the look on Mrs. Vaughan's face. Her new bathroom was a source of pride and the idea of cat litter underfoot held little appeal.

"Let's just see if he'll use it. If he does, then gradually you can start moving it out of the bathroom back to its original location," I reassured her. "And, Mr. Vaughan, try to interact with him as much as possible. Play games with him, pet him, encourage him to sit on your lap, feed him, those kinds of things. He needs to know you're a friend, not a competitor."

"You hear that, Horace?" Mrs. Vaughan asked.

"I need to be a friend," Mr. Vaughan repeated dully. "Not a competitor."

"That's right!" Mrs. Vaughan declared.

"Did you know there was hail in Southern Ontario yesterday, and a tornado?" Mr. Vaughan shook his head.

Three weeks later we took X-rays of Virgil's plumbing. Mr. Vaughan's thinly-disguised attempts at friendship hadn't fooled Virgil. I was relieved that there was no evidence of bladder stones. An ultrasound performed at the veterinary college in Charlottetown also yielded normal results. Mrs. Vaughan was thrilled that her little cat was healthy but still concerned about his flagrant disregard for the litter box. We scheduled an appointment for his final booster and I planned to discuss behaviour modification therapy.

When the day arrived, Mrs. Vaughan, accompanied only by Virgil, strode into the exam room. She seemed oddly subdued. I wondered if she was just worried about Virgil or like all of the great teams – Laurel and Hardy, Wayne and Schuster, Sonny and Cher – she needed her sidekick, even if he was almost seven feet tall and preoccupied with the weather (maybe because he was closer to it than the rest of us).

As usual, Virgil darted about the exam room, an exuberant explorer of his world. A crack in the tile fascinated him for several minutes. The sliver of paper that stuck out from underneath the cupboard door was even more exciting. But the greatest discovery of all was the doorstop, a serendipitous find when Virgil had jumped into the air for no apparent reason and landed on it. Startled by the subsequent twanging, he studied it for a moment then raised a tentative paw. The doorstop proved to be a far more interactive and entertaining toy than the crack or the paper.

While Virgil repeatedly swatted it in delight, I turned to Mrs. Vaughan. "He's such a great little cat," I grinned. "So full of life."

Mrs. Vaughan smiled at Virgil like a doting parent.

"So," I continued, "now that we know there's nothing physically wrong, we have to find out why he's doing what he's doing and find a way to change the behaviour. I think … "

"Dr. McBride," she interrupted, "we won't be needing those tests. Virgil is perfectly fine. I don't know quite how to tell you this but, well, it's the new hung toilet." Mrs. Vaughan paused. "Horace hasn't quite mastered it."

In the silence that followed, I stared at Mrs. Vaughan .

Mistaking my silence for doubt, she added emphatically, "I caught him red-handed!"

I struggled to keep a straight face. Mrs. Vaughan seemed completely unaware of her unfortunate choice of words.

When we emerged a few moments later, Mr. Vaughan was seated in a far corner, reading the newspaper as he waited for his wife and cat. He barely glanced up when the exam room door opened and offered no opinion on the sweltering day outside. Across from him, a harried young mother with a squawking infant and a howling cat was doing her best to soothe both. Clients were lined up to buy food, talk cat, and make appointments. Bernie was in the middle of a hot flash and was trying to wiggle out of a sweater as she waited on them.

Teddy Angelopoulos had just purchased a bag of low-cal treats for Sherman.

"Aha! How is my favourite doctor?" He thrust a plate of Greek pastries in front of me. "I have brought some special treats from Mrs. Angelopoulos today."

My mouth began to drool as I studied the treats and narrowed my decision down to two. I had never met the famed Mrs. Angelopoulos but I loved her dearly anyway.

"Take both," Teddy urged.

Ever the gentleman, Teddy then circled the room with his mouth-watering delicacies, even pausing to admire the screaming baby who was by now turning a ghastly shade of purple. At the Vaughans, he stopped in amazement.

"Oh my goodness! Mr. Vaughan! How are you!" Teddy smiled in delight. Balancing the plate in one hand, he shook Horace's hand with the other. "One of my best customers," he beamed. "And this must be the lovely Mrs. Vaughan."

He reached for Mrs. Vaughan's hand and kissed it. "So pleased to meet you."

Mrs. Vaughan permitted herself a smile.

"Tell me, my dear, how did you like the bouquet of azaleas? Mr. Vaughan tells me they are your favourite flowers."

Before Mrs. Vaughan could answer, Deidre Hunter burst through the doors at the end of her seeing-eye dog's lead. Tibet, a Golden Retriever, was a lovable goofball without an ounce of common sense. He was supposedly a certified guide dog, but must have graduated from correspondence school. Of the few thoughts in his head, none involved leading the blind. Smelling food, he thrust his gigantic paws on Teddy's chest and sampled what he could before Deidre managed to regain control.

Struggling to protect his wife's baking from dog drool, Teddy didn't see the storm cloud that darkened Mrs. Vaughan's face as she stared at her husband. But I did. And I knew for certain that Mrs. Vaughan had not been the recipient of those flowers.

Into the melee wandered a plump woman with curly red hair. She hovered uncertainly at the door. Bernie had given up all pretense of efficiency and stood behind the reception counter, a hand-held fan to her face. Her sweater and silk scarf were tossed carelessly over a chair. Since all the staff were occupied, I side-stepped Tibet, who was scouring the floor for crumbs, and approached the woman.

"Can I help you?" I asked, raising my voice to be heard above the confusion.

"I … I don't know," she replied. "I wanted to make an appointment with Dr. Doucette."

"I'm sorry. He's not in today."

"I hear he's wonderful," she said dubiously, glancing over my shoulder.

Teddy, overhearing our conversation, nodded in agreement.

"Aha! He is a truly wonderful veterinary man. But Dr. McBride here," Teddy spread his arms wide, "she is also wonderful too. My Sherman, he has had more things stuck in more orifices than you can imagine! And still … " Teddy paused for effect, "still he loves his Dr. McBride."

I smiled encouragingly even as a hideous odour filled the room. Its epicentre was either Tibet or the howling baby. Mr. and Mrs. Vaughan had been immersed in an animated discussion. As conversations around them slowed to a trickle, I heard Mrs. Vaughan's strident voice.

"Three hundred and fifty dollars!" she snapped. "That's how much it costs to find out you should sit down to pee! And blaming it on the cat! You're the one who should have got neutered!"

In the silence which followed, the woman smiled nervously and began backing up.

"Thank you," she said, her hand on the door. "Perhaps I'll come back another time."

Chapter 10

Andy MacLachlan rushed through the doors with a blood-soaked bundle in his arms and two little girls at his side.

"Somebody hit Charlotte right in front of the house," he gasped. "The guy didn't even stop!"

I dropped my charts on the counter. "Come with me," I ordered, racing to the treatment area. Jim materialized at my side with a stethoscope as Andy gently laid Charlotte on the examining table. I pulled back the towel. Even as I put the stethoscope to my ears, I knew there was nothing I could do. Charlotte's small body had been crushed and dragged by a ton of steel. Her breathing was ragged as pain surged through her.

Controversy rages over free-roaming domesticated cats. As a veterinarian I had seen a number of cats hit by cars, often unavoidably. But for the driver to speed away, leaving an animal to suffer, denies a basic tenet of what it is to be human – compassion.

Andy's little girls stared at me in mute appeal. Tear trails snaked down their faces, the kind of faces that children wear in the summer: small, golden brown, smudged with dust and orange Popsicle. At five, Lily just reached to the top of the treatment table. Her eyes were wide as she stood on tiptoes and peered over the edge. Nine-year-old Meghan held back. She wore a pink gingham sundress that hung down to her knees and a pair of dirty white sneakers. One lace was undone. Andy was a single parent, struggling to balance fatherhood with the demands of his job.

Kneeling on the floor, he pulled the girls toward him. "Charlotte is hurt really bad," he said softly.

"But can't … can't you do something?" Hiccupping between sobs, Meghan looked from her father to me.

"Charlotte is suffering right now," Andy explained, trying to keep his voice even. "Dr. McBride is going to take that pain away."

"And then can she come home?" Lily asked innocently.

Meghan noticed the syringe I was holding. "No!" she cried, horrified. "You've got to fix her!"

"Don't cry, Megs," Lily said, reaching for her sister's hand. "They are going to fikth her." Raising her other hand to her mouth, she popped in a thumb.

"We got Charlotte when Megs was just a baby. Remember how she used to sleep with all your stuffed animals, honey?" Andy asked.

Meghan nodded as her small body shook with sobs.

"And we couldn't tell which one was Charlotte sometimes?" Andy continued, while Jim tried to raise a vein for me on Charlotte's hind leg. "You used to read to her. What was that story you both liked so much?"

Meghan hesitated. "Charlotte's Web," she answered at last in a voice as soft and small as she was.

The vein in Charlotte's right hind leg had collapsed. Jim reached for her left leg.

"Can I hold her?" Meghan asked suddenly. Andy looked at me.

"Sure you can, sweetheart." Touching her shoulder, I guided her to a chair in the recovery ward. "Come on over here."

Meghan climbed into the large rocking chair, which was also a favourite of the resident cats. Every day the staff spread a clean blanket over top. Having salvaged it from his grandmother's house, Hughie refused to part with the chair. It was comfortable, like an old friend, and had no doubt sheltered many a small child in its lifetime.

Gingerly, I lifted Charlotte from the table and placed her in Meghan's outstretched arms. As she stroked the little cat, Charlotte began to purr. Jim knelt on the floor, the edge of his hand pressed against the saphenous vein that runs down the inside of the leg. Charlotte's veins had constricted due to the shock and trauma her body had suffered. I poured a small amount of alcohol over the fur on her leg to accentuate the vein and prayed that I would hit it the first time.

Meghan's tears had dried on her face. She seemed unaware of her father standing close by, clutching her sister's hand. She stroked Charlotte's ears and face, softly whispering her name. When I saw and felt the slight bulge of the vein, I gently inserted the needle. Drawing back on the plunger, a faint red wisp of blood entered the syringe and I knew I was in. Slowly, carefully, I emptied the contents of the syringe. The overdose of barbiturate would painlessly end her suffering.

Within seconds, Charlotte started to relax. Her breathing slowed, then stopped. Meghan continued to stroke the body, still warm with the echoes of life. Around us, movement ceased, voices hushed. Andy wiped his eyes and looked away.

"Is Tharlotte asleep now, Daddy?" Lily asked.

As Meghan hugged the small body close, I laid my stethoscope on Charlotte's chest one more time. Although I knew she was dead, this was the final act after which I could say quietly to the owners, "She's gone." Then their grieving process could begin.

With a shock, I recognized the unmistakable sound of a heart beating, loud and strong. Affirmation of life. Yet I knew I had injected directly into the vein. Had the needle somehow become dislodged? I repositioned the stethoscope then I realized it was a child's heart I heard. A child who had watched a ruthless driver drag a piece of her innocence with him. A child who, perhaps for the first time, realized that for all the wonder in the world, there is darkness too. I removed the stethoscope from my ears and draped it around my neck.

"Bye bye, Tharlotte," Lily lisped as Meghan cradled Charlotte in her arms.

"Let me know if you need anything," I whispered to Andy.

Meghan looked up at me. "Thank you," she said. As tears welled up in my own eyes, I left the family alone to mourn.

When I returned, they were gone. Charlotte lay on the examining table wrapped in a flannel baby blanket. Jim cradled a tiny front paw in his hand while Hilary took an ink impression of her paw print. Absorbed in their task, they barely looked up when I entered the room. Following euthanasia, the hospital always made a donation in memory of the cat to the Companion Animal Trust Fund at the vet college and sent a sympathy card to the owner. But including a paw print with the card had been the staff's idea: it was their farewell, their way of sharing in the family's sorrow. Sometimes, they strove for half an hour trying to get it just right.

At home that night, I curled up on the sofa with my own three cats. When I finally closed my eyes, it was Meghan's face I saw, small and freckled, dwarfed by luminous brown eyes as she thanked me for euthanizing her cat.

※ ※ ※

The glorious days of summer arrived as the earth's northern hemisphere leaned closer to the sun. There were beach barbecues, softball games played with a beer in one hand and a glove in the other, and, as always, a parade of unwilling patients and apologetic owners at Ocean View.

For Meghan MacLachlan, this summer was a time to be endured rather than enjoyed. She avoided her friends and spent much of her time on the computer or playing alone with dolls. On her bedside table, she kept a photograph of Charlotte with the paw print we had sent. She had nightmares and couldn't sleep. When Andy suggested a new kitten or even a puppy, though Lily was delighted Meghan wouldn't even consider the idea.

So I was surprised when Bernie flagged me down in the hallway.

"There you are, luv," she puffed. "It's Mr. MacLachlan with those wee lovely girls. He doesn't have an appointment, but he was wondering if you were available."

I glanced at my watch. "Sure!" I replied eagerly. "Do they have a new kitten?"

Bernie hesitated. "Not exactly."

"A new puppy?"

"No."

I slipped into a fresh lab coat and studied the chart that Bernie held in front of me. "A bird?" I hissed.

Bernie nodded sympathetically.

"What about Bedford Shore vets?" I asked, beginning to panic. "They do birds."

"Closed."

"Closed?" I repeated. "Who closes at noon on a Saturday?"

"Lots of places," Bernie said helpfully.

I sighed. "Put them in an exam room. And turn the lights down low. It'll help calm the bird," I added remembering the one lecture we had on pet birds in vet school.

Ever since I was a child, I've had an irrational fear of birds flapping their wings and getting stuck in my hair. (My mother attributes this to Alfred Hitchcock's horror flick, The Birds.) I think they are beautiful creatures. I think the world is a better place because they exist. I love their songs. But up close and personal, they make me sweat.

"What kind of bird is it? A budgie? Canary?" I asked.

"Um … it's a rather large bird," Bernie acknowledged before disappearing.

The rather large bird turned out to be some kind of duck. It blinked balefully at me from inside the box. I called in reinforcements.

"We found him on the beach," Andy explained. "We went right up to him and he didn't even try to get away. There must be something wrong with him."

Flanked by Hilary and Jim, I reached into the box with a large towel and hoped for the best. Surprisingly, the bird offered no resistance. Encouraged, I lifted him out of the box and onto the examining table. The resident cats had been herded into another room, and the door had been shut behind them.

"Is he sick?" Lily asked. "Maybe we could give him pancakes."

"I make the girls pancakes when they're sick," Andy explained with a smile.

"Birds don't eat pancakes, stupid!" Meghan spoke for the first time.

Lily's forehead wrinkled and she popped a thumb into her mouth.

"Meghan!" Andy spoke sharply.

Shrugging her shoulders, Meghan sat down in a chair and, picking up a book, began to read.

The football-shaped bird was a beautiful golden brown with darker bands of brown and white circling his body. He had a large, wedge-like bill and his neck sloped low against his back. As I began my exam, Meghan's eyes rose from the book but I pretended not to notice.

The bird's wings were undamaged and his short stubby legs seemed fine. With Hilary's help, I took his temperature. Not used to the normal reference range for birds, I consulted my emergency text. Then draping the stethoscope across my neck, I looked up and, shaking my head, sighed dramatically.

"I need to find out what kind of bird this is. But all my books are about cats." I frowned. "Meghan, do you know much about computers?"

Meghan nodded. "I have one at home and Mr. Avery teaches us computers at school."

"Mmm." I looked at Jim, our resident computer expert. "Can you help Jim find out what kind of bird this is?"

Jim held the door open. "C'mon. I'll take you to the computer."

Meghan looked at her dad. "Go ahead, sweetheart," he said. "We'll wait here."

Slowly, Meghan raised herself out of the chair and followed Jim down the hallway. I finished my examination then glanced at Lily, who was busy colouring a picture. Keeping my voice low so she wouldn't hear, I turned to Andy.

"I can't find anything wrong other than a lower than normal temperature, but I suspect it's something serious. A wild bird would never let you approach like that."

Andy nodded. "Meghan didn't want to come here. She said the bird was just going to die anyway. I guess she was right. Maybe the best thing … " He left the sentence unfinished as Meghan burst back into the room.

"We think it's an eider duck. A girl!" she exclaimed. "They live in the ocean mostly and they eat mussels and crust … crust … "

"Crustaceans," Jim said helpfully.

"Right!" Meghan agreed. "And she's brown because it helps her hide in the rocks and stuff when she's on land."

She thrust a picture, fresh from the office printer, into my hand. There was no doubt that the bird in my exam room was an eider duck. Meghan looked at me expectantly.

"Megs," Andy began in a gentle voice, "we think it might be best … "

"If we get a blood sample," I interrupted. "Then we can settle her into a kennel in the isolation ward afterwards and I'll call you with an update."

Grateful for the reprieve, Andy gathered the girls together. Lily had removed her shoes while she was colouring and refused to put them back on. Carrying a pair of pink Barbie shoes in one hand, Andy scooped Lily into his arms and held out his other hand for Meghan. At the door she paused and shyly waved goodbye.

Jim carried the duck back to the treatment area. Meghan was

probably right. The bird's chances were not good. But to put her down without even trying would be admitting she wasn't worth the effort. Everything that lives, dies. But not when you are nine years old.

While Jim held the duck, Hilary helped me collect a blood sample from a vein on the underside of her wing. The bird was silent and watchful. I gently palpated her body, searching for signs of trauma. Then I noticed a small dark area on her belly where the feathers seemed disheveled. I sniffed the residue on my gloves: oil.

Feathers are like roofing tiles. They overlap to keep air and water away from a bird's sensitive skin. Birds spend a considerable amount of time preening because if their feathers are not perfectly aligned, they can die from exposure. Oil on the surface of the water will stick to their feathers, causing them to mat and separate.

I didn't think such a small amount of oil could be a problem, but I decided to call the vet college in Charlottetown anyway. The receptionist paged the avian specialist, Dr. Janice Bird, who had seen the writing on the wall at an early age and decided she wanted to be a bird doctor. She confirmed that we did indeed have an eider duck at the cat hospital and we talked at length about her case management. After we spoke, I was even less optimistic about the bird's chances.

Jim, Hilary, and Tanya waited anxiously in the treatment area.

"Okay," I said with a reassuring smile. "We've got our work cut out for us. That spot of oil is like a pinprick in a wet suit. The duck is hypothermic because she can't insulate herself."

"So should we wash it off?" Hilary asked.

"That was my first thought, too," I nodded. "But the specialist at the vet college says no. First we have to stabilize her."

"Poor little thing," Jim crooned.

"She's probably ingested oil as well, trying to preen herself, and that can cause internal problems," I continued. "My guess is that she's exhausted and hungry. If we wash her now, the added stress could kill her."

"What can we do?"

I looked at the shining crescent of anxious faces. Jim was seventeen, Hilary and Tanya in their early twenties. At that moment, they seemed so young, so anxious to make a difference. What they didn't know was that over three hundred thousand birds die annually on the Atlantic seaboard alone. These deaths are not the result of massive industrial oil spills but rather intentional dumping. To avoid costly clean-ups in port, ships dump their bilge under cover of darkness. Bilge, a mixture of oil, water, detergents, and toxins, is the by-product of running engines. This slow, illegal dumping of several hundred litres is rarely detected by the inadequately equipped government agencies responsible for protecting our coastlines.

"I applaud your efforts," Dr. Bird had said over the phone, "but an oiled bird is a dead bird."

With these words echoing in my head, we set to work.

Following Dr. Bird's instructions, we prepared a solution designed to rehydrate the duck and flush her system as well as absorb digested oil from her intestinal tract. This we delivered through a tube directly into the stomach. Using the same approach, we fed her a nutritious, high-protein formula, then returned her to the isolation ward. Because she couldn't regulate body temperature, we had to make sure she was neither too hot nor too cold. Keeping her in a comfortable, warm, dark place would encourage rest and discourage preening.

While the staff tidied up and kept a watchful eye on Norma Rae, as she had been christened, I called Andy.

"Meghan seems to think the duck is going to be fine." He drew a deep breath and sighed. "I don't know what she'll do if it dies."

I wondered the same thing myself as I rejoined Jim, Hilary, and Tanya, who had gathered outside the isolation ward. The duck had tucked her head under her wing and, for the moment, was resting. We gazed at her in silence through the glass window that separated us.

Nova Scotians are a people shaped by the sea; no place in this province is more than eighty kilometres from a rugged coastline, a sheltered fishing village, or a sandy beach. We depend on the sea and she depends on us. The staff had rallied around this fragile symbol of our life here.

I decided to spend the night. An unwieldy stack of paperwork needed attention and I wanted to keep an eye on Norma Rae. Jim posted a notice on the door of the isolation ward to alert the morning staff to our unusual new patient and then drove Hilary and Tanya home. I spent a rather sleepless night on a cot in the office, drifting off sometime just before dawn only to awaken a short while later to the sound of my boss's incredulous voice.

"Do not disturb the duck?" Hughie flicked on the fluorescent lights and waited for me to achieve full consciousness. I stumbled through my duck story and Meghan's part in it.

"Emily, you look like hell," he said kindly. "Go home."

The morning's agenda appeared quiet, with only a few scattered appointments. Hughie promised to supervise Norma Rae's care so I gratefully slipped out the back door and pedaled home. The cats met me at the door, complaining bitterly about their night alone with only dry food. I opened up a can of their favourite entrée, brushed my teeth, and went to bed. At noon, my next-door neighbour decided to mow his lawn and then fine-tune it with the whipper-snipper. I gave up trying to sleep and went back to work.

I found Meghan in the isolation ward with Hilary. Jim had fashioned a name tag identifying her as a volunteer then scoured the hospital for the smallest lab coat he could find. Even so, it hung down past her knees. Meghan had rolled up the sleeves, proudly fastened on her name tag, and was paying close attention as Hilary explained the proper procedures to be followed in the isolation ward. Hilary transferred Norma Rae to a clean kennel and, armed with a toothbrush and disinfectant, Meghan scrubbed away the duck poo that seemed to be splattered everywhere. She worked quietly and talked in whispers so as not to disturb Norma Rae.

After the first day, Norma Rae began eating on her own. She particularly enjoyed the fresh mussels and clams that Meghan brought every morning from the nearby grocery store. These she crushed whole in her large gizzard; in between meals, she snacked on berries. With her bright, inquisitive eyes and throaty "korr-korr" at the sight of food, Norma Rae became a symbol of hope for us.

One day, Meghan brought in a battery of books on ducks that the city librarian had helped her find. She sat in the same chair in which she had once held Charlotte, frowning in concentration over some words that were, as yet, too big for her.

"Do you think Norma Rae misses her family?" she asked suddenly.

I looked up from the lab results I was reviewing for one of my patients. "I'm sure she does," I replied carefully. "But she has you and me, and Hilary and Jim. We're trying to do everything we can for her."

"But it's not the same," Meghan said after a moment.

I put my pen down and walked over to the chair where Meghan sat with her pile of books. Bending down, I brushed a lock of hair from her face.

"No, sweetheart," I replied. "It's not the same. But it's the best we can do."

Meghan nodded. "I know." With a small sigh, she looked back down at her book. After a moment, she turned the page.

Later that evening, I contacted the International Bird Rescue Research Centre in California. Founded in the early seventies, their successful rehabilitation rate had increased from 3% to almost 90% by the mid-nineties, mainly through trial and error. Because she appeared stable and was eating well, they suggested we bathe the duck the next day following a very strict protocol.

We never got the chance. Norma Rae died unexpectedly on her

fourth day in captivity.

When Meghan arrived that morning, clutching her bag of fresh mussels, she stared at the empty cage. I was prepping a patient for surgery. Jim, who was working for us on a full- time basis during the summer, squatted down so that he was at eye level with Meghan. He spoke with her for a moment, then straightened up, her hand in his.

As with all creatures, each of us has our own destiny, but it is intertwined with the destinies of others. Perhaps in Norma Rae's weakened state, she succumbed to an internal pathogen; perhaps she merely fulfilled her destiny. Clients, galvanized by the little duck's story, wrote letters of protest to the federal government. Jim's oceanography professor devoted a lecture to the devastation caused by illegal bilge dumping. And Meghan, although it would be years before she understood, was learning to open her heart again.

In the midst of it all, we returned Norma Rae to the sea.

Later that summer, I caught a glimpse of Meghan riding bicycles with a gaggle of happy little girls along the quiet street behind the hospital. Her hair whipped behind her in waves of brown against the canvas of a blue summer sky. She waved to me and long after she was past, I could hear the echoes of her laughter in the rustling leaves of the maple trees.

Chapter 11

I looked around Hughie's office in dismay. From a monstrous duffel bag, hockey gear flowed over the desk, spilling onto the floor and across the room. A pair of woolly striped socks hung on the back of the chair.

"I'm taking up hockey," Hughie explained.

"I can see that. What was wrong with basketball?" I whined, thinking of the one small gym bag that got neatly tucked away in the office on game days.

"Em, that's winter. I need something to keep me in shape over the summer," Hughie explained, patting his belly.

"Yeah. You are getting a bit of a bulge there." I began sorting through the hockey gear on the desk. "Have you seen Omar's file? It was right … oh, gross!"

Omar Zowarski's medical records lay trapped underneath a men's athletic cup and jock strap. Hughie blanched and whisked them out of sight. Gingerly, I grasped the edge of the file between my thumb and forefinger and held it as far away from me as possible as I made my way down the hall.

Hughie poked his head out the door. "They haven't been used yet," he hissed.

Ignoring him, I knocked on the door of the exam room with my good hand and entered the room. Thelma Anne Zowarski, or Taz as Hughie affectionately referred to her after the Tasmanian Devil of Loonie Tunes fame, nodded crisply.

"Good morning, Dr. McBride."

A former financial analyst with the federal government, Thelma

Anne had been a formidable opponent of tax-evading corporations and departmental inefficiencies. She was a crisp little woman, wafer-thin with neat edges and penetrating brown eyes. She stared at Omar's medical record as if she knew where it had been.

"So, how's my handsome boy this morning?" I cooed, tickling Omar's ears.

"Fairly well, considering." Thelma Anne allowed herself a brief smile.

Omar Zowarski should have been the lead harpist in cat heaven for several years. He had a host of life-threatening diseases but stubbornly defied the odds. In addition to chronic kidney failure, hypertension, arthritis, flaky skin, and dental disease, Omar had a bad heart. He and his mother were snowbirds, wintering in Louisiana and migrating back to Halifax in the spring.

My counterpart in Louisiana was one Nathaniel Julius Pitt IV, DVM. He was descended from a long line of Pitts who served the medical community as gynecologists, dentists, midwives, and general practitioners. Nathaniel J., the black sheep of the family, had been drawn to animals. Last winter he had saved Omar from dying on foreign soil when the cat collapsed in Thelma Anne's condo one morning while she was scrambling eggs. Still in her bathrobe, a frantic Thelma Anne raced to the hospital where Dr. Pitt withdrew 250 mL of fluid from Omar's chest. A few weeks ago, I had removed another 300 mL of fluid and adjusted his medication. Omar was circling the drain but in spite of that seemed content.

"You're doing a good job." I smiled at Thelma Anne as I examined Omar. Miraculously, he was gaining weight, thanks to Thelma Anne's tenacious care. He was a gentle old soul who long ago had resigned himself to regular vet visits and rectal thermometers. I finished my exam and, while Omar fastidiously removed all traces of the lubricant, updated his chart.

"I consulted a psychic," Thelma Anne said.

I looked up. "Pardon me?"

"In Louisiana. One who specializes in animal communication."

"Oh?"

"You remember Charles?" Thelma Anne continued.

I nodded. Charles, a high-maintenance Siamese with a fondness for lima beans and potato chips, had died the previous summer after leaping off the balcony in pursuit of a blue jay.

"The psychic said that Charles was doing well on the other side."

"That's, uh, that's really great," I nodded.

"She also said that Omar is suffering from deficiencies."

I put my pen down. "Deficiencies? What kind of deficiencies?"

"Oh, you know," Thelma Anne brushed my question aside with an impatient wave of her hand, "the usual kind."

Like anyone on the downward slope of ninety, not all of Omar's body parts were working together. He had chemical and hormonal imbalances in some areas and excesses in others. Dr. Pitt and I were trying to maintain an equilibrium with a low protein–low phosphorus diet, heart medication, and antibiotics for his dental problems. For the most part, things were going as well as could be expected and Omar was a happy old-timer.

Thelma Anne snapped open her briefcase. Instead of a calculator, a sturdy pen, and the usual assortment of files that organized her life, it was filled with identical brown bottles.

I squinted at the labels. "Spices?"

"Alternative herbal therapy," Thelma Anne corrected me. "Each tincture counterbalances a deficiency."

I hesitated. "What do you do with them?"

"Well, that depends," Thelma Anne replied. "Some I mix with his food. Some I rub on the affected area."

"Did Dr. Pitt recommend these herbs?" I asked.

"Oh, good heavens, no." Thelma Anne shook her head. "I buy them online."

I glanced at Omar on the examining table. Eyes closed and paws tucked underneath his chest, he was blissfully unaware of the controversy brewing above his head. When I suggested as tactfully as possible that "alternative" and "herbal" did not necessarily mean harmless, Thelma Anne bristled. Taking a deep breath, she inflated her tiny frame to its full height.

"Why is the medical community so skeptical of alternative therapies?" Thelma Anne demanded.

There are hundreds of herbal and alternative remedies on the market. Some have scientifically proven claims, but many more do not. I explained that in order to build our knowledge, it is important to know if anecdotal claims can be reproduced using scientific methods. In the end, Thelma Anne reluctantly agreed to withhold any alternative treatments until I could research possible side effects and reactions with Omar's current medications.

The rest of the morning was quiet, with just a few routine appointments and an otherwise healthy kitten suffering from an upper respiratory infection. I settled in the office with a bladder-busting large tea from Tim Hortons and began poring through books on pharmacology. While the benefits of alternative therapies like choreito powder for cystitis and glucosamine for joints were well-documented, it was difficult to find much information on herbal medicine for animals.

The private line in the office rang with a shrill persistence from somewhere underneath Hughie's hockey paraphernalia. It took a minute to find the small black cordless phone amid the hockey gear.

"Hello?"

"Emily. It's your mother. Are you busy?"

"Well, I … "

"Eugenie's son, Darvel, has just been arrested!"

Eugenie was Mom's cleaning lady. On cleaning day, I often found her and my mother playing cards at the kitchen table and sipping sherry while the work piled up around them. She was almost as old as Mom and lived just outside the city in a tiny bungalow with her toothless and perpetually cheerful husband, Stedman. Together, they had raised nine children. The youngest, Portia, was an A student in Grade 12. Darvel, on the other hand, had been in and out of trouble since he popped out of the womb. His good looks and charm could usually salvage most situations.

"Arrested?" I repeated in disbelief. "For what?"

Mom hesitated. "For growing marijuana."

"He was growing marijuana? Where?"

"I can't divulge that information, Emily."

"What?"

"I plead the fifth." (Mom loved to watch American legal dramas.)

"Mom, this isn't Law and Order. You don't get to plead the fifth. Did Eugenie know about it?" A thought suddenly struck me. "Oh my God! Were they selling it?"

"Oh, Emily, don't be ridiculous. She gives it away to people who need it. They can't arrest a person for that."

"Uh, yes they can, Mom," I sighed.

"Then there's something wrong with this country when the government can tell a person what kind of plant they can and can't grow in their own backyard! I give away my lilies every spring."

"Yes, but Mom, people don't smoke lily bulbs and get high. And wait a minute – it's in her backyard?"

"Emily, I have to go," Mom said suddenly. "I hear someone at the back door."

I strained but heard nothing.

"I'll call you later. Bye, dear."

A dial tone hummed in my ear. Slowly, I hung up the phone. For the second time in the space of an hour, I found myself face to face with the issue of alternative therapies. It was hard to focus on Omar and Thelma Anne when my own mother saw nothing wrong with growing a little marijuana and sharing it with friends. Fortunately, with a busy outpatient clinic, I had little time to think about either.

It was early evening before I had a chance to call Thelma Anne with the results of my research. I had contacted a leading feline specialist who agreed that some of the herbal tinctures could be harmful given Omar's precarious health and current medications.

Thelma Anne answered on the first ring. "I suppose you want me to stop all the treatments," she declared.

"Well," I hedged, seeking a common ground, "not all." Thelma Anne had been a loyal client for ten years. While I didn't want to offend her, Omar already had three paws in the grave. I didn't want to be responsible for the fourth.

"We definitely have to stop the melatonin," I began. "It affects the nervous system and will interfere with his other medications. It shouldn't be given to any animals with heart, liver, or kidney disease."

"What else?"

I took a breath. "Absolutely no essential oils. Never. Not only can they burn the skin, but a cat's liver can't process the terpenes in essential oils."

"I see. What else?"

"Ginseng. It can cause increased blood pressure and with his heart condition ... " I left the sentence unfinished as an odd hum, a sort of whirring sound, on the other end of the line distracted me. Perhaps it was just a bad connection. Or perhaps Thelma Anne was gathering strength, twirling faster and faster until she was just a blur, teeth gnashing and drool flying from her mouth as she morphed into the Tasmanian Devil.

"Can I still rub garlic on his kidneys?" Taz asked through the static.

Garlic taken internally can cause anemia, but if Thelma Anne was willing to stop the other treatments, then I (and Omar) could live with a little garlic. He might smell bad, but at least it wouldn't kill him.

"You know, I'm not a crackpot," Thelma Anne ventured.

I hastened to assure her I didn't think that for a minute, although secretly I thought she was walking a fine line. While there is definitely a place for anecdotal folk wisdom within the health-care system, we can never assume that a human treatment is safe or appropriate for another species. Thelma Anne grudgingly agreed.

Even so, a week later poor Omar was in trouble again. The phone rang while I was in the shower. Naked, worried, and trailing water, I ran to the bedroom. Early-morning phone calls were never because you won the lottery. It was Bernie calling to tell me that Thelma Anne was rushing Omar to the hospital. He was having difficulty breathing.

"Have Hilary put him on pure oxygen," I told her. "I'll be there shortly."

By the time I arrived, Thelma Anne was hovering anxiously in the treatment area with Hilary and Omar. I removed the lid on the oxygen therapy kennel and listened to Omar's chest. With Hilary's help, I withdrew the buildup of fluid around his heart that was making it difficult for the lungs to expand. Almost immediately, Omar began to relax as his breathing became less laboured. Back in the Plexiglas kennel, he studied his surroundings with interest.

Thelma Anne raised her arm. Little rivers of blue ran under the fine covering of skin that covered her hand as she pressed it against the box. "We've been together a long time, haven't we, old friend?"

Omar leaned against the box and stopped, puzzled by the quarter-inch of cold Plexiglas that separated him from the security and familiar warmth of that hand. And then, accepting his fate without complaint as he always did, Omar curled up into a ball and slept.

"We'll leave him on oxygen for a while," I said quietly, "then see how he does on room air."

Thelma Anne nodded but didn't look up. Her hand still rested against the box.

For the moment, Omar was stable. Leaving Hilary to monitor him, I downed a cup of coffee and began outpatient appointments. In between, I checked on Omar, who continued to do well. By noon, we were able to transfer him to the recovery ward. Susan offered him several varieties of low-protein food, which he sniffed politely but refused. Distraught, Thelma Anne ran across to the grocery store and returned with a tin of salmon. The aroma of fish was soon wafting through the air; encouraged, Omar rose to his feet. So did every other cat in the ward. Soon everyone was clamouring for salmon and we had a revolt on our hands.

Hughie tapped on the glass. "How's it going?" he asked when I stepped outside.

"Pretty good. He's stable. He's eating." I shook my head. "This guy's got more than nine lives."

Hughie grinned. "He's got Taz."

"Oh," he added as I turned to leave, "can you pick up the autoclave? It'll be ready by one and I'm going to be tied up in surgery."

Our mini autoclave, used to sterilize instruments, was a fussy little machine; wonderful when it worked, a terror when it didn't. It was a regular at the repair shop.

"I would, but I rode my bike this morning."

"Here!" Hughie tossed me his keys. "Drive carefully."

"Cool," I grinned. Hughie had purchased a sporty new car last fall. I couldn't believe he was letting me drive it downtown. I was just putting on my jacket when Thelma Anne emerged from the recovery ward and asked Bernie to call her a taxi.

"Nonsense!" Hughie declared. "Dr. McBride is heading downtown on a hospital errand. She can drive you home."

Thelma Anne peered at me over the rim of her glasses. "Well, if you don't mind … "

"No problem at all," I smiled.

Together, we headed out into the parking lot. Omar had survived another crisis, the sun was shining, and in my hand I held the keys to a shiny black Honda Accord coupe with a sun roof, state-of-the-art stereo system, and an all-leather black interior. Life was good.

Good, that is, until I spied the Jeep in Hughie's parking spot. With a sinking heart, I remembered that this was hockey night. Hughie never drove the Accord on hockey night. Both the rink and the post-game drinking establishment were in a less-than-desirable part of town. Thelma Anne stared at our transportation in stunned silence.

Hughie's Jeep was a blight on the automobile landscape. In the days preceding the annual motor vehicle inspection deadline, Hughie scrambled to make the creature roadworthy. It had barely passed this year after a brake job, new muffler, some electrical work, and do-it-yourself rust repair.

"Do the seatbelts work?" Thelma Anne asked, peering in through the window.

"Most of the time," I assured her.

Thelma Anne climbed inside, wedging her small, sensibly clad feet between a McDonald's bag full of garbage and a soggy rawhide bone.

"Sometimes the door doesn't quite close all the way," I explained through the passenger window. "Stay clear."

Clutching her briefcase to her chest, Thelma Anne stared straight ahead while I thrust all my weight against the door and heard a satisfying click.

"There!" I skirted around the back of the Jeep and hopped into the driver's seat, blithely repeating Hughie's familiar refrain, "It's got a great engine."

Thelma Anne glanced at me but said nothing as she buckled her seatbelt.

As we approached downtown, noon-hour traffic thickened and coalesced into a melting pot of cars and pedestrians. Tourists in dazzling white runners and new golf shirts clutched their walking-tour maps as they gawked at historic buildings. In the still, humid air, a thin film of sweat had glued my back to the driver's seat. Even Thelma Anne's face had assumed a rosy glow. Atop the Canadian Broadcasting Corporation building, a digital sign alternately flashed "29°C" and "Have a nice day." Thelma Anne picked up a journal from the floor of the Jeep and began fanning her face.

"Dr. McBride," she began, "I have a confession."

I slammed on the brakes, pitching Thelma Anne forward until the seatbelt yanked her back.

"Oh!" she gasped. "I'm sorry, Dr. McBride, I should have waited till we reached my condo to tell you." When I didn't reply, her eyes followed my gaze.

"Oh!" she gasped again.

Right in front of us, a large – very large, not-from-these-parts kind of large – snake lay coiled indecisively on the black pavement.

"Is that a boa constrictor?" Thelma Anne gasped for the third time in less than a minute. "On South Park Street?"

I put on the four-way flashers and hopped out of the Jeep, not sure what to do. The long line of cars behind me began to honk irritably. The snake didn't appear injured but soon would be if he decided to make a slither for it across four lanes of traffic. A curious crowd of onlookers was beginning to gather on the sidewalk.

The guy in the car behind me rolled down his window. "Move your ass, sister!"

I flipped him the proverbial bird.

Still firmly attached by her own seatbelt, Thelma Anne leaned over into the driver's side. "Psst, Dr. McBride," she hissed through the open window. "The hockey stick!"

I stared blankly at her.

"There's a hockey stick in the back of the Jeep by the case of beer."

It was a Eureka moment. Bypassing the beer (with some reluctance), I grabbed the stick and a pair of Hughie's hockey gloves. The snake eyed my approach warily, his tongue flicking back and forth as he tried to figure out his best move. Thelma Anne had hopped out of the car. Clutching a small brown bottle, she began sprinkling its contents around the snake.

"Valerian root," she explained. "It has a calming affect."

I wedged the blade of the hockey stick between a couple of serpentine coils. "You never stopped the herbs, did you?" I grunted, using both hands to steady the stick.

"Not exactly," Thelma Anne admitted.

I pressed the stick against my body for support and wrestled the snake onto the blade. For a moment, he dangled precariously and then had the good sense to wrap his body around the lifeline. The crowd on the sidewalk clapped appreciatively, parting to let Thelma Anne and me through as I deposited him safely on the sidewalk. A tourist wielding a video camera panned on the crowd and then resumed filming the snake's rescue, adding his own colourful commentary for the folks back home. His wife was alarmed; the travel brochures had made no mention of gigantic urban snakes in Canada.

"Well, it's a good thing we're in Canada!" her husband declared. "Who else would have a hockey stick in the back of their car in July!"

An officer from Animal Control arrived a few moments later. Someone must have had the presence of mind to call for backup. The name on the man's uniform identified him as Harold S.

"There's another Harold in accounting," he explained, securing a pair of goggles over his head.

The crowd leaned in for a closer look as Harold rummaged through a black canvas bag. With a flair for the dramatic, he withdrew a two-pronged head immobilizer for reptiles and flourished it in the air. It had a shiny chrome finish and a telescoping leg that extended or retracted at the push of a button. I had to wonder just how serious the runaway snake problem was in this city to warrant such a purchase.

"This baby is state-of-the-art," he declared.

And indeed, the snake appeared to have met its match. Harold studied his target and the surrounding terrain with the painstaking stealth of a golfer on the green. His were the keen eyes of a man accustomed to battling wits with other species. The snake was no fool, however, and quickly tucked his head among the multiple coils of his two-metre-long body. Despite Harold's best efforts, the snake refused to expose his head.

"They can be stubborn," he sighed.

"Dr. McBride can get him with the hockey stick," Thelma Anne declared. "You hold the bag open," she ordered Harold.

Harold looked skeptical but did as he was told.

The snake and Hughie's hockey stick had a certain rapport. In less than a minute the snake was, as they say, in the bag. The crowd began to disperse now that the noon-hour show was over. Harold quickly pulled the drawstring tight.

"Just another day at the office," he grinned. He stuck the immobilizer under his arm and, whistling cheerfully, slung the bag over his back. The snake would be cared for at the shelter until the owner came forward or a suitable home could be found.

"Good work, Dr. McBride," Thelma Anne said when we were back in the Jeep. "You know, I think the valerian root really helped."

By the time I had dropped Thelma Anne off and picked up the autoclave, Hughie was finished in surgery and about to start his afternoon appointments.

"You were gone a long time, Em," he remarked.

I flopped in a chair and closed my eyes. "It's a long story."

Omar was doing well. Since I wasn't on duty until five o'clock, I decided to run up to Mom's for a late lunch and a quick visit. I hadn't seen her in over a week. When I arrived, Eugenie's car was in the driveway so I parked on the street. As I walked up to the back door, the pungent smell of marijuana hit my nostrils. Mom and Eugenie were playing cards at the kitchen table. When I opened the door, they quickly stubbed out their cigarettes. Mom grabbed a dishtowel and began fanning the air.

"Mom!"

"Emily! What a nice surprise! How are you, dear?"

"What are you doing?"

"Oh, it's just so hot in here," Mom replied, wiping her forehead.

"Uh-huh. Yes, it is," Eugenie smiled affably.

"Eugenie and I were just having a game of cards, weren't we, Eugenie?"

"Yes, indeed," Eugenie agreed. "Crazy Eights."

I looked at the ashtray and then at Mom.

"Oh, Emily. For heaven's sakes," she sighed, lowering the dishtowel. "That's the last of it. We were just celebrating. Darcel's been released. It was all a misunderstanding. Some kind of technicality."

Eugenie nodded, a broad grin on her round, freckled face. "That's right. Uh-huh."

"Besides," Mom added, "marijuana is a valued medicinal herb. Even the medical profession agrees. It's good for my joints." She winked at Eugenie and the two of them burst out laughing.

"Oh, my, yes indeed," Eugenie giggled.

Chapter 12

I FIRST MET PASTOR AXELROD AND THADDEUS on a stifling Thursday deep in July. I remember the date because Friday was laundry day, a fact irrelevant in itself except it meant that by Thursday, my clean-clothes options were limited. On this particular Thursday, I was forced to wear a pair of pants purchased several years ago. In my twenties, this wouldn't have been a problem, but now that my thirties had a foot in the door, a few extra pounds had crept in through the crack. (It wasn't my fault. Tim Hortons was right next door.)

The morning shift at Tim's knew me well: a large Iced Cappuccino and an apple fritter to go materialized on the counter even before I said good morning. For good measure, I got a dozen doughnuts as well. The staff would whine if I returned empty-handed.

I grasped the box of doughnuts with one hand and the Iced Capp and apple fritter with the other. Leaving was easy. I exited Tim's backwards, using my behind to open the door. (It could use the exercise.) Getting back into the cat hospital was more challenging. Both hands were occupied and my behind could only push, not pull.

Sensing my predicament, a gangly passerby held the doors open. I thanked him and scooted inside. The staff were all busy so I headed for the office, a line of cats trailing behind me and the intoxicating scent of fresh doughnuts. The office door was closed. An "ENTER AT YOUR OWN RISK" sign in Hughie's familiar scrawl was posted at eye level. Mrs. Tuttle was probably hard at work on the accounts inside.

The second exam room was empty so I slipped inside, unseen. The exam rooms had two doors: one leading in from reception and the other leading out into the treatment area. I sprawled in one of the chairs and bit into my apple fritter. Sighing, I leaned back and chewed in bliss. All too soon the fritter was gone and I still had some Iced Capp left in my cup. I eyed the box of doughnuts for the staff and with only a tiny twinge of guilt, selected a Boston cream.

I had never been a delicate, graceful child, despite my mother's best intentions. When ballet lessons failed to produce the desired result, square dancing lessons followed. I was popular because I could burp on demand and talk like Bugs Bunny, but no one wanted to actually dance with me. The lack of grace continued with eating habits. And after all, I grew up with three brothers. At mealtime, he who hesitated went hungry. As an adult, I learned to slow down in public, but in private I wolfed down meals and licked the plate clean.

And so it was with carefree abandon that I sank as many teeth as possible into that Boston cream doughnut, savouring the heavenly blend of chocolate, vanilla custard, and dough. When a trickle of custard escaped down my chin, I tilted my head back so the contents of my mouth wouldn't fall out and expertly scooped up the wayward filling with my tongue. Napkins were for sissies.

At precisely this moment, the door to the exam room opened and a sparse-looking man with a cat carrier entered. I recognized him immediately as the man who had held the door open for me, and began to chew furiously.

"Oh, sorry, luv," Bernie apologized. "I didn't know you were in here."

Normally, I would have chewed a bit longer before swallowing. The large lump of dough went down after several attempts, but not without a struggle. The man stared at me in morbid fascination.

"Dr. McBride, this is Pastor Axelrod," Bernie declared, placing a heavy emphasis on Pastor. She nodded significantly, as if I was given to churlish behaviour and foul language with our non-clerical clients. "He's here today with Thaddeus for a checkup."

"Yes," the pastor replied, without the slightest trace of warmth normally associated with a man of the cloth. "We've met."

"Hello," I said cheerfully, extending my hand. The pastor eyed it warily as if he might catch something and then slowly raised his hand. He had the grip of wilted lettuce.

"Sorry," I continued, slipping into a white lab jacket that someone had left draped over a chair. "I didn't realize I had a nine o'clock appointment."

Bernie picked up the box of doughnuts. "Ta, then," she smiled. "I'll leave you to it. Lovely to meet you, pastor."

It went downhill from there.

While I chased Thaddeus around the room, the pastor sat silent and erect, his hands in his lap. The bony fingers of one hand tapped against their counterparts on the other like some sort of religious Morse code. Every so often, Thaddeus would stop to look at his owner and blink a message back. I could only speculate about what the two were saying.

Finally, Thaddeus stopped long enough for me to bend over and pick him up. As I did so, I heard the unmistakable sound of tearing cloth and the sudden sensation of open space combined with a change in temperature. The seam in the back of my ill-fitting pants had given way. The pastor was sitting directly behind me and undoubtedly saw and heard the same thing. Gingerly, I placed Thaddeus on the examining table and, with perfect posture, turned to face Pastor Axelrod. He hadn't moved or changed his expression.

"Could you excuse me for a moment, please?"

The pastor nodded with a slight dip of his head. Thaddeus yawned and jumped back down to the floor. I backed out of the room and fled to the treatment area where I ditched the short lab jacket in favour of a full-length lab coat.

Back in the exam room, Pastor Axelrod sat like a wax figure, pink stains on each side of his pale face. Thaddeus, however, was on the move again. I grabbed one of Carter's favourite toys and dangled it in front of him. The toy resembled a fishing pole. A fuzzy ball laced with crinkle foil dangled from a cord attached to a short wooden stick. Few cats could resist the gaudy apparition as it flitted through the air, and Thaddeus was no exception.

"Gotcha!" I grinned as my magic wand lured him up onto the table. Dogs love to please and usually extend this courtesy to their veterinarian, but cats have to be lured into thinking any act of compliance was all their idea. While Thaddeus examined the toy in delight, I examined him. Pastor Axelrod continued to watch the proceedings in silence. I wondered if he was tired of ministering to the sinners of this world or if he was just plain odd.

With one hand under his chest, I gently raised Thaddeus's front feet slightly off the table so I could examine his internal organs with the other. He happily kneaded the air in front of him. In the eerie silence, I maintained a running commentary for my own benefit as much as the pastor's.

"Normal-size kidneys, smooth, non-painful. Bladder's good, half-full. Small intestine feels good, like slippery big worms, that's normal. Large intestine … let's see. Bit of stool in there, normal volume and texture. Make sure you go the bathroom when you get home," I told Thaddeus and, grinning, looked up at the pastor.

"Thaddeus appears to be in good health. You're doing a fine job," I announced. At this point, most of my clients would smile at the compliment, but the pastor was a tough nut to crack.

The rectal thermometer beeped, indicating it was "done". I removed it and Thaddeus immediately jumped back down onto the floor.

"Normal," I said out loud. "Good boy, Thaddeus!" Confident within the security of a full-length lab coat, I bent down to vaccinate him. Thaddeus didn't flinch as I inserted the tiny needle tip into the scruff of his neck and injected the vaccine. As soon as I was done, he hopped into his owner's lap.

"So, we should see you and Thaddeus back in one year for an annual checkup." I rose cheerfully to my feet without incident. "Do you have any questions?"

Even as I asked, I was aware of a foul smell that grew exponentially fouler with each passing second. Thaddeus jumped off the pastor's lap and calmly strolled toward his carrier. Both the pastor and I gazed down at the spot he had vacated. Nestled in the folds of the pastor's trousers were several well-formed nuggets. The pastor looked up dismally as I stared at his crotch and tried not to laugh.

"Right." Clearing my throat, I pulled open the drawer and offered him some paper towels. I wasn't about to remove them myself. "Here you go." The pastor removed each nugget with care and deposited them in the plastic baggie I held in my outstretched hand.

Veterinary medicine can be messy. In this case, the thermometer and the added stress of a visit to the vet probably gave Thaddeus an urge he normally wouldn't have felt for an hour or two. Why he chose the pastor's lap was anyone's guess. We stared at each other for a moment, the pastor and I. He sat rigid in his chair while I stood over him, a bag of cat poop in my hand. I said the one thing that came into my mind.

"Would you like us to do a fecal analysis?"

Pastor Axelrod summoned the strength to shake his head. "No, thank you." He rose to his feet.

The appointment had not gone particularly well. Thaddeus liked my company but the pastor and I had certainly not bonded. I was oddly unsettled by this fact. God's right-hand men are supposed to love humanity. It didn't bode well for me in the hereafter if I got a bad report from one of them. I picked up the toy.

"Here, why don't you take this for Thaddeus?" I smiled and held it out to the pastor.

The pastor shook his head. "That's not necessary."

"Oh, we have lots more," I said blithely. For Thaddeus's added enjoyment, I rubbed a liberal amount of catnip into the crinkle ball at the end and handed it to Pastor Axelrod.

The pastor looked dubious but accepted the gift. Then he picked up the carrier and turned to leave. At the door of the exam room, he hesitated.

"Dr. McBride," he said, turning around, "I'm sure you are a very good veterinarian. And thank you for seeing Thaddeus on very short notice. But may I remind you that gluttony is one of the seven deadly sins." He reached into his pocket and pressed a business card into my unsuspecting hand. "We welcome all faiths," he announced. With that, he picked up the carrier and strode into reception.

Back in the office, I studied the card as I debated whether or not to have another doughnut. Embossed in gold letters across the top read "Road to Redemption Church, Pastor J. P. Axelrod." Underneath, a thin figure, not unlike the pastor himself, was stooped under the weight of a heavy pack as he traveled what was presumably the winding road to redemption.

"Whaddaya got, Em?" Hughie plopped down in a chair and reached for a doughnut.

I showed him the card. "Did you know gluttony was one of the seven deadly sins?"

"Em, I'm Catholic. I know all about sin." Hughie bit into his doughnut.

I sat down in front of the computer, and typed in "seven deadly sins." The response was overwhelming. I had been raised in the United Church, arguably one of the most innocuous, mild-mannered religions on the planet, and it didn't spend much time on the seven deadly sins.

Besides gluttony, the other six unacceptable behaviours were, in no particular order, wrath, lust, sloth, pride, envy, and greed. I studied the list, noting with satisfaction that Mom's list for her children had been a lot longer. That's not to say we followed it to the letter, but we were familiar with the basic concept.

When Pastor Axelrod and Thaddeus reappeared Monday morning, I was surprised but calm. I had read up on the sins and felt I was in control of most of my vices. For good measure, I was wearing a full-length lab coat.

"Pastor Axelrod! What brings you back so soon?" I asked, my lips curling in the imitation of a smile.

"Something's wrong with Thaddeus."

If possible, the pastor's long face had lengthened over the weekend. He had cut himself shaving and several little tufts of toilet paper were still anchored to his chin and neck. Although I tried hard to ignore them, invariably my eyes drifted downward as he spoke. I was fascinated by one in particular that bobbed up and down as it rode his Adam's apple.

"He wouldn't eat his supper last night," the pastor continued. "Or breakfast this morning."

Thaddeus was certainly not himself. The cheerful, fleet-footed extrovert was gone and in its place, a creature as morose as his owner. I couldn't find anything wrong upon physical examination. When I reached for the thermometer, the pastor recoiled but this time we got through the procedure without the need for paper towels and a baggie. However, Thaddeus's temperature was on the high side of normal.

"He may be having a vaccine reaction, which is not uncommon," I told Pastor Axelrod. "Sometimes, they can feel under the weather for a few days, just like a person might."

This was something most people could relate to. Everyone had a friend, or a friend of a friend, who reacted badly to a vaccine prior to traveling abroad. The pastor nodded knowingly.

"Or it may be something else entirely," I cautioned.

Pastor Axelrod's head slowed and came to a complete stop. He looked at me. "Such as?"

"Well, let's not get ahead of ourselves," I replied, backpedaling. "I'd like to give him some fluids. He's a little dehydrated because he's not eating and the fluids will make him feel better. We can wait and see how he does overnight or I can run some blood work now. Which would you prefer?"

The pastor reached over to pat Thaddeus, who was sitting quietly on the examining table.

"I choose the latter," he said, clearing his throat. "That is what I would choose for myself so that is what I must choose for this animal."

Despite his cold exterior, possibly reserved for a glutton like myself, it was obvious that the pastor cared very much for his little cat. "I'll just get one of the techs to give me a hand," I told him.

I returned a few minutes later with a bag of lactated Ringer's solution to rehydrate Thaddeus, a blood collection kit, and Jim. In just over a month, Jim would be entering his first year of a science degree program at Dalhousie University in his quest to become a veterinarian. He still planned to work part-time on weekends and holidays, but I would miss his full-time enthusiasm and quirky sense of humour.

"Pastor Axelrod!"

"James!"

The two shook hands while I looked on in surprise. "Do you two know each other?" I asked.

"I mow the pastor's lawn," Jim explained.

"Well, if you can call it a lawn," the pastor sighed. "There's more weeds than grass. It's the devil's handiwork," he joked.

Jim chuckled and shook his head as he gently restrained Thaddeus. "You got that right."

An amiable conversation followed about lawns in general and Rita Chen's flock of plastic Canada Geese in particular. I kept my head down.

"I hope Thaddeus is going to be okay," Jim said at last. "Dr. McBride is the best."

The pastor glanced over at me. I could tell without looking he didn't share Jim's enthusiasm.

Fortunately, Thaddeus was just as co-operative for the blood collection as he had been for fluids, which made me look good. The pastor checked his watch and decided to wait for the results. I joined Jim as we walked down the hall to the lab.

"So," I remarked casually, "you know Pastor Axelrod. What religion is he?"

Jim shrugged. "I dunno. They meet Wednesday and Saturday nights. He preaches, they sing."

I nodded thoughtfully as Jim prepared the blood sample for analysis. "Does he have a family? Kids?"

"Nope. He's kind of like a priest. He took a vow of celibacy." Jim rolled his eyes as if this was not a choice he would consider. "He pays pretty good, though," he added.

In case I might appear too curious about a man who had declared himself celibate, I busied myself with paperwork while Jim ran the tests. The results were all normal, so at this point, a vaccination reaction was the most likely possibility. I suggested to the pastor that we wait to see how Thaddeus was doing in the morning and reassess his situation at that time if necessary.

By chance, I overhead the pastor's conversation with Bernie at the reception counter a few minutes later. Carter had stolen a crinkle ball from the supply cupboard and was madly chasing it through the waiting room, leaving a wake of destruction in his path. As I straightened the books he had knocked off the coffee table, I heard the pastor ask Bernie for a crinkle ball.

"Thaddeus seems to have misplaced his," he announced. "Do you have any more?"

"Yes, luv," Bernie smiled. "Right behind you on the shelf."

Pastor Axelrod rummaged through the jar for the brightest, fluffiest ball. "Odd," he remarked casually. "The stick and line are intact but the ball is missing."

A little warning bell began to tinkle in my head. It became more insistent when Thaddeus threw up in his carrier. The pastor got down on his hands and knees and peered inside.

"Has he been throwing up?" I asked, joining him.

The pastor looked up. "No. Why do you ask?"

I took a deep breath.

"It's possible that Thaddeus might have an obstruction."

"An obstruction?" The pastor uncoiled himself from the floor and rose until we were eye to eye. "What kind of an obstruction?"

The kind that happens when the vet insists you take a toy you don't want and the cat swallows it and then you have to have surgery to remove it, I thought. Instead, I replied in what I hoped was a calm, professional voice, "You say the ball is missing?"

"Yes."

"Is it possible that it's under the fridge or stove perhaps?" I asked, grasping at the proverbial straw. "You'd be amazed at how much stuff cats send there. One of our clients found a year's worth of catnip mice when she pulled out the fridge to do some spring cleaning."

Bernie chuckled encouragingly but the pastor remained stone-faced.

"The rectory is small and simply furnished. And very clean," he added.

Of course it would be, I thought. Sloth and greed were both on the list.

"It's possible that Thaddeus may have swallowed the ball," I said slowly, wishing I was anywhere else than face-to-face with a man who not only looked like Ichabod Crane but appeared to possess similar personality quirks. "Although it's quite large," I continued. "I don't know how … " My voice trailed off.

"If this was the unfortunate course of events," the pastor asked, drawing a deep breath, "would the crinkle ball … pass?"

I shook my head. "I don't know. I'd like to take some X-rays."

Pastor Axelrod glanced heavenward at the ceiling tiles. A few were spotty where an unattended sink in the dentist's office upstairs had overflowed a couple of days earlier. Hughie hadn't gotten around to replacing them yet.

"X-rays are how much?" he asked, still staring at the ceiling as if the answer could be found there.

"We take them in pairs," I answered. "A front view and a side view – to get the best interpretation. It's $55 for the pair."

"I see." The pastor was silent for a moment. "And this is to see if he has an obstruction?"

I nodded. "It's certainly possible, yes."

"From a toy you gave him."

"It's possible."

I waited. The pastor continued to breathe. Rather vigorously, I thought. At last he turned to look at me. The hair gel which had been restraining a sweep of hair over his forehead was starting to lose its grip.

"Then we must do what is best for Thaddeus," he announced.

I was glad the pastor took the news so well but then, wrath was on the list, too. For that I was grateful. Whoever had come up with that list was a genius.

The pastor was late for his Bible study class. Before he left, I assured him I would call as soon as we had a chance to look at the X-rays, then I carried the apprehensive Thaddeus back to the radiology unit. Anxiety and resignation are a workable combination. We got good X-rays on our first try without even a squeak of protest from the patient. While Susan developed them, I saw my next patient, an outgoing calico named Abigail Joy. She was a joy; a perky little two-year-old with an effervescent personality. When I popped into the treatment area to pick up a dose of vaccine for her, Susan beckoned me over to have a look at the X-rays.

"Crap!" I shook my head. Something was wedged in the pylorus, the narrow opening between the stomach and the small intestine. "Have Bernie clear my schedule for the next couple of hours," I told Susan. "That's going to have to come out."

I finished my appointment then went to find Hughie. He was glued to the computer screen in the office and obviously in the middle of a technical crisis. "Microsoft Word for Dummies" lay sprawled on the desk.

"Oh, for God's sake!" Gulping a mouthful of coffee, he pounded on a few keys. When that didn't work, he pounded on a few more.

"Hughie?" I waited a moment. When he didn't reply, I repeated more forcefully, "Hughie!"

"What?" he replied with a trace of annoyance.

"I have a problem."

"Bigger than mine?"

"I may have lost a client because of something I did."

Hughie snorted. "I may have lost a couple of thousand." With a deep sigh, he swivelled in his chair and turned to look at me. "All right," he sighed again, folding his arms across his chest. "What did you do?"

I began my tale of woe, beginning with the doughnuts and ending with a sick cat. Hughie drummed his fingers against the arm rest and when he thought I wasn't looking, stole a peek at the computer screen. When I was done, he leaned back in his chair, silent.

"So what do you think?" I asked him.

"It pains me to say this, Em. We should probably do the surgery at no charge since this guy didn't even want the toy in the first place." He shook his head. "Can the day get any better?

"Sorry."

Hughie shrugged. "It wasn't your fault. Well, actually, it was," he acknowledged, then turned back to the computer.

"Did you try rebooting?" I asked him.

"Rebooting?" Hughie looked at me blankly.

I called the pastor with the results of the X-rays. He was understandably concerned about Thaddeus but grateful we were offering to do the surgery for free.

While I scrubbed, Hilary shaved Thaddeus's belly and prepared him for surgery. I checked his vital signs and, satisfied, picked up my scalpel. I made a long incision through the layers of skin, fat, and muscle, gradually exposing the stomach. In order to prevent spillage and resulting contamination of the abdominal cavity, I attached suture lines to each end of the stomach. Hilary held the stomach upright with hemostats clamped to each end of the suture lines. Thus positioned, I could safely open the stomach. Using the X-rays as my guide, I gently pried the obstruction free from where it had lodged like a plug in a bathtub, preventing the stomach from emptying.

"Gotcha!" Carefully I deposited the item in question in a dish on the instrument tray.

"Hmmm," Hilary murmured, "it doesn't look like a crinkle ball."

"No, it doesn't, does it?"

Puzzled, I began poking at the object with my hemostats. It was caked with debris and had been pulverized by the stomach acids, but it definitely was not a crinkle ball. Hallelujah! Praise the Lord!

I closed the stomach incision and removed the suture lines at each end. After making sure there was no leakage, I began closing first the layer of muscle, then the layer of fat, and finally, the skin. We turned off the gas anesthetic and waited for Thaddeus to wake up.

While Hilary monitored his vital signs, I gave the mystery object a closer look. It appeared to be some kind of plastic, almost like a balloon or surgical gloves. As I prodded, I uncovered a few unmistakable pieces of a rolled latex rim about the circumference of a loonie. I stared at the dish in disbelief.

For the second time in my short career as a feline veterinarian, I had removed a condom from inside one of my patients. But this time the owner was a supposedly celibate man of the cloth, not a twenty-year-old punk rocker. And Thaddeus was an indoor cat. Lust certainly appeared among the seven deadly sins, although since it required at least two people, it was somehow a lesser evil on the seven-deadly-sin meter than gluttony.

"Wow!" Hughie whistled when he heard the news. "You're the go-to girl for rubber removal. I've been practicing for eighteen years and I've never removed one from a patient." His mood had improved when the reboot successfully restored the client database. "What are you going to tell the pastor?" he asked.

I smiled sweetly. "That he's got a surgery to pay for."

Chapter 13

UNREQUITED LOVE. Who among us hasn't been a victim of the blonde cheerleader, the star athlete, or, in my case, the treasurer of the chess club? To be fair, I was the kind of girl who played baseball with the boys rather than dated them. And I was so shy, the boys I did like never knew.

Not so Mary Beth Izzard. She threw her arms around my boss and looked up at him in wide-eyed adoration. "Dr. Doucette!" she sighed. "How can I ever thank you?"

"Oh!" a startled Hughie replied as he awkwardly patted Mary Beth on the back. "Just part of the job."

"No," Mary Beth declared, shaking her head. "You are a great man. So devoted to cats. And so patient with us owners. I'm going to do something special for you."

Hughie looked alarmed. "Thank you, but that's not necessary."

"I insist."

Hughie glanced at his watch. "Goodness, look at the time," he announced. "I must be getting back to work."

"Oh, yes, of course. How selfish of me!" Mary Beth released her grip. "You'll be hearing from me, Dr. Doucette," she called to his retreating back.

Sighing happily, Mary Beth turned toward Bernie and me at the reception counter. Her cat Vincent yawned and stretched at the end of his leash. He had been named after the famous impressionist painter, partly because Mary Beth worked in an art gallery but mostly because he was missing half an ear, the result of a territorial dispute.

"You are so fortunate to work with such a wonderful man," Mary Beth sighed again.

I nodded solemnly. "I've been blessed."

My quirky boss had a knack for dealing with people and he was a gifted veterinarian. I had seen him pull more than one rabbit out of the proverbial hat in my short time at Ocean View, but Vincent only had an overgrown nail pressing against his foot pad. Hughie had merely snipped the offending claw with a pair of $1.99 toenail clippers and Mr. Van Gogh was healed.

Mary Beth tugged at her dress. Designed for smaller chests, narrower hips, and flatter tummies, it had shifted during her visit. Mary Beth barely scratched five feet but made up for it with four-inch heels. These she dug in firmly against the downward slope of middle age.

"Well, girls, I must dash. I'll be late for my Dead Sea salt scrub." She waved a cheery goodbye as she held the door open for Vincent, who strolled through at a leisurely pace.

True to her word, the following morning Mary Beth sent an extravagant goody basket laden with plump, polished fruit, gourmet cheese and crackers, and exotic chocolates. Unfortunately, Hughie wasn't due at the hospital until noon. By the time he arrived, all that remained was the gilt-edged card, a banana, an apple, and a box of crackers. He rifled through the tissue paper at the bottom then looked accusingly at me.

I shrugged. "I tried to stop them."

Hughie held the card out in front of him and read it aloud. "It says 'To the staff and most especially Dr. Hughie. Purrs and leg rubs, Vincent.'"

I smirked.

"Need I point out that you get gift baskets from a guinea pig, Dr. McBride?" Hughie peered at me over the rim of his bifocals. "Besides," he continued, "I'm Dr. Hughie. All I get is some fruit and a lousy box of crackers?"

"I know," I shook my head. "It's terrible. They're vultures."

Hughie glanced at the chocolate wrappers on my desk and shook his head. "Gluttony, Dr. McBride, is an ugly thing and, need I remind you, one of the seven deadly sins." With a deep sigh, he clutched the box of crackers against his chest and disappeared down the hall.

"What about the fruit?" I called after him.

Mary Beth had been married for five years when her husband caught the seven-year itch early and decided to carve out a new life for himself in Alberta. It was Mary Beth's fervent wish that he be mauled by a grizzly or swept away in an avalanche, whichever came first. She doted on Vincent and, by extension, Vincent's doctor. For his birthday last year, Mary Beth had given Hughie a silk necktie dotted with smiling cat faces; for Christmas, a framed eight-by-ten photo of herself and Vincent dressed as elves.

Mary Beth volunteered with a cat rescue league and occasionally brought in feral cats, which Ocean View neutered at a reduced rate. The group nursed injured, abandoned cats back to health and tried to find them good homes. Its devoted members were small in number but big in heart, often supplementing funds raised from bake sales with their own money. One day, Mary Beth brought her friend and fellow cat rescuer Johanna Simms to Ocean View.

In her late thirties, Johanna was stunning. Her thick blonde hair was pulled back in a simple ponytail that highlighted her tanned face and exquisite features. Soft tendrils brushed against the side of her face and, in an unconscious gesture, she tucked them behind her ears. She could have been a supermodel, but instead she worked for a landscape company hauling mulch and designing gardens. Traces of dirt lingered under her fingernails. Hughie dissolved in the passionate glow of her forget-me-not blue eyes as she described the horrible conditions under which the two young female cats, probably sisters, had been found. Throwing his own policy manual to the wind along with Mrs. Tuttle's latest directive, he readily agreed to spay the two feral cats at no charge.

"Oh, Dr. Doucette," Mary Beth sighed, clasping her hands together reverently, "words fail me. You are too good."

Hughie smiled modestly as Johanna looked on in approval. "Well, we like to help out where we can," he replied. Bending over, he peered inside the large carrier.

"Be careful," Johanna cautioned. "They're a little wild."

"We've had a lot of experience working with feral cats," Hughie assured her. "I'm sure everything will be fine."

"They'll be putty in your hands, Dr. Doucette," Mary Beth beamed. Turning toward to Johanna, she added, "He has such a way with animals."

Hughie picked up the surgery admission form and quickly scanned it. "We normally call clients after surgery with an update," he explained, looking at Johanna. "Do we have your number?"

"I just bought a cell phone," Mary Beth said eagerly. "You can reach me any time, day or night." She wrote the number on a piece of paper and handed it to Hughie.

"Remarkable woman," Hughie commented after they left.

"Mary Beth?" I asked.

"Johanna. What she's doing with those cats." Hughie shook his head in admiration as he reached down to pick up the cats. The carrier, which had been ominously silent, roared to life and rocked in his grip. "And she's a landscaper. Fascinating."

By the end of the day, he was a little less enthusiastic. The two cats he had offered to spay for free did not particularly want their ovaries and uteruses removed. They had strong opinions which they unleashed at random. The other surgical patients became defensive and soon everyone was hurling insults back and forth. Neither sister could be held for an intravenous injection so both were induced with gas anesthesia, a much more costly and time-consuming procedure. Both were in heat, complicating the surgery. By the time he was finished, Hughie's on-again, off-again war with his sciatic nerve was on. He spent his afternoon at home with an ice pack and a bottle of extra-strength Tylenol.

"Dr. Doucette!" Mary Beth cried when she saw him hobbling down the hallway that evening. She and Johanna had arrived to take the two sisters to their foster home.

"I'll be fine," Hughie said stoically. "It's an old basketball injury," he added with a touch of pride, glancing at Johanna.

Mary Beth clucked in sympathy. "Well, Dr. Doucette, this may brighten your day." She pulled a long, narrow box out of her tote bag and held it out for Hughie.

For a moment, I thought she had given him flowers. Instead, he unrolled a quilted wall hanging of a calico cat gazing up at the moon.

"Wow," he said, in genuine admiration. "This is beautiful!"

"It's from all of us," Mary Beth beamed. "Our quilters' guild made it for you."

"Are you a member as well?" Hughie asked, turning to Johanna.

Johanna nodded. "That's how Mary Beth and I met, actually."

"We're just a bunch of cat-loving, quilt-crazy divorcees," Mary Beth declared.

"You shouldn't have gone to all this trouble. I was glad to help out," Hughie said, shaking his head.

"It was no trouble at all," Mary Beth smiled. "Besides, quilting gives us a chance to sit around, drink some wine, and man-bash!" she continued happily. Suddenly, she clapped a hand over her mouth.

"Oh! Dr. Doucette! I didn't mean you! We think you're wonderful!" Mortified, she turned a blistering shade of red and fanned herself vigorously with one hand. "Oh my goodness! What will I come out with next?"

It didn't take long to find out. Hughie's genial good humour, buoyed by painkillers, prompted Mary Beth to add, "You could join our club, Dr. Doucette. As an honorary member, of course," she added quickly.

"You wouldn't have to quilt."

I expected Hughie to smile politely as he explained that he had a hectic, unpredictable schedule with many commitments. Instead, he seemed to be mulling the arrangement over.

"How often do you meet?" he asked casually.

"Every second Tuesday." Mary Beth held her breath.

"Well … ," Hughie hesitated, "maybe once in a while I could come and give a little talk about cats."

"Oh, Dr. Doucette!" Mary Beth clasped her hands together.

Glancing at her watch, Johanna picked up the carrier. "We should be going," she told Mary Beth, who nodded reluctantly. "Thank you so much, Dr. Doucette."

"My pleasure," Hughie replied.

"Yes, thank you!" Mary Beth echoed as she trailed up the hallway behind Johanna. At the door leading into reception, she turned around and shyly wiggled her fingers in farewell. "I'll call you," she giggled.

I turned to Hughie and shook my head.

"What?" he asked defensively.

"You're going to join a quilters' club?"

"It's a quilters' guild, Em," Hughie corrected me. "Besides, it's honorary."

※ ※ ※

A few weeks later, Hughie found himself in front of the Chebucto Women Quilters' Guild discussing the importance of neutering to a group of divorced, man-bashing quilters. I was giving the same talk to Wilma Twohig and her cat Hank. The latter had decided a life with Wilma was preferable to life on the street. He had moved in a month ago and had been happily marking his new territory ever since. I suggested that neutering was the best way to eliminate the behaviour.

"Will neutering him make Janine like him any better?" Wilma asked.

Janine was Wilma's six-year-old bulldog. At first, Wilma had been concerned that Hank would be afraid of the dog. She needn't have worried. For Hank, it was love at first sight. In Janine's opinion, however, Hank was a blight on the landscape she had ruled effortlessly for six years. Hank followed her everywhere, ate from her food bowl, and slept on top of her. With a deep sigh, Janine would move from one location to another only to have Hank climb back on top of her and knead in ecstasy.

Hank, like Mary Beth, was oblivious to the fact that the object of his adoration just wasn't interested.

"Unrequited love," Wilma sighed. "Isn't funny? They're just like people."

Despite my best efforts in the weeks that followed, Hughie remained annoyingly close-mouthed about Johanna Simms, until she made an appointment one morning for her cat Gwennie. I had heard from Mary Beth about this miraculous little cat and Johanna's devotion to her. The more I learned, the more I agreed with Hughie that Johanna was an incredible person.

Gwennie looked up at me and squeaked a friendly hello. She was a chunky mackerel tabby with a little pixie face and eyes as large and round as her mom's, though instead of blue they were a bewitching grey-green. When she looked at me, I had the odd feeling that she could see inside.

She was also partially paralyzed. Three years earlier, Gwennie had been hit by a car. Because the nerve pathway had been damaged, Johanna had to manually express her bladder twice daily. Despite several surgeries to repair broken bones and internal trauma, she never regained the use of her hind legs. She had, however, developed a unique crawl-hop and was surprisingly quick when stalking a mouse or evading capture by Johanna's two-year-old niece.

She loved the back yard and when Johanna was home, the two spent most of their time there. Some days, Johanna loaded Gwennie into a Fisher-Price wagon and strolled through the quiet neighbourhood with Ralph, her neighbour's pug, who grunted along contentedly beside them. Johanna had tried introducing other cats for companionship but Gwennie scorned them all; it was Ralph, with his spotty skin rash and an overbite, that she adored.

Indoors, Johanna had created a stimulating environment for Gwennie. She hid food so that Gwennie had to "hunt" for it. She took a carpentry course and built an access ramp up to a window perch. She scattered cardboard boxes throughout the house: cozy hideaways that could also be bitten and shredded if the occupant so desired. According to Mary Beth, Gwennie had more toys than Heinz had pickles.

Johanna looked at me anxiously. "Do you think it's serious? She's had blood in her urine before but it always goes away."

Hughie held up the blood-tinged sample that Johanna had collected in a pill vial. "What I'd like to do is get a sterile sample that I can check under the microscope," he told her. "If we find any bacteria, we'll know it wasn't from the bottle."

"Right," Johanna nodded.

"We go directly into the bladder with a fine-tipped needle and withdraw a small amount of urine. It just takes a minute," he explained, palpating Gwennie's bladder.

Unfortunately, it was too small to take a sample safely, so Johanna agreed to leave her at the hospital for awhile. The staff treated Gwennie like a visiting dignitary and vied for her attention. Throughout the morning, someone was always cuddling her or taking her on a tour through the hospital. It was hard to find help for the more mundane tasks like laundry, trimming toenails, or autoclaving instruments. Gwennie was a diminutive sun around which worlds orbited.

By early afternoon, we were able to get a urine sample. A few drops of urine on the test strip revealed the presence of blood, an elevated pH, and an increase in protein, all consistent with inflammation of the bladder wall. Susan spun some of the urine in a centrifuge. Taking a small sample of sediment from the bottom of the tube, she then prepared a slide for me to examine under the microscope. There was an abundance of bacteria, red and white blood cells, and some cellular debris. With Johanna's consent, we sent off the remaining urine to the lab at the vet college in Charlottetown to determine what antibiotics the bacteria were sensitive to. In the meantime, I decided to start Gwennie on a broad-spectrum antibiotic.

When Johanna arrived to pick her up, Gwennie's body erupted with joy. She was bright, alert, and eating well. She nuzzled Johanna's neck and purred in ecstasy, her front feet kneading against Johanna's shoulder. Although concerned, both Johanna and I were optimistic about her recovery.

When I read the faxed lab results a week later, I felt less confident.

The lab had cultured Pseudomonas aeruginosa. A common bacterium in soil and water, it is a dreaded pathogen because of its resistance to most antibiotics. Pseudomonas aeruginosa almost never attacks healthy tissues but there is hardly any tissue it cannot affect if the tissue defenses are compromised in some way, as in Gwennie's case.

Hughie's shoulders slumped as he quickly scanned the page. Of all the familiar antibiotics we deploy in the war against disease, the lab had found only two that were effective against this pathogen. Both were costly and could cause irreversible kidney damage. Gwennie would need to be admitted to the hospital for a ten-day course of treatment. The drugs were only available in injectable form and she would have to be on IV fluids to protect against kidney damage.

"We'll have to test her blood daily, too," Hughie said. "If there's any evidence of kidney damage we'll have to stop the antibiotic right away."

I hesitated. "And if we have to stop the antibiotic, what then?"

Hughie didn't answer.

It was a dishevelled Johanna who arrived promptly at nine the following morning, clutching Gwennie against her chest. She looked like she hadn't slept all night. Her normally shimmering hair hung limply, like a wilted plant, and her eyelids were weighed down with worry. She managed a smile as Gwennie chirped in delight upon seeing Hilary.

"We'll just get our blood sample so that we can check her cell count and blood chemistry before treatment. That way we'll have a baseline that we can use for comparison," Hilary told Johanna as she reached for Gwennie. "Then you can come back and visit with her," she added kindly.

Johanna nodded. She watched Hilary's retreating back in silence until she disappeared altogether through the doorway into the treatment area. With a sigh, she lowered herself into one of the chairs in reception. My next scheduled patient had evidently gotten wind of what was up when he saw his owner hauling the cat carrier up from the basement and had vanished into thin air. Enjoying the brief lull, I sat down beside Johanna.

Johanna was worried but trying not to show it. To help take her mind off Gwennie, we chatted for a few moments about gardening. I was hoping to start with a little herb garden and if that survived my erratic lifestyle, move on to flowers. Johanna had some good suggestions.

She jumped anxiously to her feet when Hughie emerged through the door leading into the treatment area. "Is she okay?" Johanna asked.

"She's doing great," Hughie assured her. "We've got her settled in a kennel with an IV line running and she's eating some breakfast. We'll be testing her creatinine levels every day to make sure the drug isn't causing any problems."

Johanna nodded, not trusting herself to speak.

"Now, with all the fluids she's getting, her bladder will need to be emptied more often than usual. No one's usually here overnight, so she'll have to go home and come back in the morning. I'm sure you'd rather have her home with you at night anyway," he added kindly.

"Oh, yes," Johanna whispered.

I knew from Mary Beth that in the summer Johanna's schedule was very hectic. She rose early and sometimes worked until dusk, but she always went home at noon and suppertime to care for Gwennie. I wondered how she was going to manage.

Then my boss, who hated house calls, said an amazing thing.

"If you like, I can drop her off in the evening and pick her up in the morning any time you're stuck. It's on the way."

"That's very kind," Johanna replied, "but I've made arrangements with the landscaping company so that I can spend more time with Gwennie. They're very understanding."

Hughie nodded. "Well, if you're ever stuck, let me know."

"I will," Johanna smiled. "Thanks."

Hughie looked like he was about to say something more but his next appointment had just arrived: the dynamic tabby duo of Gilbert and Sullivan. Reluctantly, Hughie said goodbye and headed into the exam room where the pair appeared hard at work on a new opera.

Over the next ten days, Gwennie thrived on her status as day patient with benefits. She ate well and endured her IV line with stoic good cheer. We tested her blood daily for evidence of kidney damage but found none. Mary Beth visited almost every day, sometimes with Johanna, sometimes alone. Once in awhile, she was lucky enough to corner my boss in the ward and relate to him, in great detail, Vincent's latest exploits. These he handled with good humour and grace, even though he was perpetually pressed for time.

At the end of her stay, we sent another sample of Gwennie's urine to the lab for culture. There was no trace of the bacteria so we stopped the antibiotic, but as a precaution Hughie recommended another culture and antibiotic sensitivity test in seven to ten days.

Gwennie seemed her old self once she got back home. But as the days progressed, she became increasingly listless. Johanna attributed this to the unusual weather that had descended upon the city, smothering everything in an invisible shroud of heat and humidity. Residents of the city were flocking to the beaches and bars in record numbers. My own mother had abandoned the stifling bedroom of her two-storey home and pitched a pup tent in the backyard.

Since just over a week had passed, Hughie suggested it was a good time to bring her back for another urinalysis. Ocean View was air-conditioned and therefore a popular destination with clients, if not their charges. Given a choice, most cats preferred the oppressive heat to a visit with their vet. Gwennie was the exception. We placed her on her side and gently stretched her to collect a urine sample. For this relatively simple procedure, Hughie cradled the bladder with one hand; with the other, he inserted a small-gauge needle and withdrew a sterile urine sample. Gwennie purred throughout the whole procedure and cat-napped upside down in Hilary's arms when we were done.

Hilary carried her outdoors, and the little cat lifted her head as the sweet summer air reached her nostrils and tickled her curiosity. Thanking us, Johanna hopped into the truck, her blond ponytail swinging from side to side as she cautiously backed up in the congested parking lot. She waited patiently as a group of carefree teenagers sauntered past. Then, with a small wave, she drove out of the parking lot and disappeared from view.

Hughie held the door open. As Hilary scooted back into the hospital, I turned to Hughie.

"So," I asked, "how goes it with you and Johanna anyway?"

Hughie hesitated, then summoning a grin, answered, "You know how it goes, Em. You win some, you lose some."

I was about to quip that Mary Beth might still have him when it suddenly occurred to me that he really liked Johanna. For once, I said nothing. His face unreadable, Hughie walked back inside the hospital where Mrs. MacKenzie waited with her affable Siamese, Leonard.

"Well hello, Leonard. How are you doing?" Hughie asked, lifting up the carrier and peering inside. "And how's that grandson of yours, Mrs. MacKenzie? Robbie, isn't it?" he added with a smile. "Still taking piano lessons?"

The elderly Mrs. MacKenzie beamed. Taking Hughie's arm, she described Robbie's latest exploits while my boss gently guided her toward the exam room. Their voices faded and finally disappeared altogether as the door closed behind them.

Benny and I attended my high school fifteen-year reunion that weekend. I had grown up on the outskirts of Halifax and attended the same high school as my three brothers before me. It was demolished a few years after I graduated, due to irreparable mold problems, and rebuilt on a new site. The old lot remained vacant. We rambled through the tall grasses littered with broken glass. Occasionally, we discovered pieces of brick scattered among the purple asters and stinking willies where once were hallways crammed with noisy teenagers and harried teachers. In a corner of the large field was a rusty backstop, all that was left of the softball diamond where I had learned to throw a windmill pitch that defied most batters.

Since Benny and I had attended the same feeder junior high school for awhile, we knew some of the same people. It was fun to sit down with old friends at the party that night and reminisce about the common history and thread of time that bound us together even though the building we shared was gone. What defined us wasn't a building, or winning the city football championships, or getting new computers for the school. For most of us, it was the teacher who returned a C+ report with the quiet words, "You can do better," or the friend who carried your books to school because you broke your arm.

And, as my thoughts drifted to Johanna and Gwennie, I thought maybe what defines us more than anything else is the courage to love unconditionally.

Hughie and I were sitting in the office when Gwennie's report came back from the lab a few days later. He studied it for a moment, then wordlessly handed it to me. Gwennie's infection was back; perhaps it had never left her. And this time it was resistant to all antibiotics.

"Damn it," Hughie said quietly as he reached for the phone.

※ ※ ※

On Saturday, after a busy outpatient clinic, Hughie and I got into his car and drove to Johanna's home. We were quiet, exhausted by the day and what lay ahead. We drove in silence with the windows open. I fiddled with the radio until I found a station playing a mindless ditty, then sat back and let the wind wash over me. When we reached Johanna's house, Hughie slowed down, bringing the car to rest against the curb. He got out of the car and wordlessly picked up his briefcase from the back seat.

Within the grey infrastructure of the city, Johanna had created a small oasis of lush gardens surrounding a gurgling pond. A flagstone path led to the bench under the willow where she sat with Gwennie in the dappled light. Johanna, her eyes red and swollen, held a cordless phone in her hand.

"One of Ian's housemates just went to get him on the phone," she explained. Ian was Johanna's ex, a musician and recording engineer living in Vancouver. "I've been in touch with him about Gwennie over the last few weeks. He wanted … he wanted to say goodbye to her."

The oppressive heat had broken and in its place, a gentle forgiving breeze lapped at our clothing and rippled through Gwennie's fur as we waited. Birds flitted in the green canopy overhead while neighbouring squirrels nattered at each other. Somewhere in the distance, a lawn mower droned.

And then a new sound rose into the air, silencing all the others. Gwennie's ears twitched as a familiar voice sang to her, for the last time, a lullaby as sweet and pure and beautiful as she was. Ian's voice cracked when Gwennie meowed in recognition. Then, gathering strength, he continued and finished the song.

Thanking him, Johanna hung up. Hughie reached for his syringe and my tears began to fall.

Chapter 14

"The bum! Him an' his no-good brothers."

Dulcie Huzzy gripped the edge of the counter, her dry orange hair bristling in indignation. Bernie nodded politely, only half-listening to Dulcie's tirade as she filled out Evelyn Burnett's pet insurance form with one hand and answered a ringing phone with the other.

Undeterred, Dulcie continued. "So I says to Billy, I says, 'Billy, he kin get into the flat! You gots to get your key back!' Billy just looks at me like I has ten heads and shrugs 'is shoulders."

Dulcie grabbed Evelyn's arm. "Can you believe it?"

Before Evelyn could answer, Dulcie forged ahead. "All he cares about is the next pint," she fumed, hoisting a dozen cans of cat food on the counter. "So you knows what I did?"

Evelyn had no idea but feared the worst. "What?" she asked, her eyes wide.

"I kicked 'im out," Dulcie declared with pride. "Then I opens the window and dumps out all his clothes. An' his toothbrush," she winked. "I doesn't give a rat's big, hairy you-know-what if I don't have sex for the rest o' me life!"

"That'll be $18.95," Bernie said.

Dulcie hauled a coin purse out of her pocket and began counting out exact change. Her own cat had died a few years ago, but she bought food regularly for her neighbour's cat, Junior. Junior hadn't seen the vet in years, but Dulcie made sure he had good food to eat.

"Let's see now … twenty-eight, twenty-nine … none of 'em gots the brains they was born with!" Dulcie declared.

Bernie murmured sympathetically.

"Oh, you don't knows the half of it, dearie. The stories I got up inside o' here … " Dulcie tapped her head significantly. "Should write a book, I should. T'would be a best-seller."

"There. $18.95." She pushed the change across the counter to Bernie. As Bernie picked among the coins, Dulcie continued.

"You know how I knows someone bin in the apartment?" she asked, her eyes narrowing.

Curiosity got the better of Evelyn. "Did you find something?" she asked.

"Oh, did I find something, she says! Indeed I did, my love." Dulcie lowered her voice. "You knows that temperature control thingie at the back of the fridge?" she asked in a conspiratorial tone.

Evelyn nodded.

"Well," Dulcie paused for effect. "Someone turned the knob, probably when they was reachin' for a beer, and my milk froze." She folded her arms across her chest in satisfaction.

"I see," Evelyn said, not really seeing at all.

"But how do you know it wasn't what's-his-name?" Bernie asked.

"Billy? Because the bum was down at the camp for three days!" Dulcie replied smugly.

"Oh," Evelyn said. "I never would have thought of that."

"I knows," Dulcie said kindly. "Not many would. But I watches the detective show with dat Chris fella. He's a detective in New York. I told Margie, I says, 'Margie, I doesn't go to Bingo on Thursday night. Dat's my TV night.' Oh, I talks too much – just tell me to shut up," Dulcie said pleasantly.

A taxi tooted in the parking lot.

"Keep yer pants on!" Dulcie muttered as she stacked the cans.

Bernie offered her a bag as several cans clattered to the floor.

"Oh no, my love. 'Tis bad for the environment," Dulcie replied, retrieving the wayward cans.

The taxi tooted again.

"Lord thunderin' Jaysus!" Dulcie declared as she carefully made her way through the double doors with a leaning tower of tins. "Who peed in your cereal? I'm comin', I'm comin'!"

No sooner had she gone out than a fire truck rumbled into the parking lot. Although the siren was off, there was a sense of urgency as five firefighters tumbled out of the truck that straddled several parking spots in front of the hospital. One of them was clutching a cat carrier.

The men strode single file into the hospital, bunching up at the reception counter. Each was wearing heavy work boots and yellow firefighter's pants held up by suspenders. Underneath the suspenders were regulation-issue white tees that emphasized tanned, muscled arms and flat stomachs. Hot on their steel-reinforced heels was Dulcie Huzzy.

"Where's the fire?" she demanded of no one in particular. Selecting a comfortable chair, Dulcie settled in to watch the proceedings.

The man holding the carrier looked at Bernie with earnest brown eyes. He was tall, his dark hair short and neatly trimmed.

"Hello," he said. "I'm really sorry but we don't have an appointment. We're on call," he explained. "But it's a quiet day and we were just wondering if the vet could have a look at Spotty here."

Hilary turned to Susan. "Maybe I should go to vet school," she whispered.

"Well, now, of course we can see your wee cat." Bernie flashed her recently whitened teeth in a benevolent smile. "That's what we're here for." She put the two phone lines on hold so as not to be disturbed and picked up a blank medical chart. "Follow me, please, gentlemen."

Like obedient ducklings, they formed a line behind her.

"Oh, my," Bernie smiled again as she ushered them into the exam room. "There's so many of you," she clucked happily, closing the door behind her.

Normally the model of efficiency, Bernie seemed to be taking an awfully long time to collect a name, address, phone number, and reason for the visit. She finally emerged about ten minutes later just as I was getting ready to tap on the door.

"What lovely young men," she whispered. "Call me if you need anything. I'll be right here. Oh, and Dr. McBride," she touched my arm as I turned to leave, "remember I know how to help with X-rays now."

"Bernie, you hated getting into all that gear," I reminded her.

Bernie shrugged. "People change."

I entered the crowded exam room and was immediately engulfed by the scent of fresh laundry mixed with the earthy smell of men who work hard in the outdoors. It was a pleasant smell, reminiscent of the times I curled up beside my dad as he read a bedtime story or we watched TV.

The reason for this visit and the centre of everyone's attention rose slowly to her feet as I approached. She stood still, her upright tail quivering in excitement as she waited for me. While I gently stroked her and told her how beautiful she was, she began kneading the table. She was mostly white except where random patches of black had gained a foothold, including an endearing spot over her nose and right eye.

"This is Spotty," one of the men said. "She's our version of the firehouse Dalmatian. Oh, I'm Nick, and these guys are Vince, Bobby, Ace, and Stan."

I shook everyone's hand. Except for variations in name and hair colour, they looked like they had all been chiseled from the same slab of granite.

"She's not been eating well," Nick continued. "And she seems to be vomiting more than usual."

"We thought at first she was just missing Nick," Bobby added.

"I was away on a course," Nick explained as he patted Spotty. She had resumed resting on the examining table.

"The girls always miss Nick when he's not around," Ace grinned.

Nick shook his head and looked at the floor. He was handsome in a boy-next-door kind of way and his crooked front tooth only made him more appealing.

"Spotty's part of our fire prevention program in the schools," Vince explained. "She adores the attention and the kids love her."

It was clear that the men of South Central Fire Station 128 loved her too. They crowded around as I began my examination. Her eyes seemed a little sunken and she was definitely dehydrated. When I examined her mouth, I noticed her gums were tacky and her breath bad. I lifted her rhinestone-studded pink collar to feel her lymph glands and her thyroid. As she purred softly, I worked my way down her body, listening to her heart and lungs, palpating organs, examining her skin and fur. Rather than the smooth sheen of a healthy cat's coat, Spot's fur was coarse and unkempt. Together, these symptoms were leading toward an inevitable conclusion.

"Have you changed her food recently?" I asked as I made notes in her chart.

"Only a few more treats than usual," Bobby offered, "just to get her to eat."

"How old is she?" There was no birth date recorded in the medical record. I assumed Bernie had forgotten to ask in her firefighter-induced euphoria.

"We don't know," Vince shrugged. "Nick found her wandering in the parking lot a few years ago. She was starving."

"We fed her and that was that," Nick smiled. "She decided to stay. She doesn't mind the siren, the hustle and bustle of a fire station – she's just a great little cat." Spotty looked up at the circle of anxious faces.

"She knows if you're having a rough day," Ace said fondly. "She'll just come and sit beside you."

"Same with the kids," Stan spoke up for the first time. "She seeks out the shy ones. Makes them feel special. She gets tons of fan mail," he added. "We keep all the letters in her scrapbook. She even has a commendation from the mayor's office."

The men grew silent. "What do you think is wrong?" Nick asked at last.

"Well," I began, "it looks like she has some kidney problems. I'd like to run some blood tests if that's OK. That'll give us more information."

"Whatever you need to do, Dr. McBride." Nick looked around the room as all heads bobbed in agreement. "We have a Spotty fund."

"Poker night," Ace explained. "The proceeds go into the 'Spot Pot.' Helps us keep her in the grand style to which she is accustomed. Stan's contributed the most," he grinned, poking Stan in the ribs.

"They cheat," Stan said, shaking his head in disgust.

Smiling, I opened the door to the exam room. "I'll be right back. I'm just going to get one of the techs to help with blood collection."

As soon as the door opened, I was swarmed by the female staff. Even Mrs. Tuttle looked up from her adding machine to see what all the fuss was about. We drew straws – broken-off cotton ear swabs that doubled as decision makers. After painstaking deliberation, Chelsea, our second-year vet school summer student, drew the longest stick and headed happily up the hall with me.

Inside the exam room, Chelsea gently cradled Spot in position. Using her thumb as a tourniquet, she raised the large vein in the front leg. I poured a small amount of alcohol over the site then withdrew enough blood to run a thyroid test, a complete blood count, and a serum chemistry profile. Their pagers silent, the men had decided to wait with Spotty while we ran the blood work.

I hovered nearby as the chemistry machine whirred efficiently on the counter, painstakingly recording and analyzing data as it had been programmed to do. Even though I was expecting the worst, my heart sank when the machine printed out the results on a strip of paper, a sterile, black-and-white rendering of the verdict. I slipped the strip of paper into my pocket and headed back to the exam room.

Spotty had settled on Nick's lap. A couple of the men stood, others were seated quietly as they talked amongst themselves. They looked up when I entered the room. Closing the door behind me, I took a deep breath.

"I'm afraid I don't have very good news," I began. "Spotty's kidneys are failing."

No one spoke. A couple of the men shifted uncomfortably. Nick kept his head lowered as he continued to pat Spot. Her slow steady purr rose above the silence.

"One of the measures we use to determine kidney function is the creatinine level in her blood. High normal is 150. Spotty's was 1100." I paused. "That's the highest I've ever seen."

"Is there anything we can do?" Nick asked, looking up.

"I'd like to start her on intensive fluid therapy right away," I explained.

"Will that fix the problem?" Nick's voice was calm, relaxed. It was the voice of someone who had been trained to help others, to remain cool under pressure, to hide fear.

"I hope so," I replied. "We'll know in a couple of days."

Nick rose carefully and, cradling Spotty in his arms, gently transferred her to me.

"I'll be in touch," I promised, "and you're welcome to visit any time."

The men nodded, thanked me, and filed out of the exam room. In her excitement, Dulcie leapt to her feet.

"There's no fire then, eh?"

"No, ma'am," Ace replied.

"Well, that's good then," Dulcie said agreeably as she joined in the procession. She looked up at Bobby. "Probably a false alarm?"

The words were no sooner out of her mouth than Dulcie was suddenly airborne, tripping over a seventeen-pound box of laundry detergent that someone had inadvertently left beside the reception counter.

"Lord thunderin' Jaysus!" she hollered on her way down.

Several of the men rushed to her assistance.

"Dulcie Huzzy," she beamed, extending her hand upwards from the floor where she lay sprawled amidst the cans that had spilled out of her pockets. Bobby and Stan helped her to her feet but once vertical, Dulcie was unable to bear weight on her right foot.

"Should I call an ambulance?" Bernie asked anxiously.

"Oh, no. We can run her down to the emergency department," Nick offered. "It's on the way."

"In the fire truck?" Dulcie grinned. "Oh my. Weren't it lucky you boys were here!"

"Yes, ma'am," Bobby smiled as he and Stan formed a chair with their forearms. Draping an arm around each thick neck, Dulcie wiggled her behind into place. The men straightened up and Dulcie was raised high into the air, a dazed smile on her face. As the procession began to move once more, Dulcie's hand fluttered a queen-like goodbye . Nick followed with the cat food. Vince brought up the rear with Dulcie's lime-green coat and a flowered vinyl purse draped over his arm.

"Won't that sister-in-law o' mine be some jealous," Dulcie rejoiced. "That's Mary Buggit in Big Tickle, Newfoundland. Any o' you boys from back home?" she asked Bobby.

"I am," Ace announced. "I grew up in Corner Brook."

"Well, then you must know some Buggits. There's hundreds of 'em. Buggits begattin' Buggits. If one of them Buggits even hangs her knickers next to hubby's drawers on the clothesline, there's a baby nine months later."

Dulcie chortled at her own wit. The men laughed too as they piled into the truck, Dulcie's good-natured humour a temporary reprieve from their worry.

We kept Spotty at the hospital for two days as we ran a continuous IV drip. I hoped the intensive fluid therapy would not only rehydrate her but jumpstart her renal function by flushing the kidneys. The firemen visited as often as they could. Vince even brought his two little girls one evening. I opened the kennel door so they could pat her. The older one leaned in on her tiptoes and kissed Spotty on the forehead.

"You have to get better, Spotty," she whispered, "so you can help all the kids."

I felt my throat tighten. It had been a tough couple of weeks, especially after Johanna's little cat, Gwennie, had to be put down. But in spite of my best efforts, Spotty was no better. She brightened up when anyone visited and she licked a little food off Nick's fingers, but otherwise she slept. Her creatinine levels remained unchanged.

I called the internal medicine specialist at the vet college in PEI, hoping he might have a suggestion, a rabbit we could pull out of a hat. Instead, Tony Eldridge, in a voice at once gentle and pragmatic, advised me to prepare the client for the worst.

Nick and Bobby arrived the following morning to take Spotty home to the fire station she loved and the men who loved her. She was happy to be disconnected from the bag of fluids and the IV line. For a few minutes she licked the shaved area where the catheter had been, then lay down exhausted. Nick picked her up and held her close before putting her in the carrier.

"So there's nothing more we can do?" he asked, his face temporarily hidden as he secured the latch on the door of the carrier.

I shook my head. "I'm so sorry. I wish I had better news. She's such a dear little cat."

"Well, we'll take her home and spoil her rotten," Bobby said quietly.

The three of us gazed at the mysterious little white cat with the black spots who had been found starving in a parking lot three years ago and who had brought joy to so many hearts since then.

"It's going to be hard on the kids," Nick said.

As he picked up the carrier and she knew with certainty that she was going home, a deep, rich cadence rose in Spot's throat. It was going to be hard on the adults, too, I thought to myself.

I gave Nick her home-care instructions and prescribed half a tablet of anti-nausea medication daily. The fluids we had given her would make her more comfortable for a few days, but that was just temporary. Since Spotty's time was limited, the men had decided among themselves not to prolong her life with daily trips to the vet's for fluid therapy and injections. Instead, they would keep her comfortable at her home in the fire station.

I popped a few cans of low-protein, low-phosphorus food into a bag. "If she'll eat, this will be the best thing for her."

"How long do you think she has?" Bobby asked.

I hesitated. "Maybe a few weeks."

For a moment no one spoke. Then, thanking me for all that I had done, they turned to leave.

"Home we go, missy," Nick said with a bright smile. "Everyone's waiting to see you."

I watched them leave, wishing, not for the first time in my life, that I could fix the unfixable.

※ ※ ※

Weeks passed. The early mornings were cool now. An ambitious person could start the day in shorts and sandals, though most waited until the sun rose higher in the sky. School would be starting soon, but without Spotty there would be a very different fire prevention program for the city's elementary school students. Our own summer student, Chelsea, would be heading back to university in another week.

"I'm going to miss that good-looking guy," she said, as she gnawed on a slice of pizza.

"Which good-looking guy?" I asked.

"I don't remember his name. He works at the fire station. He just bought another case of food."

"Another case? What do you mean?"

"I left you a message. Didn't you get it?" she said, seeing the look on my face. "The cat's doing great."

With Bernie on vacation and Chelsea working in reception, things hadn't been going smoothly. I hoped she would be a better veterinarian than she was receptionist. I raced to the phone and dialed the number for the fire station, hoping Nick was in.

"No, my love," a vaguely familiar voice said, answering the phone on the third ring. "The boys is out on a call."

I hesitated. "Dulcie?"

"In the flesh."

"It's Dr. McBride."

"LORD THUNDERIN' JAYSUS!"

I waited for the pack-a-day coughing fit to subside then asked, "What are you doing at the fire station?"

"I works here, dearie," Dulcie answered with a touch of pride.

"You work there?"

"Oh yes, love. Three weeks now. Their housekeeper just up an' left. Moved to the big T.O., don't ya know."

Dulcie lowered her voice. "The boys was tryin' to make do, but oh, it were a mess," she confided. "Needed a woman's touch. I tells that Nick about my pickle, you know – the dumb ex-boyfriend and all his crazy brothers. An' he tells me about his pickle – no housekeeper. An' then Nick, he says to me, he says, 'Dulcie, would you like to come work at the fire station?' And I says, 'Indeed I would!' And that dear, wee Spotty. I just loves her."

I jumped in. "How is Spotty?"

"Oh grand, just grand. There's talk about her going back in the schools once fall comes."

I sucked in my breath. "She's alive then?"

"Alive?" Dulcie's throaty cackle was music to my ears. "She's about the livingest cat I ever seen! Caught a mouse the other day an' put it on my bed. Playin' with all her toys. Eatin' up a storm. Them boys is some happy."

I leaned back in my chair. Spotty was alive! Not just alive but thriving. How? How do they do it, these little creatures that capture our hearts and hold us hostage? Although I didn't know it then, Spotty would live another ten wonderful years as South Central Fire Station's spokescat for fire prevention. She traveled to all her engagements, including annual trips to the vet, in a fire truck.

"I have my own little room in the back," I heard Dulcie say. "Spotty sleeps with me when Nick's off duty. An' that Bobby, he fixes up my TV and now I git 116 channels. Can you believe it? Me. Dulcie Huzzy. 116 channels!"

Chapter 15

IN THE SIXTIES, THEY WERE CALLED PEDAL PUSHERS and every girl on the block had a pair. In the nineties, they were born again as capris – snug, form-fitting pants that reached mid-calf. My mother decided she wanted a pair for an upcoming bridge function at the golf club.

"That's what you can get me for my birthday, Emily," she declared. "Elsie Simmons has a pair and she just loves them."

Mom normally hung out in track pants and a comfortable pair of sneakers, but who was I to argue with Elsie Simmons? Elsie had fashion sense and a lot of money to support it. I had neither. Besides, I would rather have a root canal than roam aimlessly through a shopping mall in search of the perfect birthday gift for my mother, who was in her seventh decade. I went to Sears, grabbed a pair of size 12 pale blue capris off the rack and paid cash. I was in and out in ten minutes. Life was good.

Mom got lots of presents for her birthday but her favourite gift was the capris. She ran upstairs to try them on while family and friends partied downstairs. Led Zeppelin blasted from the stereo. My seventeen-year-old niece Jessie was in charge of the music and had been told to go "retro." For her, that was the seventies. Most of Mom's friends had taken out their hearing aids and were having a wonderful time.

"Ta da!" Mom announced as she descended the steps, stopping in the hallway to pirouette.

George, Mom's octogenarian neighbour, flashed an enthusiastic thumbs-up with the hand that wasn't buried in the chip bowl.

Jessie studied Mom for a moment and then said something.

"What, dear?" Mom hollered above the music.

"I SAID, 'NANNIE, YOU NEED A THONG!'" Jessie hollered back.

"Oh, yes, sing us a song!" Joyce McCormack clapped her hands together in excitement. She turned to Ricky Meisner, the grinning young man besides her. His ears had perked up at the mention of the word thong. "She has a lovely voice, you know," Joyce confided.

The old neighbourhood hadn't changed much from the days when I was a kid. Most of my friends' parents still lived here long after their children had gone, although it was increasingly difficult for them to maintain their homes. Sixteen-year-old Ricky had struck an entrepreneurial gold mine when he and his family moved into the neighbourhood a couple of years ago. Armed with his father's lawn mower, a rake, and a big smile, he was in huge demand, and overnight became a teenage lawn maintenance tycoon. He had heard the Led Zeppelin music, smelled the food, seen Jessie, and invited himself in.

Mom just smiled and flitted out to the kitchen for more hors d'oeuvres. After the crowd had gone and we were cleaning up, she turned to me, dishcloth in hand.

"Emily?"

"Yeah, Mom?"

"What's a thong?"

And so, back to Sears I went, this time to the lingerie department with my seventy-five-year-old mother in tow. How time changes our relationships. I remember Mom dragging me to Sears for my first bra when I was eleven. They were called training bras in those days, although I have no idea why. What were we training them for, anyway? It's not like they were going to run a marathon. I preferred my unisex undershirt and was horrified when the clerk marched into the dressing room with a measuring tape to "fit" me.

In the course of raising four children, Mom had mostly chosen function over form when it came to clothes. Even now, a rainbow of sturdy, sensible underwear that could be used as parachutes hung from

Mom's clothesline on wash day. I could only imagine what the neighbours would think when a thong appeared in their midst, undulating in the breeze.

I rifled through a bin and pulled out the first one I found in Mom's size. It was red.

"How does it work?" Mom asked as she held it up in the air.

"Dr. McBride!"

I whipped around to find Herbert Grant standing behind me. Herbert was a retired history professor living in Tatamagouche, a small seaside community on Nova Scotia's Northumberland Shore. Every year, Hughie and I made a house call to Herbert's seaside home, where fourteen cats lived the life of royalty.

"Hello, Herbert!" I smiled, giving him a warm hug. "What brings you to the city?"

"Some friends of mine are performing in a play at Neptune Theatre. I thought I'd come and heckle them," he chuckled. "What about you?"

"Oh, we're just doing a little shopping," I replied with a casual shrug.

"Emily's helping me find a thong," Mom said.

Herbert's smile widened.

"This is my mom," I said, hastily making introductions.

"How do you do?" Herbert said graciously as he shook Mom's hand. Her thong dangled from the other.

"I'm just fine, thank you. I'm not sure of this colour, though," Mom said, shaking her head.

"Well," Herbert pursed his lips thoughtfully, "I suppose you should consider what you'll be wearing over it."

"Yes, good point," Mom agreed. "It would be more economical to get one that goes with everything."

"Flesh colour is usually a good choice," Herbert suggested.

I suppose after seven decades and four children, I too might feel comfortable discussing the pros and cons of buying a red thong with a man I had just met. Leaving Mom and Herbert to discuss undergarments and other matters of interest to seniors, I wandered aimlessly through the racks of Daisyfresh, Jockey, and Sears' Best.

"Goodness, I must be going," Herbert said at last as he glanced at his watch. "It was a pleasure to meet you, Mrs. McBride."

"Likewise," Mom smiled.

"Goodbye, Dr. McBride," he waved. "Have a wonderful day."

"Such a lovely man," Mom declared after he left. "So knowledgeable. A little chubby for my taste, though."

At the counter, she laid down her latest acquisition, a flesh-coloured thong with a touch of lace. The bored clerk looked at the thong and then at Mom.

"There's no returns on underwear," she hinted darkly.

Mom flashed her a bright smile. "Oh, I won't be returning it, dear. I always wear thongs under my capris," she added with a touch of pride.

We grabbed a quick bite to eat at a new sushi joint in the mall. Then I took Mom home and headed back to work. When I arrived, there was a note on my board to call Herbert. He answered on the first ring. We chatted amiably for a few minutes about cats before Herbert could bring himself to the point.

"Dr. McBride? I was wondering," Herbert paused. "Well, that is, if you don't think it's too presumptuous … "

"Yes?" I prodded.

"Would it be terribly inappropriate if I asked your mother to accompany me to the theatre this evening?"

I opened my mouth to speak, but nothing came out. The only sound was the air whistling in and out of Herbert's nose as he waited anxiously for my answer.

"Oh, dear," he sighed, "I've overstepped."

"Oh no, not at all," I hastened to assure him once I found my voice. "I was a bit distracted. One of the cats just knocked some papers onto the floor," I lied. Carter, who had been sound asleep on the desk, opened one eye and blinked accusingly at me.

In the years since my dad died, my mom had had to make many adjustments. She, like the rest of our family, was devastated by his loss. Gradually, she made her way back to old friends, met some new ones, and rediscovered the joy in living. But never before had anyone asked my permission to take my mother out on a date. I gave Herbert my blessing.

"Have her back before midnight," I joked.

"Oh yes indeed. Of … of course," Herbert stammered.

Smiling, I hung up the phone. Meredith and Murphy Gilcuddy were waiting for me in the exam room. A short, robust woman in her mid-forties, Meredith worked for City Parks and Recreation and had an eye for detail. Murphy was her big, orange tabby.

Over the last year, I had been treating Murphy for asthma with little success. He seemed better in the summer months when he ventured outdoors. But when the days turned cooler, he preferred to spend his time sprawled on the radiator or in Meredith's ample lap. Lately, he had lost his appetite. I wasn't sure if it was the asthma or a new problem.

Meredith passed me a coil notebook in which she had recorded daily food and water consumption, frequency and consistency of bowel movements, and urinary output. Ninety-nine out of one hundred clients would stare at me blankly if I asked how much their cat drank in a day. Meredith knew the amount to the millilitre, after allowing for evaporation.

"He's not nearly as playful either," Meredith added. "I bought him a new catnip mouse yesterday and he just looked at it. You know how he feels about catnip," she reminded me.

Indeed I did. Murphy had just appeared on Meredith's verandah one morning and watched through the window as she nibbled her toast and read the paper. At suppertime, he was still there, curled up on a chair. Meredith opened the front door and he strolled in, tail held high. The next morning he was whisked to the vet's for a checkup and vaccinations.

We had left him alone in the exam room for a few minutes while I showed Meredith the products for flea control on the shelf in reception. In the absence of any authority figures, Murphy had poked around in the cupboard and discovered the container of catnip. By the time we returned, the brochure rack had been shredded and a plastic cat skull used for demonstration purposes was riddled with tooth marks. Murphy was sprawled in the middle of the mess, gazing contentedly into space with half-closed eyes.

Today, he didn't even glance my way when I opened the drawer that housed the catnip. I sprinkled some in front of him but after a few polite sniffs, Murphy just sighed and tucked his paws underneath his chest.

"The last time he ate was … ," I rifled through Meredith's notes, "yesterday at 7:50? Six crunchies?"

Meredith nodded, her face a knot of concern.

"Any vomiting?"

"No," she shook her head. "He walks over to the food bowl like he wants to eat but then he just walks away. I've tried a dozen different foods."

I studied Murphy, who was still hunkered down on the examining table.

"Do you have a yucky old hairball in there, big guy?" I scratched the side of his neck and he leaned his big head into my hand.

Because cats can't stand a hair out of place, they are conscientious groomers. As a result, fur can collect in their stomachs, making them feel nauseous and uncomfortable. In most cases, it passes harmlessly through the digestive system or is thrown up in the form of a hairball. These long torpedoes of matted fur mixed with a stew of stomach contents are generally found by owners on top of the bed, on the Oriental rug, or en route to the bathroom, barefoot, at three in the morning.

In extreme cases, the cat is unable to pass the mass of fur, which becomes very dense and can cause a blockage that requires surgical removal. I always tell owners to rejoice when they find a hairball and think of how much money they saved.

"Should we take an X-ray?" Meredith asked.

"Well, we could," I agreed, nodding, "but a normal X-ray probably wouldn't show something like a hairball unless it had been there a long time and had started to calcify. And I'm reluctant to do an exploratory surgery just yet."

"Oh, dear." Meredith wrung her hands. "What are we going to do, then?" She was a woman of action. Waiting was not one of her strongest suits.

Murphy was wondering the same thing. He clambered into Meredith's lap and the two of them stared at me with big eyes. In the end, we agreed that Murphy should stay for the day so I could keep an eye on him, do some routine blood work, and administer fluids since he was a little dehydrated.

"If he doesn't improve or if he gets worse," I added, "we can do a set of barium X-rays, which would show if something is blocking his digestive system."

"Yes, I guess that's best," Meredith sighed. Clutching Murphy to her chest, she followed me to the recovery ward, where we settled him in a kennel.

"Bye, sweetheart," she whispered. "Be a good boy."

"We'll take good care of him," I said gently.

Meredith nodded. Slowly, she picked up her coat and, draping it over one arm, left the ward. The big cat stoically watched her departure from behind bars.

With the exception of the lovable but needy Siamese, who as a group seem to suffer from separation anxiety and want everyone to know it, most adult cats in a veterinary hospital appear to accept their fate; Murphy was no exception. We gave him 200 mL of fluids under the skin but, because of the volume, we had to move the large-gauge needle several times. Murphy took it all in stride. When Carter and his protégé, little Patrick, tore through the treatment area in pursuit of a buzzing housefly, Murphy watched with interest.

Despite his outward calm, I was worried that stress might trigger an asthma attack. We syringe-fed him a small amount of food and then put him back in his own familiar cat carrier instead of the kennel in the recovery ward. Carrier was a poor description for the portable condo on wheels, which boasted a private lavatory, down comforter, and snack bar. Meredith had it custom-built and Murphy loved to lounge in it when he was home. He fell asleep with his head resting on top of a blue teddy bear.

By evening, he seemed much brighter, and I decided to send him home on a trial basis. Although he showed no interest in eating on his own, he had kept down all the small meals we had given him. I felt he would be happier in his own environment and more likely to eat.

Meredith took a day off and spent it recording Murphy's activities instead of those of the city recreation department. When he wasn't sleeping, these were limited to peeing in the litter box and not covering it, turning up his nose at every can Meredith opened, and hissing at the mackerel tabby who boldly sauntered down the sidewalk in front of his house.

Distraught, she called me that evening. "He's still not eating, Dr. McBride. And not only that, Pierre is missing. I think I left a window open," she moaned. "I've been so distracted lately. Not my usual self at all."

Pierre LaFleur was Meredith's budgie. The opinionated LaFleur was quick to bite first and never ask questions. Meredith had offered to take him after her neighbour, his hand bloodied from the most recent beak-raking, had loaded the unrepentant Pierre into the car for a one-way trip to the vet's. Under Meredith's care, the feathered fascist's personality had improved, but only marginally. He was allowed free range when Meredith was home but otherwise lived in a spacious flight cage. For the most part, Murphy ignored him.

"Do you think he'll be okay? Can budgies figure out their way home?" Meredith asked.

What I knew about birds could be balanced on the head of a pin. I suggested she let her neighbours know that Pierre was missing in case someone had seen him and recommended that she bring Murphy back in for an X-ray. I was worried that there might be something going on besides a hairball.

The following morning, a distraught Meredith had grabbed the first clothes she encountered in her closet, the car keys, and Murphy. She was already waiting anxiously at the door when Bernie arrived at 7:30 a.m. Murphy howled piteously at the injustice of being pried out of bed at so early an hour. Apart from being a little out of sorts over the personal inconvenience, however, he seemed fine. He purred at my touch and thrust his big head against mine, the cat equivalent of a handshake between friends.

Even though he wasn't acting like a sick cat, we repeated the blood work and took four views of his chest and abdomen while Meredith waited. Hilary had just finished rinsing them when a cat having seizures was rushed into the hospital. Meredith decided to wait at home with Murphy while I dealt with the emergency. I promised to call her as soon as possible. Even so, the X-rays hung from the rack for three hours before I finally had a chance to look at them.

With my emergency case stable and resting comfortably, I grabbed a red licorice from Susan's bag of candy in the cupboard, followed by a second. I decided she still wouldn't notice if a third went missing. Then, still chewing, I grabbed Murphy's X-rays, slipped them onto the viewer, and flicked the switch.

The X-ray film came to life against the lit backdrop of the viewer. Immediately, I knew what had happened to Pierre. Murphy may have had a hairball in his stomach that had passed over the last few days. But the reason he wasn't eating today was because he was full. I could see a few small bones and what might have been a beak working their way through his digestive system.

I went to the office to call Meredith, but sat down and stared at the phone instead. There were a million things I had to do. The patient in isolation needed an injection of antibiotics and anti-nausea medication. The lab had to be called for results that should have been here yesterday. My message board was full and I had a stack of charts to update. My stomach growled. And I couldn't bring myself to pick up the phone to tell Meredith that Murphy had eaten his adopted brother. Perhaps it would be better if I simply told her that Murphy did not have a blockage and was doing well.

Tired of my dithering, the phone took matters into its own hands and rang shrilly.

"Dr. McBride?" Bernie poked her head into the office. "Ms. Gilcuddy is on line 2."

Wearily, I picked up the phone. "I'm sorry to bother you, Dr. McBride," Meredith blurted out, "but I just couldn't wait any longer. My stomach's all in knots."

"No need to apologize," I told her. "I was just about to call you. How's he doing?"

Meredith sighed. "About the same. He's still not eating. Did you find anything on the X-rays?"

"Well," I took a deep breath, "I'm afraid … "

"Wait!" Meredith interrupted. "Murphy's just walked into the kitchen. He's sniffing something on the floor."

I exhaled slowly.

"It's a piece of toast!" Meredith lowered her voice to a whisper. "He's reaching out to touch it. Maybe he's going to ... no, wait!" she paused as Murphy took a detour around the toast crumb and sat down to scratch himself.

"Okay. He's on the move again," Meredith continued, speaking in the hushed, reverential tones of a sports broadcaster at a golf game.

I leaned forward in my seat, listening with mounting excitement to the play-by-play.

"He's approaching the food bowl ... he's lowering his head in. He's ... oh no! He heard something. He's looking all around." Meredith held her breath, while I perched motionless on the edge of my seat.

After a minute of silence she continued, her voice barely audible. "He just picked up a crunchy. He's sort of moving it around in his mouth ... Damn! He just spit it out."

I collapsed in my chair. "Wait!" she hissed. "He's picking up another one."

I leaned forward. "C'mon, buddy," I urged Murphy silently. "Hit this one onto the green for the old doc!"

"He just swallowed it!" Meredith croaked. "He's picking up another one. And another. I can hear him crunching them! Oh, Dr. McBride! Thank you! Thank you so much!"

In her excitement, Meredith hung up before I had a chance to tell her about Pierre. I decided that was a sign. Meredith could cling to the hope that Pierre was alive and flying free somewhere in west end Halifax.

Oddly enough, Murphy never had another asthma attack after Pierre disappeared.

"It's the strangest thing, Dr. McBride," Meredith said, several months later. "No more coughing spells, no difficulty breathing. He's doing wonderfully! Do you think he could have been allergic to Pierre?"

"It's certainly possible," I agreed. Maybe Murphy got tired of waiting for the humans to figure it out and had taken matters into his own hands.

"The Lord works in mysterious ways," Meredith declared. "That's what my mother always said."

My mother, too. She and Herbert had been out several times since their evening at Neptune Theatre. The thong, a medieval instrument of torture according to my mother, had been relegated to a remote corner of her dresser.

"But just think, Emily," Mom declared. "If it hadn't been for that thong, I never would have met Herbert." She folded her arms across her chest. "The Lord works in mysterious ways."

Chapter 16

BABS BAUMGAARTEN LOVED TWO THINGS: football and felines. To be more precise, quarterbacks and tabbies. She had four of them at home – cats, that is. NFL quarterbacks she kept in her purse. The bubblegum that came with them was doled out to the neighbourhood children.

Most of Babs's cerebral cortex was used to store football statistics. If asked, though I never did, she could recite a decade's worth of data on touchdowns, yards gained, yards lost, sacks, completions, and interceptions. I wondered if she was some kind of idiot savant with an uncanny (some would say annoying) ability to retain football trivia. Beyond football and cats, she didn't contribute much to a conversation.

I ushered Babs and Brett Favre into the exam room. Brett was a large, self-possessed cat with a big personality and feet to match. When I opened his carrier, he yawned, stretched luxuriously, and began a relaxed inspection of the premises. Brett had three brothers at home. All were short-haired tabbies and all were named after quarterbacks. While Brett was overweight and built more like a defensive tackle, Joe Namath was a skinny little squirt with a large Roman nose and ears too big for his head. Joe was always getting into trouble and was a regular at Ocean View. Brett I had seen only once in the past year and he wasn't due again until August.

Babs sat in the chair, her hands folded in her lap.

"So," I smiled, "what's Brett here for today?"

Babs looked at me for a moment, then got up and walked over to the window. The reception area was empty except for the Medscape delivery man chatting with Bernie as he unloaded his trolley of medical supplies. Irish, divorced, and in bad need of dental work, he asked

Bernie out at least once a month. At least once a month she refused.

Babs turned from the window. "You don't record doctor-patient conversations, do you?" she asked.

I shook my head. "No. We don't find it works well with cats."

Babs nodded in relief. "Good." She walked back to the chair and sat down. Taking another deep breath, she exhaled slowly and having made up her mind, leaned forward in her chair. "Brett's in trouble," she whispered.

"What kind of trouble?" I asked.

Babs held a finger to her lips as the outside doors chimed. Satisfied it was just the delivery man leaving, she turned back toward me. Brett was sprawled on the floor, idly flicking the tip of his tail.

"He's a stalker."

"A what?"

Babs shot me a warning glance. "A stalker," she whispered. "I overheard a woman in the lineup at the grocery store. She was walking her little dog and they were stalked by a great big tabby cat with a green collar."

"Well, what makes you think it was Brett?" I asked.

Babs nodded significantly in Brett's direction. The bell on his lime-green collar tinkled as he rolled over on his back and gazed at my shoes.

"Oh. Lots of cats probably have a green collar," I reassured Babs. "We sell a lot of them."

"There's more," Babs said. Her shoulders slumped under the burden of knowledge. "That woman? She must live nearby. I've seen her walking the dog. Anyways, the cat followed them for a ways then disappeared. When she got home, she gave the dog his supper on the porch."

Babs looked up at me. "And then do you know what happened next?"

Without waiting for me to answer, Babs cradled her face with both hands and shook her head. Taking a deep breath, she continued. "Dr. McBride, the next thing she knew, she heard this God-awful racket, screaming and yelling. She thought her poor little dog was dead. She rushed outside and … "

"And … ?" I prompted.

Babs stole a peek at me between her fingers. "And the cat was disappearing over the fence. All she could see was a big, bushy tail!"

This time we both looked at Brett, who began washing the very body part in question. For a short-haired cat, Brett had the fluffiest, most luxuriant tail I had ever seen. It was his most prized possession and he kept it scrupulously clean.

I had to admit, the evidence was damning. Brett had always been pleasant and cordial but then, so were most serial killers. Still, I couldn't imagine the lump of inertia at my feet stalking anything other than his food bowl.

"Dr. McBride, what am I going to do?" Babs wailed, pushing her glasses back up to the starting position on her ski jump nose.

"Well, we don't know for sure the cat is Brett," I offered without much conviction.

Babs considered this for a moment then reached into her purse and pulled out a silver flask. Unscrewing the top, she took a sip then held it out to me. When I declined, she tipped her head back and took another hearty gulp. Replacing the top, she stowed the flask back in her purse and waited for me to continue, her hands folded in her lap.

I suspected that more than one of my clients packed a silver flask in her purse, but this was the first time I had seen one, much less been invited to share the contents. "It would probably be best to keep him in the house until all this blows over," I managed. Four years of vet school and this was the best I could come up with. But Babs looked relieved. After all, I was a professional.

"Besides, people do like to exaggerate," I added. "It makes the story more exciting."

Babs bobbed her head in agreement. "That's true. Thank you, Dr. McBride. I feel so much better."

I smiled agreeably but Babs's improved outlook likely had more to do with the contents of the flask than my brilliant advice.

"Can you just check to make sure no one is out there?" she asked, as she stuffed Brett back into his carrier.

Given the city's unresolved concerns about wandering cats and the polarized opinions of the public, I supposed a little paranoia wasn't unreasonable. I poked my head out the door and scouted the perimeter. Carter was asleep on the fish tank and Bernie was busy licking envelopes. The rest of the staff used a sponge but for reasons unknown, Bernie liked the taste of envelope stickum.

I gave Babs the "thumbs-up" all-clear signal. She nodded and pulled a kerchief out of her coat pocket. Tying it securely under her chin and donning a pair of sunglasses, she grabbed Brett's carrier and scuttled past Bernie, head down.

"Can't stop," she muttered breathlessly. "I'll pay later."

Puzzled, Bernie looked up, an envelope raised to her lips.

"Do you know there's three calories per envelope?" I asked her.

Bernie, who was always trying to shed a few pounds from somewhere, looked horrified. "Really?"

I nodded. "Really."

The next time I saw her, she had a sponge in one hand and a doughnut in the other. "I just did a hundred stamps with the sponge. That's three hundred calories. I can afford a doughnut," she announced proudly.

I was just thinking how hungry I was when Hughie popped into the office with two monstrous slices of pizza and two cans of pop. He plopped one of each on my desk.

"Oh! You're a lifesaver. I'm starving. Thank you!" I mumbled, tearing into my slice before he even had a chance to sit down. Tomato sauce dribbled down my chin as I took a gulp of pop with one hand and updated medical notes with the other.

Hughie handed me a phone message. "Nothing urgent," he said. Nodding, I slipped it into my lab coat pocket. The two of us polished off our pizza in companionable silence as we worked.

Throughout the rest of the afternoon, I caught Hughie glancing furtively at me whenever I was hunched over the microscope, or rummaging through the cupboards in the treatment area.

"Are you okay?" I asked him.

"Me?" Hughie looked surprised. "Great. Never better. Yup, I'm good."

Hilary looked at me and shrugged her shoulders.

It wasn't until the next morning that I remembered the note I had slipped into my lab coat pocket the day before. It had gone through the wash, rinse, and spin cycles and was now pinned to my bulletin board. Most of the writing was illegible but I could make out two words: "call" and "Dick". There were a million "Dicks" in the world but I knew without asking which one it was. I cornered Hughie in the office.

"What's this?" I asked, dangling the crinkled note in front of him.

Hughie raised his reading glasses to his face and peered at the note. "Looks like paper."

"Well, of course it's paper. Am I supposed to call," I grimaced, "Dick Johnson?"

"Oh!" Hughie had the decency to look sheepish. "I forgot all about that."

"Uh huh." I folded my arms across my chest.

"It seems like ol' Dickie's in a bit of a pickle," Hughie began in a conversational tone. "What would it be like to work there for a week?"

"Let me think. Wait! I know. Like falling into a deep, dark well, getting rabies from a bat, and going mad."

"Mmm," Hughie nodded thoughtfully.

I stared at him. "What do you mean 'Mmm'?"

"Nothing, really. The guy's a turd with a capital T." Hughie sighed and folded his arms across his chest. "He's scheduled to have surgery in a week and his associate just quit."

"Surgery for what?" I asked.

"He wouldn't say," Hughie shook his head. "But he seemed less turdish than usual. I actually felt a little bad for the guy."

"Well, he can get a locum for a week," I retorted. "That's what everyone else does."

"Apparently, he's having trouble getting anyone."

I sniffed. "Well, I'm not going."

"It's totally up to you, Em," Hughie agreed, "although he did offer to pay you double time for the week."

"Double time?" My ears perked up.

"Plus he was going to throw in a new dental hand descaler that he won at a conference. It's a nice descaler," Hughie added wistfully as he picked up the chart for his next patient. "Anyway, it's your decision."

I stewed in the office for a few minutes after Hughie had left, then picked up the phone. Dr. Dick's receptionist informed me that her boss was far too busy to come to the phone. A few hearty smacks from the gum she was chewing broke up the nasal monotony of her voice.

I was in no mood to be trifled with. "Can you please tell him it's Dr. McBride returning his call?"

In less than a nanosecond, Dick had picked up the phone. He snorted and wheezed his way through a series of compliments. When he finished describing what good things he had heard about Ocean View in general, and me in particular, he dropped the bomb.

"It's big, Emily," he sighed.

"Big?" I repeated.

Dick lowered his voice. "And painful. It's got to be removed before it's too late. If it isn't already," he sighed. "It runs in the family."

"Cancer? Oh my God, Dick, I'm so sorry." I waited for the lightning bolt that was reputed to strike the godless. How could I have been so uncaring and insensitive? Dick was, well, a dick. But I wouldn't wish cancer on anyone.

"Of course I'll work for you," I gushed, doing the redemption two-step. "We need to help each other out in these kinds of situations," I added.

"True, so true," Dick sighed again. "And Emily, let's just keep this between us. I wouldn't want people to find out. If it was anywhere else but … you know. We men are sensitive about this kind of thing."

I readily agreed and admired the man's courage.

The day that I was scheduled to begin at Dr. Dick's began in a glorious fashion. The late summer sun had summoned all its reserves and enveloped the entire province in record-breaking temperatures. Benny and I were planning a swim and evening barbecue at the beach. I walked along city streets where gardens still bloomed, humming a cheerful tune.

As I approached the bat cave that was Dr. Dick's hospital, the shadows grew longer, the streets narrower. Leaving the bright day behind me, I descended into the tiny waiting room below ground level. A matching tiny window looked out onto the sidewalk. Several pairs of feet and a skateboard went by as I waited for the receptionist to look up. To be fair, two light bulbs were burnt out so she probably couldn't see me. With her Walkman earphones wedged firmly in place, she probably couldn't hear me either. I tapped on the glass partition.

Eyes still glued to the magazine, the receptionist slid the window across. "Yes?" she sighed. Her nametag identified her as "Monique L., customer service star."

I waited. Monique's star wasn't shining too brightly. When I didn't respond, she looked up from her magazine.

"Yes?" she repeated in an irritated voice.

"I'm Dr. McBride. I'm filling in a few days for Dr. Johnson."

Monique sighed again. Closing the magazine, she wiggled off the stool and began rummaging, unsuccessfully, through her desk. The crumbs from a half-eaten muffin were scattered on the top.

Without a word, she suddenly vanished, leaving me alone with the beige walls. I studied the peeling border, which featured a pack of beagles, armed men on horseback, and a fleeing fox. The scene was repeated every three feet; a rather tasteless bit of décor, I thought, in a place that was supposed to cherish animal life, not cheer on its destruction. On the reception counter, a potted plant clung to life. I shivered although the day was warm.

Monique materialized without warning and thrust a piece of paper in front of me. "Here," she said with an authoritative crack of her gum. "This is your schedule for today."

The phone rang and the glass partition slid back into place. I stood in the middle of reception clutching my schedule until Monique pointed to a smallish door in the farthest corner of the room. Feeling a bit like Alice in Wonderland, I ducked so that I could pass through with my head intact, and entered a strange new world.

Wooden kennels, less easily disinfected than their stainless steel counterparts, occupied half the room. Instead of blankets or towels, patients lay on old newspapers in the still, humid air. Three small windows near the top were shut, presumably because the screens were torn or missing altogether. The cinderblock walls had been painted the colour of stale coffee and notices were stuck to their pock-marked skin with masking tape. Overhead, a fluorescent light fixture flickered. In a corner of the room, a small tabletop fan fought a losing battle against the hot day.

"Hi! I'm Francine," a cheerful voice announced. "You must be Dr. McBride?"

The drab room burst into bloom as a robust woman with curly grey hair entered at the end of a leash. Ahead of her, an exuberant boxer strained to greet me. Cats watched his disorderly approach with a mixture of fear and disdain while the canine patients barked encouragement.

"This is Clarence," Francine added, straining to be heard above the noise. After a year in a feline-only practice, I had forgotten how chaotic and noisy a mixed practice could be.

"Quiet, you people!" Francine ordered and shook her head in the indulgent manner of a parent as she smiled at her charges.

"Hello, Clarence," I grinned, getting down on my knees. Delighted to hear the sound of his own name, Clarence's stump of a tail quivered in excitement.

"He's had explosive diarrhea for three days," Francine warned me. "He just had his first normal poop this morning. And we're so proud of him. Yes, we are!" she declared, giving Clarence a big hug.

I nimbly tried to avoid his tongue. God knows where it had been last.

Francine was dressed in a pair of lilac scrubs. The matching top featured miniature polar bears and icebergs, an unusual combination among animal care technicians in temperate Nova Scotia. Francine had worked as a nurse in the Yukon where she and her husband Dennis met. When they moved to Nova Scotia, she enrolled in the three-year veterinary technician program, fulfilling a lifelong dream. I was immediately drawn to her warmth, good humour, and genuine love of animals. As the day progressed, I realized she was a gifted technician as well. At suppertime, while she waited for Dennis to pick her up after work, I asked her the question that had been on my mind all day.

"You could work anywhere," I said, looking up from my stack of charts. "Why do you work here?"

Francine hesitated. In the darkened ward a dog whimpered, and she called to him.

"Because I'm needed," she said with a gentle smile.

Outside a car tooted. Francine looked at her watch. "Goodness. That'll be Dennis," she said, picking up her coat where it lay waiting on the edge of a chair. "The day went so quickly."

She turned to me. "See you tomorrow, Dr. McBride. Have fun at the beach," she winked.

There is nothing better on a warm summer evening in Nova Scotia than a dip in the ocean after a long day of work in the city. One of the greatest things about Halifax is its easy access to beaches and wilderness just twenty minutes from town. Benny and I frolicked in the water and then snuggled up to a small fire on the beach, where we roasted hotdogs and drank wine. A curious seal poked his head out of the water, the three of us enjoying the calm water and spectacular sunset together.

When I got home that night, I saw the cans of leftover paint that had been sitting in the foyer for the last month with new eyes. My landlord had single-handedly painted all four flats in a weekend marathon with paint that he had purchased on a large-volume, no-return deal. Sick of the colour, he plucked one out of the pile for touch-ups and told me to take the rest. I loaded the cans into the car the next morning and hoped that Bill, my aging Volvo, could handle it. He was ninety-six in human years, although he was still capable of short trips.

Monique eyed me suspiciously when I arrived with four gallons of sage green paint.

"What are you doing with those?"

"Oh, just a few touch-ups," I shrugged.

Francine was delighted. She sent a disgruntled Monique to a nearby department store for some rollers and a drop cloth.

"Oh, and get a new overhead light fixture while you're there," she added.

Monique shook her head. "I don't think Dr. Johnson is going to be happy about this," she muttered darkly as she pulled on her sweater.

Over the next few days, we began transforming the treatment and kennel areas. Francine bought some material from the petty cash fund and made three cheerful toppers for the windows. Dennis repaired the screens so that we could open them, and the flow of fresh air lifted everyone's spirits. I found a lovely dried flower arrangement in Mom's basement, which we placed in the entranceway. Francine thought a contrasting colour for the trim would be a nice accent and I agreed. Despite her prophecies of doom, Monique was dispatched to several other stores for one more can of paint, warm towels to replace the newsprint, and a soothing tabletop fountain for the reception area. After several clients admired the changes, she even stayed one evening to help paint, though she soon collapsed from exhaustion.

"Dr. Johnson is going to be so surprised," Francine declared as she surveyed the room with satisfaction. "I've been wanting to do this for ages."

"Well, you can blame me," I grinned. "Dr. Johnson and I have had our differences but cancer … " I shook my head. "It's the least I can do."

Francine looked at me quizzically as she rinsed a paintbrush in the sink. "What do you mean?"

"Well, just that at a time like this we have to put our differences aside and help each other out." I lowered my voice. "Do you know how bad it is?"

"He's having hemorrhoid surgery," Francine said. "How bad does that get?"

※ ※ ※

"Hemorrhoid surgery?" Hughie repeated when I called in a rage. "And he told you it was cancer?"

"Not exactly," I admitted. "But he might as well have. He set me up."

Hughie chuckled. "I see Dickie's up to his old tricks. Well, I suppose the old fart couldn't get anyone to help." Hughie could afford to be charitable. Dr. Dick had had one of his minions personally deliver the new hand descaler, and I had to admit it was pretty nice.

"What else could he do?" Hughie asked cheerfully.

Gripping the phone, I unleashed a string of suggestions. "Emily, you must rise above this pettiness," Hughie chided with evangelical zeal. "In the big picture does it really matter if it's hemorrhoid surgery or cancer? No," he continued before I could answer. "The man needed help and you were there for him. This is the destiny of the human spirit. We are one." Hughie's voice had risen to a righteous fervor. He lowered it an octave and spoke quietly into the phone.

"How can the drops of water know themselves to be a river?"

"What?"

"It's from The Book of Zen. You should read it sometime," he added.

What was Hughie doing reading The Book of Zen? He read crime novels, spy thrillers, Gary Larson cartoons, and anything relating to Star Trek. It must be that new drug rep.

Francine knocked on the door and handed me the chart for my next patient.

"I've got to go," I told Hughie. I counted to ten. One hundred would have been better but ten was all I had time for.

My next patient was a Sheltie named Precious. I had to admit it was fun seeing a few canine patients for a change. And, for the most part, I had enjoyed my time in the twilight zone. Dr. Dick was back tomorrow. Determined to put his deception behind me, I opened the door to the exam room with a smile.

"Oh!" Hilda Rathbone said in surprise. "I was expecting Dr. Johnson. Just as well. Precious doesn't like him."

At the mention of Dr. Dick's name, Precious's lips curled back, exposing an impressive collection of sharp little teeth.

I took a step closer. Precious braced his front legs and countered with a high-pitched riff. At first, the notes were distinguishable, but they quickly blended into one long scream of outrage in between breaths. Apparently Precious didn't like the veterinary profession in general.

"He's got a lump on the side of his face," Hilda explained.

Oh, great.

Without taking my eyes off him, I reached for the doorknob behind me. "Oh, Francine," I called pleasantly, "could you bring me a sedative for Precious, please?" I smiled at Hilda reassuringly, then added, "As soon as possible?"

In less than a minute, Francine materialized at my side. With help from the pharmaceutical industry and a pair of Kevlar restraint gloves, we were able to subdue Precious. As I examined the lump, a creamy discharge began to seep under my fingers.

"Looks like an abscess," I told Hilda.

"Aha!" Hilda exclaimed. "I thought so."

"Oh?" I said absently as I began cleaning the wound. "What do you mean?"

"Well," Hilda took a deep breath, "I had Precious out for a walk one night and we were followed part of the way by a great big huge tabby cat." Hilda threw her arms wide so I could grasp the enormity of this suburban savage.

"Cats are so sneaky," she shuddered. "My niece has one."

"A tabby cat?" I repeated, keeping my head down as I flushed the wound with saline.

Hilda nodded. "With a green collar. And a really big tail."

Uh oh. This was sounding familiar.

"So, um, what happened?" I asked as I inserted a small Penrose drain into the wound and anchored it in place with a tiny stitch.

"Well, like I said, he followed us for a bit. Then he disappeared. I didn't think any more of it." Hilda shrugged her shoulders. "We got home. I fed Precious on the porch and went in to make my own supper. I was on the phone and I heard this God-awful commotion. There was screaming and yelling. It was horrible!"

She paused before gathering enough strength to continue. "So, I grabbed a knife from the kitchen and went out in my nightie!" Hilda shook her head. "Can you imagine?"

I couldn't.

"Anyway, when I got out there, I saw a striped bushy tail disappearing over the fence. I know it was that cat. I should have reported it to the SPCA!"

All I could think of was poor Babs. "You know," I began, "I've seen a lot of cat bites."

"Dr. McBride works in a cat practice," Francine explained.

"A cat practice?" Hilda was incredulous. "You mean a hospital that treats just cats?" She shuddered. "Really?"

"Really," I smiled. "Most cats are really quite nice. They get into fights now and then just like dogs do. And this is not a cat-bite wound."

"It's not? Are you sure? What about that cat that was following us?"

"Maybe he was just curious. But this is definitely not a cat bite. From what you've said, it might have been a raccoon."

"A raccoon? On LeMarchant Street?" Hilda raised her eyebrows. Clearly, in her opinion, a veterinarian who had chosen cats as a career path might be a few tomatoes short of a thick paste.

"The city has a lot of urban raccoons."

"Oh?"

"They're great little guys. Very clever. But they can be a bit feisty if they're cornered. Like any wild animal," I added.

Hilda clapped a hand over her mouth. "Precious might have been defending the house ... and me. Oh, the brave little dear!"

I suspected that Precious was defending his food bowl and might very well have attacked first, receiving a bite in return for his troubles.

As Hilda stroked his glossy coat, the little dog began to stir. While he was still groggy, we fitted him with a cone-shaped Elizabethan collar so he wouldn't be able to scratch the wound. Francine and I then transferred him to the recovery ward, where he stayed until he was awake enough to go home.

"Well, Dr. McBride, I'm so glad you were here," Hilda declared.

"Me too," I grinned in relief. "And I think it would be best to feed Precious indoors from now on."

It was a humiliated Sheltie who left the hospital a few hours later, his head hung low. I prescribed a course of antibiotics and advised Hilda to return with Precious in a few days to have the drain removed. She was disappointed to learn that I would be gone.

"Can he come to your cat hospital instead?" Hilda asked.

Under the circumstances, I thought it only fitting that Dr. Dick should face the wrath of Precious Rathbone. Besides, our lease allowed Seeing Eye dogs only.

"Oh, well," Hilda sighed. "Thank you again, Dr. McBride."

Precious held his tongue until he was safely outside and then complained bitterly about the service he had received. His complaints were muffled, however, within the plastic cone of shame he wore around his neck, and he soon gave up.

Dr. Dick would be back tomorrow. It was time for me to go too. I completed all my case histories and left a detailed summary for him on the desk. On the way out, Francine gave me a little hug and a bottle of wine. Even Monique slid the window across long enough to say goodbye.

I stepped out into the crush of evening traffic. In the deepening blue of twilight, a few stars competed for attention above the gaudy neon signs of the street. The fresh evening air rushed to greet me and it was with a sense of exhilaration that I pedalled home. I had emerged safely from behind enemy lines and made a new friend in the process.

In my absence, Babs had thinned Brett's bushy tail, started him on a weight loss program and replaced his neon green collar with Nova Scotia tartan. He hadn't been outside in over a week. She was thrilled to learn that he had been found not guilty and bought him a package of his favourite treats to celebrate.

I nestled happily back into my life at Ocean View. In the office, Hughie hummed a cheerful tune as he sorted through lab results, correspondence, and, at Mrs. Tuttle's unsmiling insistence, bills.

"Em, here's one for you," he said, handing me a long, white envelope addressed with Dr. Dick's now-familiar scrawl. Inside were a sizable cheque and a thank-you note.

"See? What did I tell you?" Hughie smiled indulgently.

I nodded, surprised by Dick's generosity.

"Oh, look," he added after a moment, "here's one for me, too."

As he read, Hughie's face turned from pleasantly tanned to blotchy, the skills so recently acquired from The Book of Zen abandoned. In his fist, he dangled a bill for the improvements Francine and I made.

"That cheap son of a _____!"

I took a bite of my sandwich. It was peanut butter and banana, my favourite. I chewed slowly and deliberately, relishing the taste, as I imagined myself a drop of water in a smoothly flowing river.

Chapter 17

MARY HAVERSTOCK WAS AN EX-HIPPIE who had burned her bra in the sixties and never bought a new one. Pendulous breasts hung down to her waist, enjoying their freedom under a tie-dyed T-shirt. As the tenured chair of the university's English department, Mary mingled with the higher tax brackets but wore the same pair of cherished Birkenstock sandals year-round. Her concession to winter was a pair of wool socks.

She removed her round, wire-rimmed glasses and stared at me. "Asthma?"

"Well, it could be. I'd like to run some tests on Woodstock." Ever since her first kitten, a stray found wandering at that famous festival, the parade of cats in Mary's life had all been named Woodstock. Only the Roman numeral after the name changed.

She leaned forward, her anxious face framed by black, ruler-straight hair that hung to her shoulders. "Dr. McBride, how can this happen? He eats only natural food. He drinks bottled water. And I have central vac."

The pair looked at me expectantly.

"Asthma can be an inherited disease or it can develop over time," I explained. "Just like people, cats can become sensitive to certain allergens in their environment, even when their owners are as careful as you are," I acknowledged. "Once they become sensitized, their breathing can be affected."

"How do we treat it?" Mary asked.

"Well," I began, choosing my words with care, "we could put him on a trial course of medication to see how he responds."

"Medication?" Mary's eyes narrowed. "What kind of medication?" She was bitterly opposed to the pharmaceutical industry, capitalism, and anything that wasn't grown in her own garden.

"Anti-inflammatories," I replied, knowing Mary wasn't quite ready to hear the word steroids. "But I think the best approach would be to run some diagnostic tests first."

Mary nodded in agreement. "I'm not one to pop a pill for every little ache or pain. You know me, Dr. McBride."

Indeed I did.

"Did he have supper tonight?" I asked, rummaging for a pen in one of the drawers. My hand closed around a short stalk of black licorice and I released it in disgust. Hughie had recently given up jellybeans for what he claimed was a healthier choice, and now half-eaten pieces of black licorice were popping up everywhere.

"Oh, yes. Chicken livers," Mary replied, rubbing Woodstock's chin.

My hand locked on a pen. Clicking it with a satisfied flourish, I looked up. "Cooked?"

"Of course!" Mary rolled her eyes. "I'm eccentric, Dr. McBride, not crazy."

I made some notes in Woodstock's chart, then explained to Mary that our first step would be a bronchial wash. For that he would need to be sedated, so it was important that there be no food in his stomach. I suggested she bring him back the following morning.

"Tomorrow?" Mary asked in a stricken voice. "But what about breakfast? I can't eat in front of him."

After a year in feline practice, I was no longer surprised at this reaction. Clients would, without hesitation, devour a chocolate sundae in front of their dieting spouses. But their fasting cat? Never.

"If you like, we can settle him in a kennel tonight," I told her, "and do the work-up in the morning. That way we'll be blamed for the lack of breakfast."

"Oh, that's wonderful," Mary breathed. "Although I won't be able to sleep a wink tonight without him."

I scooped the big, gentle cat into my arms. Mary followed me to the recovery ward. Except for Bert Barkhouse, who was sleeping off a three-day adventure in a moving van, the bored in-patients looked up with interest. I noticed a piece of licorice on top of the centrifuge and quickly whisked it out of sight.

"Oh, Dr. McBride," Mary said mournfully as she gazed back at the little faces behind the steel bars. "This is like a kitty prison."

I assured her that everyone was fine and would be going home tomorrow. Nevertheless, Mary decided that she should stay for a while to ease Woodstock's transition from beloved house pet to prisoner. He curled up for a snooze while she sat in a chair beside his kennel and marked English papers.

The evening passed quickly, due in no small part to a feisty little Abyssinian with an ingrown claw and multiple personalities. By the time we had trimmed the offending nail and cleaned up the wound it had left in her foot pad, it was almost closing time. I had forgotten about Mary until I saw her bob past the reception counter.

"What happened to Dr. Haverstock?" I asked Hilary, returning to the treatment area. "She looked like she was limping a bit when she left."

Hilary wrinkled her nose and pointed to Woodstock's kennel. There, next to the water dish, sat a single Birkenstock sandal. Clients often left a familiar object to help comfort the hospitalized patient in their absence. But this was our first shoe – a smelly, weathered testament to love.

As I was wondering why Mary couldn't simply have left her sweater or batik scarf, the phone rang, an ominous sound at five minutes before closing time. Tanya came rushing back to the recovery ward.

"Theodora McWhirtle's on the phone," she announced.

"Ah, one of yours, Em." Hughie visibly relaxed.

"She's found a cat covered in tumours," Tanya added, "and wants to bring him in right away."

Hughie glanced at me as he pulled on his coat. "A cat? Is Theodora branching out?"

Theodora had been one of my first, albeit reluctant, clients when I arrived as a new associate just over a year ago. She had called about a pair of guinea pigs that she neither wanted nor liked. Won over by their endearing antics and friendly dispositions, she now cared for a dozen or so rescues in her luxurious south end home. And I was their personal physician.

I shrugged my shoulders and sighed. "Tell her okay."

While I waited for Theodora, I checked on a couple of in-patients. Bernie counted the cash and balanced the day's transactions while Hilary vacuumed the floors. Tanya followed with the mop. This was generally the winding-down time of the day; the lights were dimmed and patients settled quietly in their kennels. But not tonight.

I heard an anxious rapping on the glass, followed by Theodora's equally anxious voice as Bernie unlocked the doors.

"Oh, thank you! Thank you so much!" Theodora gushed, rushing inside. "I don't know what I would have done if you hadn't been here." A heavyset policeman followed behind Theodora, with a large black cat embedded in his uniform.

"Dr. McBride!" Theodora cried as I came around the corner. "Thank God!" She motioned for the police officer to follow us into the exam room.

"Quickly," she urged him. Her face was flushed and her normally elegant upsweep was drifting downwards. I noticed an assortment of leaves cemented to one of her high heels by a wad of chewing gum.

"What do you think?" Theodora asked breathlessly as I pulled the cat free from the policeman's chest, one claw at a time. The poor man's jacket looked like it was riddled with miniature bullet holes.

"Well," I replied with a smile, "I should probably examine him first."

"Oh yes, of course!" Theodora nodded vigorously. "How silly of me.

I'm just so worried."

"It's all right," I hastened to assure her as I began to examine the cat. He was shaped like a football: narrow at both ends with a wide middle. If he was a stray, he hadn't been a stray for long.

"I was on my way to the community theatre when I saw the poor creature huddled by a dumpster," Theodora explained. "I just couldn't leave him there. And it's such a cool evening." She turned to the policeman. "He should be sitting at home in a nice warm lap. Don't you think so, Officer?"

Without waiting for his reply, Theodora continued, "Officer Turnbull was directing traffic around an accident. Some kind of minor fender-bender. But I convinced him this could be a life-or-death situation."

The policeman allowed himself a faint smile. "Well, I'm a bit of an animal lover. And it is a bit cool out there for September."

"Global warming!" Theodora sniffed. "I don't believe in it. Anyway, it's lovely and warm in here."

"A little too warm," I apologized as the policeman unzipped his jacket, revealing a ribbed bullet-proof vest underneath. "The building manager says it's some kind of seasonal changeover and that the air-conditioning system is confused." I rolled my eyes lest either of these two people thought I was buying the story.

I turned my attention back to the patient. Theodora hovered in anxious silence as I palpated his internal organs. His temperature was normal, his teeth and gums healthy. Except for the extra pounds he packed, he seemed in pretty good shape. I raised the stethoscope to my ears and listened to his chest.

"Sounds good," I said at length, draping the stethoscope around my neck. "So where are these tumours you found?"

"Oh my goodness, Dr. McBride. They're everywhere!" Theodora exclaimed. "The poor soul!"

"Could you show me?" I asked.

Theodora glanced at me in surprise. "Well, I suppose I could," she replied in a doubtful voice. Clearly, she felt this was my job.

Taking a deep breath, she leaned over the cat, her pearl necklace dangling tantalizingly close to his face. He eyed the shimmering white balls with a mixture of curiosity and restraint. "There's a good pussy," Theodora told him. "This won't hurt a bit."

With the cat's attention riveted on the necklace, Theodora began probing his abdomen with her fingers. Almost immediately, she found what she was looking for. "Here, Dr. McBride," she announced. "Feel this. And there's another large one right next to it."

As instructed, I leaned over and felt the lump of tissue in Theodora's grip.

"What do you think?" she repeated, as I felt the cat's groin and lifted up his tail.

"Oh!" I shrunk backwards.

"I knew it was bad." Theodora's eyes shimmered with the faint sheen of veiled tears. "How much time does he have?"

"Well … "

"I know they're discovering new things all the time," she interrupted. "Maybe there's an experimental program somewhere? Special diets? Radiation? Money is of no concern."

"Well … "

The policeman wiped his forehead with his hand. In the uncomfortably warm room, he was beginning to perspire under the heavy uniform and vest. "Ma'am, I … "

Theodora held up a silencing finger. "Dr. McBride, you can tell me the truth."

"These lumps you feel?" I asked. Theodora nodded vigorously. "They're rolls of fat."

Theodora stared at me, then at the cat. Officer Turnbull's

increasingly ragged snorts of breath filled the silence.

"Dr. McBride," Theodora said at last, "I appreciate that you're trying to be kind, I really do, but I've been through worse."

"I'm not trying to be kind."

"You're not?"

"No. These are rolls of fat. He will have to go on a special diet so he can lose some weight."

"Oh, Dr. McBride! This is wonderful news!" Theodora turned a rapturous face toward Officer Turnbull. "I told you she was a gifted veterinarian. Tell your friends. And thank you so much for bringing me here tonight. I'm not sure how I would have managed."

"To serve and protect, ma'am," he grinned weakly. "I'll be off then."

"There's just one thing."

The police officer, his hand on the doorknob, turned around to look at me.

"He has an abscess we'll need to repair," I explained. "It's a little nasty because it's been there for awhile."

"Oh dear. Where?" Theodora asked.

As both she and Officer Turnbull leaned forward for a closer look, I lifted the cat's tail. He had a ruptured abscess about the size of a loonie on his backside. It would need to be cleaned and surgically repaired under anesthetic.

"What are those little white things crawling around?" Theodora asked.

"Maggots," I replied matter-of-factly. "That happens sometimes with an open wound, especially if the cat's been living outdoors."

"I see," Theodora nodded. "Well, I'm just so happy you can fix him up. Now we'll have to find him a nice home and … "

She was interrupted by a dull thud as the police officer slid down the wall onto the floor.

"Good God and Heavenly Father!" Theodora stared at Officer

Turnbull in horror. "Should we call 911?"

I knelt down beside him. "Are you all right?" I asked. He was conscious but breathing heavily. I eased him out of his jacket and vest and, with Theodora's help, got him into a chair. We opened both doors to the exam room and a refreshing mix of cooler air from reception flowed through. Bernie appeared with a tall glass of cool water, which he drained.

"Sorry, ladies," he said with a sheepish grin. "Just got a little overheated, I guess. And the maggots … " He shook his head and left the sentence unfinished.

"What maggots?" Bernie whispered. "Where?"

I pointed to the cat perched on the examining table, watching the proceedings with interest. With a shudder, Bernie took a few steps back.

"Should I call anyone?" I asked Officer Turnbull. "Another police officer? Family? Friend?"

"No, really, I'll be fine." Embarrassed, he rose to his feet. His colour had improved dramatically and his respiration was back to normal, although he avoided looking in the direction of the cat. His walkie-talkie, which had been cackling intermittently with police business throughout the visit, squawked again. Officer Turnbull acknowledged it, then put his vest and jacket back on.

"I'll be going then," he announced, tipping his hat. "Goodnight, ladies. I'm glad that cat's going to be okay."

"Are you sure you're okay?" Theodora asked. "Perhaps I should drive?"

Officer Turnbull turned around, his eyes twinkling. "Thank you, ma'am, but civilians aren't supposed to drive squad cars."

"Oh yes, of course," Theodora acknowledged. As he climbed into his car and headed back out into the night, Theodora picked up her coat, which was draped over one of the chairs.

"My, though, it would have been fun," she sighed, following me back to the surgical ward.

Hilary had settled the cat and all his squiggly little companions in a kennel. I planned to give him a good meal tonight, then repair the abscess in the morning. Hopefully we would be able to locate his owner. Theodora offered to put up posters and contact the local radio stations that provided a lost-and-found-pet service. She explained all this to the big black cat, who eyed her impassively from behind the bars of his kennel.

"What a night," Theodora said, shaking her head. She sat down in a chair to remove the wad of gum on her shoe and came face to face with Woodstock in the kennel across from her. For the second time that evening, I heard her exclaim, "Good God and Heavenly Father!"

I turned in alarm. "What?"

"Is that Mary Haverstock's cat?" Theodora asked, pointing to Woodstock.

"Yes, do you know him?" I asked in surprise.

"By reputation only," Theodora replied, "but I'd know that shoe anywhere. Mary and I are members of the Halifax Chapter of the Royal African Violet Society. Mary can work wonders with an African violet, but … " She shook her head as she stared at the shoe.

"Ms. McWhirtle?" Hilary popped her head in the door. "Your taxi is here."

"Oh, thank you, dear." Theodora turned toward me. "And thank you, Dr. McBride. What an interesting evening! Goodbye, dear. Get a good night's sleep."

"I'm going to have dinner and go straight to bed," I replied before I realized that Theodora was talking to the cat.

By the time I got home that night, it was almost ten. True to my plan, I had some leftovers with a glass of wine and fell asleep shortly thereafter. It was a good plan that went awry shortly after eleven, when Hughie hit the wrong button on his speed dial. As the cats scurried for cover, I fumbled for the phone.

"Hullo?" I mumbled groggily into the phone.

There was a pause. "Emily?"

I sat up straight in bed. "Oh, for God's sake! Not again!"

"Oops. Sorry, Em. What are you doing in bed this early anyway?" Hughie asked. "It's only eleven."

"I was sleeping. What are you doing calling somebody at this hour? It's that damn redhead again, isn't it? This is the second time this month!"

"McBride, McBurney. You see my problem?"

"Wear your glasses then." I hung up the phone and tossed and turned for another hour before finally drifting off. In one of my dreams, someone who looked suspiciously like Hughie was being chased by an evil-looking creature with multiple heads. I awoke refreshed.

In fact, everyone involved in last night's drama seemed happy. Officer Turnbull was back at work. The theatre graciously allowed Theodora, one of their largest contributors, to exchange her ticket for another performance. And Hughie hadn't stopped humming all morning. Only the stray, christened Jimmy Ray by the staff, seemed upset over our failure to provide breakfast. Surgery required fasting, an unpopular concept among cats in general and fat cats in particular.

I repaired his abscess then spent the rest of the morning proving beyond reasonable doubt for Mary's sake that Woodstock was indeed asthmatic. A complete blood count (CBC) had ruled out infection while also revealing an increase in cells called eosinophils, common among patients with asthma.

We snapped a pair of X-rays, then anesthetized Woodstock and carried him into surgery for a bronchial wash. I inserted a sterile breathing tube into his airway and injected a few millilitres of sterile solution into the lungs. Using suction, I drew it back into a syringe. Again, the cells collected showed a higher than normal number of eosinophils.

We had a definite diagnosis of a treatable condition. I was pleased for Woodstock, for Dr. Haverstock, and for myself.

"See these thickened airways?" I asked Mary Haverstock as we stood side by side in front of the X-ray viewer. She leaned in for a closer look.

"Woodstock is definitely suffering from asthma," I continued. "We'll need to put him on a trial course of steroids."

Mary studied the X-rays in silence as I hastened to explain that low doses of steroids in cats posed minimal health risks. "Woodstock will be happier and healthier," I concluded.

She turned toward me, our faces only inches apart. "What about his sex drive?"

"Pardon me?"

"His sex drive," Mary repeated. "Steroids can diminish desire and cause impotence." Mary's round eyes never blinked behind her glasses.

I hesitated, never having considered the effects of steroids on my patients' sex drives. Most were neutered; sex was the last thing on their minds. Mary, on the other hand, believed neutering was unnatural and willingly assumed financial and moral responsibility for any chips off Woodstock's old block.

"We're using a corticosteroid on Woodstock," I explained. "The problem you mentioned can be true for human males on high dosages of anabolic steroids."

Mary nodded. "I used to know a weight lifter in the athletics department."

"Oh?" I remarked encouragingly but Mary remained close-mouthed as she studied the X-rays.

"Well," she said at last, "I'll try these pills if you think it's the best thing for Woodstock, and we'll see how it goes." She collected her Birkenstock, her cat, and a month's supply of prednisone. After studying the bottle suspiciously, she dropped it into her briefcase.

"Keep in touch," I told Mary as I helped her out to the car, an aging

Volkswagen Beetle. "We need to find the lowest dosage that works for him."

Mary got into her car. "Oh, by the way, Dr. McBride," she said, rolling her window down, "my friend Theodora called me today to see how Woodstock made out. She said she was in last night with a cat emergency."

"Yes, it was quite an evening," I smiled.

"She's a lovely person but … ," Mary shook her head, "all those rats she keeps in the house."

"Guinea pigs," I corrected her.

"Tailless rats!" Mary shuddered. She rolled up her window and careened out of the parking lot. Little pebbles flew in the wake of her heavy Birkenstock-clad foot.

While Mary spent the next two weeks reluctantly doling out pills to Woodstock, Theodora visited Jimmy Ray regularly. She felt responsible for his care and insisted on paying for his treatment and hospitalization until a permanent home could be found. If her own home had not been overrun with domesticated rodents, I think she might have adopted him herself. The big cat lay in her lap as she brushed his coat and told him about her guinea pigs. He was attentive and respectful, but he seemed sad. I was convinced he was lost, not abandoned. But despite Theodora's advertising campaign we had received no concerned phone calls or inquiries.

I did, however, receive a disgruntled call from Mary about two weeks after we started Woodstock on prednisone. According to Mary, he was absolutely no better.

"Those pills aren't working at all!"

"Mmm. Are you sure he's getting them down?"

"Well, of course he is," Mary sniffed. "I'm doing them myself."

I knew Mary's eyes were rolling at my failure to comprehend the obvious. In her view, I was incompetent and had spent a lot of her money proving it. Still, I had a definitive diagnosis. I couldn't understand why the medication wasn't helping.

"Anyway," Mary continued, "I'm going away for a few days so I'm just going to stop the pills. Since they're not working," she added pointedly.

I cautioned her that it would be very hard on Woodstock to stop the pills all at once. Patients receiving prednisone need to be slowly weaned off the drug to allow the adrenal glands time to return to normal function. Since Theodora was going to be looking after Mary's plants in her absence, she volunteered to give Woodstock his pills as well. I told Theodora to call me if she had any trouble.

Saturday's outpatient clinic was unusually quiet that week and I was hoping to finish on time for once. I vaccinated a handful of cats, doled out some behavioural advice, and took an X-ray on a lame cat. It appeared to be nothing more than a strain so I sent him home with some pain medication and advised the owners to keep him quiet for a couple of days. By the time I finished updating his medical record, a phone message for me on yellow note paper had appeared on the bulletin board.

I glanced at my watch. One forty-five; we closed at two. With a growing sense of dread, I walked toward the bulletin board and snatched the yellow harbinger of doom from the tack that held it in place.

"Call Theodora McWhirtle," it ordered. "Urgent." Underneath, a phone number was listed. With a sigh, I sat back down at the desk and called Theodora. She answered on the first ring.

"Oh, Dr. McBride! You'll never guess what!"

"What?" I dutifully replied.

"I believe I have just outsmarted a cat!"

I hesitated. It was a bold statement that few cat owners could make, let alone a guinea pig owner. "Is Woodstock okay?" I asked, ignoring the tic in my left eye. I was supposed to be pitching at a softball game in less than an hour.

"He will be," Theodora announced. The excitement in her voice was infectious. I sat up straight in the chair.

"I'm at Mary's house," Theodora continued, "and you're not going to believe this! Mary's a terrible housekeeper so I just did a little tidying up while I was here. I couldn't resist. I mean, who can appreciate the beauty of African violets surrounded by old newspapers and toast crumbs?"

"Terrible," I murmured, glancing at my watch.

"Anyway, when I moved some of the newspapers to dust, you will never guess what I found."

I was beginning to get an idea but I didn't want to spoil Theodora's story.

"A pile of gooey white pills," Theodora exclaimed. "Behind a pyramid of newspapers! That cat is smarter than Mary!"

I leaned back in my chair with a smug smile of satisfaction. So, I was not such an incompetent idiot after all. Woodstock was not the first cat, and would certainly not be the last, to find a creative solution to avoid taking medication.

"What do you think of my discovery, Dr. McBride?" Theodora asked with a touch of pride. "Do you want me to bring him in right now?"

"No, no," I hastened to assure her. "Try grinding up the pill into a powder and just mix it with some tuna juice so he thinks he's getting a treat. And make sure you tell Mary everything."

"Oh, you can be sure I will!" Theodora declared.

By the time Mary returned a few days later, Woodstock was already doing much better and was delighted with his daily dose of tuna juice. An embarrassed Mary actually apologized to me and made a sizeable donation toward Jimmy Ray's care. We tested him for both feline leukemia and the feline immunodeficiency virus, then vaccinated and dewormed him. Pronounced fat but healthy, he was allowed to roam throughout the hospital. He appeared destined to become Resident Number Five, until a threadbare teenager showed up one cold, wet afternoon.

She was pretty but, unlike most girls her age, doing her best to hide that fact. Her dark hair, streaked with ribbons of purple, looked like it had been cut with a pair of garden shears. She had no tattoos, no piercings, no style of dress that conformed with any teenage code. I had the feeling that regardless of her past, or maybe because of it, this girl was fiercely independent.

"He's my cat!" she announced, glaring at Bernie.

"Luv, I'm not saying he isn't your cat," Bernie began carefully. "It's just that … "

"Well, where is he?" the girl demanded.

The staff had become fond of Jimmy Ray and wanted only the best for him. This waif in army boots and lugging a tattered knapsack didn't look like she could care for herself, much less a pet. I understood Bernie's concern.

"I'll take you to see him," I interrupted. "My name's Dr. McBride," I added in a conversational tone.

Ignoring my outstretched hand, the girl tugged her jacket close against her chest. She stared at me underneath lids weighed down by heavy black makeup.

"I've been looking after Jimmy Ray since he arrived," I tried again.

"His name's Onyx," the girl replied icily.

Scowling, she followed me to the storage area where Jimmy Ray aka Onyx was asleep on a heap of warm towels in the laundry basket. The resident cats loved this room with its secret hiding places, subdued lighting, and easy access to fifty different types of food. Seeing him, the girl drew a sharp breath and held her hands up to her face.

"Onyx?" she whispered, dropping to her knees. "Onyx?"

Like threads of gossamer, her voice rippled on unseen air currents toward the big cat sleeping in the basket. His ears twitched at the familiar, yet unfamiliar, memory of her scent and sound until it broke through the sleep barrier. Opening his eyes, he chirped in joyful recognition.

I sat quietly on the step stool a few feet away. Outside the storage room doors, a skateboarder rumbled past on the concrete sidewalk. It was suppertime. As the lights changed at the intersection, I could hear the muffled sounds of cars on the side street as the drivers inched them forward, hoping to make a left turn and get home. Inside, the big, black cat purred with contentment as the girl held him close, her body trembling.

"How did you find out he was here?" I asked at last.

The girl pushed back the wall of hair that hid her delicate face. "Elmer," she answered.

"Officer Turnbull? How do you know him?"

"He volunteers at a place … a place I stay once in awhile." I looked at the skinny kid on the floor who probably went hungry sometimes so her cat could eat.

The girl misinterpreted my silence.

"It's not like you think!" she said angrily. "I rescued Onyx from some rock-throwing assholes. I take good care of him. You're not supposed to have pets at that place so I had to sneak him in, and then some jerk left the window open."

"Look, I didn't mean … " I left my sentence unfinished. The girl had gone back to ignoring me. Spying a used carrier, I stood on the step stool and hauled it down from the shelf.

"Here. You can have this carrier to travel with him. That way there's less chance of him getting lost."

She nodded. Squirming out of her jacket, she began stuffing it inside the kennel. I looked around the room. Clients were always leaving things behind when their cats boarded and never bothered to return for them. I picked up a wool blanket and handed it to her. September nights were cool. The kid was going to need her jacket, however sparse it might be.

She made a comfortable nest for him and then we eased Onyx into the carrier. "He's a little overweight," I grunted as I lifted the big cat.

For the briefest of moments, we shared a smile.

"This door leads outside?" she asked abruptly, pointing to the delivery door.

Nodding, I held the large steel door open as she slipped through. She cradled the carrier gingerly so as not to bump its purring occupant. On the sidewalk she paused.

"May," she said, turning around. "My name's May. Like the month."

Chapter 18

Most domestic housecats have three basic goals. Those are, in no particular order, a full food bowl, a twenty-hour daily rest period, and attention on demand. Occasionally, I come across a cat with an agenda different from the rest of his or her peers. RosaLeigh was one of those cats.

"There's a cat outside your door," Mavis Bennett announced one evening as she stood at the reception counter, waiting to pay her bill. "I always knew this was a good place," she joked, "but now the cats are lining up to see the vet?"

Bernie peered over the edge of the counter, squinting against the last rays of the evening sun. It was low in the sky and appeared as a golden bump on the ridge of the house next door. Long shadows stretched across the parking lot toward our door. A thin black cat sat demurely at the edge of one of those shadows and stared inside.

"Oh, 'tis probably one of the wee youngsters that lives in the house down the street. There's eight or nine of them live there and not one spayed or neutered." Bernie clucked her tongue in disapproval. "They come up in the evening sometimes for treats at the Tim Hortons."

The little cat ran off when Mavis's taxi tooted, but was back less than ten minutes later.

Her mouth opened and closed in a request silenced by the double set of glass doors. Rising on her hind feet, she pawed the door, stopping every so often to see if anyone was watching. Bernie relented and opened the door. The cat rushed inside, her tail upright in the high-noon position. In an outpouring of gratitude, she wrapped herself around Bernie's legs and purred.

"Oh, you wee, sweet puss." With considerable effort, Bernie bent down to pick her up. There had been a recent mishap in Bernie's ballroom dancing class involving a pair of high heels and an exuberant dance partner. She had been off work for several days and her dancing career was on hold for at least another couple of weeks.

"Here, Bernie," I said, holding my arms out. "I can carry her."

The little cat's head bobbed with interest as I carried her back to the treatment area. Her deep, resonating purr was interrupted several times, however, by a sneezing fit and mucous bubbled out of her nose with each breath.

While Hilary prepared a kennel in the isolation ward, I began to examine this curious little cat who, unlike ninety-nine per cent of our patients, had chosen to be here. Immediately, I noticed that she had a neurological condition known as Horner's syndrome affecting her right eye. A severe infection in her middle ear was impinging on the nerves that control the size of the pupil and the nictitating membrane, or third eyelid as it is known. Further examination revealed outer ear infections on both sides. She must have been suffering for a long, long time.

"Yoo-hoo! Dr. McBride?" I heard the familiar swish of support hose coming toward me. "Ah, there you are, luv," Bernie declared as she wound her way through the food order, which had not yet made its way to the shelves. "Mrs. Pugsley just called to say she and Hermione won't be coming to see you tonight because one of them is up a tree and won't come down."

I wasn't surprised. Hermione had a sixth sense about trips to the vet and routinely disappeared just before her scheduled appointment.

This left time to run a combo test on the stray cat before closing. With her full co-operation, we withdrew a blood sample to check for both feline leukemia and the feline immunodeficiency virus. I knew, as did the staff, that a positive result in a sick cat was very bad news. Yet this little black cat had somehow found her way to a place that could help. Surely fate wouldn't be that cruel. I held her in my arms as she rubbed my face and kneaded against my neck, seemingly oblivious to her pain.

We spent an anxious ten minutes waiting to see if the test spot would turn the telltale blue of a positive result. Sometimes it turned blue right away. Other times, it didn't and we would begin to relax, chatting about our day, our plans for the weekend, movies we had seen. Then, when we least expected it, a faint blue thief would creep in and steal our hope.

The egg timer's strident clanging announced that ten minutes of our lives had passed. We gathered around the lab counter. Hilary looked up with a triumphant grin. "Negative," she announced.

"What's negative?" Hughie asked, striding into the room and joining the huddle.

"The combo test for that little black cat." Hilary pointed to the isolation window. "She's a stray."

"Oh?" Hughie said, peering through the window into the isolation ward.

"She was waiting outside the door half the night to come in," Bernie explained.

"So, did she just open the door, waltz in, and ask if we had a vacancy?"

"Well ... I let her in," Bernie admitted.

"Uh-huh."

"Go see her," I urged. I understood Hughie's reluctance to take in yet another stray. Three of our twelve boarding suites in the Cat Nap Inn were currently occupied by stray cats, one of them pregnant. Sometimes we had to turn away paying clients who wanted to board their cats. The hospital's bills still had to be paid even in the months when expenses were greater than income. But we would never turn away an animal that needed help.

With a backward glance at us, Hughie opened the door to the isolation ward. He was still in there after I had finished all my phone calls and updated my charts for the evening. I looked in though the window. The little cat was asleep on his lap. Quietly, I opened the door and sat down beside him.

"She has Horner's syndrome," he said.

I nodded. "I noticed that."

"And the worst bilateral ear infections I've ever seen – along with a God-awful cold." He was silent for a moment, his hand caressing the little face. I noticed his lab coat was spattered with tiny drops of blood-tinged mucous.

"Tell Hilary no more food tonight," he said. "We'll schedule her for skull X-rays tomorrow and clean out those ears while she's under. I've started her on antibiotics. It's going to be a long haul."

I murmured my thanks, but Hughie brushed it aside. "Go on home. I'll see you in the morning."

As it turned out, Hughie didn't see me until almost noon. The dentist's office called that morning to say they could squeeze me in to repair the gaping hole in one of my molars. Most of the filling had fallen out a few nights ago while I was in the middle of a chicken stir-fry, although there was nothing more tooth-threatening in the meal than a few crisp veggies and a handful of deep-fried egg noodles. The sharp edges of what remained of the tooth gnawed like a hacksaw against the inside of my cheek. Despite my best efforts to control it, my tongue had a mind of its own and kept exploring the black hole in morbid fascination.

The dentist clicked her own tongue in disapproval when she peered inside. As I lay in the dentist's chair, my feet higher than my head and my mouth propped open like a live trap, I could only blink in wide-eyed alarm.

"We'll use lots of painkillers," she assured me.

By the time I returned to work a few hours later, Hughie had taken some skull X-rays and was cleaning the stray's outer ears. "Take a look," he said, nodding at the X-ray viewer.

I flipped the switch, bringing the images to life. Normally, the middle ear is full of air and appears black in radiographs. But the pictures before me revealed dense, white areas indicating pus-filled chambers in both ears. Bilateral infections are uncommon and confirmed that the infection was very advanced. Hughie applied eardrops to both ears.

"There's no evidence of polyps in the back of her throat or outer ears," he added. This at least was good news. Polyps are abnormal tubular growths that project from a mucous membrane. From the Eustachian tube they can grow either down into the throat or up into the middle ear, where they can puncture the eardrum.

"Whaddya think?" he asked, massaging the drops deep into the outer ear. While the drops would have no effect on the middle ears, they would help resolve the inflammation and infection in her outer ears.

"Wull, ah donh … " Quickly, I shut my mouth. I hadn't talked to anyone since leaving the dentist's office.

"What's the matter, Em? Cat got your tongue?" Hughie chuckled at his own wit.

True to her word, the dentist had used enough analgesic for a horse. I checked my chin for drool.

"There you go, little girl," Hughie said gently to the sleeping cat. He removed his gloves and, leaning over on the stool, turned off the anesthetic machine. Now only pure oxygen flowed into her lungs as he waited for her to wake up.

"Wha di you …?"

Hughie held up his hand. "Are you actually seeing clients this morning, Em?"

I shook my head no.

"Well, thank God." Hughie picked up the toenail clippers and began trimming the stray's nails. When he was done, he stood up and stretched his shoulder and neck muscles.

The little cat followed suit, pawing the air as she began to wake up. Hughie removed the endotracheal tube and carried her to the recovery ward. She had been under anesthetic for just over an hour, so we covered her with a warm afghan and placed a heated pad at her back.

"She's going to need a bulla osteomy to get at that mess in her middle ear," Hughie said, gently closing her kennel door. "That's not something I can do. She'll have to see an orthopedic surgeon."

Tanya was cleaning a kennel in the ward. "What's a bulla osteomy?" she asked.

"We drill a hole through the base of the skull just below the joint of the jaws to get at the middle ear," Hughie explained.

"Yuck," Tanya grimaced. "I wouldn't want anyone drilling in my head."

"It's the only way we can get at that raging infection," Hughie told her. "There's no other option. We can't allow her to suffer like this. And I'm pretty sure all you guys would quit if we euthanized her," he smiled gently.

"Dr. D," Susan interrupted, dangling a chart in front of Hughie, "your appointment is still waiting and she's not getting any happier about it."

Hughie sighed and rolled his eyes as he reached for the chart. "Em, can you call Armview Heights and see if Randawa does this kind of surgery? Otherwise she'll have to go to the vet college, and logistically that's going to be difficult."

I had never met Dr. Randawa. He was a visiting orthopedic surgeon who held a referral clinic two days a month at Armview Heights Vet Hospital.

"Oh, and Em," Hughie called out as I turned to leave, "wait until you don't sound like you just polished off a six-pack. I have my reputation to think of."

Had I been quick-witted and physically able, I would have had a snappy retort. But by the time outpatient appointments began, I could at least wrap my tongue around most one-syllable words. Armview Heights returned my call and scheduled our little stray for surgery the following week. In the meantime, we were to continue with the antibiotics.

The receptionist warned me that the surgery would be very expensive and that they would not be able to offer a professional discount. "You'll have to pay what anyone else would pay," she declared. "Dr. Randawa is not an employee of our hospital. We have no control over him. He surfs all over the world," she added as if this somehow explained their inability to control his surgical fees.

"We have to give her a name," Hilary announced when I got off the phone. "We can't just keep calling her the little black stray."

The staff debated this for some time and finally agreed upon RosaLeigh. It was a name I hadn't heard in a long time. In Grade 3, a little girl named RosaLeigh joined our class midway through the year. She was the first person I ever knew who wore braces. That didn't stop her from eating Oh Henry chocolate bars and then spending an hour afterwards removing the telltale goo from her hardware. She was kind, spunky, and loved animals. We were best friends until her family moved away a year and a half later, and I never forgot her.

RosaLeigh was a perfect name.

Because of her infection we weren't able to vaccinate RosaLeigh, so she remained in the isolation ward. She seemed fascinated by the hustle and bustle of the treatment area visible through the window of the isolation ward. Hughie fashioned her a perch from a mandarin orange box and she sat on it like a queen, surveying the daily parade of cats and owners. The staff spent every spare minute they had with her.

It was a testament to RosaLeigh's strength and will to survive that she seemed able to rise above her own pain, perhaps because she had lived with it for so long. But even more extraordinary, she seemed to sense pain in others, a fact I learned first-hand when I developed a painful infection in my tooth.

"Just the luck of the draw," the dentist had said cheerfully, and prescribed a course of antibiotics.

There was nothing lucky about it. Feeling sorry for myself, I donned an isolation-ward lab coat and sat down with RosaLeigh. Instead of kneading for a few minutes then curling up on my lap, she seemed unsettled. She raised her front paws against my chest and rubbed her little face against my own. Every so often, she stopped and looked at me. I felt the warm sting of tears forming in my eyes, not for myself, but for the selfless little creature who had endured so much.

I kissed her forehead and told her we would both be fine.

And indeed, in a few days I was. By then, it was time for RosaLeigh's surgery. We had withheld her breakfast that morning and RosaLeigh was not the least bit pleased about it. She groveled and whined and howled to no avail. Poor Hilary had been assigned the task of driving her to Armview Heights, about ten kilometres away. We lined the inside of her carrier with Hughie's favourite fleece jacket.

"No vomit," he warned her. "And especially no poop!"

We allowed ourselves a brief smile, but everyone was well aware of the delicate nature of this surgery. At best this little cat would be given a fighting chance against a debilitating and deep-seated infection. At worst, she could end up with severe nerve damage and eventually die from septicemia as the infection spread throughout her body. Her desperate cries as Hilary left haunted me.

Fortunately, Max Slocum was able to take my mind off RosaLeigh, if only for a little while. Max was a healthy six-week-old kitten with an appetite for adventure and no common sense, a perilous combination. His latest foray into a glass vase with a narrow neck and bulbous bottom was the reason for the visit. Most cats arrive in a carrier or at the end of a harness. Max arrived in a hundred-year-old Georgian crystal vase. Denise, his owner, was perfectly willing to break the vase but was worried about hurting Max in the process.

"I thought if he could get in by himself he could get out," Denise sighed.

While I considered Max's predicament, Ernie strolled into the exam room. Max twirled round in his vase for a better view. The big cat sat tantalizingly close, his great plume of a tail twitching with studied disinterest. It was more than the kitten could stand.

Pushing his little hind legs against the base of the vase with all the strength he could muster, he stretched into the neck of the vase. It was just enough for me to grip the scruff of his neck and ease him out the rest of the way. He leapt off Denise's lap and trotted happily into reception after Ernie.

Karen, Denise's friend and designated driver, was sitting in the rocker with Tina Louise. While Tina stared haughtily at Max, I scooped him up before he could get into any more trouble.

"I see you got the genie out of the bottle," Karen smiled as Max squirmed in my arms.

I laughed. "With help from one of my furry associates."

"He's quite the character," Karen agreed. "I'd love to have a cat."

"Oh?" My ears perked up. "That can be arranged."

Karen shook her head. "It's just not a good time right now. Plus I'm in a no-pets building."

"You could always move," Denise said helpfully.

"If your situation changes, let us know. We always have cats looking for homes," I told Karen as I gently transferred Max to Denise's waiting arms. "And I will see you, young man, in a couple of weeks for your booster."

"If he doesn't get into any trouble before then," Denise grinned.

After they had gone, I went back to the treatment area. Ernie trotted down the hall ahead of me, his three years of the good life swinging from side to side with each step. At the empty food bowl he looked up plaintively with a look that said, "Hey, lady, you owe me."

I opened the lid of the treat jar. It was like opening the floodgates of the Hoover Dam. A river of cats poured down the hallway and pooled in the treatment area. The general consensus was that I owed everyone. While they munched away, Susan looked up from the tray of instruments she was preparing to autoclave.

"Have you heard anything from Armview Heights?" she asked.

I shook my head.

"Do you think we should call?"

I looked at my watch. "It's only been half an hour."

"Yeah," Susan sighed. "I know."

People who work in veterinary practices make the worst clients. Maybe it's because we know too much. Whoever said "Ignorance is bliss" was right. I did call Armview around noon and while the receptionist was very sympathetic, she had nothing to report. RosaLeigh was still in surgery.

It wasn't until mid-afternoon that we heard from Dr. Randawa. I had never met the man and was startled to hear a young, cheerful Australian accent.

"Dr. ... Sahid Randawa?" I asked.

"Yup. How weird is that, mate? An East Indian with an Aussie accent? Anyhow," he continued, "your little girl is quite the charmer. The staff here don't want to part with her."

"She's pretty special," I agreed.

"Worst case of otitis media I've ever seen," Dr. Randawa declared. "I've got a drain coming out of the middle ear on each side of her head just below the jawbone. Clean them three to four times a day, keep her on the antibiotics and, uh ... ," I could hear him rifling through some papers, "call me if you have any questions. Right then, ta."

I hung up the phone and silently blessed Dr. Randawa. Only later did I learn that he was missing two fingers, the result of a disagreement with a shark. It was a testament to his skill and expertise as a veterinarian that he could perform such delicate surgery. Still, I was glad I didn't know about his shortage of digits before the surgery.

Hilary brought RosaLeigh home the following day, along with a bill for $1,800. Even though I knew what to expect, I was shocked by her appearance. She looked terrible. Her right eye was swollen shut and weepy. Pus mixed with blood oozed out alongside the flexible Penrose drains on each side of her head where the fur had been shaved away. Even though we were generous with painkillers, she was withdrawn and sad. We had done what was best for her, but she had no way of knowing that, and it tore us apart to see her so unhappy.

"It'll get better," I whispered, trying to reassure myself as much as RosaLeigh. She tried to purr but gave up in a painful coughing fit. We hoped that as the trauma and swelling around her facial nerves subsided, she would regain control of her eyelid and the critical blink response. Otherwise, it was possible one or both eyes would have to be removed.

Two weeks into her recovery, the irrepressible Max arrived for his eight-week booster, this time in a traditional cat carrier. When Denise opened the latch he sprang forward as if he'd been shot out of a pinball machine, and proceeded to bounce against everything in his path. Little Patrick, now six months old, was thrilled to have a playmate close to his own age, but quickly moved on when he heard a commotion in the Cat Nap Inn.

Karen, who had kindly driven Denise to the appointment, looked disappointed. "Where are all the cats?" she asked.

"Either snoozing or getting into trouble. You could visit RosaLeigh," I suggested. "She'd appreciate the company. She just had a major surgery."

"What for?" Karen asked.

"To get rid of nasty infections in both middle ears," I told Karen. I explained how RosaLeigh had just appeared at our door one evening, crying to come inside, and how desperately sick she was. Then I pointed to the door leading into the treatment area. "Just go through there and one of the staff will show you to the isolation ward."

Karen looked at the door hesitantly. "Okay," she nodded at last, draping her jacket over the back of the chair.

Convincing Max to go through the door into the exam room was easier. I was used to matching wits with kittens. I picked up a fuzzy striped snake and tossed it into the room. Max enthusiastically chased the airborne reptile and pounced on it.

"Wow, Dr. McBride," Denise whispered in awe as I closed the door behind us, "you're good."

Midway through Max's appointment, I excused myself to pick up a vial of vaccine from the fridge. I could see Karen through the window in the isolation ward. Her shoulder-length brown hair floated in gentle waves against her shoulders as she nestled RosaLeigh against her chest. The little cat had extended her front legs on each side of RosaLeigh's neck in a hug and gazed up at her face. I had to pause for a moment, spellbound.

They were still together when I finished with Max about twenty minutes later. Reluctantly, Karen put RosaLeigh back into her kennel and hung up the isolation lab coat she had been wearing. RosaLeigh pawed at the kennel door, her mouth opening and closing in plaintive meows. Karen was devastated. She kept trying to reassure RosaLeigh by slipping her fingers through the bars of the kennel and rubbing the little pixie face that stared out so sadly from behind them. I had never seen this kind of reaction from RosaLeigh before. The staff were always generous with their attention and the little cat had never demanded more.

Finally, Karen opened the door of the isolation ward and slipped through, closing it behind her with a gentle twist of the knob. RosaLeigh jumped onto her perch and watched as we left.

"Oh, Dr. McBride," Karen sighed. "I feel terrible. Will she settle down?"

"Oh, yes," I nodded with more confidence than I felt. In fact, RosaLeigh remained on her perch a long time after Karen left.

From a medical point of view, she was doing quite well. The infection was clearing up and one eye looked completely normal. The other would only half open in a kind of seductive, bedroom-eye gaze. And her appetite was impressive. She could put away more food than cats twice her size. But she seemed to be waiting for something now, rather than watching the action in the treatment area.

Once we were able to vaccinate her, she was allowed out of the isolation ward. Cautious at first, she soon adapted to the hospital routines. A dozen clients offered to adopt her. They played with her, held her, gave her catnip, and told her how beautiful she was. But after a thorough and painstaking inspection, suitor after suitor was rejected. RosaLeigh simply strolled back to her suite in the Cat Nap Inn and curled up on the highest shelf. No amount of coaxing or treats could convince her to come back down.

Disappointed clients could only sigh. Successful adoption has to be a two-way street. Most animals weren't choosy: food, shelter, and companionship were all they required. RosaLeigh was looking for something more. And she had found it in Karen.

It wasn't uncommon for clients and non-clients alike to pop in to Ocean View to say hello and get their "cat fix." Karen began coming in regularly to visit. One evening as I struggled against the current of backlogged appointments and phone messages, I happened to look up. Perhaps it was Hilary hobbling past on a pair of crutches with a bag of cat treats clenched between her teeth that caught my attention. It was her first shift after dropping a frozen ham, the family's intended Sunday dinner, on her foot. Perhaps it was Vanessa Rhodenizer complaining about her bill at the reception counter. Perhaps it was the unsupervised child licking the glass walls of the aquarium. Whatever the reason, when I looked up I saw Karen and RosaLeigh snuggled together in the rocking chair. The air around them was still, like the eye of a storm. Karen was reading a book. RosaLeigh lay in her lap, paws tucked under her chest and eyes closed as she purred in contentment.

Without warning, I was quickly tossed back into the swirling chaos of a busy practice. The moment passed, but not my memory of it. Just as that indefinable something called chemistry exists between humans, animals also share special connections with each other. Cats have cat friends, buds who hang out together, wash each others' faces, while other cats in the neighbourhood may be deferred to, tolerated, ignored, or even victimized. Friendships even exist between cats and crows, horses and dogs, but to me one of the most fascinating relationships is the bond between humans and animals.

Mrs. Dalrymple, a former client of mine and self-proclaimed cat psychic, would have said that Karen and RosaLeigh had known each other in a former life. RosaLeigh had certainly picked Karen above all others. So I wasn't surprised when Karen called me several days later.

"Dr. McBride," she began in an excited voice, "I have an idea."

※ ※ ※

Autumn is one of Nova Scotia's most beautiful seasons and though it marks the end of summer's T-shirts and sandals, it does so with a glorious finale. Under a rich blue sky, I drove up the tree-lined road speckled with crispy flakes of colour to Meadowlands Guest Home. A rambling structure set amidst several acres of what was once farmland, it was now a home for dementia patients with physical disabilities.

Karen, who worked here as a full-time physiotherapist, met me at the door.

"Oh, Dr. McBride, I'm so glad to see you! RosaLeigh is doing so well. The administration was already thinking of getting a resident cat," she added as she led me past reception and down a hallway. "And now, I get to be with her all the time."

Patients dotted the landscape. A few were in their rooms, lying in bed or chatting with visitors. There was a large group in the recreation room, where a game of Bingo was underway. Most of the participants stared with indifference at their cards. In another corner of the room, several residents were working on a puzzle. One woman was sitting in a chair staring at a blank TV screen.

A number of the residents looked up and waved when Karen entered the room.

"Hello, everyone," Karen began as we strolled through the crowd. "I have a special guest with me today!" No one took notice until she added, "This is one of the doctors who saved RosaLeigh."

A few people broke out into spontaneous applause and someone yelled "BINGO!"

A woman in a wheelchair grabbed my arm. "Where's RosaLeigh?" she demanded.

"Yes, where's RosaLeigh?" others wanted to know, eyeing me with suspicion.

"Now you all know RosaLeigh is with Mrs. Harnish," Karen explained. "She'll be here in a few minutes with your afternoon snacks."

Right on cue, Mrs. Harnish, accompanied by RosaLeigh, arrived with the snacks. Mrs. Harnish clearly enjoyed the fruits of her labour and was as wide as she was tall. RosaLeigh strode proudly beside her, partners in the production of such delicacies. The snacks and juice were left on a table in the corner, but no one moved. I watched in amazement as RosaLeigh began her rounds, moving from one person to another with the relaxed confidence of a TV host. Smiles appeared where there had been none, conversations sprang up around the room. Those who couldn't remember the names of their own children knew RosaLeigh's name by heart, their faces alive with joy as they stroked her soft fur.

The room dissolved into happy chatter, the silence of individuals isolated by their disease shattered by one small black cat. As the residents began drifting toward the snacks, RosaLeigh joined Karen and me. While she was happy to see me, it was Karen she adored. She stretched up against Karen's legs asking to be picked up. Karen happily obliged.

I turned to Karen, shaking my head. "It's like she was waiting for you. And this place," I added as I looked around. "Right from the very beginning."

RosaLeigh rubbed her face against Karen's in an enthusiastic outpouring of affection, her little paws gently clasping Karen's neck. I could sense the same stillness around them that I had felt in reception that night. Karen looked at me and smiled.

"I know," she said softly.

Chapter 19

"The washing machine's making weird noises again," Hilary stood with her hands on her hips and stared at Hughie. Absorbed in a reference book, he gave no indication that he had heard her.

"Dr. D!"

Startled, he looked up.

"Can you look at it?"

"Look at what?"

Hilary sighed. "The washing machine."

Hughie glanced at the big white cube that rumbled and shook on its linoleum launch pad.

"It always sounds like that. You guys put too much in at one time." He turned back to his book.

Hilary shook her head. The staff had been lobbying for a new machine ever since I had started working at Ocean View. With at least six or seven loads daily, it saw more action than washing machines half its age. Sometimes when it stopped on a whim, the staff could energize it with a swift kick to the side. The plastic Dial-A-Wash selector button had cracked, crumbled, and eventually vanished altogether. In its place, a pair of pliers clung with a death grip to the tiny metal knob that remained. New staff had to be trained on the machine's eccentricities.

"Yoo hoo, Dr. McBrrride?" Bernie appeared around the corner with the chart for my next patient. Lowering her voice, she added, "It's Mrs. Hussein."

On cue, a perfectly coiffed head popped out through the exam room door. Most clients waited politely in the exam room for the few minutes it took me to review their cat's medical history or finish the previous appointment. Patricia Hussein was not one of them.

"Dr. McBride," she called out from the other end of the hallway. "We're ready. They told me you were on time."

"God, it's great having an associate," Hughie remarked.

Patricia started seeing me because Hughie had suggested that her cat was getting fat. She came from, as they say, old money and her husband made tons of new money. A variety of professionals made sure she started each new day with perfect hair, manicured nails, and as little body fat as possible. In her early fifties, Patricia Hussein was an elegant woman. She was also, in Hughie's words, a button-pusher.

Patricia glanced at her watch when I entered the room. Donald, her Siamese cat, nibbled his toes.

"Good morning," I smiled, determined to protect my buttons.

Patricia got right to the point. "I was here three months ago for Donald's annual checkup and you said he was fine. Now look at him."

I looked. Three months ago, six-year-old Donald had been fine. Now he had a rash, sores, and bare spots where the fur was missing.

"He looks hideous!" Patricia complained.

Perched on the end of the table, Donald tucked his paws underneath his chest and stared cross-eyed at the wall. He knew he looked hideous.

"C'mon, Donald," I said, coaxing him into an upright position so I could begin my examination. Donald was a robust fellow, larger than the average Siamese. Last year, we had to remove a broken upper canine on the right side of his face. Unfortunately, he had never acquired the adult lower canine on the same side so, with nothing to hold it in place, Donald's tongue often protruded listlessly out that side. The result was a cat who looked like he had nothing sensible to add to the conversation.

I ran my hands over his coat, prying apart the fur and examining the skin. "Well, there's no evidence of fleas," I told Patricia.

"Of course there isn't," Patricia rolled her eyes.

Determining the cause of skin rashes in cats is a step-by-step procedure. I didn't bother pointing out that, for cats who go outside, fleas are the number one cause of allergic dermatitis. I began rummaging through my drawer for the Wood's lamp then realized I had left it in the treatment area.

"I'll be right back," I told Patricia, opening the door.

"Where are you going?" she demanded. Donald looked at me bleakly.

"I need to get something called a Wood's lamp. If Donald has a fungal infection, it will fluoresce under black light."

As I headed down the hallway, I could hear footsteps behind me. "I have another appointment at 11:00, Dr. McBride!"

Before I could answer, the washing machine exploded. That is to say, in the middle of a spin cycle the lid flew off its rusty hinges and crashed against the metal shelving in the storage room. Ernie, who been meditating on a stool with his eyes closed, leapt into the air and landed on the instrument drying rack. The stool, the rack, and several dozen surgical instruments clattered to the floor in a spectacular finale. Patricia screamed and ran back up the hallway.

The storage room was a soapy swamp. Since Hughie and Susan were prepping a patient for surgery and Bernie was tied up in reception, I helped Hilary haul some bags of food to dry ground. Then we threw down some towels and began mopping up the mess. By the time I returned to the exam room, Patricia was gone and Donald with her.

"The poor thing," Bernie said, shaking her head. "She yelled something about a bomb as she was racing out the door."

"A bomb?"

Patricia had two teenage children attending the local high school just down the street. In the last few weeks, there had been several bomb threats at the school, each on gloriously sunny days. The students had been evacuated and spent a few enjoyable hours lounging on the grounds while the fire department conducted a thorough inspection. No one had yet been apprehended.

"Did you tell her what really happened?" I asked.

Bernie looked at me, a faint smile tugging at her lips. "Well, I didn't really have the time, she left so fast. Are you going to call her?"

I looked at my watch and shrugged. "Maybe in a little while."

When I finally called Patricia to explain what had happened, only her answering machine was home. She herself was probably down at the police station filing a report. I left a brief message and when I didn't hear back, rejoiced, assuming that she had taken Donald to another practice where washing machines didn't blow up.

I hoped it was Dr. Dick's. He would enjoy taking her money. A few months ago, a mass mail-out of coupons had arrived at the hospital. Included among the fast-food offers, carpet-cleaning specials, and bargain jewellery was a two-for-one deal on bottled water for pets. The local distributor was none other than Dr. Dick. Someone at Ocean View had cut out the miniature photo of his head from the coupon. It was discovered several days later on the hazardous waste disposal. After that, it appeared taped to a bottle of euthanol. One day I found him in my gym shoe.

In spite of the horror of her last visit, Patricia returned to Ocean View about a month later. Donald looked worse than ever. I resumed from where we had left off at the last appointment. With a brand new washing machine humming confidently in the background, I reached for the Wood's lamp.

"He needs to detoxify," Patricia announced.

I looked at her. "Pardon me?"

"Detoxify," she repeated. "Don't you do that?"

I thought for a moment. "Well, I shower regularly. Oh, and sometimes I drink prune juice," I added.

While Patricia stared at me, I flicked off the overhead lights and scanned Donald's body with the black light. He didn't appear to have a fungal infection. When I turned the lights back on, she was still staring at me.

"Dr. McBride, I'm talking about a deep, purging, inner cleanse. The air we breathe is polluted, and our food is full of poisons."

"You bring up a good point," I interrupted. "Food. We need to change Donald's diet."

"That's what I think too!" Patricia's head bobbed in amazed agreement.

"It's possible that Donald is having an allergic reaction to his food."

Patricia's eyes grew wide. "Yes, I've been reading about that on the Internet." She leaned in closer.

"I think we should try a three-month course of a hypoallergenic diet."

"Can you order it in for me?" she asked breathlessly.

I paused for dramatic affect and cleared my throat. "We have it here."

"Oh!" Patricia leaned back in awe. "Here at the hospital?"

I nodded smugly. "We like to keep up to date on the most current research."

"Well!" Patricia was speechless. She folded her arms across her chest in approval. I felt like I had just brought home a straight-A report card. For once, the woman had nothing negative to say. We were sailing uncharted waters. I waited for her to make the next move.

"What about vitamins?" she asked, narrowing her eyes as she studied me closely. "I think Donald needs a shot of vitamins."

Donald no more needed vitamins than an all-expenses-paid trip to the moon. In the early days, I had tried to convince Patricia not to spend her money on unnecessary treatments. Now rather than waste my breath, I usually agreed to any practicable suggestions that weren't harmful. Patricia could then complain about her bill, which she enjoyed, and boast that she knew more about veterinary medicine than the vet. It also meant she was more likely to follow my recommendations.

I pulled out a bottle of injectable vitamins and filled a syringe. Donald didn't even blink when I emptied its contents just under the skin on the scruff of his neck. Patricia was smiling and even complimented me on the pewter cat pin I wore. My professional star had never shone so brightly. I felt like we were bonding.

"Dr. McBride, do you mind if I use your washroom?" Patricia asked.

"By all means," I told her graciously. "I'll settle Donald back in his carrier."

I had barely closed the latch on the carrier when I heard the returning click of her heels, growing louder with each step. That was fast, I thought. Mrs. Hussein was nothing if not efficient. I looked up expectantly as the footsteps stopped and the door was thrown open. Patricia stood in the doorframe and stared at me.

"Do you realize there's a picture of a man's head taped to your toilet seat?"

"Really?" I had left him taped to the tube of Preparation H in the cupboard.

"An old man with curly hair," Patricia grimaced. "It was very disconcerting, given what I had gone there to do."

Since the image was not much larger than a postage stamp, I wondered how Patricia was able to get such a good look at it.

"And," Patricia paused, "there was no toilet paper."

"Oh, sorry. We keep it in the cupboard beside the toilet," I explained.

"Never mind," Patricia dismissed me with a flick of her hand. "I'll wait till I'm home." Tucking the bag of hypoallergenic food under her arm, she picked up Donald's carrier and strode to the front desk.

"Call me," I said hopefully.

When I didn't hear from her, I phoned several weeks later for an update. I was concerned that if Donald was allergic to his regular cat food, then it could take as long as two to three months before there was any noticeable improvement. And if he was getting any treats or supplemental food in the meantime, it could negate any progress that had been made.

Patricia's husband, Victor, answered on the fourth ring. Patricia wasn't able to come to the phone and her husband, while very pleasant, had no idea how the cat was doing or if he liked the new food. He promised to tell his wife that I had called.

When I didn't hear back this time I thought she was gone for good. Surely, Ocean View had insulted her sensibilities one too many times. But, like a wart that just won't go away, Patricia showed up several months later with Donald in tow. When she opened the kennel door, he chirped a friendly hello and strolled through the exam room like the debonair gentleman he was. The sores were all gone and his fur was growing back nicely. He looked fantastic.

"I demand a refund," Patricia announced.

Dumbfounded, I looked up.

"It was fleas," Patricia continued. "I don't know how you possibly could have got that wrong. I had to have the house fumigated and Donald professionally bathed."

I felt my neck grow hot. "When I examined him, I didn't see any flea dirt or adult fleas. There was nothing. It's written right here in my notes."

"Well, apparently you didn't look hard enough."

This was not going well. "Did you continue to feed him the hypoallergenic diet?" I asked tersely.

"Well, of course!" Patricia retorted. "I didn't want to waste that money too."

I hesitated. "So what made you think it was fleas?"

Patricia rummaged through her purse. "Here!" she said, thrusting an empty Chanel N°5 bottle toward me.

I held the bottle up to my face. Its tiny occupant was deceased.

"Where did you find this?" I asked.

"In the bed. Donald likes to sleep under the covers." Patricia folded her arms across her chest.

"Do you mind if I take a look at it in the lab?"

"Have you not seen a flea before, Dr. McBride?"

"This one looks a bit … unusual."

"Well, Victor says it's a flea. And I think he would know."

I opened the door. "No harm in making sure."

"I want it back when you're done," Patricia called after me.

Back in the treatment area, I examined the insect under the microscope. It had a broad body with six legs. The middle and hind legs, which ended in hooked mitts, were distinctive. Just to be sure, I hauled the parasitology book off the shelf and began leafing through it.

"What are you looking at?" Hughie asked.

I stepped aside so he could have a look. "Be my guest," I grinned.

Hughie bent over the microscope and adjusted the focus. "Where did this come from?" he asked after a moment.

"Patricia Hussein's bed."

Hughie looked up, a smirk on his face. Then he turned back to the microscope for a second look.

"Her husband says it's from the cat," I told him.

"Interesting," Hughie observed dryly. "He's an MD, isn't he?"

I nodded. "Infectious diseases."

Back in the exam room, Patricia was flabbergasted. "A louse! But where could it have come from?"

There was only one place where this particular louse, commonly known as a "crab" in some circles, could have come from and I wasn't going to be the one to tell her. I advised Patricia to continue with the hypoallergenic diet and we scheduled another recheck in six weeks.

She never showed up for the appointment. Bernie called and left a message on her answering machine but the call wasn't returned. The following month, a computer-generated reminder was mailed to the house with no better luck. I never saw Patricia again, although there were sightings reported from several reliable sources who said Donald was doing well.

A tiny little creature slightly smaller than a flea had ended my professional relationship with Patricia Hussein. I gained a whole new respect for the lowly louse.

Chapter 20

I come from a creative family. My mother plays the piano and sings. My father was a talented landscape artist who could also fashion a little girl's dollhouse from wooden orange crates, leftover linoleum, and other spare parts. Even my brothers managed a little wood carving and gained neighbourhood notoriety with a teenage garage rock band. Unfortunately, the creativity gene got used up before I was born.

In elementary school, our music teacher arranged us into three singing groups named after birds. I was a crow and relegated to the back row with Jimmy Matheson, who had the unusual ability to sing and pick his nose at the same time. My best friend was a bluebird and sang up front with all the other little bluebirds while we crows cawed in the back.

Undaunted, I joined band in junior high. Mr. Chen, the frustrated band teacher, told my mother he had trouble finding "just the right instrument" for me. For reasons unknown to anyone, he finally settled on flute. By the time I reached Grade 10, he had been reassigned as a geography teacher in some remote part of the district and I joined the chess club. My flute days became a distant memory, relegated to the stuff of nightmares punctuated by Mr. Chen's cries of pain.

And then I met Lois and Crawford.

Crawford was the largest cat I had ever met. His front legs rivaled my own forearms. Orange fur radiated like solar flares from a face the size of a dinner plate. On one side of his face, the same side that was missing half an ear, whiskers corkscrewed east. On the other side, they took a more northerly turn. Lois had rescued Crawford from a life behind bars at the local animal shelter and he had never looked back. He sat on the examining table and stared at me with calculating green eyes.

"Oh, Crawford!" Lois gushed. "Look what Dr. McBride has for you!"

I held up a bag of weight-loss food for Crawford's inspection. His tail twitched ever so slightly as he held my gaze.

"Now, Crawford. Don't be like that," Lois scolded. "Mommy only wants what's best for her baby. Mommy loves Crawbaby! So does Dr. McBride!" Lois looked up at me expectantly.

I hastened to assure Crawford that I loved him too and shook the bag encouragingly. Lois beamed. Crawford was the sun around which her world revolved. I explained that he should get only a cup of the dry food daily and one small can.

"What?" Lois was incredulous. "Are you sure?"

"And no treats," I added.

"No treats?"

I shook my head.

"Dr. McBride, you have no idea how stubborn he can be! And that look – oy vey!" Lois held her face in her hands and shook her head.

I searched for the right words. It was difficult to discuss a pet's weight loss with a client who was also overweight, but I didn't want Crawford developing diabetes or heart disease because of his weight.

"He is big-boned," I began carefully, "but he still needs to lose about six pounds. That may take as long as seven or eight months. You need to be firm."

"Oh, I'm such a schmo!" Lois declared. "But he's my baby!" She grabbed the big cat off the table and clutched him to her chest. Although miffed, Crawford was no fool. Well aware of who buttered his many slices of bread, he submitted to Lois's enthusiastic outpouring of love and stared at me over his mother's shoulder.

I turned away from his silent accusation. "Let's get him back in his carrier and I can tell you about our exciting new Weight-Watchers for Cats program."

Lois rolled her eyes. "Dr. McBride, you're young and skinny so I'm going to make allowances. There is nothing exciting about a weight-loss program."

"Ah, but there is," I grinned as we lowered Crawford into the lower half of his carrier, then reattached the top half. He was too large to fit through the traditional way so whenever the big cat had to be transported, the entire carrier had to be disassembled.

When we were done, I showed Lois our Fat Cat Wall of Fame, featuring patients who had successfully completed the program. Feline participants were required to return to the hospital every six weeks for a free weigh-in. If they had lost weight, both the owner and the cat received a small gift. Ever since we started the reward program, compliance among clients had skyrocketed.

Lois giggled and clapped her hands in delight. "Oh, what's the first reward, Dr. McBride? Tell me!"

I shook my head. "You'll just have to wait for six weeks."

"Dr. McBride!" Lois admonished, waggling a finger at me. "Meanie!"

Following behind Lois, I gripped Crawford's carrier in two hands and waddled into reception, where clients and cats in various stages of their appointments mingled. A couple of the resident cats were idly watching the proceedings from the top of the food shelves. Little Patrick blinked in wide-eyed wonder from his basket underneath the coffee table. At first, we had been concerned that he might lose his eye due to the nerve paralysis affecting the left side of his face. Happily, his third eyelid, the white membrane sometimes visible in the corner of a cat's eye, had developed to the point where it functioned as a normal eyelid and kept his eye moist. Unlike a regular eyelid it blinked across his eye, more like a lizard than a cat, and it could be a bit disconcerting for new clients.

"Oh, Dr. McBride, he's beautiful! They're all beautiful!" Lois breathed as she clasped her hands together reverently. "This place is Heaven."

I helped Lois and Crawford out to the car, a rusty, gas-guzzling monster with a hood ornament. Lois slipped inside and rolled the window down a crack. The top of her head was level with the steering wheel.

"'Bye, Dr. McBride!" she called out as she began backing up. She turned to look at Crawford in the front seat, nearly side-swiping the car beside her. "Say bye-bye to Dr. McBride, Crawbaby."

Crawford sent a baleful glance my way. "He loves you!" Lois translated.

Waving gaily, she chugged out of the parking lot in a cloud of blue smoke. From behind, the car appeared to be driving itself. It paused indecisively at the exit, first signalling to go left, then right. While the right-turn signal was still flashing, the car had a complete change of heart and went straight, much to the disgust of the driver behind.

When I didn't hear back from Lois, I assumed all was going well with the new diet. Crawford didn't seem to be the fussy type. Susan made a routine follow-up call a week later and learned, however, that Crawford was refusing to eat his new food. When she suggested mixing his old kibble with the new, Lois confessed that she had already tried that. He wouldn't even eat his mouse cookies. Wary of preservatives, Lois concocted her own treats from "all-natural" ingredients, shaping them like little mice and baking them for twenty minutes.

"He wouldn't eat homemade soup from the spoon either," Susan continued.

I looked up. "Does he usually?"

She nodded. "At the table – in his own chair."

"Well, tell her to bring him in as soon as possible," I told Susan. I was concerned that Crawford could be developing a condition known as hepatic lipidosis, or fatty liver disease. Failure to eat can trigger changes in the liver, and an irreversible downward spiral begins.

"I already did," Susan explained. "She can't."

"Why not?"

Susan shrugged. "I don't know."

I picked up the phone. "Hi, Lois. It's Dr. McBride. Susan tells me Crawford won't eat anything. Can you bring him in? It's really important that we see him as soon as possible."

"Oh, Dr. McBride, I can't," she whispered.

I glanced at my watch. Benny and I were supposed to be meeting friends at a lovely little Greek restaurant that had just opened. And I despised house calls. Cats always know I'm coming and vanish before their owners even hang up the phone. Besides, if there's anything seriously wrong, they need to be admitted to the hospital anyway.

But there was something in Lois's voice, a kind of quiet desperation that tugged at me. Against my better judgment, I offered to pop in on my way home and have a quick look at him.

"For free, you mean?" Lois asked hopefully. "Oh, would you? I'm so worried about him. I was just being firm like you said."

I hung up the phone. As I packed my medical bag, I found myself hoping that Crawford merely had a cold and had lost his appetite. Otherwise, I may have inadvertently caused a serious health problem by insisting that he needed to lose weight.

I arrived at Lois's home shortly after six. It was a small, defeated-looking bungalow perched on the edge of a sprawling urban shopping centre. A decade of parking lot litter was firmly welded to the wire fence that enclosed a tiny yard. Opening the gate, I stepped into Lois's world.

Almost at once, I heard the sweet, haunting tones of a flute. I didn't recognize the music, but the passion and skill of the musician were unmistakable. I walked up the cracked concrete steps. Rivers of orange stain from the rusting wrought-iron railing poured down each side. At the top, weeds sprouted from a chipped plastic pot. The doorbell didn't appear to work so I knocked on the screen door. Like most homes with screen doors and cats, its mesh was pockmarked from years of abuse.

"Lois!" a voice bellowed from somewhere within. "Door!"

Immediately, the music stopped. Dishevelled and out of breath, Lois arrived in the doorway a few moments later. She was wearing the same threadbare sweater and a shapeless pair of pants. They had been worn and washed far more frequently than the manufacturer ever intended.

"Oh, Dr. McBride!" Lois cried, throwing her arms around me. "Thank you for coming!"

I followed her down a dingy hall to the kitchen. Clumps of orange fur, presumably Crawford's, clung to the equally dingy carpet.

"Bob, this is Dr. McBride," Lois declared, making introductions. Her tone implied I was personally related to God, or at the very least the Pope. Bob, clad in striped pyjamas and a checkered housecoat, barely looked up from behind his newspaper.

"All this fuss for a cat," he grunted.

"Shift work," Lois explained in a whisper as we continued down the hall to the den.

In contrast to the chaotic kitchen with its sink full of dirty dishes and sticky floor, the den seemed content. There was a single decorating scheme and that was CAT. The large needlepoint cheetah over the fireplace dominated a room filled to overflowing with cat ornaments. Lois noticed me staring at an arrangement of artificial flowers which rose from the head of a wide-eyed china cat on the floor.

"Can you believe it?" she asked. "Someone actually threw this gorgeous vase out in the trash! I saw it one day when I was still working and brought it home."

"Unbelievable," I agreed, shaking my head.

A music stand with a flute resting at the base stood in the far corner of the room. "Was that you playing?" I asked.

Lois nodded shyly.

"It was beautiful."

"Oh, Dr. McBride," Lois put her hands on her hips. "You are such a schmoozer," she giggled.

Crawford looked up from his blanket on the sofa, a plaid monster from the sixties. Here in the comfort of his own kingdom, he seemed much more relaxed.

"Crawbaby, did Mommy wake you up?" Lois leaned over and smothered him with kisses.

Crawford yawned and stretched luxuriously. He certainly didn't seem distressed, but according to Lois he was refusing to eat or play with any of his toys. He didn't even want to go outside and spray the next door neighbour's prize rose bush, as was his custom. All he wanted to do was sleep.

A shadow loomed over Lois as she knelt on the floor. "Is supper ready?"

Bob stood in the entrance to the den. He had changed into a navy blue uniform with a yellow badge on the arm. I couldn't read what it said, but I guessed he worked as a security guard, maybe at the nearby mall.

Lois scrambled to her feet. "Oh, Bob. I didn't know you were there." She brushed the hair away from her face. "It's all made up. Do you think you could just heat it up in the microwave?"

Bob stared at her for a moment, then turned and left the room without a word. Lois's whole body sagged, like a balloon left alone and forgotten long after the party is over.

"We'll just be a few more minutes," she called to his retreating back. "I can heat it up for you then. Would that be okay?"

The front door slammed shut. Poised between the hallway and the den, Lois hesitated. Then she turned back toward us and lowered herself onto the sofa. She sat with her hands clasped in her lap and watched in uncharacteristic silence as I examined Crawford.

Other than mild dehydration, I could find nothing physically wrong. Puzzled, I leaned back.

"So, what do you think?" Lois asked, a worried frown creasing her face.

I shrugged my shoulders. "I'm sorry. I can't really know what's going on without further tests."

Lois was silent for a minute. Outside, the day was rapidly losing ground to the evening shadows. Not quite ready to give up, the sun still struggled for purchase, its long fingers of light extending through the branches of a nearly naked maple tree into Lois's den. Maples were the first native trees to herald the arrival of spring in Nova Scotia; they were also the first to give them up as the days grew shorter and the nights cooler. Crawford ambled over to a swivel rocker where a single sunbeam pooled on a cushion.

"Is there anything I can do at home?" Lois asked as he hopped up onto the cushion. "I can't bring him in."

I hesitated. Crawford wasn't acting like a sick cat. No vomiting, no diarrhea, no fever. And yet, his refusal to eat anything was a sign something was wrong. He would have to be syringe-fed or have a tube inserted into his stomach through which food could be delivered. Otherwise, his liver could suffer irreparable damage. Syringe-feeding can be difficult – most cats would rather swim the English Channel – and accidentally forcing food down the trachea can result in pneumonia, possibly leading to death.

With grave misgivings, I gave Lois some syringes to try feeding Crawford at home. In a timely coincidence, the cheerful little Scottish rep for one of the food companies had left a sample case of a brand new food designed for anorexic cats. It was very palatable, high in calories, and easily forced through a syringe. I gave Lois half a dozen to try, and warned her that if his liver was damaged, it may take as long as six weeks for him to begin eating on his own.

Lois sighed and took a deep breath. "Oy vey!"

I patted Crawford one last time and, slipping into my jacket, headed out to the car. A cold drizzle had enveloped the city. Shivering, I hopped inside and turned the heat on full blast. The wipers clicked in time to an old Beach Boys song on the radio, both trying to keep the miserable weather at bay. Lois was standing on the front steps, her sweater pulled tightly around her. As I pulled away from the curb, she waved goodbye and slowly receded into the distance.

At dinner that night, Benny and I made plans to go hiking in Cape Breton on the weekend. It was worth the five-hour drive to see the glorious fall colours of Cape Smokey and the Cape Breton Highlands National Park. I was worried about Crawford, but I knew Hughie would be on call if Lois ran into any problems.

"Have a good time. Don't worry about a thing," Hughie had replied breezily when I told him of my plans. He grabbed a chart and was rushing up the hall to his next appointment when he screeched to a halt halfway there. "Don't come back sick!" he hissed, pointing a warning finger at me. "It's bad for business."

We had been short-staffed most of the fall as people took turns being sick. Schedules were constantly being adjusted, appointments changed, and overtime hours accumulated. Hughie was the only one who hadn't caught the bug as it made its rounds, which was lucky since he not only worked full-time as a vet but also ran the practice, with firm guidance from his bookkeeping despot, Mrs. Tuttle. Her lips had grown increasingly tight as the busy fall progressed and Hughie lapsed into his old ways.

Benny picked me up at the hospital at four o'clock on Friday afternoon and we drove straight through to a bed and breakfast in Ingonish. While an undergraduate, I had spent my summers working as a dining room waitress at the world-renowned Keltic Lodge in Ingonish Beach. Benny, on the other hand, had spent his summers underground in the gold mines of Yellowknife. He made three times more money than I did, but was poorer for never having seen the breathtaking beauty of the Cape Breton highlands.

Within the park, there is a special place not marked on any map. From the road, it looks like nothing more than a small gurgling brook. For those who venture further, it is an untouched wilderness of gently cascading waterfalls, giant rocks worn smooth by glaciers, and calm, pristine pools. One summer, while working at Keltic, I had the somewhat mixed good fortune of dating Jimmy Angus MacIsaac, kitchen boy and native son. Jimmy Angus was a hard-working, hard-drinking daredevil who washed pots, peeled potatoes, and in his spare time hiked all over the highlands. On a sweltering summer day deep in July, he took me to "The Hole," as the locals called it. Water that began up in the highlands as snow and ice had, over millennia, carved a smooth passage through granite rock. At "The Hole" (an ugly name for such a magical place), a thin film of fast water washed over a moss-covered natural waterslide that plummeted into a pool of water fifty feet below. I couldn't wait to show Benny my secret garden.

It rained the entire weekend. When it wasn't raining, it drizzled, spat, showered, and at one point snowed. But none of that really mattered. There would be other times. In my wildest dreams, I never thought I would fall for Benny Mombourquette, the boy-next-door who peed on my doll's tea party. Yet, he was also the boy who understood my sorrow over a dead rat when everyone else in my junior high class laughed at me, the boy who quietly took that rat and buried him in the woods. Benny understood me before I understood myself.

Who was it who said you have to go away to come home?

Much to Hughie's chagrin, I did get sick and was off work for two days after I got back. Besides the constant nausea, I had a skull-splitting headache and mucous dribbling out of my nose. But, in spite of that, I couldn't be happier. When I returned to work, it was with renewed vigour. No question was too mundane, no client too irritating, no cat too aggressive. I loved them all.

Hughie, on the other hand, was exhausted and cranky. He was sitting at the desk, staring at the tax bill and grumbling to himself when I entered.

"Dr. McBride, isn't it?" he asked, peering at me over the rim of his bifocals. "So nice to see you again. I must say, you seem unusually chipper for a sick person."

"Well, I'm feeling better. I ... "

Hughie held up a silencing hand wrapped in gauze. "I'm sure you had a wonderful time gallivanting around Cape Breton getting sick," he added, narrowing his eyes.

"What happened to your hand?" I asked.

Hughie sighed. "Does the name," he shuddered, "Crawbaby ring a bell?"

"Crawford? How is he?" I asked breathlessly.

"Oh, I'll be fine, by the way," Hughie added. He gently unwrapped the gauze around his hand, exposing mottled purple flesh riddled with tooth marks.

I leaned over for a better look. "Oh, gross. It must really hurt."

"Four hours in Emergency," Hughie declared as he rewrapped his hand. "Yes, I could have used an associate in my time of need." He sighed deeply and leaned back in his chair, raising his eyes heavenward. "But alas, it was not to be."

As Hughie told his tale of woe, I murmured suitably sympathetic noises. Apparently, Lois only had to syringe-feed Crawford once. The big cat loved everything about his new food – the smell, the taste, the texture, even the pretty pink can it came in. Lois was so delighted, she fed him on demand. Crawford did a lot of demanding. In three days, he had eaten enough for a week. With that much food going in, one would expect to see something coming out.

But not Crawford. His colon hung onto that food like a bear holds onto honey. I had warned Lois about the dangers of megacolon, a condition not uncommon in overweight cats, where the bowel becomes "lazy" and eventually dysfunctional. Alarmed that he was developing a bowel disorder, she had rushed him in to Ocean View and Hughie's waiting hands.

Poor Crawford. His pleasantly fat world had been turned upside down when I insisted he go on a diet. Another trip to the vet hospital had only heightened his insecurity. In his opinion, nothing good ever came out of these visits. When Hughie had tried to palpate his abdomen, Crawford lost his mind and, as it turned out, a good portion of what had been stored in his colon.

Standing up, Hughie grabbed the tax bill off the desk and stuffed it into a shirt pocket.

"I have to go," he announced. "I have a date."

I rolled my eyes. "With one of the ER nurses?"

"Mrs. Tuttle," Hughie sighed as he struggled into his jacket. He zipped it up with his good hand and picked up a file folder off the desk. "The nurse is Friday night." Whistling cheerfully, his good humour restored at the thought, Hughie turned to leave. At the door he paused and rested a hand against the doorframe. I looked up.

"What? Did you forget something?"

Hughie smiled. "That's a beautiful necklace, Dr. McBride."

Before I could say anything, he charged out the door and down the hall in his usual breakneck fashion, arm raised in a cheery farewell as he shouted some last-minute instructions to Hilary. I raised my hand to my throat and felt the new pendant that rested there – a beautiful, old-fashioned locket that had belonged to Benny's grandmother. The warmth from it seemed to spread throughout my body.

"Dr. McBride," Susan called out. "Mrs. MacIntosh is here with Sharisse."

"I'll be right there." Smiling to myself, I tucked the necklace back under my lab coat and stood up. There would be more time to dream later.

When my shift was over, I stopped at Lois's on the way home. She was thrilled to see me and showed me into the den. Grabbing Crawford off the sofa, she dangled him in front of me. The big cat hung motionless, suspended by his armpits.

"Oh, he loves you, Dr. McBride!" Lois cried.

Love was the last thing on Crawford's mind. His ears flattened against his skull in silent disapproval as his exposed belly hung loosely. It was larger than ever.

"Kiss-kiss," Lois urged.

I managed a quick peck on the forehead. Lois cuddled her beloved a few moments longer then gently placed him back down on the sofa. He quickly leapt down and strolled into the hallway, where he could watch me from a safe distance.

"Where's your flute?" I asked, looking around.

"At the pawn shop," Lois replied with a bright smile. "I'm buying it back in instalments."

I nodded. We were both silent for a moment, smiling at Crawford who sat in the hall batting at a strip of peeling wallpaper. The flute, in my hands, was an instrument of torture; in Lois's, it became something magical that transported her beyond this drab little house. And she shared that magic with Crawford. "Isn't he a good boy?" she sighed lovingly.

"He is," I agreed. Reluctantly, I gathered my belongings and stood up to leave. Lois followed me down the hallway.

"Oh, Dr. McBride! Wait just a minute."

She rummaged around in the kitchen for what seemed like an eternity. Crawford had joined her and the two chatted amiably as cupboard doors opened and closed, utensils rattled, and a microwave hummed.

Lois found a cardboard box and filled it with some buttered slices of banana bread, a bowl of homemade soup, and for dessert, chocolate pudding. Then she waddled toward me, arms outstretched.

"Now you take this home and put some meat on your bones," she ordered.

She held the door open for me as I wiggled past with some difficulty. There wasn't much room for the two of us and a box full of food. At the bottom of the steps, I turned around to say goodbye. Crawford stood with his mom at the top. A few dead leaves scurrying past in the crisp breeze caught his attention, but he didn't move from Lois's side. Radiant, Lois bent over to pat him.

Chapter 21

VETERINARIANS, AS A GROUP, are more comfortable in scrubs than the latest runway fashions. When forced together socially at conferences, they gather in small groups and make feeble attempts at conversation while clutching their glasses of wine. A few of the more prosperous manage animated discussions about the stock market. But when the conversation turns to animals, as it always does, the entire room comes alive.

"Worst case of worms I've ever seen!" "Did you see the pus that came out of that abscess?" "You'll never guess what I pulled out of her stomach."

All vets have their miracle stories about patients who defied death in spite of cold clinical facts that screamed "Impossible!" I've seen a number of patients who have beaten the odds and gone on to live full, happy lives. One cat stands out in my mind, not because of a single miracle, but because of many. His name was Mike.

It had been a quiet evening at the hospital. The second storm of the season was predicted to start around suppertime, and after the first one the citizens of Halifax were taking no chances. Several weeks earlier, the predicted "rain, at times heavy" had turned into a brawling storm that deposited fifteen centimetres of snow and drifts twice that height on the city. Blasted by the local media for that error in judgment, forecasters had been issuing storm advisories all day for what so far was a cold night with a few flurries and scattered showers.

Shortly after 7:00 p.m. the doors flew open and three firemen rushed inside. One of them was carrying a limp bundle wrapped in a blanket.

I barely recognized Nick's familiar face. He and his men looked like coal miners at the end of a shift. Their eyes gleamed under a layer of soot that covered their exhausted faces. Water dripped from their helmets and thick yellow coats as they followed me into the treatment area.

"What happened?" I asked, grabbing my stethoscope. Susan positioned herself across from me on the other side of the table, ready to assist.

"Bad fire in the west end," Ace explained as Nick gently placed his bundle on the examining table. "We found this little guy in the basement. And two others upstairs." He shook his head.

I peeled back the blanket. The shivering wet cat underneath barely acknowledged my presence. He was breathing, but his heart rate was slow and his gums were pale.

"This guy's in shock." I draped the stethoscope around my neck. "Susan, get me a bag of lactated Ringer's and set up the thermal blanket."

The men stepped back from the table so we could work. Susan shaved a small patch of fur on the cat's forearm then disinfected the area with Betadine solution. I tore open a sterile catheter and, while Susan used her thumb as a tourniquet to raise the vein, I tried to insert the needle. After two unsuccessful attempts, we were finally in the vein. Cat veins are tiny compared to those of dogs, and when an animal is in shock the veins constrict even further. I breathed a sigh of relief when the fluids began to drip unobstructed into the cat's foreleg. Satisfied that we had good positioning, I taped the catheter in place and transferred the patient to a thermal blanket. The circulating warm water would help raise his core temperature, which was below normal. Susan held an oxygen mask over his face.

"Do you think he's gonna be OK?" Bobby spoke for the first time.

I shook my head. "I don't know. He doesn't appear to have any burns, but I'm worried about his lungs. I can hear a fair bit of crackling."

The men nodded knowingly. Smoke inhalation can cause serious and irreversible damage to the delicate tissues of the lungs. As the cells break down, fluid is released into the lungs, causing the sounds I heard.

"Bobby's had him on oxygen since we found him," Nick said.

I looked at Bobby, then at all of them. Their shift was over. Relief crews had arrived. But instead of going home to a hot meal and a shower, they were here with a bedraggled cat clinging to life. Nick shifted his weight forward from one tired leg to the other. He had removed his hat, as had the others, and held it under one arm as he gazed at the cat.

"Why don't you guys go home?" I suggested. "You've done all you can. He's stable right now. We'll see how he does overnight and I'll call the station house in the morning."

Reluctantly, the men agreed and followed their muddy trail back out front where Bernie was busy with a mop. Nick apologized for the mess they had made on her clean floor.

"Oh, don't be daft, luv," Bernie smiled kindly.

I returned to the treatment area, where Hilary was blowing the cat dry with warm air from the hair dryer. Then we transferred him to the oxygen therapy unit so he could breathe oxygen-rich air without having a mask held over his face. I could only hope that with supportive care, his body would begin to repair itself.

When I arrived at work early the next morning to check on my patient, his owners were already there, a young boy and his mother. They both had dark wavy hair and the same wide-spaced eyes.

"They were waiting by the door when I got here at 7:30," Hilary whispered.

I flipped through my patient's chart. His temperature was normal but he hadn't eaten. Hilary had made a note that his lungs were "noisy." I opened the door to the recovery ward.

"Dr. McBride?" The woman rose from the chair beside the cat's kennel. She was dressed in jeans and a plaid work shirt. Her tired face, bare of any makeup, was etched with lines like used tissue paper.

"I'm Maggie Newcombe," she said, extending a hand. "And this is my son, Peter."

Peter's faced was pressed against the bars of the kennel. His small fingers had found their way through the bars and were busy scratching the cat's ears. He acknowledged my introduction with a friendly wiggle of his free hand.

"Hello. Are you my cat's doctor?"

"Yes, I am," I smiled.

"Are you good?"

"Pretty good. I didn't always get straight A's in school, though."

"Yeah, me neither," Peter sighed, glancing at his mother.

"Is Mike going to be OK?" she asked quietly.

I shook my head. "I don't know. The firemen who found Mike got him on oxygen right away, but there's definitely lung damage. We'll know more over the next forty-eight hours," I added gently.

"We went to a movie," she said. "I didn't even want to go. I was tired. If I'd just stayed home this wouldn't have happened." She covered her face with both hands, her voice breaking. "We lost everything."

Peter turned and looked up at his mother. "Not everything, Mom. We still have Mike."

In the silence which followed, Mrs. Newcombe's face struggled with several different emotions. Then, resolutely brushing away her tears with the flannel sleeve, she smiled as she bent down to hug her son. "I'm so proud of you," she whispered. Peter rested his head against her shoulder, his small arms encircling her neck.

"Okay, Mom, that's good," he said after a moment. "I'm almost nine."

"I know," she smiled, ruffling his hair.

I opened the door of the kennel so that Peter could reach inside. His mother and I watched for a moment as the little boy silently patted his best friend, then laid his head on the blanket inches from Mike's face and whispered to him. The cat's eyes closed, calmed by the child's gentle touch and familiar smell.

"We got Mike just before I found out I was pregnant with Peter," Maggie said softly. "Phil, my husband, found him in the middle of winter in the parking lot of the building where he worked."

She shook her head. "He was in really bad shape, not neutered, broken leg, terrible cold. He was basically starving to death. You could feel every bone in his body. I cried when Phil brought him home."

"Tell what he liked to do, Mom," Peter urged.

"It was the strangest thing," she continued, smiling at her son. "After we got him fixed up, he started sleeping on my belly. This was even before I knew I was pregnant. And the bigger I got, the more he liked it. I just thought it was the heat, you know. A nice warm spot. And then Peter was born." Maggie looked at her son fondly. "You were such a fussy baby!"

Pete looked up with a grin and rolled his eyes. I winked at him.

"He had colic," Maggie explained. "Phil and I used to be up all night. After a while we started noticing that whenever Mike came into the room, Peter stopped crying. So we started letting Mike sleep in the crib. Phil's parents were horrified."

"Tell what Grammie Newcombe used to say." Peter's eyes twinkled in anticipation of a punch line he had heard a hundred times.

Maggie shook her head. "Grammie Newcombe used to say that when God was giving out brains … "

"… Mommy thought he said trains," Peter chimed in, "and she didn't want any!" He laughed in delight. Eight-year-olds have their own unique sense of humour.

"It's just that I knew …" Maggie paused, as she gazed at Mike lying quietly in his kennel, his head resting against her son's hand. "I knew he would never hurt Peter."

Within every family, some stories, some shared experiences, become part of that family's identity and are retold at every family gathering. The bond between Mike and Peter that began even before Peter was born was one of those stories. A small grey and white cat was the one thing tying this family to a life they used to know and memories that they used to share, with hope for the future. But even from where we stood, I could hear Mike's raspy breathing.

Maggie passed me a business card from the hotel where they were staying. "The room number's on the back. Call me if anything changes," she said in a low voice. "Good or bad."

I nodded and attached the card to Mike's medical record.

"Peter, put your coat on," Maggie said after a moment. "We have to go."

Peter gave Mike one final scratch then reluctantly closed the kennel door and struggled into a bulky winter jacket.

"Scarf and mitts too," Maggie told him.

"Mom, guys don't wear scarves and mitts," Peter sighed dramatically.

"My guys do," his mother replied, handing him the offending winter wear.

Peter reminded me of the Pillsbury doughboy as he waddled down the hall, his boots clumping against the floor with every step.

"Hey, Dr. McBride," he called out as he turned around and started to walk backwards. "Don't worry about Mike. He's gonna be fine." Peter waved goodbye. "See ya later, alligator!"

"In a while, crocodile," I told him.

In reception, I could hear Peter's excited voice as he grabbed his mother's arm. "Did you hear that, Mom? She knew the right answer. See? You don't always have to get A's to be smart."

I smiled, remembering one of my dad's favourite expressions whenever my brothers or I said something particularly enlightening: "Out of the mouths of babes!" Dad had only a Grade 8 education; at fourteen, he had to leave school to help support the family. In spite of that, he was one of the smartest people I ever knew and a non-stop reader, always thirsting for new knowledge.

But even my dad couldn't predict the future. I couldn't share Peter's assurance that Mike was going to be okay. For the moment, however, he was stable. With both Hilary and Susan keeping a watchful eye on Mike, I began my appointments.

Mid-afternoon brought Dulcie Huzzy of South Central Fire Station and a cod-cheek casserole.

"For that poor family what's gone an' lost their home … and those poor cats. I'd be clear outta me mind. Lord thunderin' Jaysus!" Dulcie shook her head. "Here you go, dearie," she said, thrusting a large container and a loaf of homemade bread into my arms.

She followed me back to the treatment area and stared through the window of the recovery ward while I stored the casserole in the fridge. "Is the little fella gonna make it?" she whispered.

I shook my head. "I don't know, Dulcie. I hope so."

Dulcie was silent for a moment as she studied the IV line and the untouched plates of food. "You be strong, little one," she urged him in a quiet voice. "You gots people what needs you." She looked up at me with a smile and patted my hand.

The staff and I kept a close watch on Mike throughout the day. He didn't seem any worse, but neither was there any improvement. Maggie popped in to visit while Peter was at school. She and her husband wanted to keep his routines as normal as possible.

"I don't know what to do," she confided. "Peter is convinced that Mike is going to be fine. I guess that's because he's always been fine." Her forehead wrinkled as she recalled Mike's adventurous past which included, but was not limited to, a stint in the dryer on the fluff cycle, a tour of downtown Halifax as a stowaway in a taxi, and surgery to remove a sewing needle and thread. By my count, Mike had used up eight of his nine lives.

"So maybe he still has one left," I said gently.

Maggie sighed. "I hope so."

But by evening Mike still hadn't eaten, despite the smorgasbord of temptations in his kennel. Even his favourite food from the grocery store was untouched. In desperation, I pulled out a few chunks of codfish from Dulcie's casserole stored in the fridge and put it on a dish. I didn't know too many cats that could resist fish, but Mike showed no interest. Somewhere between Archie Muncaster's ingrown toenail and Puss-Puss Jones's thyroid recheck, I decided to stay the night. It wasn't that there was much I could do; I just didn't want Mike to be alone. Not tonight.

After everyone had gone, I settled on the sofa in the recovery ward to read a book. By day, the hospital pulsed with life. But at night, the hospital assumed a completely different persona as it rested. Sights and sounds that went unnoticed during the day were a comfort at night: the gentle hum of the refrigerator, the warm glow of the nightlights. Cats dozed peacefully in their kennels, or meditated – it was hard to tell which.

At some point, I drifted off to sleep with Tina Louise in my lap. The other residents were confined to their respective kennels at night after one too many frat house parties. Carter, the ringleader, had learned to open cupboard doors and on more than one occasion, we discovered IV lines gnawed through and plastic catnip containers riddled with punctures. A curfew was instituted for everyone except Tina Louise, who never got into trouble.

Sometime around four in the morning, I awoke. My book was on the floor and Tina Louise nowhere in sight. The reading light was on. Shivering, I pulled on my sweater, then got up and walked over to Mike's kennel.

"It was the cod cheeks," I told an ecstatic Maggie the following morning. "That got him started and he hasn't stopped."

"Cod cheeks?" Maggie asked. "Is that some new kind of cat food?"

I wanted to keep Mike for a few more days for observation but he had other ideas. By eleven o'clock, he was hollering for lunch. By suppertime, he was rattling the bars of his kennel and trash-talking the other inmates. I sent him home that evening in Peter's arms. Maggie's husband, Phil, gingerly carried Dulcie's prized casserole and the bread. His wife's eyes shone with restrained tears, overwhelmed by the kindness of a woman she didn't even know.

"Cod cheeks!" Peter exclaimed. "I didn't even know cod had cheeks. You learn somethin' new every day, hey Mike?" The little boy lowered his head and kissed the soft, furry head. "Cod cheeks," he murmured.

As the weeks passed, Mike continued to do well and the Newcombes began to reassemble their lives. Eventually, they bought a bungalow in a kid-filled subdivision outside the city, but they quickly learned that Mike could not travel more than ten minutes in a car without getting rid of something – pee, poop, pet food, and sometimes all three in the same trip. He was anxious for days afterward. Reluctantly, they had Mike's medical records transferred to another veterinary clinic just minutes from their new home.

The following Christmas I received a family Christmas card from the Newcombes. Everyone wore big smiles, except Mike in his red Santa hat with a bell on the tip. Apparently, just after the photo was taken, Mike swallowed the bell and the family spent a few anxious days before it reappeared in the litter box. He was doing well and loved the new neighbourhood. He had befriended a Lab across the street. In a double dose of good fortune, the dog's owner was a little girl Peter's age who had pet mice. Peter was in Grade 4, enjoyed school, and wanted to play for the Montreal Canadiens when he grew up. If that didn't work out, then he was going to circumnavigate the globe in a hot-air balloon. The story could have ended here, happily ever after.

But it didn't.

It was two years before I saw Mike again. In the passage of time, some things stay the same, some things change. Susan, Hilary, and Bernie still worked full-time but Tanya, who hated snow and anything to do with winter, was moving to Alberta with her boyfriend. When we teased her about it, she would retort, "They have chinooks, you know!" Jim was almost finished his science degree and would be applying next year for vet school, but he still planned on working with us during the summers.

My hair was shorter now, which made it easier to pluck the random threads of grey that had begun popping up overnight. And, much to my mother's relief, I had finally "settled down." Last spring, Benny and I had purchased a small home not too far from Hughie's, who was delighted to have his favourite pet-sitter nearby. Mom was eagerly awaiting grandchildren, although she already had half a dozen. I told her it would be a long wait, and she reminded me that I wasn't getting any younger.

Mike had changed too. When he was brought into Ocean View for a second opinion, I was worried by his appearance. He was eleven now, but looked like a much older cat. His fur was unkempt and dull. Apparently, he had lost two pounds in just over a month. According to Maggie, he was eating well and was still his old self: by day, self-appointed guardian of the yard, and by night, loyal bedfellow. He and Peter were inseparable.

Their vet suspected one of the diseases frequently seen in older cats – hyperthyroidism, kidney disease, diabetes, even cancer – but all the test results had been normal. Normal test results in a cat who is losing weight rapidly are worrisome.

Peter listened to our conversation with growing concern. "What about cod cheeks?" he asked hopefully. "It worked the last time."

Dulcie Huzzy and her "boys", as she called the men of South Central Fire Station, were still regulars at Ocean View. And Spotty still arrived for her appointments in a fire truck. I knew Dulcie would make a dozen cod-cheek casseroles if she thought it would help. I wished it were that simple.

Despite our best efforts, Mike continued to decline. Eventually, he started vomiting and then stopped eating altogether. I referred him to the Atlantic Vet College in Charlottetown. There he underwent an extensive diagnostic work-up, including an exploratory surgery with multiple organ biopsies. Using an endoscope, the team also put a feeding tube in place to allow for nutritional support during his recovery.

Dr. John Plover called me late one night after outpatient clinic. Dr. Plover had been one of my favourite clinicians during my fourth-year rotation at vet school. We affectionately referred to him as "the Piping Plover," after the endangered shorebird, because he loved to sing. His voice frequently echoed throughout the halls of the vet school and adjoining small animal clinic. He was kind and gentle with both patients and students. We chatted pleasantly for a few moments and then he broke the news.

"It's not good, I'm afraid. Mike has diffuse intestinal lymphoma." He paused. "It's relatively advanced."

Even though I was expecting bad news, I felt my body go limp. So this was it.

"I've discussed all the options with the owners," he continued. "Chemotherapy, palliative care with steroids, no therapy, or euthanasia."

"What's his prognosis if we don't do anything?" I asked, already knowing the answer.

Dr. Plover hesitated. "A few weeks at best."

Sighing, I hung up the phone. I switched off the light in the office and carried my stack of updated medical charts to the front desk for Bernie to file in the morning. Outside, a few random flakes of snow brushed against my skin, mysterious soft white kisses that appeared from nowhere in the clear, starlit night.

I took the old two-lane road home, preferring its gentle twists and turns to the wide-open efficiency of the main highway. When I turned into the winding driveway that led to our cedar bungalow, I knew Benny would have supper waiting for me. I knew a fire would be burning brightly in the wood stove and three cats would be curled up beside it in their respective baskets. I was so grateful for all of it.

Maggie called a few days later when she returned from Charlottetown with Mike. She and her husband had decided against chemotherapy but both felt guilt-ridden.

"Mike's survived everything life's thrown at him," Maggie cried softly. "We really can't afford chemo but at the same time, what if there's a chance that he might get better and we don't do anything to help him?" The anguish in her voice was unmistakable.

As a pet owner and a veterinarian, I had been in her position many times. And there was never one right answer. Together, we decided to try a two-week course of steroids. Not only do they possess anti-tumour properties, but they also reduce inflammation and stimulate appetite. If nothing else, Mike would feel more comfortable on the steroids.

"He won't eat any of the really good cat food we bought," Maggie sighed. "What should I give him?"

"Give him whatever he wants," I said gently. "We know he's living on borrowed time and the most important thing is to keep him comfortable and happy."

Maggie took a deep breath. "Thank you," she said. "For all you've done."

"I wish I could do more," I told her.

"You gave us hope two years ago when we had none. I'll never forget that, Dr. McBride."

I promised Maggie I would make a house call when it was time. But Mike had other plans. When his two-week supply of medication was finished, Maggie and Peter popped into the hospital for a refill. Peter cheerfully plunked Mike on the weigh scale. I glanced at the result and assumed the scale hadn't been reset to zero. We lifted Mike off the scale, I reset it and then we weighed him again with the same result. Mike had gained a pound in two weeks.

"He's eating on his own," Maggie smiled.

I listened to Mike's heart and lungs and took his temperature. "So what's your secret?" I asked Peter.

"Cod cheeks," he announced proudly.

"Peter insisted," Maggie said. "We know it's not a cure," she added, looking at her son. "But we found a recipe. Daddy bought the fish and we cooked it up. It was a real family effort."

Over the next few weeks, Mike's activity level increased and his coat began to shine as he returned to his normal, all-you-can-eat self. I removed his feeding tube since he was eating everything he was offered, including macaroni and cheese, roast chicken, strawberry ice cream, and the occasional tin of cat food. I cautioned the family not to get their hopes up as the improvement would only be temporary. His tumour would return soon and probably with a vengeance.

"I know," Maggie said with a wistful smile. "But he's happy today. And so are we."

※ ※ ※

Mike was in for his second-year recheck last week. Despite Mike's dislike of cars, Peter insists that his beloved cat come to Ocean View Cat Hospital because we are the only ones who know about the healing power of cod cheeks. Twenty-six months after his diagnosis, Mike is still in remission and is getting fat. As I discussed a weight-loss program with Maggie, Peter looked up with a wide grin.

"It's your fault, Dr. McBride. You told us to feed him whatever he wanted."

I grinned back. "I did, didn't I?"

The End